MW01256602

The Play

A Novel

KARINA HALLE

First edition published by
Metal Blonde Books November 2015
Publisher's Note: This is a work of fiction. Names, characters, places, and incidents either are the product of the author's imagination or are used fictitiously. Any resemblance to actual events, locales, or persons, living or dead, is entirely coincidental.

Kindle Edition

Cover design by Hang Le Designs
Edited by Kara Maclinczak
Metal Blonde Books
P.O. Box 845
Point Roberts, WA
98281 USA
Manufactured in the USA
For more information about the series and author visit:
http://authorkarinahalle.com/

ISBN: 1518896375
ISBN-13: 9781518896378

For Bruce, pit bulls, and other misunderstood beings who are rarely given a second chance in life.

Also by Karina Halle

The Experiment in Terror Series

Darkhouse (EIT #1)

Red Fox (EIT #2)

The Benson (EIT #2.5)

Dead Sky Morning (EIT #3)

Lying Season (EIT #4)

On Demon Wings (EIT #5)

Old Blood (EIT #5.5)

The Dex-Files (EIT #5.7)

Into the Hollow (EIT #6)

And With Madness Comes the Light (EIT #6.5)

Come Alive (EIT #7)

Ashes to Ashes (EIT #8)

Dust to Dust (EIT #9)

Novels by Karina Halle

The Devil's Metal (Devils #1)

The Devil's Reprise (Devils #2)

Sins and Needles (The Artists Trilogy #1)

On Every Street (An Artists Trilogy Novella #0.5)

Shooting Scars (The Artists Trilogy #2)

Bold Tricks (The Artists Trilogy #3)

Donners of the Dead

Dirty Angels

Dirty Deeds

Dirty Promises

Love, in English

Love, in Spanish

Where Sea Meets Sky (from Atria Books)

Racing the Sun (from Atria Books)

The Pact

The Offer

The Play

Table of Contents

PART ONE 1
Prologue 3
Chapter One 13
Chapter Two 28
Chapter Three 43
Chapter Four 59
Chapter Five 69
Chapter Six 86
Chapter Seven 93
Chapter Eight 109
Chapter Nine 129
Chapter Ten 148
Chapter Eleven 163
Chapter Twelve 185
Chapter Thirteen 202
Chapter Fourteen 229
Chapter Fifteen 247
Chapter Sixteen 271
Chapter Seventeen 293
PART TWO 311
Chapter Eighteen 313
Chapter Nineteen 334
Chapter Twenty 357
Chapter Twenty-One 381
Chapter Twenty-Two 409
Chapter Twenty-Three 421
Chapter Twenty-Four 437
Chapter Twenty-Five 459
Chapter Twenty-Six 478
Chapter Twenty-Seven 487

Chapter Twenty-Eight 496
Chapter Twenty-Nine 512
Chapter Thirty 522
Epilogue 535
Acknowledgments 547

"I'll awake you from this living sleep"-
Matador, Faith No More

Part One

Prologue

Edinburgh, Scotland

1987

It had started to snow the night before. The boy woke up on the floor by the fire, like he sometimes did when the winds blew in too cold and mum didn't pay the electric bill. But by the time morning came around, the fire was out, just smoldering ash, and he couldn't feel his fingers or his nose, the only things sticking out of the itchy flannel blanket.

Despite the cold and the damp that coated the small, dark living room, the boy woke up happy. Today was his special day. He was turning five, and his mother had promised, *promised* him last year, on his last birthday, when he had no presents at all, that when he turned five and became a big boy, he could go to the toy store and get whatever toy he wanted.

He had spent most of the year flipping through discarded catalogues he found in the housing complex's rubbish (sometimes he'd have to wait on the sidelines while some rough, unpredictable characters looted around for food or something they could pawn), looking for toys that caught his fancy. He would find them, rip the pages out, and take them to the bedroom he shared with his mother, hiding them in the inner pocket of the single coat he had.

When he wasn't so lucky with the catalogues, he would flip through the magazines he found at the library. That's where he spent most of his time. He wasn't in school, though he should have been at this point, so his mum had to put him somewhere while she did her business. The library was the best place for him. In the chaotic slums of Muirhouse, no one in the library noticed the little boy in his ill-fitting, threadbare clothes, sitting on the library floor for hours, looking through magazines and dreaming about a different life.

The truth was, as his birthday came around, he didn't care at all about what toy he ended up getting. He just wanted something he could call his own. And even though he knew that boys like him should want army figurines and cars, he just wanted something comforting. A stuffed animal, maybe a bear or a dog. He loved dogs, even the ones who belonged to his neighbor that barked all night and tried to bite if you got too close. He loved those dogs, too.

The boy got up, shivering even with the blanket draped around his shoulders, and went to go look out the window. His large grey-green eyes widened in awe. The grime and dirt of the godforsaken streets below were completely wiped away by a layer of clean, white snow. It was the first snowfall in Edinburgh this year, and he couldn't help but think that it was all for him, for his special day. With cold, fumbling fingers, he pulled his cross necklace out of his shirt and kissed it as thanks to God.

He wanted to tell his mother about the snow, so he ran across the thin rug, ever covered in tears and cigarette burns, and to the bedroom.

He really should have knocked first. In his excitement he forgot one of the few rules his mother gave him: "If I have a friend over, you must sleep in the living room," and, "If my door is closed, never open it."

But he opened it.

The window had a crack in it, and the frozen wind was seeping in, blowing the faded curtains around. Below the window was the bed, where his mother, clad in a dirty negligee, was currently sleeping facedown.

A naked man was standing over her, smoking from a pipe.

The boy froze, but it was too late. The man saw him, slammed down the pipe in anger, and in a second was across the room, holding him by the throat.

"You think you can judge me?" the man hissed in his face with rank breath that smelled of onions and blood. The boy closed his eyes and shook his head fearfully.

He had seen the man a few times before—his mother had so many male friends. They would all disappear into the bedroom. Sometimes for hours, sometimes for minutes. He would hear coughing, laughing, and cries of excitement on good days. On bad days, he would hear shouting, his mother crying, things being thrown around the room. On those bad days, his mother would be covered in cuts and bruises. She wouldn't talk to him, and she wouldn't go outside. He just stayed by her side, bringing her weak tea from teabags that had already been used a few times, because that's all there was left.

"Do you?!" the man yelled again and squeezed and squeezed his neck. The boy couldn't breathe at all. He thought this terrible man with the purple, bulbous nose and the mean eyes, was going to kill him.

In some ways, he wanted him to.

"Hey," his mother said from the bed, slowly stirring. "What's going on?" Her voice was ragged, and slurred as she sat up. "Leave my son alone."

The man released his grip, and then looked behind him to glare at the woman. The boy pawed at his own raw throat, wheezing, trying to say he was sorry, but nothing was coming out.

It didn't matter. The man suddenly whirled around and backhanded the boy across the face. It made his head explode with shards of glass, and he went flying backwards.

He banged into the doorframe and landed on the ground with a thump, and prayed to the same God who had made it snow that he would never feel this pain again.

But this wouldn't be the last of it. He had a whole life of pain to get through first.

"You shut up," the man yelled back at his mother.

She looked frightened to death but still managed to tell her son to get up and go in the bathroom and lock the door.

The boy could barely move, but somehow he did it. He got to his feet, his head pounding, coughing hard, and went into the bathroom. The floor was wet with urine. Clumsily, he slid the lock in place and sat on the toilet and waited.

There was shouting and more shouting and then finally a door slammed.

A few gentle knocks at the door and he knew his mum was okay.

"You better get ready," she said to him when he opened the door a crack. She smiled at him quickly with crooked, yellow teeth, and gathered a robe over her frail body, her chest bones protruding like prison bars. "It's your birthday and I haven't forgotten what I promised you."

Her voice cracked over the last words and she quickly hurried away, shoulders slumped, head down.

Soon the two of them were fully dressed and trudging through the snow, heading to the bus stop. The boy couldn't help but smile at everyone and everything they passed: the scary people who slept on the street and talked to themselves, the dogs that shivered and ran away, the rats that feasted on dead things on the side of the road. None of that mattered to the boy because the world seemed bright and pure and all for him. He kicked at the snow and watched it fall to the ground and told his mum that this must be what heaven was like, walking in the clouds all day long.

She wiped away a mascara-stained tear and agreed.

The bus ride took a long time, but eventually they found themselves at one of the large concrete shopping centers. This was the boy's big moment, what he'd been looking forward to for a year.

He didn't even notice the odd looks that he and his mother sometimes got; he was so focused on that toy that the whole world seemed to slip away. Despite the bump at the back of his head, his cheek that was swollen and slowly growing purple, this was the happiest day of his life.

"Now we don't have much time," his mother said. "So hurry and pick out your present and I'll pay for it."

The boy heard the urgency in her voice and suddenly he was so overwhelmed. There were action figures, superheroes, cars and trucks, horses, dolls, stuffed animals, building sets, art supplies and Lego, and a million other things he wanted. He stood there, completely dumbfounded, and looked around and around, his heart thumping in his chest.

"Please," his mother said again. She was at the cashier, ready to pay. He was suddenly so afraid that if he didn't pick something right that second he wouldn't get anything at all. At the same time, he was old enough to know that they didn't have much money, so anything fancy and expensive was too much.

Panicking, he headed toward the stuffed animals. They were all crammed into a box—giraffes, bears, dogs, cats. They all looked like they needed a home, and it broke his heart to think he could only take one of them.

But he had to make a choice. He was gravitating toward a stuffed puppy when he noticed a lion half-buried in the pile, only his sly feline eyes and furry yellow mane poking out. It was no place for such a majestic beast.

The boy plucked the lion from the animals, so soft and huggable in his arms, and ran over to his mother with it, hoping she hadn't changed her mind.

She looked at the lion and smiled. He had done well.

After she paid, he hugged that lion with all his might. It felt so good to hold something, and it felt like the lion was holding him back, thanking him for the rescue.

"What is the lion's name?" his mother asked quietly. There was so much sadness in her voice that it nearly broke the spell the boy was under, that dizzy spell of love.

"Lionel," he said after thinking about it for a moment. "Lionel the lion. And I love him."

"And you know he loves you, don't you?" she said, wiping her nose on the sleeve of her faux-fur coat. It smeared her red lipstick. "Just as I love you."

His mother didn't tell him that she loved him all that often so he was surprised to hear it. It made his birthday that much better.

Soon they were back on the bus, but this time they weren't headed back to the house. The roads were unfamiliar, and the city was slowly left behind them. The yards got bigger, the snow deeper.

"Where are we going?" he asked. "This isn't the way home."

"We're going to see some friends of mine," she said.

The boy didn't like that. He hugged his lion tight to him. He didn't like her friends.

She put her hand on his shoulder but wouldn't look at him. They were the only people on the bus which made him feel even more alone.

"Don't worry," she said eventually. "They have boys your age there."

That didn't make him feel any better. He didn't get along with other kids, whether they were his age or not. He was shy and often got picked on for being too quiet. That only made him sink more into himself, where it was always safe and comfortable.

Eventually the bus stopped by huge iron gates and a stone wall, and the mother grabbed his hand, holding her purse close to her as they shuffled out into the snow. The bus pulled away and the boy wished he could have stayed on it. They were in the hills, in the middle of nowhere, and even though his home was cold and dirty, it was still *home*.

The boy couldn't read the sign on the wall so he asked his mother what it said.

"It says we are welcome," she said, hurrying him along until they were standing in front of the gates. She pressed a buzzer on the intercom.

The boy stared through the iron bars at the giant mansion on the hill. He didn't like it. Something about it, maybe the bars on the windows or the overgrown ivy, or the way it bared down on them, like a brick beast, ready to pounce. He was grateful at that moment to have a lion like Lionel, but it didn't stop him from digging in his heels.

"Come on," his mother hissed, yanking him forward until they were climbing up the stairs.

The front door opened, and a tall, thin man with a beak for a nose and slicked back hair appeared, peering down at them.

"Welcome, Miss Lockhart," he said, and then gestured for them to come inside.

The man was speaking to them still as they stepped into the mansion, but the boy wasn't listening. He was struck by the cold all around him. From the sickly yellow lights to the industrial feeling walls and floor—everything screamed inhospitable. There were bad vibes here, a place that held nothing but wicked things.

But his mother pulled him along down the lifeless hall until they were in an office. They both sat down in leathery chairs across from the man, and she handed him an envelope from her purse.

"I trust this is all in order," the man said, his voice deep and emotionless.

His mother nodded. "It is." She paused and looked at her boy with eyes that held a world of regret, before talking to the man again. "I hope you'll take care of him. It's not his fault. It's mine."

The man only nodded, looking over the papers.

"What are you talking about?" the boy asked her. "When are we going home?"

"Son," the man said, staring into him with beady eyes. The boy swore he could feel them trying to poke holes into his soul. "This is your new home."

He couldn't comprehend what the man was saying. He shook his head and looked to his mother, but she was crying and getting out of her chair.

"Mum!" he yelled, dropping his lion so he could grab her coat with both hands. She nearly dragged him out of his chair.

He scrambled to his feet as she went for the door, but he was held back by the man, who had a strong, merciless grip on him. "Mum!" he screamed again, arms outstretched.

She paused at the door, only briefly, mascara running down her cheeks.

"I'm so sorry, Lachlan," she sobbed to the boy, gripping the doorframe until her knuckles were white. "I love you. But I just can't have you in my life. I'm so sorry."

"But mum!" Lachlan screamed, his voice ripping out of him. "I'll be good! I promise. You can take Lionel back to the store, just take me back home, please!"

His mother only shook her head and whispered, "Goodbye."

Lachlan continued to cry, to wail, to try and get out of the man's grasp, as he watched his mother walk away and disappear out of sight.

"Please!" he bellowed, such a large sound from such a small boy. He felt his feet give way, and the man was now holding him up, legs dangling beneath him. "Please come back, mum, please! Take me home, take me home!"

"This is your home," the man said again. He brought Lachlan's head back to his mouth and whispered in his ear, wet and harsh. "And if you don't stop screaming and making noise like a little twat, you're going to get twenty lashings from my belt. Is that what you want for your first day here at the Hillside Orphanage? Is it?"

But Lachlan couldn't stop screaming. He couldn't care less about being beaten. He'd been hit that morning; he'd been beaten many times before. The true pain was the pain he felt inside, raging through him, tearing him apart. He felt like he was drowning in ice water and the flood was starting in his soul.

"Fine then," the man said, and threw Lachlan to the ground. He picked Lionel up from the floor and held the lion up in the air. "If you don't shut your bloody mouth, you'll never see this again. I'll give it to another boy."

It was all Lachlan had. He shut up. Whimpering, he clamped his lips together, his chin shaking. The man gave him the lion, and he held on to him with all his might, until the fur was wet with tears.

His fifth birthday was the last one he would celebrate for a very long time.

Lachlan would never see his mother again.

He would never go home.

And the flood in his soul would never truly subside.

Chapter One

San Francisco – Present day

KAYLA

"How long do you have to be absent of dick before you're considered re-virginized?"

Steph and Nicola look at me sharply, as if I've asked something that's just blown their minds.

"Kayla," Nicola admonishes.

"What?" I ask with a shrug and tilt my head at her. "Out of the three of us here, you're the one who'd probably know. We practically had to shove dick in your face before you started getting it on with Bram. So, were you re-virginized or not?"

"I had a vibrator, you idiot," Nicola says, sitting back in the booth and giving me the eye. I know that eye too well. It's the "What the hell is wrong with you, and why are we still your friend?" look.

"Vibrators don't count," I tell her. "I'm talking actual peen. Was it like losing it all over again when Bram gave you the ram? The Bram ram. Wham, bam, thank you Bram?"

She rolls her eyes and exchanges a look with Steph. It's only been a few weeks since Nicola reconnected with Bram, and she and her daughter Ava had moved out of my apartment and in with him. While I'm still a bit wary about Bram at times, mainly because hot Scottish men can't be trusted, I have to say I miss having Nicola and Ava around. It's kind of lonely without them, and I'm prone to just sitting around at night, eating frozen meals and watching reruns of *The Vampire Diaries*.

Of course, part of the reason I'm all alone and pigging out on preservatives is because I decided to take a vow of celibacy a few weeks ago. It's not just no sex—it's no flirting, no dating, no Tinder, no nothing. Boys, men, I'm not even giving them a second glance.

And I'd like to say that it's all working out for me. I may be alone at home most of the time, but I'd rather be battling my urge to drink wine and online shop than to sleep with another guy who wouldn't know a woman's clit if it slapped him in the face. Hell, I'm sure when I jerk my hips, it literally *is* slapping them in the face, and yet they pretend like it doesn't exist.

Not to mention the dates that go nowhere, the men who seem to have potential but then see you only as this half-Asian princess that they want all sweet and subdued, and meanwhile I'm all slapping them with my vag and cursing my head off.

It's much, much easier this way. Less stressful.

"You all right there, Kayla?" Steph asks.

"Yes, why?"

"Because you're holding onto the edge of the table like you're about to go all Hulk on us."

I look down at my hands, my knuckles whiter than my already pale skin. I slowly let go. Maybe I'm stressed after all.

"Are you sure this whole no men thing is a good thing?" she asks, taking a sip of her beer.

Truthfully, having her question it is exactly what I want to hear. Any excuse to just throw it out the window. But still, I'm nothing if not determined.

"It's the right thing," I tell her, raising my head and forcing myself to relax. I reach for my glass of wine, even though it's my second glass and I'm already lightheaded. "It's the only way," I add gravely.

"And why are you doing this again?" Nicola asks.

I look at her and her deep brown eyes, then over to Steph and her baby blue ones. My two best friends, dressed to casually impress in foreign labels and independent designers. The two of them are the reason I'm doing this, with their happy, shiny faces and commitment to those damn McGregor brothers. Nicola just settled down, happily, with Bram, after their massive falling out, and Stephanie is married to his brother, Linden. It doesn't help that I'd had a fling with Linden a long time ago, way before he and Steph got together, back when they were just friends. It's not that he broke my Grinch heart (it's three sizes too small), but sometimes I'm reminded of what I could have had and what I don't have.

I'm jealous, that's really what it comes down to. And when I get jealous, even of my friends, I can turn into a mean little ninja. And I don't want to be a mean little ninja, just a regular one (though I do miss being a sex ninja). So, swearing off men meant swearing off disappointment.

At least, it's supposed to. It's easier when I'm alone at home, at work, at my mother's, at the gym, or even out for dinner. Anywhere where temptation is limited. Tonight though, Steph and Nicola practically dragged me out of the house and took me to our hangout, The Burgundy Lion pub in the Haight district, for a girls' night. Being around booze and boys is never a good idea when you're abstaining from dick. Luckily, I left the house wearing no makeup, yoga pants, and a baggy t-shirt that says "No Pants Party," so it's not like the guys will be clamoring to talk to me. Unless they think the "no pants" thing is an invitation.

"I'm doing this because my battery operated boyfriend always knows the right spots and I let my fingers do the talking," I explain with a tired sigh. "And I'm sick and tired of dating in this stupid city. I'm just spinning my wheels, wasting my time, and I swear the men are just getting stupider. I can't even get laid properly anymore. It's like all the men in San Francisco are either taken, gay, or afraid of greedy vaginas."

They exchange another glance, this secret kind of communication they seem to have now. My theory is that having a McGregor dick inside of you gives you a form of telekinesis. They are forever bonded by Scottish cock.

"What?" I say. "It's true. And you both would agree, if you didn't have your own vaginas snatched up by those kilt-lifters."

"Would you stop saying vagina?" Nicola says. "The word is ceasing to have meaning."

"Yeah, for me."

"Hmmmm. If Kayla ceased to have a greedy vagina, would she even exist at all?" Steph muses with a twinkle in her eye.

"Whatever," I tell them, taking a large gulp of a Napa zinfandel. "My life will be easier this way. You'll see."

Nicola's phone rattles on the table and she peers at it. "Bram's on his way."

I groan, putting my chin in my hand and letting it slide over my face. "Ugh, why? I thought we said it was a girls' night. The last thing I want to see is you two making eyes at each other and your stupid innuendo."

"Linden's coming too," Steph says sheepishly.

I give her a hard look.

"Sorry," she says, not really sorry at all. "But if it makes you feel better, Linden and I are boring and married, so that whole swoony, making eyes stuff is over."

"Oh, please," I say while Nicola makes a similar sound of disbelief. "You're even worse than Bram and Nicola, because you've got a case of the smug marrieds. Remember Bridget Jones? I'm Bridget. And you're…the rest of them."

Nicola nods. "It's true." Then she looks to me brightly. "So you just need to meet your Hugh Grant."

I glare at her. "She doesn't end up with Hugh Grant!"

Nicola frowns in confusion.

"Oh, like you'd even want a Mark Darcy," Steph supplies. "Besides, Linden and Bram aren't coming alone."

Oh god. Something cold washes over me.

"What? Who are they with?" I ask slowly. If it's a guy, I'm going to be very upset, particularly if he's a single guy.

Another glance. I can practically hear the giggles in their heads.

"Their cousin, Lachlan," Steph says.

Lachlan McGregor. As if there aren't enough damn McGregors in the city already, let alone the world. I haven't met Lachlan yet, score another point for staying at home, but Steph and Nicola haven't shut up about him from the few times they've met. He's a rugby player, he's so mysterious, he's so built, blah, blah, fucking blah. All the stuff that I never needed to know because that sort of shit is my sexual kryptonite, especially in this city where a rough and wild man is a needle in a very metrosexual haystack.

"Why would you do that to me?" I cry out, patting down my messy top knot. "I came here in my pajamas. I don't have any makeup on, my hair isn't even brushed. Jesus, are my teeth even clean? Do I stink?" I quickly sniff my pits and then breathe into my hands. Mmmm. Eau du Wino.

"Do that to you?" Steph repeats. "I didn't know he was coming until an hour ago. Hell, I didn't know they'd be stopping by at all."

"Argh," I say, running my fingers under my eyes, checking for puffiness. "I should have known they would. They practically live here."

"Well, I do work here," Nicola points out. "And Linden's best friend James runs the place. And, well, so what if Lachlan's here? You don't have to sleep with him."

I reach for Steph's lilac Balenciaga bag, a present from Linden that I've always wanted to steal, and rummage through it for a compact and some makeup since I didn't bring a single thing with me, not even money since we usually drink for free at the Lion.

"Of course I don't have to sleep with him. But I don't need the temptation. And what if he's still around when my vow wears off? I could get my own Scottish dick before he jets back to the homeland."

"I thought you were against Scottish dick," Steph says.

"I'm against McGregor dick. And didn't you say that Lachlan isn't his real cousin anyway. He's adopted?"

She nods. "Well, let me make this easy on you, hon. Even if you were your usual cock-gobbling she-devil, I don't think he'd be interested."

I pause. "Hey, cock-gobbling is *my* word. Don't be stealing my shit. And also, why, is he gay?" One of my brothers, Toshio, is gay, and I wonder if I can set the two of them up.

"I don't think so," Steph says. She looks at Nicola. "Actually, I think Bram said he had a date with some Justine woman."

Nicola scowls. "Yeah. Same Justine that Bram went out with, remember?"

"You said it wasn't really a date though—that his dad set them up," I point out.

"Yeah." She pouts at the memory anyway. She and Bram had a pretty tumultuous start together. In fact, they pretty much hated each other. Then she had to get all sappy and fall in love with more than his dick.

"Okay, so he has a girlfriend," I say to Steph. "You could have just said so."

"I think it was just a date or two, I don't know," Steph says. "Regardless, he's kind of hard to get to know."

"Yeah, really," Nicola says, nodding vehemently. "I think he's said two words to me and he's over at our place *a lot*."

"I don't need a guy to talk in order to fuck him. Which I'm not. Because of my vow and shit."

Nicola gives me an eyebrow raise and holds it for ten seconds. Such talent.

"You'd miss the dirty talk too much," Steph says with a grin, and I know she's thinking about her husband and his filthy mouth.

"Hey," I say, thumbing my chest. "I talk dirty enough for the both of us."

"You definitely do with us, anyway," Nicola says.

I snort, pulling out Steph's compact and peering at my face. Even without makeup I know I don't look *that* bad.

From my mother's side I got high cheekbones, her dark eyes, and long, black lashes that don't need any mascara. From my father, I got full lips and freckles. But still, I could look a lot better. My cheeks are blotchy from the alcohol, my thick mess of hair is unruly, and I'm dressed like a bag lady.

And you're all the better for it, I remind myself. *Untalkative Scottish peen is the last thing you need.*

"Yeah, you're right," I say.

"Huh?"

I look at Steph blankly. "Oh, sorry. I was talking to myself. I do that. You know this."

"There they are," Nicola says. I can hear the stupid grin in her voice.

I sigh and look back to the front door of the bar. Beneath the low lighting, amid the wood finishing, green and brass décor, and the rigged jukebox that only plays James' music, steps in Bram, Linden, and Lachlan McGregor. The Scottish trifecta of hot guys.

But even as that thought hits my brain, I blink, my eyes trained on Lachlan because I'm finally taking him in for the first time. I realize that "hot guy" is an understatement. While Linden and Bram are stupidly good-looking in their charming, handsome ways, Lachlan is a whole other beast.

Because, he basically *is* a beast.

Lachlan is a good half a foot taller than Bram—and that says a lot already because Bram is pretty tall—and nearly twice as wide. Like a redwood tree, he goes up and up and he's solid and probably unmoveable, and I already have this urge to run across the bar and slam into him, just to see how immense he is. I have a feeling I would bounce right off of him. I mean, his physique seems lifted from a superhero comic, from his thick arms that are covered in masses of dark tattoos, and his expansive, firm chest, to his mountainous shoulders and v-shaped torso. Even dressed in a plain moss-green t-shirt and dark jeans, he looks larger than life.

And I can't stop staring. I don't even care because everyone else in the bar is staring at the Scottish trifecta, even though I manage to glide my fingers over my mouth to make sure I'm not actually drooling. He's probably the most stunning man I've ever laid eyes on, and I immediately want to rub myself all over his face. If that's not love, I don't know what is.

While Bram nods his head in our direction and Linden waves, Lachlan's eyes scan the crowd intently, almost like he's a cop searching the place for suspects. Or a criminal looking for opportunity. There's a hint of electric danger in his searching gaze, and for a moment I wonder what it would be like to be looked at the same way. I'd probably burst into flames.

Unfortunately, as they get closer and Lachlan's eyes finally meet mine, I see nothing but indifference in them.

I quickly look away, suddenly aware of how I must appear, and curse myself once again for letting my friends drag me out here when I could be watching Damon Salvatore instead. At least I don't care if *he* sees me in my pajamas.

All the better for your vow, I tell myself. I refrain from adding a *shut up* rebuttal. See, talking to myself again.

"Hey sweetie," Steph says to Linden, grinning at him like an idiot, just as I called it. I ignore the pleasantries the couples make and stare down at my wine instead, waiting for the dreaded introduction. My eyes slide over to the floor and I take in their shoes—shiny dressy ones for Bram, Keds for Linden, and hiking boots for Lachlan. They look worn and beaten and oh so large.

"Kayla," Bram says, almost delicately. I love how they treat me like I'm a bomb they're about to diffuse.

I slowly look up to meet his dark eyes.

"This is our cousin, Lachlan." He steps aside slightly and gestures to the beast of a man. "Lach, this is Kayla."

I play it cool. I nod and say, "Nice to meet you."

What I really want to say is, "*Can I please lick your face?*" Because it's a damn good face, especially up close. He's all frowny, like he's trying to figure out why he should care who I am, and it makes a deep line appear between his eyes and I kind of want to run my finger over it. His eyes themselves are this vivid, sharp hazel, leaning more toward green. There's a deep hollow beneath his cheekbones, his wide jaw is lined with a perfectly scruffy beard, and his hair is brown and thick and tuggable. Then there are his lips. They're show-stopping lips. They are lips I need between my legs.

At that thought, the heat builds in my core, and I can feel my face flushing.

It just makes him frown more.

"Kayla," he acknowledges. His voice is very low and very rough, like he belongs in a 40s noir film, and his Scottish brogue is a million times thicker than Linden or Bram's. My name coming from his mouth sounds like some kind of Gaelic dessert. Naturally that thought puts an image of him spreading me open on the table and eating me like a dessert.

Jesus. I need a cold shower, stat.

"We should get a bigger booth," Nicola says, and her voice brings me back to reality. Even though I don't want to tear my eyes away from Lachlan and all his brooding, hulking glory, this is the perfect time for me to be smart and get the hell out of here.

I quickly finish the rest of my wine before getting out of the booth. I move myself away from Lachlan, afraid that being close to him is something like orbiting around a black hole, and prepare my excuses to leave when Bram reaches out and touches my arm.

"Kayla, can I talk to you for a moment?" he asks, and I stare at him in surprise. He looks serious for once, and for some reason I feel like a little girl who's gotten herself into trouble. Probably because I'm usually getting into trouble.

"Okay," I say quickly and shoot Nicola a worried look. She just shrugs, seeming surprised herself, and the rest of them move over to a bigger booth.

Bram pats the table of the booth where we were just sitting. "Have a seat. I have something to ask you."

"If you're asking me to move in with you, the answer is no," I tell him, reluctantly sitting back down.

"Ha ha," he says dryly. "Actually, I wanted to ask you a favor." He pauses, his dark brows coming together "You work for The Bay Weekly, right?"

"Yeah," I say slowly. I think about quitting my job every day, but I don't tell him that.

He clasps his hands in front of him, showing off a shiny silver watch that probably cost a fortune. "As you know, I'm still trying to get funding for the apartment complex. Lachlan is here to help—he's made a lot of smart investments himself over the years, so he has money, and charity is dear to his heart as it turns out. But we're missing more investors, and we've been trying to do everything to secure more."

I nod along, not understanding how I can help at all. Even though Bram has rubbed me the wrong way a few times, the guy actually has a heart of gold and has been trying to get funding for his apartment complex in the city. He bought it all with his own money, and he's been opening the apartments to lower income families, the sick and elderly, and other people in need. As Nicola explained it, he can only do this on his own for so long before he runs out of money, and so far the city of San Francisco hasn't been so giving with something it so desperately needs.

"So I was thinking," Bram goes on, "that maybe you could put in a good word in the magazine. We need all the publicity we can get."

I grimace in disappointment. "I'm sorry. I'd help if I could, but I work in advertising. I handle the retail ad accounts. I mean, I can maybe get an ad or something…"

Bram shakes his head. "Thank you. I can get ads. It's just…an article, an editorial, anything would really help."

Even though I don't mind my boss Lucy, it's Joe, the editor of the paper who is a real asshole. If I could get what Bram is talking about, I'd have to go to him.

Still, Nicola is my friend and Bram's heart is in the right place. I sigh. "Okay. I'll talk to the editor tomorrow and see what I can do. I couldn't write the article, but I'm sure someone else could. *If* they're interested."

"Nicola said you went to school for journalism. Why couldn't you write it? It would give it more of a personal spin, don't you think?"

I feel a familiar pinch of regret in my stomach. "I went to school for communications," I correct him, "and got sucked into the ad world. I can write, but…they wouldn't let me, even if I tried. They'll give it to a staff writer. But they're all good. I'll see what I can do, okay?"

He smiles at me. Handsome devil. "Thank you, Kayla. You're not as black-hearted as they say you are."

I raise my brow. "I beg to differ. I'm in advertising, after all."

Even though I'm ready to leave, something makes me sit down with the rest of them. Linden, Steph, and Lachlan are on one side of the booth, so Bram and I slide in beside Nicola, just as a waitress comes by bringing more drinks. The glass of wine slides toward me, and I groan inwardly knowing it would be rude of me to leave now.

"What was that about?" Steph asks us.

"Just seeing if Kayla can pull some strings at the Weekly," he explains, then looks over to Lachlan.

His cousin gives a sharp nod, his eyes flitting to me and back to Bram. I've barely made an impression on the man, and usually people say I'm forgettable (not always in the most flattering way, but still).

"That would be great if you could," Nicola says from down the table. "Would save Lachlan from going on another date with Justine."

Bram laughs at that, and Lachlan leans back in his seat, palming his light beer. Holy crap. His hands. I get such a lady boner for men's hands, and his are large, wide, and strong looking. If he could touch me like he's touching his beer, I'd be in so much trouble.

Lachlan gives Bram a dry look, and I notice the light scarring on his forehead and cheekbones, the way the middle of his nose is just a bit crooked. He looks like a bruiser, a fighter, a player. My mind adds that information to the recent discovery about his hands, and I feel like I'm about to implode.

"The things I do for my cousin," Lachlan comments, and I'm lost in the roughness of his accent. His tone borders on amusement, even if his face remains as stony as ever.

"More like the women you do for your cousin," Linden jokes. Lachlan doesn't say anything to that.

Ah, so he's a womanizer like the other McGregors. I thought as much. I mean, how can you look like that, all manly, primal, rugged, with those lips and eyes, and not have women falling at your feet. Hell, if I hadn't made a vow and actually had makeup on and fresh breath and didn't have a live audience, I would be under the table, trying to put his dick in my mouth. I bet it's glorious.

I sigh inwardly. It doesn't bother me that he's a player because I am too. Or I used to be. So I guess *that's* what bothers me. I'll never be able to sample the goods. Even though abstaining is for the best, I need to get laid something fierce, and Lachlan McGregor would be the man to do it. Over and over again.

That is, of course, if he even finds me attractive. Or anything at all. And from the way I catch his gaze briefly from time to time and see nothing readable in those hard, mossy eyes, I know that's not a possibility. Maybe he really is hung up on this Justine girl, despite the joke that Nicola made it out to be.

Thankfully James comes over to join our group and asks if we want more drinks, and I take the opportunity to escape. Steph and Nicola protest, saying they'll cab with me later, but I can't sit there for a single moment longer with the Scottish beast across from me.

I quickly wave goodbye, barely focusing on Lachlan, and then I hightail it out of there. As soon as the cab drops me off, I head straight to my apartment and into my burgeoning stash of battery operated boyfriends.

I don't waste any time whatsoever. I didn't need any more foreplay, I got enough staring at Lachlan, as one-sided as that seemed. I'm already wet from just thinking about him, so I lie back on the bed, plunge the dildo deep inside, and imagine it's his cock slowly pounding me. I imagine his taut, hard, impossibly sculpted muscles above me, a feverish intensity in his eyes, his brogue calling out my name.

Then the fucking batteries in my vibrator die, and I'm left with a stuttering fake penis. I groan in frustration, throwing it to the side, then finish myself off with my hand.

First the men in this city disappoint me, then my vibrator does.

I fall asleep reinstating the thought that anything penis-shaped needs to stay far, far away from me.

Chapter Two

KAYLA

The next morning I wake up feeling slightly worse for wear. This is my punishment for having three glasses of wine last night. It doesn't take much to get me tipsy, and unfortunately that also means it doesn't take much for me to feel like shit the next day either.

Somehow I manage to get up before my last snooze alarm goes off, and I take a cold shower. Literally. Some days I feel it's the only way to really wake up and knock some sense into myself, which means I'm subjected to freezing cold water at least a couple of times a week. It's no secret that I'm, how does my mom put it, a "fanciful girl," and that I need to regroup my thoughts from time to time. Also, it makes your hair extra shiny.

Afterward, I decide to take some extra care with my appearance to make up for looking like crap last night, and I drive to the office just before I can get reamed out for being late.

Not that my boss, Lucy, would ever yell at me, even though I'm late constantly. She doesn't really say anything half the time, which is both a good thing and a bad thing. No criticism, but no praise, either.

When I first graduated university, I had all these grand ambitions. I mean, who didn't? I thought I was going to waltz out of school and straight into an amazing new career. Bram hadn't been too far off with his presumption that I could write. In school, my major was in journalism, with a minor in advertising. Both of those careers seemed to appeal to the two different sides of me—one visual, one internal. Both creative.

But the world was a cruel bitch, and the job market was flooded with thousands of naïve dreamers like myself. I was lucky as hell that, after interning on the production side of things at the Bay Area Weekly, a position opened up. I was an assistant to retail and classifieds advertising. I worked three long years, taking any shifts possible, under two different bosses, until finally I was able to move on up. I took over the classified's account, then eventually the retail account.

It's an okay job. Nothing exciting whatsoever, which I guess makes it less than okay. But from the point of view of someone who just wants a job for the sake of having a job, I'm doing all right. Since I've worked there so long I have full benefits, three weeks' vacation a year, and a paycheck that allows me to pay rent in San Francisco, which is a miracle on its own.

But it's not what I want to be doing with my life, even though I haven't really allowed myself to dream about that. I mean, I'm thirty. I *know* I'm immature as anything, but even so, I should have that shit figured out already. Hell, I thought I would have a lot of things figured out by this point.

Steph and Nicola had it easy in a way. Both of them knew they wanted to work in fashion, and though they've had to jump through hoops to get where they are, they made it work. Stephanie owns her own successful clothing store and Nicola, even though she's still working as a bartender, is branching out with her own designs.

Then there is me, who wants to help and create and express, but isn't sure how. All I know is that working from nine to five in something I don't care about is creating an even bigger void in my heart. When I've complained about this to my friends, they both tell me to take the leap and find out what I want to do. When I complain to my mother or brothers, they tell me I should be grateful to have the job I have, to be able to pay rent and put food on the table. The problem is, in this scenario, everyone is right.

I will say, ever since Bram brought up the whole interview feature piece thing that he propositioned me with, something inside of me has been waking up, like a dormant volcano. At first I thought it was because I was also thinking of erotic scenarios involving Lachlan, but now I realize that it's because I'm imagining what it would be like to write something. See my name in print. Have *my* words seen. Make a difference in people's lives in one way or another.

So while I'm sitting at my desk, twirling my ponytail around my pen, and pretending to read emails, I'm really wondering what it would be like to sit in the open offices across the hall, where all the writers are, pursuing something with passion.

I look at Candace, the ambitious assistant that I share with classifieds girl, and tell her I'll be right back. I gather up my courage and head down the hall to my boss's office. My courage isn't for her, it's for who I know I'll have to talk to after.

Her glass door is open so I knock on it lightly. "Lucy?" I say, and open it to see her peering at me over the top of her computer through her large glasses.

"Hey Kayla," she says. "What's up? How was Margarita Monday?"

"Didn't happen," I say. "Just went to the usual bar for a bit." I've become somewhat known for Margarita Mondays. I don't even like the taste of tequila all that much, but I love fruity cocktails and Mexican food, so for the last few years, I've been going out every Monday to a Mexican restaurant. Sometimes Steph and Nicola go with me, sometimes people from work, sometimes a guy I'm screwing. But obviously since I made the decision to abstain from dick, I haven't been out lately.

"Listen," I continue. "I have a friend who has this apartment complex in SOMA and he's renting the units out to people in need. You know, affordable housing. But he's fronting the bill all himself because he can't get any investors. I think he just needs a bit of extra help. I was wondering if maybe someone, one of the writers, would be able to write about it. Give it some publicity. It's a worthy cause and I think it's something the city really needs."

Lucy shrugs. "I'd help if I could. Unless he wants to put in an ad. You'll have to ask Joe. Maybe he can find someone." She shoots me a quick smile. "That's really nice of you to want to help the cause."

I nod and roll my eyes at her before leaving her office and stalking off down the hall. Why is everyone so surprised when I try and do something nice? It's not like I'm one hundred percent pure evil. Just like forty percent. That's less than half.

Taking in a deep breath, I seek out Joe's office, which is located at the end of the floor, between all the different departments. I've only been in there a few times, and Joe is pretty much the stereotype of your disgruntled, ornery editor. You would think I'd know how to work him a bit better because of that, but maybe we were too much alike.

His door is closed and I can hear him yelling at someone inside, so I wait a few minutes. I watch some of my colleagues in their cubicles. Some are furiously typing while wearing ginormous headphones, others are on their cellphones while talking and transcribing notes, others are just staring blankly at their screen. Then there is my friend Neil who is running a file over his nails, his expertly arched brows furrowed in concentration.

Every one of the writers—Neil excluded—looks invested, involved, and dedicated to what they are doing. It stings, just a bit, knowing I don't have that in my own life.

Finally the door opens and Mia, a writer I know, scampers away with her eyes down, papers in her hand, her cheeks flush with either anger or humiliation.

Oh great. So he's in a bad mood, too.

Before I can change my mind, I knock on his door and call out, "Sir?"

"What?" he barks, and I take that as a sign to come on in.

Joe sits at his desk, dress-shirt sleeves pushed up to his elbows, showing off the ape-like quality of his hairy forearms. His hair is slicked back which only accentuates his crazy widow's peak, and it looks like he has some kind of food stains on his collar. His office is a mess of loose papers, copies of the magazine, and discarded paper coffee cups.

"Oh, you," he says, derisive. He barely looks at me. "You work with the ads. Why are you here?"

I step in, just a foot, in case I get sucked into his vortex of mess, and say, "Actually, I have a story idea and Lucy told me to run it past you."

That makes him pause. "Story idea? You? Let me guess, you want to make your margarita Mondays into a column?"

How the hell did he know about that?

"No, wait," he goes on. "Something about dating in the city and what a drag it is."

I frown. I have no idea how he knows about my dating woes either. Maybe I'm more of an open book than I thought.

"No," I say slowly, crossing my arms. "It's actually for a charity of sorts." I go on and explain about Bram's project, hoping that by the end of it he'll be somewhat impressed.

No such luck. His eyes have totally glazed over. He rubs at them and sighs.

"See if someone will write about it. If no one will, you're out of luck."

"Well, what if I write it?" I ask.

"You?" He practically stutters. "No, no. We may be laughed at from time to time, but we're trying to bolster our serious image, not detract from it. Writing isn't your forte."

"How do you know?" I ask, unable to bite my tongue.

He looks at me sharply. "I'd ask for you to prove me wrong, but I don't have the time." He sighs and looks down at last week's copy in his hand. "But the story does fit into our new agenda. Go find someone to write it for you."

At that moment I want to kill Bram for putting me in this position. Still, I thank Joe and leave the office. I set my eyes on Neil and march over to him.

"Neil," I say sweetly, putting my hands on his shoulders and giving them a massage.

"What did I tell you about sexual harassment in the workplace?" he says mildly, his nails nice and shiny, his attention focused on an inbox of a million emails.

"You told me it only counts if I have a cock."

He makes a small sound of agreement. "And if you had a cock, I'd be all over you. Remind me again why you haven't set me up with your brother?"

I squeeze his shoulders extra hard, hoping I'm hurting him. "Because you're a total manwhore and I love Toshio to death. I'd hate to have his heart discarded on the streets of the Castro."

"For one," he says, wincing at my touch, "that's so cliché. The Castro? Get with the times, Lieutenant Sulu. That's where the uncouth hang out. For two, he'd find someone else in a minute. I've seen how cute he is. Just like you. And by the way, if I'm a manwhore, you're a cockslut. Own it, bitch."

I roll my eyes. "Look, before we get all racist and crude—"

"Whatever, I've called you Sulu for the last five years. Just like you won't stop calling me Diego. And I'm not even Hispanic."

I ignore him. "I need a favor from you. Actually, I need a favor for a friend, but I'm having troubles, um, fulfilling it."

"Ugh, favors," he says. I take my hands away. "Don't stop," he commands, patting his shoulder quickly.

I keep massaging. "It's a good deed."

"Double ugh. And why are you doing good deeds?"

I shrug. "I don't know, I just am. But I need your help." For the third time that day, I explain Bram's predicament.

"But this isn't even the guy you're fucking," he points out. "Aren't you still on that stupid vow of cocklessness?"

"Yes I am, and no, I'm not fucking him, but he is my friend's boyfriend."

"I don't buy it. Why are you really interested?"

Because he asked me, I want to say. Because it's nice to feel needed, like I have the power to make a difference. And because, well, maybe because there is a hot piece of rugby playing ass attached to the deal.

"Because I just am," I say. "Now can you write it up?"

"No," he says.

I groan loudly and step away, throwing my hands dramatically in the air. "Why not? *Please?*"

"Kayla, honey, I'm swamped as it is. Why don't you ask someone else?"

I look around me. Even though half the people in the office seem to be a big fan of Margarita Mondays and enjoy it when I have too many tequila sunrises and end up dancing on rickety tables, I don't think they like me enough to write something I suggested. It's kind of their job to come up with ideas, not mine.

"Or, why don't you write it?" he suggests.

I glance at him, raising my brow. "Really? I said that to Joe but he laughed at me."

"Joe laughs at everyone. It's his thing. Along with being a grumpy old man who either needs to fuck or get fucked, I'm not sure which one." I grimace. "I say write it anyway and hand it in. I'll even help you with it, editing and all that. Clean it up. You said you went to school for journalism, didn't you?"

"Communications," I mutter. "Majoring in journalism."

He waves his hand at me, stopping to admire his nails as they catch the light. "That's good enough. Half the people in here don't even have degrees. I don't. Just blind luck and a pretty face."

"Well." I lean against his desk and give him a pleading look. "Can you give me some pointers?"

Neil spins around in his chair, hands folded at his stomach over his crisp, deep purple shirt. His lips twist into an amused smile and I'm reminded of a villain in a movie. "First, honey, you need an angle."

"I just told you the angle. Rich guy does good."

He makes a sound of disgust and throws his head back. "Boring!" he yells. Someone in the background yells at him to shut up but he just waves at them dismissively. He props his elbows on his knees and points his fingers at me. "No. No rich guy does good. No one cares about rich dudes, and unless they're an Oscar-winning actress by the name of Susan Sarandon, people generally don't care what rich people are doing, good or not."

"Not true," I point out. "All the gossip mags are about the rich and all they are doing wrong."

"Find another angle," he says.

I try and rack my brain. "The city needs this though. Everyone is always complaining about the lack of affordable housing. People all over the world poke fun at our homeless populations. This is a solution. It should be a good thing no matter who does it."

"Look, there are tons of people doing good every day. Most people don't care unless you make them care. We're all too trained to shut down from all the shitty, shitty details of life and the billions it screws over. We're all selfish and self-centered, serving our own needs until someone makes it affect us personally. So, how can you do that?"

Jeez. All these years I worked with Neil, partied with him at clubs, held his hand while he cried over some guy with a mustache, and he's never seemed as smart as he is right now.

"Well, Bram is hot."

"That helps..." he says, perking up noticeably.

"And his partner is even more so," I tell him, and I find myself smiling dreamily as Lachlan filled my head. "He's a rugby player from Scotland."

He sat up straight. "Is he a big deal?"

"Oh," I say with a smirk. "He's big."

"You know this personally? What about your vow?"

I exhale, loud and exaggerated. "No, I do not know this personally. I just saw him last night at the bar. And he... he's...just such a *man*. I can't explain it. He's probably the hottest guy I've ever seen. And he's built like a redwood."

"Like a North Cali redwood?" he asks excitedly.

"Just like," I tell him, happy I have someone to talk about my sudden obsession with. "He's covered in tattoos, he's got money, he's got lips you just want to suck on."

"Amongst other things."

"And I think someone mentioned he's good at what he does. He was in the World Cup for Scotland a few times I think."

"*Shiiiiit*," Neil says with a grin, waving his hand in the air like he's sprinkling pixie dust on me. "Kayla, there's your angle. The hotness. And the celebrity."

"You just said no one cares about celebs doing good. And I'm not sure he's a celebrity just because he was in the World Cup of Rugby. No one watches that."

"Well, he's a celebrity back home, maybe. And if he's not, you'll write him as one. That's always more interesting. Besides, you know the audience for this magazine—women and the gays."

I smirk at him. "Has anyone ever told you that if you weren't so gay and cute, you'd be totally offensive?"

"That's how I get away with it," he says with a wag of his brows. "So, go and do this. Interview him. Forget the other guy. And see if you can get some photos of Mr. Redwood. Nude, preferably. You know lots of rugby players pose for nude calendars. It's, like, their thing."

My smile suddenly fades. Interview Lachlan? "Can't I just, you know, write about him without actually talking to him?"

He stares at me like I'm a moron. "How will you know what to write if you don't know him at all?"

"I could ask Bram," I say hopefully.

"No," he says. "You have to interview the guy. Why is this an issue? You should be jumping all over this. And then him."

I tug at my hair nervously. "Well, it's just that...he's not, like, super friendly. Or talkative. And I don't think he likes me."

"You mean he hasn't fallen for your charm yet?" he asks caustically.

I give him all the glares. "Not yet," I tell him. "But it's not like I was even trying last night."

He shrugs. "So go try. You want this story, you have to work for it. Looks like writing it might be the easiest part." He wiggles in his chair, all self-assured, seeming happy that I'll learn what a hard job he actually has. I won't give Neil the satisfaction.

"Fine, I will," I say, then strut back to my office. I hear him hollering "Good luck!" behind me.

It isn't until I get back to my desk that the butterflies start swarming in my stomach, and not the good kind. The nervous kind. Ugh. This is so unlike me.

Before I can think it over, I dial Bram's number and hope I don't catch him in the middle of doing something with Nicola. You can never predict her hours, nor their horniness.

"Kayla?" he asks, obviously surprised.

I plop down in my seat and wheel it away from Candace who is pretending not to watch me. The girl watches everything I do, like she's taken job shadowing just a little too far.

"Yeah. Hi, Bram."

"Did you talk to your boss?"

"I did, but listen...I'm going to write the article."

"That's fucking fantastic."

"But I have to interview Lachlan, not you."

He pauses. "Lach? Why? What's wrong with me?"

"Because you're not newsworthy."

"And my cousin is?"

"Well yeah. I mean, have you seen him?"

"Have you seen *me*?"

"I have Bram. Sorry. You're not my type."

He snorts in disbelief. "Anyone with a cock is your type."

"Hey!" I yell into the phone. Candace jumps and a pen clatters on her desk. "I'm telling you how it is. Now give me Lachlan's number or there won't be any kind of story on your apartment at all."

"Okay, okay, fine," he says quickly. "Calm your tits."

"You calm your tits," I retort. He gives it to me, and I write it down. It's international, obviously.

"Can I just text him, since it's long distance?" I ask.

"Sure," says Bram. "But I think you'll get more out of him if you talk in person. He's not very talkative on the phone."

"You don't say."

"Aye," he says. "But listen, whatever you guys end up talking about, don't ask Lachlan anything too personal, okay?"

I straighten up, my interest piqued. "Why?"

He sighs, loud and exaggerated. "Just don't, Kayla. I know you. You're all up in everyone's faces and privates lives, and we all think it's cute, but he's not like that. If you be yourself, you'll just scare him. He's a private person. He's got… well, just be professional. If you dig too deep, he'll probably snap at you and you won't get anything."

"Snap at me?" I repeat. "Is he a dog?"

Or a beast?

"Eh," Bram says. "He's just guarded, and he has no time for bullshit. So keep the focus on what's important."

"Uh-huh."

"Which is…"

Those lips. Those hands. Those eyes. But I say, "The housing situation."

"Correct. Hey, did I ever say thank you for doing this?"

"No. You didn't."

Then I hang up on him before he gets a chance to say anything. He deserves it for that dig about how I shouldn't be myself around Lachlan, as if my personality is some sort of plague.

Before I lose my nerve again, I enter the long ass number into my iPhone and text him. Well, actually I stare at the screen for a few minutes, then I type a few different sentences and erase them, and then I stare some more. Everything that Bram said about him makes me even more anxious than I was before. I mean, I can handle people. Believe me. I'm not afraid. But I'm out of my element here. I'm not a journalist, despite what I learned in school, and suddenly I feel a whole load of pressure on my shoulders.

Finally I text him: *Hey, it's Kayla, Nicola's friend. I met you at the bar last night. Bram wanted my weekly magazine to do a story on the housing situation and my editor thought it would be a good idea if I interview you. Is that okay?*

And then I wait.

And I wait.

And I wait.

Hours pass.

"Expecting a call?" Candace asks a little too brightly.

It's about 4:30 p.m. now and I just looked at my phone for the one millionth time. I've also rechecked the phone number I wrote down. I've barely done anything today except wait for that damn response. I'm not very good at multi-tasking.

With my face propped up by my hand and my shoulders slumped, I can't even bother giving Candace a look.

The phone beeps.

"Nope, not at all," I say, grabbing the phone like it's precious and I'm Gollum.

A response from Lachlan: *All right.*

The fuck? Just all right?

I quickly text back: *Okay, great, thank you. When would you like to meet? Where?*

I press send and pray it doesn't take another six hours for him to respond.

It doesn't. *You know the city better than I do. I'm free anytime.*

Okay, so we're making progress here.

Do I feel giddy? I feel giddy.

My office is near the ferry building, so I ask him to meet me at Blue Bottle Coffee at noon. It won't give us all the time in the world, which is both a good thing and a bad thing. A good thing because I'll probably get right down to business and not do the things that Bram thinks I'll do (aka ruin everything). A bad thing because it means I only get an hour to stare at him.

I'll take what I can get.

Chapter Three

KAYLA

After work I swing by my mother's house. She lives across the bay on Alameda Island, just outside of Oakland, in the same house where I grew up. It's a gorgeous narrow Victorian with gables and iron details. Out front there is a rose garden bordering the small yard that looks out onto the road where people and tourists bicycle past on warm days. It smells like childhood and sunshine and peace. The garden was always my mother's pride and joy, but these days the roses are overgrown and pretty much fending for themselves.

A lot of the house is slowly succumbing to decay. My mom isn't young and isn't in the best of health. She turned seventy-one this year, something I hate to think about. My parents were much older when I was born. In fact, my oldest brother Brian is fifteen years older than me. My youngest brother, Toshio, is six years older. I wasn't even supposed to have been born at all—my mother would describe me as a miracle surprise. The girl she had always wanted.

And I'm glad I was that miracle. My parents gave me so much love growing up to the point where I was spoiled, while my brothers acted overprotective, babying me to a fault. But shit, if it's not hard having an aging parent, especially when you've just turned thirty and still feel like a kid—like you still need them.

My father died from prostate cancer when I was just twenty-three years old. It's something that haunts me every day. He was sick for a long time and in a lot of pain, so when it happened we were glad he was no longer suffering, but even so...nothing can replace that loss. My father, for all his faults, was someone I loved without question, someone I idolized for as long as I could remember. I didn't think I could *ever* get over his death, but little by little, year after year, I tried to move on. I had to.

My mother never had such luck. Her health has been testing her ever since. It was like she lost a part of herself when he died, and she hasn't been the same. I worry about her all the time now and try and stop by the house as much as I can, which is way more than my brothers do. They only come by when I force them to, either to say hello and check in, to give her money, or to do repair jobs on the house. I know what they want for her—to move into a small apartment, or maybe even assisted living. But my mom hangs on to the house for dear life. She'll never ever leave.

And I know the minute she goes into a home, that's the moment we'll lose her forever. The house is all she has left.

So even though it's out of the way, I head on over there. She's lonely *and* alone, and it's something I understand a little too well.

It's the start of August and even though summer is fickle in the city, on Alameda it's warmer. I water her roses, run out to get groceries from the closest store, tidy up, and then settle down on her couch with her white fluffball of a cat, Mew Mew, to tell her the somewhat good news.

"So guess what?" I say.

She looks up from her knitting and gazes at me with so much...devotion...that I suddenly feel, I don't know, unworthy of it. Funny how your mom can do that to you.

"What is it, sweetheart?" she asks in her gentle, lilting accent.

"Well, I'm branching out at work. I'm writing an article, and it looks like if all goes well, they'll print it."

She smiles broadly and I'm struck by how flawless her skin still looks for her age. Despite everything, she looks like she's decades younger. I hope those Japanese genes have been passed down to me.

"That is wonderful. Oh Kayla, that makes me so happy for you."

"Yeah?"

"Oh, yes. Look at you. You're practically glowing. I was wondering if you would find that passion again."

I purse my lips. I've always thought of myself as a very lively, passionate person. Had I really been lacking it that much?

"Well," I say, trying to downplay it, "I mean it all depends on how well I write it. They don't usually run articles by people who aren't staff writers...or writers. You know, in general."

"Yes, but when you were younger, I remember the stories you would write for the school paper."

"Yeah, but those stories were, like, movie reviews and what band was in town that weekend."

She shakes her head, still smiling elegantly, and goes back to her knitting. "It does not matter, sweetheart. I read every article, and I knew you had a talent. I knew you would go back to it."

"Even though I'm old now."

Her face falls slightly. "You are not old, Kayla. *I* am old."

I sigh. "I'm sorry…I don't mean that. It's just, I felt like at this age I would have had my shi…my stuff sorted out. My life on track."

"Your life is on the track it is meant to be on. This is not a contest or a race. Don't compare yourself to others, only to the person you were yesterday."

Yeah, but how do I explain that sometimes I feel worse than the person I was yesterday? Like I'm spinning my wheels before going backward. Losing character instead of gaining it?

But I don't want to trouble my mother with that. I try not to trouble myself with those kinds of thoughts either, it's just that they sneak up on you sometimes.

"I know," I tell her. "I guess it's never too late."

"No, it's not," she says. "Just remember to keep an open mind. To take chances."

I manage a smile. "Oh, believe me, I do."

She studies me for a moment, seeing something inside me. I'm not sure what it is.

"I loved your father very much," she says, her needles clacking against each other. The statement seems to come out of left field. "Very, very much."

"I know you did. And he loved you."

"He still does." She gives me the sweetest, saddest smile. "Even though he's changed his residency to heaven, I still hear from him from time to time. I know he's okay. I know he's waiting for me."

My eyes begin to water. We don't talk about my dad too much, maybe because every time he's mentioned, the tears start to flow. My mother doesn't cry though. She takes it all so gracefully, even though I know how sad she is, how half of her soul is missing.

"Don't cry, sweetie," she says gently and leans over, putting her hand on mine. "It's okay, really. I'm just telling you because I don't want you to be afraid of love."

"I'm not afraid of love," I say defensively, wiping a tear away with the palm of my hand.

She gives me a thin smile. "It's been a few years since Kyle."

Freaking Kyle. Why is she bringing him up? Kyle is my ex. Ex-fiancé. We started dating in college and stayed together for a long time after that. But things just weren't working between us. There wasn't anything wrong with Kyle, it was just that...I don't know, I guess I got cold feet. But it wasn't because I was afraid of love. He just wasn't what I wanted from life.

"I'm happy, Mom," I reassure her. "I loved Kyle, too. He just wasn't the one."

"Oh, I know he wasn't. I know that. You did the right thing. But when you do meet the right one, I just don't want you to run away. I don't want you to be scared. Love is something you have to fight for."

I roll my eyes. "Once again, Mom, I'm not afraid of love. I *love* love!"

It's just that I happen to love fun and sex more.

She watches me closely. "Good. I'm just trying to say that even though I love your father and I'll never be the same without him, the bad outweighs the good. Even if I knew I would lose him, I would have still fallen in love. I don't regret a thing. I just want you to know, to realize, that even if you lose love, it's never really gone. It stays in you forever. The risks of love are always worth it."

I sigh, feeling a brick in my chest. "Okay, okay," I say, but I'm not sure what else there is to add. I know how it must look to my mother, always perpetually single ever since I left Kyle. But I swear, I'm not afraid of love. There's just no one out there for me and I've made peace with that. If you can't find a man to share your heart with, well...share your vagina with him instead.

Of course, at the moment I'm not doing that either. Maybe that's why I'm getting so worked up and frustrated about life.

I leave my mom's and head back into the city, my mind running over her words. She tells me not to be afraid of love, but it blows my mind how she can even say that. She said she would never be the same without my father...how can that not scare you? How can you just keep going with that loss, believing in love even when it's left you? The amount of hope and faith involved is staggering.

That night, I barely sleep a wink. It isn't just what my mother said. It's my nerves. Stupid nerves. I can't remember the last time I was nervous. I don't *get* nervous.

And yet here I am, a nervous pervous, thinking about the interview tomorrow, feeling all the pressure that wasn't there before.

I'm still anxious when I wake up. I head into work, feeling like I swallowed a ball of electricity. I'm like this all the way until before lunch, then it intensifies until I'm practically jumping out of my skin.

I have to admit, the excitement, even over something so simple, is intoxicating. I decide to roll with it, to stay positive. I'm going to win this man over. I'm going to get the best interview of my life. Well, so far, the only interview of my life.

I grab my bag and head to the washroom to make sure I'm looking just right. I'm wearing skinny black capri pants with zebra print loafers, and an eggplant silk blouse that shows just a hint of what little cleavage I have. My hair is loose today, long and wavy, and so shiny it resembles a pool of oil (thanks to me going overboard this morning with hair glosser). My dad was from Iceland (that's actually where my parents met), and while I inherited my mother's thick black hair, I also inherited his wavy texture that goes AWOL when it's humid.

I look...respectable. Maybe even hot, especially if I toss my hair over my shoulder and slick on some nude lip gloss. I hope he'll take me seriously and want to bone me at the same time.

I make some last minute adjustments, ignore the texts coming in from Nicola and Stephanie *and* Bram who are all wishing me luck (and therefore making this out to be a bigger deal than it actually is), and make my way across the streetcar tracks to the ferry building.

Blue Bottle Coffee is an SF institution and kind of a hipster mecca, and just as I suspected, there's a giant line snaking out into the building's airy hall. The café attached has limited seating, but I was hoping that once we got our coffees we could go outside and stare at the ferries and the Bay Bridge. I mean, *pretend* to stare at the ferries and the Bay Bridge, while I'll be scoping out his ass. Thank god for dark sunglasses.

But for the life of me, I don't see Lachlan anywhere.

I casually fish my phone out of my purse to check, but there's nothing on the screen except for my Orphan Black wallpaper. I get in line for coffee instead and hope that I'm not being stood up.

I'm almost at the cashier—five minutes have crawled by and I want to stab everyone in the line with a stir stick—when

I feel a presence to the side of me. It's more than a presence. I feel *eclipsed.*

"Kayla?" Just one rough, Scotch-soaked word and I'm dessert all over again.

Play it cool, play it cool.

I turn to face him. I look up. And up. And I give him the biggest grin in the world. I'm surprised my tongue doesn't loll out of my mouth.

"Oh, hi!" I say, way too enthusiastically. "Lachlan, right?"

He frowns. Obviously not endeared by my raging awkwardness.

"Uh, yeah. Sorry I'm late. Still finding my way around."

I know I should look away. Say something else, even. Maybe, "It's not a problem, what would you like to drink?"

But I can't. I am rendered speechless by this man. I am Jell-O, putty, and other soft, moldable substances. I am anything but Kayla Moore when I am around Lachlan McGregor.

So I stare at him. Black jeans, nicely fitted, a dark grey flannel shirt that looks cozy enough to sleep in and plays up the breadth of his chest and shoulders. In the natural light of the ferry building, his eyes are lighter, leaning more towards grey-green, like the water of San Francisco Bay. The more he frowns at me, his lightly tanned forehead scrunching together into deep, craggy lines, the more I like it. I feel like I'm being examined. Scrutinized. And he looks rough. Dangerous. I want him to spill all his secrets.

"Miss?"

I barely hear the words uttered from behind me. Lachlan looks over my shoulder, then tilts his head at me.

"You're wanted," he says in his thick brogue.

"Oh?" I ask coyly.

He jerks his chin at the barista at the counter. "It's your turn."

Right. That. I smile again and I know it reads pure goof. So much for being sexy. Or even tolerable.

I turn and give the barista my attention. I quickly order an almond milk latte for myself.

"What would you like?" I ask Lachlan.

"Tea, black," he answers.

"Oooh, black tea, living dangerously," I tease him.

He doesn't smile back. He just stares at me, brow furrowed, like I'm too stupid to live.

Well isn't this going just great? I remind myself that I'm not here to win Lachlan over, to be sexy, cute, funny, or anything that I normally am. I'm here to write about Bram's stupid charity. I find myself cursing the Scot once again.

I pay and then step off to the side while we wait for our drinks.

Lachlan reaches into his jeans and pulls out two rumpled dollar bills, holding it out for me.

"What's this?" I ask.

"For the tea," he says gruffly and shakes it at me.

"Thanks," I tell him, "but it's on me. Don't worry."

He grunts something then reaches over to the counter and sticks the money in the tip jar, which gets an appreciative thank you from the overworked barista.

Thankfully he gets his tea right away and my latte doesn't take long either, so we don't have to stand around awkwardly while I think of things to say. I spent all morning going over questions I was going to ask him, but now that he's here, standing in front of me, I can barely remember where I work.

"So," I say to him, wishing I had wrote my questions down on my phone instead of on the notepad. That I forgot at the office. Of course. "Do you want to take a stroll outside?"

He nods, taking a sip of his tea, his eyes darting everywhere else except at me.

I clear my throat and we walk away from the coffee shop and past the shops. It's actually a good place to meet someone you don't know—there's lots to look at.

But of course all I want to do is look at him, even though I get the feeling that my eyes constantly roving all over him isn't that appreciated. It's just that it's hard when you're walking beside a beast of a man. I feel so tiny in his shadow.

"Have you done interviews before?" I ask.

He gives me a sidelong glance. "Have you?"

I grimace, feeling sheepish. "Uh, well, not really. This is my first one. I mean, legitimately. In university I wrote for the school paper, but that was a fucking long time ago."

He nods. Another sip of tea. "Bram mentioned that."

"What else did he mention?"

"That this could help get him some attention."

"Him?" I repeat. "Aren't you in this as much as he is?"

Lachlan shrugs. "Not really. I just helped out with what I could."

We come to the doors leading outside to the docks and he holds one open for me. Well, at least he hasn't forgotten his manners.

"Thank you," I tell him. He makes a dismissive noise in return.

The air is beautifully fresh outside and seems to clear my head. The sun shines down with ferocity we rarely see this time of year.

"So, back to you," I say, bringing it around. "Have you done lots of interviews before? I mean, I don't know, you must be used to it with rugby. Aren't rugby players celebrities over there?"

Another nod. "I've done some."

We pause at the railing overlooking the ferries, watching seagulls wheel overhead, and I wonder if I should start taking notes. Then again, he hasn't really given me any information.

"And what rugby team do you play for back in Scotland? I heard you represented the country at the World Cup."

"I play for Edinburgh. And I was in the last two world cups."

"Did you win?" I ask hopefully.

He turns his head to look at me and shakes it ever so slightly. I could swear he almost looks amused. "No."

"Aw, that sucks," I say because I'm not really sure what the right response is.

He shrugs. Leans against the railing and stares off into the distance. The breeze ruffles his hair slightly, golden brown highlights catching in the sun.

I do the same and lean on the rail beside him, my arms looking like toothpicks in comparison to his, his sleeves rolled up to showcase thick forearms. I glance over the tattoos, words and images, and when I look up, he's staring down at me. I'm not sure he realizes how intense his gaze can be, and it takes a lot for me to look away.

"Do your tattoos tell a story?" I manage to ask.

He keeps on staring, completely unreadable. Then he looks down at his arm and it flexes beautifully. "Everything tells a story."

Now it's my turn to give him the eye. "Do you mind elaborating?"

"Will my tattoos help with the article?"

"It might," I tell him, starting to get a bit frustrated at how unforthcoming he is.

But still, he doesn't elaborate.

"So how was the no pants party?" he asks, adjusting his stance so he's facing me.

I blink at him. "What?"

He looks me up and down. "When I first saw you, you had a shirt on that said 'no pants party.'"

He's joking, right? I find myself scrutinizing him just as he does to me. Then his mouth, that gorgeous, luscious mouth, quirks up, just a bit. It's subtle but it's the closest thing I've seen to a smile.

"Pants are usually a waste of time," I tell him. "The only reason I'm wearing them now is because my work expects me to be 'professional,'" I add, using air quotes.

"How would they know if you're wearing pants or not?" he asks, and then cranes his head to look at my ass.

I'm both flattered that he's looking and hella confused as to why. I frown. "Huh?"

"Oh," he says, bringing his gaze back to me. "In the UK, pants is another word for underwear. Thought you had a predisposition to go commando."

I laugh. "No, no. Well, I do. I mean, underwear is a waste of time, really. But no, the shirt was about…anyway it doesn't matter."

"I agree," he says.

"About what?"

"Pants being a waste of time."

My mind goes wild. I'm picturing him not only without any pants on, but with no underwear either. I try and keep my eyes focused on his upper body instead of looking for a dick imprint and getting an idea of what nude Lachlan really looks like.

"Of course," he continues, "it's smart to wear them during a match. You'd be surprised how many times your shorts get pulled down during a tackle."

And my imagination explodes. "The other guys pull down your shorts?" My brain is suddenly bombarded by images of him wearing tight little shorts while other big, burly men pull them down. Dicks flying everywhere.

He looks me over. "Have you ever seen a rugby game?"

"No. But if you wear shorts and other men are constantly pulling them down, I may have to start watching it."

"Do you watch any sports?"

I consider that. "I watch baseball. But only when the Giants play. But in general, no. I don't think it's good for my heart. I tend to get a little worked up. I'm known to throw things."

"You'd fit right in with Scotland, then. We're a passionate bunch when it comes to our teams. Passionate and a little nuts."

"You consider yourself a little nuts?"

"Well, of course. Isn't everyone?"

I nod. He has a point. "Yeah. I'm definitely not normal."

"No, you aren't."

I glance at him sharply, not sure whether to be offended or not. "Hey."

He isn't bothered. "Bram said you were a handful."

I roll my eyes and make a noise of disgust. "Of course Bram said that. But listen, your cousin is full of shit."

"He said you were thirteen going on thirty." Again, his lips twitch into that almost smile. Well, I'm glad he finds that amusing above all else.

"I *am* thirty," I say bitterly. "And he's the one who acts like a teenager. Same with Linden. Both your cousins are in a state of arrested development."

"Can't argue with that."

"But they aren't really your cousins, are they? That's probably why you're so different."

The air around us seems to sharpen. The line between his brows deepens and his gaze turns hard. "They aren't really my cousins?" His voice is like flint.

Oh shit. I feel like I've said the wrong thing.

"Um, you're adopted, right?"

His jaw tenses and I'm absolutely terrified that maybe he didn't even know he was adopted. Holy fuck, did I just ruin absolutely everything forever?

A million beats pass. I feel like the pause goes on for eternity. This silence is deadly.

Then he says, "Yes, I'm adopted."

How do I recover? What do I say?

"Sorry," I apologize. I put my hand on his forearm and feel the warmth of his skin. Then he stares down at my hand and I quickly remove it. "I didn't mean to get personal."

"Mm-hmm," he grumbles, and looks away. His posture is rigid, muscles strained. I pissed him off. I know it. Why do I have to be so good at pissing people off?

"Sorry," I say again, nearly helpless.

He clears his throat and downs the rest of his tea. It must be scalding hot still but he doesn't even wince. "Listen, I better get going. Hope you got what you wanted. I'm sure Bram would love to talk some more about the project."

Shit. Shit, shit, shit. He can't go now! We didn't even talk about the project at all! What the fuck am I supposed to write about?

"Um, uh," I stammer. "Maybe we can meet again when you have more time? I feel bad, I haven't asked you anything important yet."

He straightens up and nods at me, avoiding my eyes. "I'll see you later, aye."

And then he walks off. I stand there feeling stupid and watch his taught, perky ass disappear from sight.

"Kayla, you are a total fucking idiot," I say out loud, which prompts a cautious glance from a passerby. I sigh and lean against the railing, staring down at the choppy water. Bram hadn't been kidding when he said I shouldn't ask him anything too personal. And I guess adoption is always a personal thing. It just really sucks since I felt like we were finally having a good rapport with each other. Getting answers from him was like getting blood from a stone, and I finally felt like I was breaking through.

And of course I had to go and mess it all up, because that's what I do. Maybe if he wasn't so damn good-looking, I would have been able to think better. I decide to blame my vagina for robbing my brain of its much-needed blood supply.

I bring out my phone and text Bram.

It didn't go too well, I type and press send.

He responds almost instantly. *I had a feeling. What happened?*

I asked the wrong question and he pretty much shut it all down.

What did you ask him?

I groan as I type. *I mentioned the fact that he was adopted. I guess he didn't like that.*

Bram's response takes a while. The dots flash as he types on his end, and I know he's just going nuts. Finally it comes through as: *That was stupid.* I guess he erased whatever he was going to originally say. Probably smart. I don't normally feel bruised but after all this, I'm strangely fragile.

Yeah, I fucked up. Sorry. But I'll write what I can. I may come to you with some questions if that's okay.

No worries.

And though Bram said no worries, that didn't mean I wouldn't worry.

I take a deep breath and make my way back to the office where I sit down and pretend to concentrate on my *real* job for the rest of the day.

Chapter Four

LACHLAN

I hate interviews.

I mean, I really, *really* despise them. So when Bram told me that his girl's friend would be contacting me, wanting to interview me for some San Francisco weekly magazine, I immediately said no.

Don't get me wrong. I want to help him out. After all, I'm here, aren't I? I'm supporting him the best I can, putting my own money in. I've always had a soft spot for charity, and even though I hadn't seen my cousin for years, I have a soft spot for family too.

But interviews are a whole other thing. Nothing is worse than having to talk about yourself, especially to someone who will twist your words around. The number of times I've been called "difficult" and "temperamental" by a news article or interview is high, high enough that I just full-on stopped doing them. It became less about the game and more about whatever salacious items they could drag up about me, and that's a game that I just don't play.

And the main problem is, there's a lot about me that they can bring into the light. Not necessarily things that I'm ashamed of, but stuff that shouldn't concern anyone else except me. Privacy is everyone's given right, and the problem with the world today is the fact that everyone thinks they have a right to it, too. So fucking what if I play for Edinburgh? Does that mean the public has a right to know about my personal life, my private life? No, it doesn't.

Bram's a persuasive guy though. He said the article could help us secure the extra funding that he needs. Then he mentioned that the girl, Kayla, is trying to get her break in writing, so she won't be like any of the journalists I've been subjected to.

He was right about that. The girl is kind of a hot mess. She's hot too, even though she looked like she just rolled out of bed the first time I met her. But more than that, she gives me the impression of a runaway train that's about to implode. Not exactly professional journalist material. So with that in mind, I said yes. Let her interview me if Bram thinks it will help.

Of course he had to warn me of a couple things about Kayla. One was that she was a notorious man-eater, and if I wasn't careful, she'd be climbing me like a bloody tree. And two, she has no filter and was bound to say the wrong thing and that I should take it easy on her if that happened.

Well, she didn't climb me like a tree. I can't say I was disappointed because when you've had women throwing themselves at you over the years, the novelty can wear off really fast. But even though she wasn't getting handsy with me, she was letting her eyes roam all over my body like she was exploring a new planet.

What she did do, though, was come out and say something incredibly stupid. I guess stupid is a strong word, but the mention of my adoption did seem to come out of left field. I knew she regretted it immediately—her face flamed a shade of pink and I could see the utter embarrassment in her eyes—and I probably should have taken it easy on her.

I couldn't help it though. The fact that Bram and Linden's aunt and uncle adopted me when I was a teenager is nothing I'm ashamed of. I just don't like that some girl I barely knew somehow knew that about me. It's not like I went around announcing it, and that was only the tip of the iceberg. I wondered what else she knew. It seemed no matter where I went, my past couldn't leave me alone.

So I snapped at her. I won't be surprised if she also describes me as "difficult" in the piece, if she's even going to write it still. I'm not exactly the kind of guy you want to donate money to, no matter how hard I've been working on changing that back at home.

After I left her there at the waterfront, I went straight back to the flat I was temporarily renting. I resisted the siren song of alcohol and immediately put on shorts and running shoes and went for a run along Central Basin until the ocean spray and the exhaustion calmed my nerves.

Being back in my flat though, this small, cold space that's so far from my real home, has this ability to pull me back down. Now I feel really bad. I keep seeing Kayla's dark eyes flash with humiliation, the way her shoulders slumped as I nodded goodbye. I don't know the girl at all, but something about her, maybe it's her boldness, her enthusiasm, makes me care that I was a premature arse to her.

I glance at my phone and think about texting her, just to say I'm sorry. It would at least appease the traces of guilt that are creeping through me. But I'm nothing if not prideful.

I text Bram instead.

I think I might have been a dick to your friend.

He texts back: *Don't worry about it. She's tougher than she looks.*

Has she said something?

She's always saying something. Want to come to the Lion tonight?

Part of me wants to say yes. Especially if Kayla is there and I can apologize in person. But I'm in a mood and I know my moods well. I shouldn't be in a bar, I'm apt to drink too much and get in a fight, and that's really the last thing I need right now.

The truth is, I'm counting the days until I go back home: all fourteen of them. The injury to my Achilles tendon is fully healed and I'm due back in Edinburgh mid-August to start training again with the team. I won't be on right away—I've missed too much sitting on the sidelines and resting up—but it's a start. It's kind of pathetic, actually, how much the game controls my life—how much passion it brings me and how lost I am without it. The fact that I'm getting late in my career is something I try not to think too much about.

Then of course there is Lionel, who I miss like fuck. And everyone who works with me at the organization, my brother Brigs, my mate Amara, my teammate Thierry. Even though my life back home felt like it was stalling for a while, like it was missing something, coming here makes me realize that Scotland is where I truly belong. I might go back still feeling bereft—that void that swoops in when you're lying in bed, in the dark at night and wishing your chest wasn't aching for something *more*—but at least I know it's home.

I text Bram that I'll catch him some other time, then settle down to watch the telly. I make it through a few stupid American shows and half a baseball game before curiosity grabs me by the ankles. I find myself grabbing my iPad and searching through Facebook for Kayla. I barely have a Facebook account myself, and what I do have is locked down and private, but even so I can't help but want to find out more about her. I'm aware that I'm being a wee bit stalker-ish and I can't exactly explain why I'm doing this, but it's happening.

Short of adding Kayla as a friend, which is weird and unnecessary, I go on Nicola's Facebook page and search through her pictures until I find the ones with Kayla in them.

I have to admit, for all her crass attitude, Kayla is actually a really beautiful girl. Dark, wicked eyes, long shampoo commercial hair, and just enough freckles to make her seem young and innocent, even though I know she's anything but. She's got a strange brand of confidence, which is always a bonus. You can tell from the way she smiles, just free and wild. Uninhibited. That perfect body doesn't hurt either.

But I'm not creeping on her out of anything other than curiosity—she's not really my type. Sure, gorgeous girls can be great for a quick shag, but anything beyond that is usually futile. They're too shallow, too vain, too vapid. And once they discover that I'm more than just a rugby player, when they find out who I really am, what I'm really like...they tend to run the other way.

They *always* run the other way.

Believe me, I've seen them all, been with them all. But I'm not like Bram. I'm not proud of it. The honest truth is, after a while, being a player starts to get tiring. I'm thirty-two years old, and the days of sleeping with anyone who throws themselves at me is over and done with. And as for relationships, well, I've never been one to get too close to anyone. I'm just not built for it. Being alone has suited me my entire life and I don't see that changing anytime soon.

Which is why it's really draining that I've had to go on a few dates with Justine already. She's an all right girl—at least she's easy on the eyes. Our conversations have been pleasant, and I seem to appease her with a simple kiss goodnight. But I feel pretty lousy leading this girl on.

Once again, it was all Bram's idea. Justine's father is loaded and has been known to make a lot of investments around the city. He's hoping that if we get on her good side, she'll put a good word in for us and then, bam, we'll have enough to continue.

But because Bram is now happily attached to Nicola (thank god, since I couldn't stand another day of hearing the lovesick fool pine for her), it all falls on me. I got way more than I bargained for when I came over here.

And I know that Justine can see through it all. At least I hope she can. I'm not exactly wooing her, and it's been a long time since I've tried to woo anyone.

As if she can sense what I'm thinking, my phone suddenly lights up with a text from Justine.

What are you doing tonight? it reads.

I run my hand through my hair and sigh. I suppose anything would be better than lurking on Kayla's photos and dreaming about home. Maybe getting out of the flat, out of my head, would be good for me.

Not much, I text back. *You?*

Her reply is immediate, like she already had it all typed out. *A new restaurant opened up on Grant. I was wondering if you wanted to grab a bite and check it out.*

I sit back on the couch and stare at the phone for a few moments. In some ways, this is no different from doing an interview. And even though this project isn't my baby, it is Bram's. I have my own projects back home in which I work tirelessly for, every single angle. I know what needs to be done.

I make plans to meet Justine and then get ready, slipping on a black dress shirt and grey trousers instead of my usual jeans and t-shirt.

Fifteen minutes later and I'm stepping out of a cab in front of some restaurant called Salt Air. There's a line of overly fashionable people outside, and it's exactly the kind of scene that I hate, the type of people who make me uncomfortable. All that judgement. All that ignorance. Give me a fucking pub that smells of stale cigarettes over this chi chi, Instagrammed crap any day.

"Lachlan." I turn to see Justine walking toward me. As usual she's dressed to impress, her simple red dress clinging to her long, lean curves. Her chocolate hair is piled high on her head, showing off stunning cheekbones.

Being a gentleman, I hold out my arm for her. "You look beautiful," I tell her honestly.

She takes my arm and shoots me a coy smile. "You know, this is our third date and I think that's the nicest thing you've ever said to me."

I nod, pressing my lips together before I say, "I call it as I see it."

We don't wait in line and instead go straight to the hostess who seats us right away. I guess Justine really does have a lot of power in this city. We get a secluded table in the corner where candles flicker in the dim light. Though the restaurant has this sparse, industrial vibe, there's no denying that it's romantic.

At least, it's supposed to be romantic. And as we order the wine and look over the menu, I know that's all that's on

Justine's mind. She shoots me flirtatious glances over the menu and her foot brushes up against my leg more than once. Though she's very demure about it all, there's no question what she wants.

"So how was your day?" she asks me. I can tell she's just trying to make conversation.

"It was fine," I tell her, and mentally decide to get the rib-eye, even if it comes with some kind of weird South American green sauce.

"You know, Lachlan," she says, swirling her glass of shiraz around, "I don't think I know a thing about you. Even still."

Frowning, I glance at her briefly. "There isn't much to know."

"No? It's hard to tell. You don't say very much. You're very quiet."

There's nothing I hate more than having to hear that. I lean back in the chair and stare at her for a few beats. "I only speak when I have something to say."

She stares right back until I can see she's getting uncomfortable. She looks away and then brings on that big white smile. "Luckily I like the strong, silent type."

I've heard that before. They all say that. None of them mean it.

"But," she goes on, "you know a lot about me."

That's because you don't ever shut up, I think.

"Tell me about your childhood," she says innocently. "Your past."

A sour taste fills my mouth. I take a sip of wine and a deep breath. I can't help but give her a hard look. "My past belongs to me and no one else," I say, my voice sounding rougher than I mean it to.

She's taken aback. "Oh." She looks down at her hands.

"That's what I always say," I add quickly, remembering what an arse I was earlier in the day to Kayla, who also didn't mean any harm. "The future is a more interesting topic. Don't you think?"

Now she's grinning bashfully, brushing a piece of hair off her face. I know she thinks that I'm talking about her and our future together, when nothing could be further from the truth. So I take the opportunity to talk about Bram and the housing project, and my hopes that we can make the future bright for so many others.

It seems to work. For once she seems to listen, maybe because for once I'm actually talking. Maybe if I had just opened my mouth on the first date, there wouldn't have had to be three.

"I'll tell you what," Justine says to me when we're finished with our dessert. "There's an event coming up next Monday, a cocktail party. Daddy will be there. I could introduce you two, and maybe he can help with the apartment. Sometimes he feels…what's the word?"

"Philanthropic," I suggest.

"Sure," she says, and from the look in her eyes I'm wondering if she knows what the word means. "Are you interested?"

I give her a lopsided smile. "Most definitely."

Even though a cocktail party with the elite is another thing that raises my hackles, I know I would be a fool to pass it up. Not when we are so close.

That night a Town Car drops her off at her apartment overlooking the bay. By the way she's leaning against me in the backseat, her hand running up and down my thigh, I'm not surprised that she asks me in for a cocktail. I'm almost tempted, too. I haven't gotten laid in a very long time and I'm itching to burn off some steam.

But my principles hold me in check. And with everything set for next Monday, the chance to maybe, hopefully, win over the final investor, going the extra step isn't needed. It will only complicate things, and that is the last thing I need before I leave the city.

When I fall asleep though, I'm not thinking of Justine, but Kayla of all people. I saw how opening up, getting off my grumpy high horse, and just trying to be a little more sociable led to what I had wanted to begin with.

If I see Kayla again, I'll ty and make it different.

Chapter Five

KAYLA

I spend the next two days trying to write the article. It's freaking hard. Between visiting my mother, going for dinner with my brother Toshio and his boyfriend Sean, and trying to make my weekly fencing lesson, plus working my normal job, I barely have any time. Thank god I'm not dating anyone at the moment because sex trumps work, always. No wonder all the journalists I know are single.

The article sucks anyway. I know it does. And I know that if I was a stronger writer, I could probably craft some magic out of it. But I don't know what I'm doing, I'm unpracticed and unseasoned, and Lachlan left me with nothing.

Of course, I'm the one who spent too much time ogling him and not enough time asking the questions that I needed to. Nicola had mentioned that the San Francisco Chronicle had done a story on them a month ago, but it hadn't drummed up any serious interest. That's why Bram wanted me to write it for The Bay Weekly. It needed that human aspect, instead of being cut and dry.

Unfortunately, because I barely had any human interaction with Lachlan, I didn't think I brought that human aspect to the table. I'm about to erase it and start all over again when Neil ventures into my side of the office.

"So, honeypie," he says, leaning over my desk. "Where's the article? Let's give old Neil here a looksee."

"Ugh," I say. "The interview went horrible."

"Oh, I bet it wasn't all that bad," he says while he nudges me out of the way to stare at the screen. He glances it over, his lips moving as he reads the words.

He gets to the end and turns to look at me expectantly.

"What?" I ask.

"Kayla. That's garbage."

"What?!" I shriek, even though I know it's the truth. "It's not garbage."

"I know you can do better than that." He jabs his finger at the screen. "All you've got here is blah blah blah boring shit about charity. And then a quote from a Scottish World Cup rugby player who helped out with what he could." He shakes his head at me. "Helped out? That's all you got?"

I glare at him and shove him out of the way. "Well, I told you that it didn't go well!"

"But Joe won't run this. I can't even edit this. It's boring, Kayla, and you my dear are the opposite of boring. Go back to him, get another interview, and inject some of that personality of yours into this piece."

"But my personality is why everything got fucked up to begin with!"

He puts his hand on my shoulder and stares down at me with mock endearment. "Kayla. Get your head out of the gutter, put on your big girl panties, and go try again."

I hate that he's right. But he's right. If I think I deserve a shot at a new career choice, I'm going to have to earn it, and I sure as hell didn't with this pile of stink.

When Neil leaves, I take out my phone, swallow my pride, and text Lachlan.

Hey, it's Kayla. I just want to apologize for the other day. I'm really sorry if I said the wrong thing. It wasn't my intention to offend you.

I know I'm texting with kid gloves here, but I feel it's the only way to ease into this situation.

I wait and thankfully it doesn't take long for him to text back.

That's all right. It's a touchy subject, and I shouldn't have been such a wanker.

Wanker. I love the Scottish idioms. And the fact that he said that can't mean he's all that mad and disgusted with me.

I decide to chance it and text: *I totally understand if you say no to this, but would it be okay if we try again? I promise I won't be an idiot.*

Sure. Can you meet me tonight at six o'clock? The field at Avenue D and 9th.

Tonight? I wasn't expecting for him to say yes, let alone to want to meet up so soon. And in a field of all places? I quickly google the address because I have no idea where it is. Treasure Island pops up. I've only been there for a music festival. Other than that it's the lump of rock along the Bay Bridge between San Francisco and Oakland.

Still, it's not too far from work so I tell him I'll meet him, even though the clouds are coming in fast and dark today.

This time I'm going to be prepared. Even though I have a crapload of work to do, I pass off as much as I can to Candace, and then go through my interview questions again and again, before I copy them out on my phone's notepad as well as a physical notepad.

By the time five o'clock rolls around and it's time to go, the skies outside open up and dump a deluge of rain on the city. It rarely rains in San Francisco—usually we just get clouds that seem to hold their breath but never let loose—but I grab the umbrella under my desk.

Treasure Island is close by, but I still have to go over half the Bay Bridge with everyone else in the city, so by the time I actually get to turn off from the traffic, it's nearly six. Thankfully the rain has let up a bit as I crawl along the wide streets until I spot the field.

To my surprise there's a game of some sort going on. When I pull the car over to the side of the road and park, I can see it's a rugby match. I turn the car off and watch through the windows as the rain patters down. I can't make out Lachlan in the mix of men, and my eyes scan the sidelines where people in rain slickers and umbrellas are watching. He's not there either.

I sit in the car for a while, until the windows start to fog up, then I grab my umbrella and head out. The rain is down to a light drizzle, but the field is wet and muddy already. The people at the sidelines are talking with each other and slapping the players on the back as they come in off the field. Some head back to the line of cars. I guess the game is over.

And then I spot him, the last one walking off the field and the one holding the ball. It's called a ball, right?

It doesn't matter what it's called, because just like that, I'm stunned by the sight of him. No, floored. My knees actually feel weak, and I dig my heels down into the grass to try and keep upright.

Lachlan is soaked from head to toe. Slick. Splashed with mud. And wearing cleated shoes, black shorts that would cling to him under normal circumstances, and a thin grey t-shirt that looks plastered on. There is absolutely nothing left to the imagination and I try and commit every step he takes into my memory to draw upon later. I feel like if I don't see another man for the rest of my life, it doesn't matter, because this vision will eclipse them all.

And he knows I'm staring. He doesn't care. As he comes closer and I tear my eyes away from his massive thighs, the rigid outline of his six-pack, his nipples poking through that wet shirt, those tattoos—damn those tattoos!—I see what can only be described as a smirk on that gorgeous face.

"Hello," he says, stopping a few feet away and tucking the ball under his arm. It makes his bicep flex beautifully.

I tilt my umbrella back to stare up at his face. A lock of wet hair sticks to his forehead. Drops of rain trickle down his nose, over those full lips, and down his throat until they settle at the base of his neck. Oh god, to lick that throat.

"H-hi," I say before composing myself. I smile. "I really didn't expect to see you playing rugby."

He runs the back of his hand over his forehead, wiping away the rain, and eyes the sidelines where the rest of the team is leaving. Raindrops drip from his lashes. "Aye," he says with a nod. "It's just a pick-up league. Been playing with them a few times."

I want to follow his gaze but I can't. I don't want to look away from this sight, and even if I do, I'll hit him in the face with the umbrella. I can't risk starting off on the wrong foot again.

"Well, I'm sure you're giving one side an unfair advantage," I say. "Did they have to fight over you?"

He looks at me, tilting his head, and though he's not smiling, his eyes just might be. "They don't know who I am."

I nearly laugh. "How do they not know who you are?"

He shrugs and takes the ball out from under his arm, and starts spinning it between his hands. He frowns and looks everywhere. I've noticed he has a hard time looking at me sometimes. "I didn't tell them."

"Huh. Well, I don't know anything about the game, but I'm pretty sure they've figured out that you're more than just a Scottish guy who plays a few pick-up games every now and then."

Lachlan nods, considering. "Maybe." Finally his eyes meet mine briefly. "So did you watch the match?"

"Just the end," I admit. "Did you invite me here so you could show off?"

A flash of a smile. Well, more like a close-lipped smirk, but it transforms his whole face. It makes his eyes go soft, sensual, and his lips turn devious. He goes from looking like a dangerous dog to a puppy. I can't help but grin back instinctively.

"Maybe," he says again, and for one delicious second, bites his bottom lip. "Did you like what you saw?"

My eyes widen. Is he flirting with me? Was that flirting?

Oh my god.

If it was, it's like he just handed me the key to heaven.

"Relax," he says, taking a wide-legged stance in front of me. "I'm joking."

And just like that, he takes the key back.

"I didn't think you had the ability to joke," I tell him, ignoring my dashed hopes.

"Most of my jokes are in my head," he says mildly. "Honestly though, I figured if you learned a bit more about rugby, it would help the article." He pauses. "You know. Give it a time, a place, some action."

Hmm. He's actually right about that. It would bring the article from passive to active. I would start off by describing him on the field, soaking wet, his clothes sticking to every surface like glue, every curve of taut, sculpted muscle on display, the way his large, strong hands cup the ball, just like he'd cup a woman's ass. My ass.

Shit, my article is going to veer off into erotica territory pretty soon.

I realize he's staring at me for a response, and I haven't said anything. That smirk is still there, his brows raised expectantly.

I look at him and shrug. "Sorry. If you're going to be playing rugby in the rain and you look like you do, you can't blame a girl for staring."

He licks his lips, a flash of pink tongue. "It's okay. I'm used to it."

I bet you are.

"So, do you want to learn?" he asks, forehead all wrinkled and serious again.

"Of course," I tell him. "Can I play?"

That catches him off-guard. "What, now?"

I shrug. "Why not?"

He points at me with the ball. "Because you're wearing that."

I look down at my clothes. I'm in grey skinny jeans that I bought from Steph's store, a black blazer, and a simple white t-shirt. My shoes are leopard print kitten heels. It's kind of my quasi-professional work look when I'm feeling lazy.

"And it's raining. And muddy," he adds.

"I'm not afraid of getting dirty," I say, bringing on the sass. "Give me a minute."

I leave him wide-eyed and hurry back to the car, closing my umbrella. I open the back door, take off my shoes and blazer, and throw them on the back seat. I quickly put my hair back into a ponytail then run barefoot back over to him, nearly slipping a few times.

If he's going to teach me rugby, he's going to teach me properly.

"Okay, I'm ready," I tell him, stopping at his side. The rain is starting to soak through me pretty fast but luckily it's warm out.

His eyes rest on my chest briefly. Also lucky that I'm wearing a bra. At least, I think that's lucky.

"I do think you're a bit nuts," he says, scratching at his cheek with one finger.

"Technically, I'm wearing more clothes than you are," I point out. "And whatever. Mud comes out in the wash easily."

"There's a reason we wear boots with cleats."

I look down at his shoes, which look more like runners than boots. Then I look at my wet, grass-stained bare feet with bright orange nail polish. "If I slip, I slip. Maybe I'll bring you down with me."

Now he's frowning at me like I ought to be committed. "Suit yourself," he says with a shake of his head. He turns and walks off to the middle of the field. I stand and watch him for a few moments before he looks over his shoulder and jerks his head, gesturing for me to follow.

I walk—carefully—through the wet grass, getting into muddy territory. Because we've been in a drought here, the field is probably more dirt than grass the further you walk in, which means the middle of it all is just a mud bath.

And yet here I am, playing barefoot rugby in the rain with a man who can only be called the hottest guy on earth. I feel a buzz of excitement run through me, my heart hammering in my chest as I come to his side.

He points the ball down the field. "That's your end." He points to the other side. "That's my end. In layman's terms, the object of the game is to rack up the most points by scoring the most tries or kicking goals."

I raise my hand. "Wait, you can kick the ball? Like soccer?"

He breathes in through his nose, nostrils flaring, and I know he's fighting the urge to roll his eyes. "Like football," he corrects. "Soccer is called football everywhere else but in America."

"Is rugby still called rugby?"

He squints at me. "Yes."

"Then who cares?"

There's the eye roll I was waiting for. He sighs, and even though he's back to being all brooding again with that sharp crease between his brows, I'm taking silent pleasure in making him annoyed enough to respond like a teenage girl.

"All right," he continues. "So, you can either score a try or kick a goal. But you can't just kick the ball around the whole game, that's not how it works. Your main objective is to score a try, meaning to get over those lines over there."

I can barely see through the rain, but I just nod.

"And you do that by either kicking or running with the ball."

"So it's like football," I say. "Sorry, *American* football."

"No, love," he says to me, and I can't ignore the flash of heat in my chest from that term of endearment. "It's nothing like it. For one, you can't pass forward. You can only pass laterally or backward. For two, rugby players don't wear padding.

We rely on brute force and strength to make it through a tackle."

My eyes rest on the hard breadth of his chest and shoulders. No wonder he's built like a fucking tank.

"I saw some guy earlier wearing a funny helmet, though," I say.

"That's a scrum cap."

"Scrum cap," I repeat.

He tugs at his ear. "It's to protect these during a scrum or just during play."

"Do you guys bite each other's ears off?" I exclaim. "This is worse than boxing!"

He gives me a placating look. "No. Not on purpose anyway. But if you don't wear them, you could end up with cauliflower ear."

I grimace. "Ew. What the hell is that? Wait, no, I don't want to know." I can already picture it.

He shrugs. "I've been lucky, and I wouldn't care regardless." He runs a finger over the scar at his eyebrow, another on his forehead, another on his cheek, the middle of his nose. "Your face is bound to get fucked up at any point in the game. We aren't the prettiest bunch of men and most of us take pride in that."

"I beg to differ," I blurt out. "I mean, I think you're pretty. I mean, maybe that's not the right word..."

He gives me a dry look. "It's definitely *not* the right word."

But your eyes are like storm clouds and sunshine, framed by wet ferns, I think dreamily. I am so fucking glad he can't see this bullshit inside my head.

"Back to the game," he says.

"Right!" I clap my hands together. "Let's get dirty."

"Still a few rules though," he says patiently. "When the person with the ball is tackled and brought to the ground, they must either release it or pass to another player."

"Look, if you tackle me, I'm pretty much dead," I tell him.

"I'll go easy on you," he says.

"Oh, you don't have to."

"I can tell you won't go easy on me." He says this slowly, forcing me to focus on those lips, that hint of a smile.

"Definitely not," I admit, feeling fired up. "I'm going to bring you to your knees."

He studies me carefully for a moment, as if he's taking what I say seriously, then says, "We'll see about that."

He turns his back to me and places the ball on the ground, seeming to line it up between the goal posts at the far end.

"What's the other rule?" I ask him, wiping rain off my forehead.

"Normally you can't tackle around the neck or head. But for you I'll let it slide."

"What about your crotch?"

He looks back at me and frowns. "That's off limits, too."

"Just during the game, or like always?"

He laughs. Actually lets out a laugh and it's a beautiful sound. "Just keep in mind that we don't wear a cup in rugby."

My mouth drops. "Ever?"

He shakes his head and picks up the ball, holding it out in front of him. "I've had my nose broken a few times, my face smashed, my shoulder dislocated, my ribs broken, my Achilles tendon torn. I've had a million cuts and bruises. But I've never had any injury to the family jewels."

"That's good to know."

Another laugh. "Is that right?" Then suddenly he springs into action, dropping the ball and then kicking with one sweep of his leg, his thigh muscles bulging beneath his tiny shorts.

The ball goes soaring down the field, landing short of the end.

"Oh come on," I say, standing there as he starts to run off.

He doesn't stop, just waves at me to follow. "Are you going to play or not, you pansy?"

Pansy? I don't think so. And so even though it's extremely unfair that a tiny Asian barefoot girl has to run down a wet field after a Scottish pro rugby beast, I do it anyway.

Because, really, like I'm going to let this man get away.

I sprint down the field as fast as the slick mud and skinny jeans and short legs will let me. I know it's futile to even try, but Lachlan starts to slow down.

"You want me to catch up with you?" I yell at him, nearly slipping.

He stops near the ball. "I realize the cleats give me an advantage."

"Oh sure, the *cleats*."

He goes for the ball and I know I'm close enough to tackle him.

"Well what the bloody hell are you waiting for?" he says to me, stooping over, the ball in his hands. "This is when you tackle me so I either release the ball so you can get it or I'd pass to another player. Either way you need to prevent me from making the try."

He's just given me permission to put my hands all over him. I am not going to pass this up.

I run at him, yell some kind of warrior cry, and fling myself at his upper body. It really is like throwing yourself against a brick wall. I bounce off, my legs sliding back through the mud, and I grab on to his shirt for dear life as I fall to the ground.

Of course it doesn't bring him down. All it does is stretch the neck of his shirt and I'm hanging off him like a monkey. But I refuse to let go.

"If you don't let go, you'll rip my shirt right off," he says, staring down at me, rain pouring off his face.

"That's the idea, isn't it?" I yell back. "You gotta give me something here."

He drops to his knees beside me in the mud, his thigh pressed against mine. I can feel the heat of his skin through my jeans which starts an inferno between my legs. I've never been so close to him. All his wet, glistening skin, close enough to lick. His immense size makes me feel so small and easily overtaken, and he smells like sweat and rain, a deadly cocktail.

I swallow hard, my breath heavy in my chest. He gazes at me through wet lashes, those eyes of his laced with intensity that I can feel deep inside.

I have to be professional. I have to hold it together. And the vow, think of the stupid vow. But damn, if he kissed me, that would unleash a beast of my own. There would be nothing stopping me from ripping off the rest of his clothes and fucking him here in this muddy field.

God, I pray, briefly closing my eyes, *I know praying for dick isn't a new thing for me, but if you could please make muddy field sex with Lachlan McGregor happen, I'll erect a church in your name.*

"Here," Lachlan says, voice gruff. My eyes snap open as he pushes the ball out ahead of us. "You tackled me. This is me releasing the ball."

No, no, no. Forget the game. Make a play on *me*.

But Lachlan hasn't forgotten the game. He nudges me with his elbow. "Go get it."

I toss my hormones aside for the moment, give him a brave nod, and reach for the ball.

The minute it's in my grasp, feeling so large and heavy that it makes me want to come up with a million sexual innuendos, he bellows at me, "Now, run!"

Agh! Those are some powerful lungs. I scamper to my feet and immediately start running back down the field toward the goal. I slip a few times, my feet slapping the mud, but it's basically like running on ice.

I fall backward, completely ungraceful.

Splat!

Mud flies everywhere.

"Are you okay?" I can hear Lachlan yelling in the distance.

Though I'm winded, I take a deep breath and quickly get to my feet. I'm not going to stop now, even when I can hear him approaching close behind me.

I start running again, my own muscles straining as I try and go as fast as I can without eating shit. I don't care that I'm absolutely filthy, that I'm scampering like a colt, that I can barely see through the rain in my face. I'm going for the try and I am fucking loving it.

I'm only a few yards from the end. I know Lachlan is going slow, that he's going to let me win, but it doesn't matter because—

Splat.

I slip again and faceplant straight into the mud. I immediately try and get to my feet, but I feel Lachlan looming over me like a storm cloud. He steps on either side of my body, straddling me, then drops to his knees, so my sides are between his legs.

"Nice try," he says gruffly.

"Is that a pun?" I say, spitting out grass. I attempt to turn over but his tree-trunk thighs grip me in place. I'm not complaining.

"It would have been a pun if you made the try," he says. "You didn't. I stopped you."

"I fell," I say through gritted teeth. "I was already down."

I hear him grunt from behind me. "And I wasn't about to tackle you. So let's just pretend you didn't fall, and I brought you down, like in a normal game. Now release the ball."

"Fuck that," I mumble, holding the ball tight beneath me.

"It's the rules," he says, leaning over me so his lips are near my ear. I can't be sure but I'm almost certain he has an erection and its pressing against the top of my ass. He said he wasn't wearing a cup so it has to be all him.

Please let it be all him.

"Fuck your rules," I manage to say.

He pauses. "No rules, then? All right."

I feel him lean back, easing off me slightly.

Then his hands are down at my shoulders and underneath my arms and his fingers are going crazy.

I yelp in surprise. My fucking god, is he *tickling* me?

"What?" I cry out before bursting into nervous giggles. "You can't tickle!"

"No rules," he says, and I can hear the enjoyment in his voice.

"Stop!" I yell, laughing again. "Please, this is torture!"

"Release the ball."

But I can't. I'm laughing too hard, my body attempting to curl up into a ball even though I'm between him like a vise.

"I'm going to bite your leg," I warn him, trying to twist around and see if I can get a nip of his grass-stained knee. I'm flexible but I'm not that flexible.

"Release the ball."

"Fine!" I shout, but since I can't move I can't even get it out from under me. "Fine, you win, you can have the ball."

Suddenly he gets up and I'm free. I roll over onto my back and stare at him, holding up the ball. If he was one step closer to my face and his shorts weren't so tight, I could try and see up them.

He looks down at me, not smiling, but there is a hint of triumph in those expressive eyes.

I shake the ball at him. "Aren't you going to take it?"

He continues to stare. I can't tell what the hell he is thinking. I feel like he's trying to memorize me.

After a few beats and as the rain falls down on us, he takes the ball with one hand then grabs my hand with the other.

"Come on," he says. "I think we've had enough for today."

I'm hauled effortlessly to my feet, my body mere inches from his. We're both breathing hard, like we just had epic sex. I can only imagine.

"Hope that gave your article some insight," he tells me, voice low and eyes focused on mine. I watch the streams of water run down his face. I barely feel the cold that's slowly seeping into my bones, the feeling in my muscles that warns me I'll be sore tomorrow.

I nod, licking my lips, tasting water and salt. "I think it will."

He glances at my car in the distance, brows furrowed. "We should probably go clean up and get dry."

"Sure," I say, hoping that this might turn into the two of us cleaning up and getting dry…together. "Do you need a ride home? How did you get here?"

"I took a cab," he says, taking a step away from me and tucking the ball underneath his arm.

I look at his outfit briefly, not wanting for my eyes to get trapped in the tractor beam that is his body. I could literally stare at it all day, every single muscle and ripped line that his wet shorts and t-shirt display. "You took a cab in that?"

"I was dry at the time. And anything goes in San Francisco, doesn't it?"

I grin at him. "It sure does. How about in Edinburgh?"

He looks away and shrugs. "Just about." He jerks his chin at my car. "How about we get moving? You don't want to catch a cold standing around here."

He starts walking to the car and I wait just a moment to watch his ass go before I catch up with him.

Chapter Six

LACHLAN

I didn't really know what to expect when I told Kayla to meet me at the rugby match. I just figured if she could see the game being played, maybe it would help her with her writing. It would give her more than what I gave her before, which was nothing.

The only problem was the game ended a half hour earlier than usual because of the weather, so she only got a few glimpses of it before it was my turn to show her the ropes. I know she thought I arranged it all so I could show off, even though nothing could be further from the truth.

All right. So maybe there was some truth to it. But I had no idea that she actually wanted to play with me. She took off her fancy shoes and work jacket, and got down and dirty in the mud with me, without any hesitation.

This solidified that the girl was nuts. Clearly. But there was something about her brand of crazy that intrigued me, maybe even more than it should have. Enough so that when she pulled up to the flat I've been renting near AT&T Park, I did something I never thought I'd do.

I invited her inside.

I haven't had a girl in my home for a long time, whether it be in Edinburgh or San Francisco, and I didn't think I'd start now, especially when I was so close to going back to Scotland. And even though it's because I'm being polite, because I don't want her to drive home shivering cold and wet, it still surprises me.

"Do you want to come upstairs?"

She stares blankly at me, her eye makeup starting to gather underneath her eyes. We are both dirty, muddy wrecks and I feel bad that her car is taking the brunt of it.

I try to smile, not wanting her to get the wrong idea. "It doesn't seem right for you to drive home like this."

"Do you have a stash of women's clothes upstairs?"

"No. But I have some dry, clean clothes you can wear. Just till you get home." I glance at her thighs and trim waist. My clothes will be absolutely swimming on her, but still.

"Okay," she says, smiling, color coming to her cheeks. I get her to park in the empty space that's leased to my unit and we head upstairs.

I wish I'd tidied up a bit. "Uh, sorry it's a shithole," I tell her as we walk inside the flat.

She looks around and shrugs. "Looks like a man lives here. I'm okay with that."

I watch her briefly, her jeans clinging to her legs and perky arse, her long hair sticking to her back. She's pretty toned all over and proved to be in great shape earlier today. I need to stop checking her out though.

"I'll get you something. Be right back," I tell her before disappearing into the bedroom. I grab a clean towel from the linen closet, then fish out the smallest t-shirt I have, which will still dwarf her, and a pair of clean drawstring running shorts.

When I come back, she's staring at the weird art on the walls. "This all you?" she asks as I hand her the clothes and towel.

I shake my head. "Nah. Came with the place. I haven't been here long enough to settle in. No personal touches."

She thanks me for the towel and starts fluffing her hair with it. "When do you leave?"

"Two weeks," I tell her. "Actually, less than that." I gesture to the washroom. "Did you want to shower?"

A coy smile tugs at her lips. "Is that an invitation?"

I stare at her, not sure what to say.

She laughs. "Just kidding. Go ahead, I'm fine with this."

I swallow, give her a nod, and shower fast, even though the hot water begs me to stay longer. I wrap the towel around my waist and look at myself in the mirror. Without a shirt, every tattoo on my shoulders, arms and torso is on display, and I hope she doesn't ask me about them again. They each represent a part of my life, and some of those parts, a girl like her just wouldn't understand.

When I come out the washroom, I'm surprised to find her sitting at the table with a notepad and pen in her hand, her phone beside her. She's wearing my clothes, which look strangely becoming on her. They look…right.

She looks up at me and her eyes widen. To her credit, she blinks and immediately averts her eyes back to the paper. I quickly go into my room and throw on jeans and a t-shirt before coming back out to the living room.

"So," she says, and I notice she's trying not to meet my eyes.

I take a seat across from her and study her. She's tapping her pen against the table, reading over the jotted questions on the paper, chewing on her lower lip. Her mascara is still smudged beneath her eyes, but other than that she looks fresh, her skin like cream. I guess she can feel my gaze because she finally looks up. "So," I prompt her and gesture to the work in front of her, "what's this?"

Her mouth twists sheepishly. "I realized that I still haven't interviewed you properly."

"You really aren't much of a journalist, are you?" I say. I know I don't sound like I'm joking, but I am. Still, Kayla's mouth turns down at that and I realize she's far more sensitive about this whole thing than I thought.

"No," she says after a beat. "I'm just trying."

I don't like hearing that melancholy in her voice. It's such a change from the coy, flirtatious girl from earlier. "You're doing a great job," I reassure her.

"Do you mind?"

I shake my head. "Ask away." I pause. "I promise I'll be a gentleman this time."

"Don't get me wrong, I like it when people say what's on their mind," she says. "I'm not so different."

"No, you definitely aren't."

She looks at me, eyes soft, and I can't help but stare back at her. You could get lost in those eyes. They're so dark, like wandering in the woods at night.

I clear my throat, realizing I'm scrutinizing her, and she sits up straighter, a faint blush coming to her cheeks. "Okay," she says. "Well, the one thing I want to know is…why is this such a passion project for you?"

"Bram's initiative?"

"Yeah," she says, tapping her pencil against her lips. "What made you hop on a plane from Scotland and come to help him out? Are the two of you really close?"

I watch her for a moment, but her expression is hopeful, innocent. She doesn't realize she's almost getting too personal again. "We're not that close, but I take family very seriously. Truth be told, I misunderstood Bram. From his social media, from what my parents would say about him, I just assumed he was a playboy who wouldn't grow up. And while that was true, I also didn't think he was the type to be charitable. But what he's doing proves the guy is really invested in making a difference. He wants to do more with his life. He wants to be seen as more. And that's something I can relate to."

"This is almost turning into a bromance," she says under her breath.

"Also," I add carefully, "I believe in his vision. The under-represented are the underdogs. They are the ones fighting a fight that no one can imagine. He's giving a home to those people, the ones who have been cast aside. The strays. The wounded, the ruined, and the lost. Society can't begin to understand their problems, and it rarely provides a solution either. Though Bram's complex is small, it's a start. Big things start somewhere. Great things can come from this."

She's scribbling furiously as she writes it all down. I eye her phone. "Would it not be easier to record this on your phone?"

She smiles but doesn't look up. "It feels more authentic this way." She reads it over, her lips moving, then raises her brow, impressed. "So do you think you'll go back to Scotland wanting to do something similar? Follow in his footsteps?"

My lips twitch into a small smile. "I might."

Her brows furrow. She's assessing me, trying to read what I mean. I know better than to turn her away from the subject matter. This is really about Bram, not me.

We talk a bit more about the next steps needed in the development, my rugby career, and some things about Scotland. To her credit, she manages to keep the questions at a shallow level, even though after a while I want to flip the tables on her and start asking her questions. Not to even the score—just because I'm getting curious. I hate to admit it, but I want to know more about her—this crazy, flirtatious, ballsy, ambitious, yet sensitive girl. From the things I've heard from Bram compared to the things I've seen, I'm starting to think she's a bit misunderstood too.

But I don't ask her. Because that's not why I'm here and that's not why she's here, no matter how I catch her glancing at me from time to time. Funny how it annoys me when Justine casts a sly glance, but when Kayla does it…it's flattering.

That's just my ego talking though. Sometimes it can be as big as the moon. Other days it's not much more than a seed.

When we're all done, I get up from my chair and say, "That went well. I hope you got everything you need."

She stares at me for a moment, then says, "Oh," and gets to her feet and starts shoving her stuff in her purse. "Yes, thank you. That should be it. I think I already have the angle and everything."

"Good," I say, feeling strangely awkward. "If you need anything else, just ask." I don't think I've ever talked this much in a long time, and even though saying goodbye should be simple, somehow it's not coming across that way.

I watch as she slides her shoes on her feet. I suppress a grin from the sight of her in my baggy workout clothes and leopard print heels.

She looks up and catches my eye, flashing me a playful smile. "Maybe I'll start a new fashion trend."

"You can pull it off," I admit, folding my arms across my chest.

Her eyes rest briefly on my forearms, then she looks away, slinging her purse over her shoulder and heading for the door.

"Oh, wait," I tell her. I go into the kitchen and pull out a plastic bag, then take her wet jeans, shirt, and a tiny pair of pink underwear that were drying near the sink and shove them inside. I walk over to her and hand her the bag. "Don't forget your clothes."

She tugs at the t-shirt she's wearing. "And what about your clothes? Will I see you before you leave?"

I shrug. "Maybe. If you don't, keep them."

She frowns for a moment, then raises her chin. "I'm sure I'll get them to Bram soon. Well…thanks again for agreeing to meet with me."

"Thanks for being a good sport."

"Ha," she says, opening the door. "I have a feeling I'll be cursing you tomorrow when I can't feel my calves."

She wiggles her fingers at me and leaves. I stand there for a moment, watching her sashay off, her perky little arse eclipsed by my shorts.

I go back into my flat and close the door. I lean back against it, close my eyes, and exhale. I can still see her walking away in my mind.

Chapter Seven

KAYLA

I'm such an idiot.

Seriously. I really thought that if I conveniently forgot my wet clothes behind at his place, it would give me an excuse to go back and get them. But fuck, this dude is not like the others. It's like flirting with a block of ice. And yeah, I could see it slowly melting over time—I mean, I'm still convinced he had an erection when he was pinning me to the ground—but Lachlan doesn't have much time here. Which means I don't have a lot of time to try.

"What about your vow?" Nicola asks as Ava noisily sips on her smoothie. It's Saturday afternoon and the three of us are in a coffee shop, celebrating the fact that I'd finished my article and handed it in to Neil yesterday, who is going to fix it up and hand it in to Joe. I'd spent three days writing it and rewriting it until finally I was happy with it. Neil was happy with it. And Nicola just read the whole thing, looking damn impressed.

Naturally though, the conversation shifted to Lachlan. Well, me bitching about Lachlan, this beast of a man who seems forever off-limits.

"My vow?" I repeat, confused as to what that has to do with anything.

I look over at Ava who is coloring in her book, her tongue sticking out in concentration. I put my hands over her ears and say, "*Fuck* my vow."

When I release Ava, she looks at me then her mom, and says, "Auntie Kayla said a bad word again."

Nicola smiles at her adoringly then gives me a mock stink-eye. After having the two of them live with me for so long, Ava knows the drill very well.

"I knew you wouldn't last very long with your…drought," Nicola says, rather smugly I might add.

"Hey, I'm still going," I tell her. "But for Lachlan, I would make the exception. In fact, if by some grace of god I was able to get in his pants, I swear I'd never touch another man again."

She looks startled at that. "Jeez. Be careful what you wish for, Kayla."

I wave my hand at her dismissively before sucking down my iced coffee. "It doesn't matter. It won't happen. He is completely immune to my charms. I mean, I was running around in the mud, *soaking wet* in a white t-shirt. I was writhing beneath him. It was practically like having sex. And yet…nothing. Later on at his place, he was about to take a shower, and I made a joke about joining him. You should have seen his face."

"Did he look disgusted?" Nicola says, already sympathetic.

"No," I tell her. "But thanks for thinking he might have. He just looked…I don't know. I can't read him at all. It's like he didn't even hear me."

"Maybe he didn't," she says.

"He heard me," I say, leaning back in my chair and folding my arms. "He's just not interested."

"Well, you can't be everyone's type," she tells me, taking one of Ava's crayons and coloring a square before Ava swats her away.

"I refuse to believe that."

She sighs and looks up at me. "I have to say though, I didn't think he would give you this much." She nods at the article on the table I printed out from my work computer. "I mean, whenever I've spoken to him, he's only responded in monosyllabic caveman grunts."

She's not exactly wrong. Half of his responses to me are in the form of grunts and other manly noises, but I feel more adept at distinguishing those noises. "Getting him to talk is kind of like pulling teeth. The whole time I was asking him questions, I was terrified I was going to say something wrong and set him off like a bomb again."

"I wonder what his deal is," Nicola muses.

"Yes!" I exclaim, slamming my palms on the table. Ava and Nicola both jump. "What *is* his deal? Can you find out for me?"

Nicola's face scrunches up. "I told you, the guy barely talks to me."

"Yes, but Bram would know."

She shakes her head. "I don't think so. Bram says he barely talks to him either, and when he does, you can be sure it's nothing personal."

"I need to talk to Bram," I say, nodding to myself.

"Well, come to the Lion tonight," she says. "I'm working a short shift so Bram is meeting me there. I'm sure he'd like to read the article, too." She looks at her phone to check the time. "Speaking of, I better drop Ava off at my mom's and get ready."

I hug the both of them goodbye, then order decaf. I don't need the caffeine because I already feel like I'm flying. This article really has me all jazzed about life, which is kind of a weird thing in itself. And it's scary. Because what if this doesn't work out the way I want it to? What if Joe just takes the article, prints it, and that's it? I go back to my regular job, being bored out of my mind. What if I work forever in advertising, doing the same old shit every single day? I don't know if I can do it, now that I know something better is out there, something that makes me feel...alive. It would kind of be akin to living your life in darkness and someone giving you the sun. Okay, scratch that—that's *way* too schmaltzy and dramatic. But still...it would suck balls. And not the good kind.

Naturally my thoughts drift to Lachlan after that. I really need to get that man out of my head, but every time I picture his face, that body, that gravelly voice that holds a million secrets, I get this rush inside me, like birds being let loose from a cage. That, combined with the article, and I feel like I'm starting to go a bit insane. Perhaps I just need to put my head down and conjure up that black shriveled heart of mine that doesn't get too excited about anything.

But curiosity killed the Kayla, and later that evening I find myself at the Lion.

The moment I walk in, I'm accosted by drunken hollers and James's angry music—Faith No More, *again*. It's Saturday night and everyone in the city seems to be pre-drinking here before they hit the clubs. I quickly scan the bar, looking for Bram, but I keep making eye contact with a few guys that I know I shouldn't. I have to admit, it would be nice to just find a cute one and have a random hookup. Maybe it's the lack of sex that's turning me into a crazy person. In fact, I'm pretty sure that's exactly what it is. So much sexual frustration and no place for it to go.

But to be honest, even though getting laid would help in the short term, it wouldn't do shit in the long term. I'd just feel empty afterward, because when it comes down to it, a random hookup with a random guy isn't what I want at all. I know exactly what I want, and I can't have it.

I spot Nicola at the bar, slinging drinks. She's slammed, but as I come over, she catches my eye and gestures to the booths by the washroom. There's a hint of warning in her eyes, which makes me pause, but she's in no position to explain. People are practically throwing money at her. James, at the other end of the bar, gives me a nod but he's equally busy.

I make my way through the crowd to the other side of the bar and finally see Bram sitting in the booth, nursing a few fingers of Scotch.

Sitting across from him is Lachlan, his big hand curled around what looks like a glass of water.

I hate to use the term clench, but that's exactly what my body does when I see him. I clench, my thighs squeezing together, as if I can already imagine his cock inside me.

Damnit, I need help.

For a moment I stand there, wondering if maybe I should just turn around and leave. I'm only here because I want to talk to Bram about Lachlan, not actually see Lachlan, and the fact that he's here makes me both turned on and absolutely terrified.

But then Lachlan looks up beneath his baseball cap and sees me. He doesn't smile. That would be asking too much. But he stops frowning for a moment as he eyes me up and down, so I'll take what I can get.

I swallow the lump in my throat, throw my shoulders back, and walk over to them, my eyes going from Lachlan to Bram and back to Lachlan again.

"Hey," I say to them, standing at the end of the table.

"There's the woman of the hour," Bram says, but to my surprise it's Lachlan who moves over in the booth to make room for me.

I give Lachlan a grateful smile and sit down next to him. Tonight I'm wearing a black fringe skirt with bare legs and when he glances down at them briefly, his own thighs so close to mine, I hope he likes what he sees.

If he does, though, he doesn't give any indication. He doesn't say anything at all, just takes a sip of his water. I watch his throat as he swallows until I can tell that Bram is staring at me.

I tear my eyes away to glare at Bram, but he's already shaking his head like I'm being ridiculous. I ignore him and pull the article out of my purse, unfolding it and holding it out.

"Did you guys want to read the article?" I ask, and Bram immediately snatches it from my hands.

I glance at Lachlan. "It's all about you. You really should read it first."

He gives me a fleeting smile and scratches at his beard. "I'll read it when it goes to print. Seems more special that way."

Bram looks over the paper at Lachlan for a second, frowns, then goes back to reading. I drum my fingers anxiously along the edge of the table, waiting for his final verdict.

"Well, well, well," Bram finally says. He hands it back to me and gives me a charming grin. "I'm impressed."

"Really?"

"Aye. Reads like the real thing. Thank you," he adds emphatically. "I think that this could really help."

"I fucking hope so," I tell him. "I wrote the shit out of this thing."

"That you did. And you made Mr. Rugby here sound like an angel." Bram picks up his drink and raises it to Lachlan in a mock toast.

Lachlan grunts in return before excusing himself. I quickly hop out of the booth, and as he gets out, his arm brushes against mine. I nearly burst from the sensation, that quick whisper of hot skin that sends my whole body ablaze.

He saunters off toward the bathroom and I watch that ass in those jeans for as long as I can. It's becoming a bit of a habit. The best habit.

"Look at you," Bram says teasingly.

I whirl around and glare at him. "Look at me what?"

"You," he says, then nods toward the washroom. "Him. You are such the smitten kitten."

"Smitten kitten?" I repeat, sitting back down. "You've been hanging around Nicola too long."

"I don't think I've ever seen you so hung up on someone before," he adds.

"What?" I exclaim. "That's ridiculous! I'm always hung up on someone."

He presses his lips together, shaking his head. "Nope. Not like this. I know your looks. You're practically drooling."

"Bullshit," I say, leaning across the table and looking him in the eye. "You may think you know me, Bram, but you don't. So I think your cousin is hot, so what?"

"Just hot?" he says. He swirls his scotch around his glass and grins down at it. "All right. Too bad the smitten kitten is climbing up the wrong tree."

My face twists in confusion. "Huh? Why are we still talking about cats?"

He shrugs. "I just don't want you to get your hopes up. As if you couldn't figure it out already. He's not so easily…swayed."

I roll my eyes. "Believe me, I've figured that out."

And yet when Lachlan returns and asks if I want something to drink, my heart starts dancing to a hopeful beat.

"Hmmm," Bram muses, watching him go.

"Let me guess, he never normally buys girls drinks," I say.

"Not that I've seen," he says. "Then again, he doesn't drink much anyway."

I want to press Bram more about that, find out why. With his bruiser personality, Lachlan doesn't seem like the straight-edge type. But if it's something personal, I know Bram will shut me down.

Soon Lachlan comes back with another glass of water for himself and a Bellini for me. He slides it along the table to me and says, "This is thanks. For the article."

Oh. So he wasn't buying me a drink because he finally realized I was hot stuff. Damn.

"Did James make you pay for that?" Bram asks.

He nods. "I guess the courtesy doesn't extend to family. I don't think the guy likes me much."

"James doesn't like any guy who's bigger than him," Bram points out.

"Except for Linden," I say. "But that's a twisted bromance right there." I give Lachlan a grateful smile and move down so he can sit next to me again. "Well, thank you for the drink. You're the one who was gracious with his time and my fumbling questions."

He nods, pulling down the brim of his cap slightly, fidgeting. After a few beats he says, "You know, I've been meaning to ask you what kind of exercise you do."

I tilt my head at him and he quickly continues, "You played really well on that field. I mean, you were tireless."

"Oh," I say, and exchange a look with Bram. "Thanks. I usually just go to the gym in the mornings but I take fencing lessons once a week."

"Fencing?" he asks. "That's....rare."

I smile sweetly at him. "I'm a rare thing." I don't look at Bram, but I know he's not looking too impressed at my flirting skills. I go on. "It helps me stay disciplined but lets me get my anger out at the same time."

"You struggle with discipline?" he asks, and I can't tell if he's kidding or not.

"Isn't that obvious?" I say, and find myself shifting closer to him.

He considers that, his eyes softening as he looks at me.

"Plus," I add, "it gives me a booty. No flat ass for me."

"Definitely not," he says, and I can't help but beam, my nerves tingling all over.

Bram clears his throat. Loudly. I narrow my eyes at him, annoyed that he's interrupting whatever kind of banter Lachlan and I have going. Doesn't he realize what a big deal this is? Bantering with Lachlan is like unlocking another level in the game. Plus he just complimented my damn ass.

But before we can get back to it, Linden comes into the Lion, strutting toward us with a big smile on his face.

"Hello, hello," he says to us and plops down beside Bram.

"Oh great, the Scottish trifecta," I say underneath my breath.

"You'll be changing your tune in a minute, missy," Linden says. "Because I've got some pretty fucking awesome news."

The three of us stare at him expectantly. He licks his lips and smiles triumphantly. "One of my clients is a sponsor for the Outside Lands Festival. I guess he was feeling generous today because he gave me five VIP passes to the festival next weekend."

"Nice perk," Bram comments.

"Obviously I'm giving them to you," Linden says.

"But there are six of us, including Steph and Nicola," I say. "So we can't all go."

"It's all right," Lachlan says. "Count me out for the festival."

I'm hit with disappointment. "Don't be silly," I tell him. "You're the guest here, you're definitely going. It's a San Francisco institution. *I'll* not go. I'm pretty sure Linden wasn't inviting me anyway."

And when I look at Linden and see the sheepish glint in his eyes, I know it's the truth. When it comes to him making plans, sometimes he conveniently leaves me out of them until Steph gets angry. But I can't say I don't do the same either.

"Oh, for fucks sake," Bram says. "I'll buy my own damn VIP passes. There. Problem solved."

Lachlan shakes his head. "Don't worry about it, mate. I'm not a fan of music festivals anyway."

"You don't like music?" I ask.

He frowns. "I love music. People, not so much."

I can't help but smile. "Maybe we are more alike than I thought."

I swear there's a ghost of a smile on his lips.

"Ah, but the people who attend Outside Lands are scantily clad girls who drink shitloads of wine and dance in their bikinis to music that isn't even playing yet," Linden says. "Easy place for you to pick up a few girls, wouldn't you say?"

The fuck? I glare at Linden. I just know he's suggesting this shit to piss me off.

"Nah," Lachlan quickly dismisses him. "Not my crowd, not my scene."

"Elton John is headlining on Sunday," Bram adds, and I can tell he's kicking Linden under the table because Linden is giving him the "what did I do?" look. "You can't pass up a legend."

Lachlan grunts in response. I think it means "we'll see."

The rest of the evening turns to talk about music festivals and bands. So many Scottish accents at once. Lachlan doesn't provide much conversation and neither do I, we just sit there listening to Linden and Bram get in arguments over which band is better, Massive Attack or Portishead. In a way, it's kind of nice. Their incessant yammering provides background noise and ensures that both of them are wrapped in their weird brotherly world. Which means Lachlan and I are in a world of our own.

Not that we even talk to each other, not that he's even aware of being in this private world with me. It's just nice to sit beside him and enjoy his presence, feel his heat, smell the warm amber of his skin. Being in the shadow of this beast is strangely comforting. He both kickstarts my heart and calms my nerves, and I can't help but think that Bram is right. I do have it bad for him. Really, really bad. I am a smitten fucking kitten. And I'm starting to think it's more than just in a physical way. I don't know the guy at all—and it seems that nobody does—but I feel drawn to him, like our blood is made from magnets, pulling us together.

The sad part is, though, that all these crazy feelings are in my head. And that's probably where they're going to stay.

When the night gets on and Lachlan leaves to go home, I feel the loss. I don't think I've ever felt sad over a guy, but all this Scot has to do is leave my vicinity and I miss him. Maybe I just miss staring at those lips, wondering what it would be like to take them between my teeth, what they would feel like against my mouth. Maybe I just miss taking in his tattoos, inventing stories for them in my head—the lion on his forearm is for his pride, the cross on his bicep is for the time he worked as a Trappist monk brewing strong beer in the Alps (I don't know, it might be true). Maybe I miss fighting the urge to run my fingers over his beard, his nose, touching every faint scar on his face.

Or maybe I just miss the one-sided cat and mouse game that he doesn't even know he's playing. It's the thrill of the chase, it's how every small smile he gives me, every word he speaks, is a victory in itself. It's challenging me constantly to try and win him over. And if there's anything I've learned recently, it's that I like to be challenged.

When I lie in bed later that night and stare out the window at the streetlights, I realize that, for the first time, my bed feels empty. Like it's missing someone. And not someone who leaves in the middle of the night or the next morning. Someone who will stay.

The truth creeps in like an oil spill.

I, Kayla Moore, am a lonely, lonely girl.

...

When I walk into the office on Monday morning, there's no denying I have a little extra swing in my step. Even though my piece won't come out until Friday, I'm feeling good. Fantastic even. This is *it*. This is my new life. I've pushed aside all my woe is me crap from the weekend and am focused on the positive. Once that piece comes out, not only will it (hopefully) help Bram and Lachlan, but it will say to the world, "Hey fuckfaces! Hey, every person who's doubted me! Look at me! Look what I've done with myself!"

But as I walk past Neil in the hallway on the way to lunch, he looks like the bringer of bad news.

"Kayla," he says, pulling me to the side. "I need to talk to you."

I've never seen him act serious before. "What?" I ask, wringing my hands together. "Everything okay?"

"Sort of," he says. He examines his nails for a moment then looks up at me and sighs, looking completely apologetic. "There's been a change to the article."

I stand up straighter. "What change?"

"It's still being printed, don't worry," he says quickly. "It's just that, uh, well sweet cheeks, Joe won't run it with your name. He's putting down my name as the byline."

"What?!" I exclaim, loud enough for people to stare.

"Sorry!" he says, whispering harshly. "I didn't want it that way, but Joe says no one knows who you are. But the good news is that he's running it. Yay." He gives a tiny, desperate jump for joy. "Right?"

I can't even speak to him. I push him away, whirl around, and march toward Joe's office. I hear Neil yell behind me, "Don't do it, it's not worth it!" but fuck that noise. This is *my* article. My chance. It's worth it.

Joe's door is closed so I quickly rap on it, trying to take a deep breath, to control my rage which is totally out of control.

"What is it?" he asks brusquely from the other side.

I open the door and step in, shutting the door loudly behind me. He looks up in surprise then cocks his head and shakes it.

"Yeah, it's me," I say bitterly. "You know why I'm here."

He looks back down at his papers. Always looking at fucking papers. Use a damn computer like the rest of us.

"I know you should talk to the damn editor with a little more respect," he says gruffly. I've dealt with enough gruff from Lachlan this last week so it doesn't intimidate me in the slightest.

"You're not running my name with the article!" I tell him, hands waving all over the place. "I wrote it. That's not fair. That's like…that's like…"

"It's business," he says with a sigh, pinching the bridge of his nose. "The article is good, and you should be proud. And it might even get some attention, which is what *you* wanted for this goddamn charity nonsense. But it won't help if it's from someone who works in advertising. All the credibility is gone."

"Then…then, let me work *here*. You said I can write. You said it's good. So then make me a staff writer."

He shakes his head. "Kayla, you're just fine at what you do. The weekly can't run without ads. Let the writers handle their work. They've been at it for years. You've written one," he jabs his finger in the air, "thing."

"Then let me keep my name to the article and let me write more things," I plead. "Let me try again. I can prove myself, I know I can. I can do more than just book fucking ads!"

His oversized, hairy nostrils flare at that. He carefully folds his hands in front of him. "Look. Originally you weren't going to write it anyway. Just appreciate the experience and be proud that it was good enough to get printed, though I'm sure Neil did more than his fair share of cleaning it up. If you look at it that way, I'm sure he deserves to have his name on it just as much as you." He clears his throat and starts rummaging through the mess of paper cups and sticky notes on his desk. "Now if you'll excuse me, I'll go back to pretending you didn't barge in here with this terrible self-entitled attitude, and you can go back to doing what you normally do. Got it?"

I press my lips together until they hurt. I so want to yell, scream, hurl things at him. But that won't get me anywhere. I hate, hate, *hate* admitting defeat, but that's what this is—utter defeat.

I leave his office, refusing to look at anyone who might have heard my outburst, and head straight into the bathroom. I'm relieved to find it empty, and I rush over to the toilet stall, put the lid down, and sit. With my head in my hands, I breathe, breathe, breathe, and try to hold it all together.

Breakdowns aren't common for me. Not the ones that seem to tear you from the inside out, like this one is threatening to do. And I know it's dumb that I'm feeling this way when I should have seen it coming. It's just an article. One thing I wrote. And I was an idiot to think it was going to lead to something, that it was going to change my life.

But I can't ignore the disappointment. It hurts. More than that, it's embarrassing. I've told everyone I know about this and so many people are going to be looking for it come the weekend. Yeah, I did good...but it's not the same.

I stay in the bathroom stall my whole lunch break, fighting back tears, swallowing my anger. Then, after a while, I push my pity aside and turn on myself, my next best target. I berate myself for freaking out on Joe like I did. He's an ass and definitely not in the right, but I could have lost my job—my real job—by talking back like I did. That was hella risky and I wasn't thinking straight. Even though the whole thing is just awful, what I really need to do is go back to Joe and apologize for freaking out.

But my pride can be a lioness, and instead, when I'm finally calm and composed, I go back to my office, sit down, and commit myself to my real job—the one I'm paid to do. The only one I know how to do.

Mondays fucking suck.

Chapter Eight

KAYLA

Naturally, I have a hard time shaking it off. I lay low all week, shutting myself away from the world. The only person I see is my mom, and I'm not even planning to go over because I know she'll ask about it and I don't want to let her down. But she sounds so sad and helpless over the phone, maybe even weaker than normal, and I can't say no.

"Do you want to talk about it?" she asks me from her chair, watching reruns of The Nanny on TV, while I make dinner for us. I ended up telling here there were changes with the article but I didn't go into details.

"Not really," I say.

"That's okay. Talk when you're ready. Just remember what I told you last time—you're on your own track."

Yeah, but my track is officially going nowhere.

I spend the weekend shut in as well, eating a pint of caramel waffle cone ice cream and binging on Netflix. I know that the Outside Lands Festival is going on, I know that Steph and Nicola are getting aggravated by my inability to answer the phone or respond to their texts. I even get a text from Bram on Friday that says, "Kayla, what happened?" assuming that he's read the article that *Neil* wrote. But still, I pretend that it doesn't exist.

When I wake up on Sunday morning though, it's not my alarm that seems to be blaring in my head. It's my buzzer.

I groan and slip on my leopard print robe and pad my way over to the intercom.

"What?" I say angrily into the speaker, eyeing the clock on the microwave. It's nine a.m. and I'd planned on sleeping all day long.

"Hey!" Steph yells, voice crackling. "If you don't let us upstairs, I'm calling your mother."

Ugh. And she would, too. Steph and my mom love each other.

"Fine," I say, buzzing her in, unlocking my door, and then going into the kitchen to make myself a pot of coffee. All the caffeine is needed before I can deal with today.

Moments later, Steph and Nicola barge into the apartment.

"What the hell, Kayla?" Steph exclaims, tossing her purse on my sofa. Both of them look like they've just rolled out of bed, wearing pajama pants, flip-flops, and hoodies. "Where have you been?"

"I've been right here," I say tiredly, opening the bag of coffee and inhaling deeply.

Steph walks right over to me, looking me up and down, as if checking for signs of injury or bodysnatching. "You're ignoring our calls, our texts..."

I shrug and measure out the coffee into the filter before pressing the on button. "Didn't feel like being social this week. Sorry."

"Bram told us about the article," Nicola says quietly. "We read it. It's excellent, Kayla, really. He's *so* happy with it... but...what happened?"

I sigh heavily and turn to face them, crossing my arms. "You mean why is my name not on it?"

"Yeah," Steph says. "Who is Neil? Is that the same Neil we've met?"

I nod. We've all partied together.

"Yeah, the same one. He edited it and Joe thought it would be better if his name went on the byline, since I'm not actually a writer."

"That's bullshit," Nicola says, frowning. "We're not pulling your leg when we tell you it's great. I mean, really, you should be proud of yourself."

Am I proud of myself though? I don't know.

I turn away. "Well, it is what it is. I'm over it."

"If you were over it, you wouldn't be avoiding your best friends," Steph says, putting her hand on my shoulder. "Do you need a hug?"

I swat her hand away and back up. "Absolutely not." I look at them both. "Why are you both here at such an ungodly hour? Who gets up at eight a.m. on a Sunday?"

"Your friends," Steph says imploringly, "who want to make sure you're up and ready to go to the festival today."

"Oh, hell no," I say, shaking my head vigorously. "I'm not going to that. I've already missed two days. What's the point of going to the third?"

"Two days that were a lot of fun," Steph says. "Don't miss the last one. It will take your mind off things, and I think you need to get out of your apartment before you start peeing into jars and letting your toenails grow long."

"Like Howard Hughes," Nicola adds.

I give her a dry look. "Yeah, I know who Howard Hughes is."

"Please. Even Ava is going," Nicola says. "She's so excited."

"Are you going to dress her up like a little fairy hipster?" I ask, picturing her daughter like all the feathers and headband wearing girls that swarm these festivals.

"Maybe."

"Well, I'm sorry to disappoint you," I tell them. "But it's Sock Sunday, and I have a lot of reading and napping to do." I kick my leg out, showcasing the fuzzy knee-length socks with Minions on them.

"Fuck sock Sunday," Steph says. "Do you know who else is going?" she adds conspiratorially.

I swallow, already feeling heat in my stomach. "Who?"

"Lachlan," she says. She adds a knowing little smirk.

"So?" I tell her, ignoring the flutter in my chest. Just the mention of his name and I feel myself light up from the inside, like a switch being turned on.

"Oh, come on," Nicola says. "Don't pretend you're still not all—"

"All what?" I challenge.

"Lovestruck."

I laugh and roll my eyes. "Lovestruck? Please. This is me you're talking about. Kayla Moore. Maneater extraordinaire." Even though that phrase has kind of lost its shine.

"Okay, not *love*struck," Nicola corrects herself. "Infatuated."

"Horny," Steph adds. "Kayla is just a horny monster with a raging lady boner."

I grimace. "It doesn't sound so good when *you* say it."

"Phffft. Whatever. The point is, you need to get laid something fierce," she adds. "This celibacy thing is not good for you."

"While that may or may not be true, we all know it won't be with him," I say, tapping my foot, wishing the damn coffee would drip faster. "And I thought he wasn't going to go. He told me he didn't like crowds and that it wasn't his scene."

"Bram bought him a VIP for today. Somehow convinced him," Nicola says. I look over at her and she gives me a hopeful smile. "You know, he leaves next Sunday for Scotland. This might be the last time you see him."

I rub my lips together anxiously.

"That's true," Steph says. "You probably should say goodbye."

I eye them both. "I don't know," I say reluctantly, even though in my heart I do know. I want to see him again. One more time. I know nothing will come of it, but I've become addicted to that high I get when I'm around him. I may not be lovestruck, but there is something so...I don't know, refreshing, about feeling like a schoolgirl again with one hell of a crush. And I think Steph and Nicola know that, too.

"Fine," I say. "I'll get ready. What time should we be there?"

"I'll come get you at noon," Steph says, smiling triumphantly as they both wave and flounce out of my apartment.

I exhale noisily and look over at the pot of coffee, which is finally done. I'll drink the whole damn thing, then I'll get ready.

...

When noon rolls around, I have to admit that I'm actually excited. It feels good to have my mind off of things, and even though I know that tomorrow is Monday and full of suckage again, and that this may be the last time I get to feel those butterflies when I look into Lachlan's compelling eyes and conveniently brush my body against his, I'm committing myself to live in the moment. Today is only about today and nothing else.

Naturally, it also becomes about looking my best. I want to look good, but I also don't want to become a parody like so many festival chicks. I settle on suede boots because I know how much dust and dirt gets kicked up in Golden Gate Park, leather shorts for the edgy factor, and a long plaid shirt over a low-backed tank top. Today is one of the few days I can get away without wearing a bra (hell, half the girls will be in bikinis), so I take advantage of that. I add a small crossbody bag and I'm ready to go.

Soon, Linden's Jeep pulls up to the curb with Steph riding shotgun. I climb in the backseat and learn that Bram is driving Nicola, Ava, and Lachlan in a little bit.

"Hey, you guys," Steph says, eyeing me in the rear-view mirror as we cruise down Geary Boulevard toward the park. "I just wanted to say that I know you guys have had your differences in the past, but you really need to start playing nice to each other."

Linden and I exchange a glance.

"I am being nice," I say.

"When am I not nice?" Linden adds at the same time.

Steph scoffs at us. "I'm not stupid. You guys fight like cats and dogs sometimes. Look, I know it's weird and awkward that you guys slept together back in the day—"

"That's not why it's awkward," I tell her quickly, leaning forward between their two seats. "It's that he was such an ass to me afterward." I thump my fist on Linden's shoulder.

"Hey," he says briefly, rubbing his arm. He glances at me with disgraced eyes before looking back to the road. "How many times do I have to apologize for being a bloody wanker?"

"How many times can you say wanker? Don't you Scots have any other words?"

"Bollocks," Linden replies.

"He *has* apologized a lot, Kayla," Steph says. "And we all know he was a different guy back then. People make mistakes."

"You slept with James," I point out to her. Steph and Linden had a very long and complicated relationship before they finally professed their love for one another. "You know about mistakes, too."

Linden freezes up and I know it's still a touchy subject for their marriage.

"Anyway," Steph says, putting her hand on Linden's and squeezing it, "for all the messed up things we've done, I just want to see you two getting along. Kayla, if you stop giving Linden a hard time, then he in turn will stop being a dick. Right?"

I lean back in my seat, folding my arms. "Why does the pressure fall on me?"

"Because you're the mature one here," Steph says, and Linden laughs. She hits him on the shoulder where I just did, and he cries out again.

"What the hell, Steph? Can you girls stop hitting me?"

"I'm serious," Steph says. "Kayla, do you forgive him?"

I sigh. "Of course I do. Bygones and all that shit."

"Good. Now cowboy, stop being a dick to her."

"I'm not."

"Stop it anyway."

"Fine."

She looks at the two of us and then nods, apparently satisfied. "Good," she says to Linden. "Because I've never ever seen Kayla act like a bumbling fool over any guy before, so I want to make sure we do what we can to make the two of them happen."

"What?" I exclaim.

"The two of them?" Linden asks. "What are you talking about?"

"Lachlan," Steph explains.

Linden cocks his head and eyes me in the rear-view mirror. "You like Lachlan?"

I bury my face in my hands and groan. "What is this, the fourth grade?" I raise my head and look at him. "I think your cousin is stupidly good-looking. Okay?"

"Don't listen to her," Steph whispers. "She's got it bad."

I can't deny that, so I don't. I say to Linden, "I thought you knew that. I figured that's why you were talking to Lachlan about hooking up with the half-dressed chicks at the festival."

He shakes his head, looking confused. "Is that why Bram was kicking me? I didn't know. I just wanted him to have a little fun. The guy could use a little fun in his life."

"I agree with that," I mumble.

We ride in silence for a little while until I see Linden glancing at me with a dumb smirk on his face.

"What now?" I ask.

"I had no idea you liked the silent type." He wags his brows at me. "I thought you liked the loudmouths more."

"Oh, like you? Please. And just because I'm a loudmouth doesn't mean I like loudmouths. Anyway, it doesn't matter. Bram already told me I'm barking up the wrong tree, as if I couldn't tell already."

Linden seems to consider that. "I dunno. He's definitely not a relationship kind of guy, seeing as he's leaving in like a week. But I don't think he'd toss you out of bed."

"Well, he kind of tossed me out of his apartment."

He shrugs. "I'm just saying. He's hard to get through to and he's not easily persuaded, as I am sure you know at this point, but he's still a dude with a dick. I say, make your moves. Again. Let him really know."

I sigh. "He knows."

"Does he? Try telling him."

"He'll reject me."

"And I'm sure you'll hold it against him for years to come," he says dryly. "But if he doesn't reject you…isn't that worth it?"

Steph grins at Linden and runs her hand through his hair. "Do you see this? Do you see what harmony and unity comes from you guys being nice?"

I try not to think she has a point. And I try not to think that Linden is right.

After driving around the Richmond district for twenty minutes, we finally find a parking spot and join the throngs of festival goers heading into the park. Linden grabs a few beers from a man on the street corner selling them illegally from his cooler and hands them to us.

I don't drink beer very often, but I down that can in seconds. Maybe it's the infectious energy in the air and the fact that I've been cooped up in my apartment for a week. Maybe it's because I keep thinking about what Linden said and I need the liquid courage.

We slip in through the crowds, the VIP wristbands working just fine, and head towards the beer and wine tents. In the distance from stages unseen, muted music thumps through the eucalyptus trees, carried by the ever-present mist.

I know I should eat lunch first, but my initial instinct is to get in one of the massive lines to buy local wine in tiny plastic cups. Steph waits with me while Linden gets on his phone and tracks down Bram and the others.

By the time we're both two-fisting glasses of red and fighting our way out of the growing mass of wine-hungry music fans, we spot Linden with Nicola and Bram, Ava sitting high on his shoulders and looking around in awe.

I don't want the first words out of my mouth to be, "Where's Lachlan?" but that's exactly what I say.

Nicola, looking cute in a sundress and jean jacket, points toward the main gate. "It's a non-smoking event. He wanted to finish his cigar."

Cigar, huh? I've never been with a guy who smokes cigars. Not that I've been with Lachlan either, though I have to admit, Linden's words are still floating around in my head. Should I really make a move? I mean...that's nothing new to me. If I want a guy and he's not coming up to me, then I'll go up to him. I have no shame.

But with Lachlan...yeah, I do have shame. And I don't want to do my same old song and dance (again) because he's worth so much more than that. But what else can I say, other than, "Hey, so I think you're really hot. Wanna screw?" That just wouldn't cut it. It's not enough.

"I'm hungry," Ava complains, while I sip my wine and think it all over.

Bram pats her legs as they rest on his shoulders. "You just ate, you little munchkin. Where are you putting all that food?"

"I want tacos," she says, pointing to a pair of dancing hippies holding tacos and beer.

I can tell Nicola is trying to stay strong, but she caves in because she wants tacos too. I mean, tacos. Who doesn't? While everyone turns to make their way to one of the fifty million taco stands lined up around the fence, Steph nudges me gently and nods her head to the gate.

I turn around and see Lachlan sauntering toward us. Even the way he walks is distinctive and one hundred percent man, almost like a guy in a Western, all shoulders and swagger, someone who's ready to fight at a moment's notice. It's intimidating and intense, and it makes me freeze right where I am. I want to play it cool and look away, but I can't.

He's dressed in hiking boots, green cargo pants, and a grey, long-sleeved Henley shirt that clings to his every muscle. I haven't seen him for a week and his beard has grown in more, the same deep brown as his hair. Combined with those ever present lines on his forehead, darting eyes, and permafrown, he looks like a mountain man about to wrestle some bears.

Yeah. Whatever plan of attack I had just got thrown out the window. I'll be lucky if I can talk to him in anything other than gibberish.

"Hey," he says when he approaches. He says this to both of us, though when he looks at me, that crease between his eyes deepens.

"Hey," Steph says. "Glad you came! Now if you'll excuse me, I have to make sure Linden orders me extra guacamole." She takes off running toward the taco stands, leaving the two of us alone. Real smooth, Stephanie.

But Lachlan doesn't seem to notice. He's staring intently at me, hands shoved in his pockets. He smells like cigar and musk.

"I saw the article," he says.

I bite my lip for a moment and nod. "Yeah. Did you like it?"

He seems confused by that. "Of course I did," he says in his thick brogue. "But why did it say someone else wrote it?"

I sigh and give him an exaggerated shrug. "I don't know. My editor thought it would be better if a real writer was accredited."

"And that's who Neil is?" His voice is oh so coarse, like he's about to find Neil and punch his lights out.

"I work with him," I explain, trying not to seem affected by it all. "He edited it. And I guess my name on the byline would have lowered credibility or something. I don't know. But if that's the case, it's better that it happened this way. I don't want to take away from what you guys are doing."

He makes a noise of agreement, nodding his head quickly, though his expression doesn't relax and his body is still tense. "I think it would have been better if it were truthful. I didn't do the interview with some cunt named Neil." His voice lowers. "I did it with you. You should have gotten all the credit."

My heart is fluttering. I don't know if it's because he's getting mad that I wasn't rightfully attributed or it's that his eyes won't quite look away from mine. I can feel his anger, his frustration. For me.

"I know," I say slowly. "But there's not much I can do."

"I could talk to your editor. He sounds like a real fuck-head. I could put some sense into him."

Put some sense into him or *knock* some sense into him? His jaw is clenched, looking volatile. Against my better judgement, I reach out and touch his arm, just briefly, my fingertips resting on his wrist. "It's okay. I shouldn't have expected anything different. I'm the ad girl. That's my job. And it will stay my job."

He takes a step closer, his face suddenly in mine, and he squints at me for a moment. "But I can tell," he says, "that you're not okay with that. Are you?"

We stare at each other for a moment, and I don't know what's going on, but I don't think I've ever felt so…fought for in my whole life.

I blink at him and he pulls back. "It is what it is," he says, finally looking away. "And what it is, is what you make it."

My mouth quirks up in a wry smile. "You sound like my mom."

"Then your mother is very wise," he says, seeming calmer now. His eyes brighten. "Want a taco?"

I beam at him. "Yes, please."

We walk up and join the gang who are still in line for the street food. Lachlan and Linden greet each other with a quick hug and a pat on the back, while Steph takes me aside for a second.

"What were you talking about?" she whispers excitedly.

"Just the article," I tell her, watching Lachlan. "Why?"

She tugs at my arm and grins at me. "Because, he was totally in your face. I thought he was going to kiss you."

I give her a look. "Again, how old are we?"

"Right," she says, leaning back and crossing her arms with her "don't even" face. "How come Carrie and Samantha could giggle over men on *Sex and the City*, and we can't? We're the same age. Same problems."

"And I'm still Samantha," I say with a sigh, remembering years ago when Steph, Nicola, and I would binge watch the show for days on end. Fictional or not, the girls were who we aspired to be. Pretty, fun, carefree, and living the life in a big city. The single life always seemed a lot more fun when someone else was living it.

After Lachlan buys me my taco and I gracefully refrain from any pink taco or fish taco jokes, we head toward the main stage where the VIP area is.

It's like a whole other world in those white tents. Not only are there cushy seats and a range of bartenders serving up whatever drinks you could want (not free though, which is kind of a rip-off), but you're constantly looking around in hopes of spotting a celebrity.

Of course, most of the people in here with us are splurging or people who have been gifted the passes, so any hopes of seeing someone like Sam Smith or Elton John are dashed. We grab more drinks—Lachlan opting for a bottle of water—and head down to the bleachers beneath the tents that overlook the field and the main stage. From this vantage point, we have an excellent view of the current band, some hipster shit that has everyone waving their hands and glow sticks.

I'm at the end, sitting next to Lachlan, no accident on my part. I kick him playfully with my foot, and when he turns his head to look at me, I'm momentarily stunned by how close his face is to mine. His beautiful, gorgeous face. It makes my blood run with mercury.

I smile before I can speak, trying not to focus on his lips. "So you said you're a music fan," I say, my mouth moving carefully. "What kind of music do you like?"

His brows lift, and it's then that I notice part of the reason he looks so intense all the time. His pupils always seem to be enlarged, dark and huge. It gives his eyes another layer of intensity.

"Oh, all sorts," he says in his rough voice. At this proximity I can feel it in my bones. "I like people with a lot of soul. The performers. The ones with stories to tell, even if they aren't their own." He pauses and looks out at the crowds, passing his hand over his beard. "Tom Waits, for one. Nick Cave. Jack White, even. A lot of the classics, too, the good old soul singers with the voices that hit you right here." He thumps his fist against his chest. "What about you?"

"I'm kind of a nerd," I say.

He frowns. "What do you mean?"

"Well, I'm not so big on rock or pop or anything like that. I just love classical. Composers. Anything with strings and a piano, really."

"That's not nerdy," he says, shaking his head.

"No? Well, I for sure can't tell you what's on the radio," I admit. "But I know what kind of music makes me feel."

He tilts his body closer to mine, his elbows resting on his knees, bottle of water in his hands. His thigh taps mine. "Do you know who Ryuichi Sakamoto is?"

"Oh, come on," I tell him. "My mother is Japanese. Of course I know who he is. And even if she wasn't, and she didn't play the soundtrack to *The Last Emperor* over and over again while growing up, I would still know who he is."

He nods appreciatively. "I saw him in Edinburgh a few years ago. Small theatre. Amazing show."

"Quit bragging," I tease.

He flashes me a smile and we go back to watching the set.

Time flies by and the festival grows to epic proportions. During Sam Smith I'm feeling buzzed from another glass of wine and I find myself swaying back and forth against Lachlan's shoulders to the music. He's so damn solid and he doesn't shy away.

It's dark out when Sir Elton John comes on, opening with "Benny and the Jets." The crowd goes nuts. I go nuts. It's impossible not to sing along to every single song, and it's like every person around us is singing along too, hugging each other, drunk and happy and united by Elton.

It's probably the wine bolstering my courage, but when "Your Song" comes on, I lean into Lachlan and put my head on his shoulder. He tenses for a moment and I hear him suck in his breath. I pray he doesn't move, doesn't shrug me off.

Then he exhales and relaxes. I can feel his beard brush against my hair as he turns his head to look down at me. I close my eyes, thinking I can fall asleep right here. With this song, with my head on his shoulder.

It feels beyond right. It feels like an answer to a question I never knew I asked.

He shifts ever so slightly and puts his arm around my waist, holding me to him.

My heart leaps, my whole body fizzing like champagne. Never has such a simple gesture turned me inside out like this. I can't help but smile with pure unfiltered joy, still mouthing the words to the song. I don't want anything to change. I want the song to go on forever, the concert to never end. I want to stay in this spot until the end of time, his large, strong arm around me, holding me to him like I'm being sheltered against the world.

And, for some reason, time does seem to still. In the dark, with the colorful lights from the stage flashing, with this tune, with this man, time stretches on. Whatever worries and cares I had before, they're gone in this moment.

I'm the opposite of alone.

Somehow we stay like this through "Daniel" as well, even though the song makes me tear up a little bit, thinking of my brothers. I feel Lachlan's thumb rub against my side, back and forth along my shirt, a slow, teasing motion that introduces some fire to the soft peace inside me.

Look up at him, I tell myself. *Kiss him now. You may never get the chance again.*

But I'm too afraid to do anything more than snuggle into him further. It's funny how prepared I was to make my move, but now that I have this, I've realized how perfect it is. And to imagine kissing him, well that has turned into a scary prospect. I'm not sure I can handle it.

The song ends and "Someone Saved My Life Tonight" comes on.

Something in the air changes. Lachlan tenses, slowly, as if he is just waking up. I hear his breath deepen and he swallows hard.

Abruptly, he takes his arm away and gets to his feet, hulking over me.

"What's wrong?" I ask him, moving back and out of his way as he steps around me and walks off down the bleachers. People raise their feet and move their bags to get out of his way, but he doesn't even look at them, doesn't even slow his heavy pace.

I turn and look at Bram who is sitting on the other side of me. He's frowning, watching him go.

"What the hell was that?" I ask Bram.

He just shakes his head. "I don't know. He has moods."

"No shit," I say, and I crane my neck to see if I can still see him. He's barely visible, heading toward the gates that lead out of the VIP area. "I'll go see." I get to my feet.

"Oy." Bram reaches out and grabs my arm. "Just let him be. When he gets this way with me, I just ignore it."

Well maybe he needs someone to say something, I think to myself.

"It'll be fine," I say, picking up my purse and heading across the bleachers, apologizing to the people who just had to clear a path for Lachlan. I quickly walk through the crowds lining up at the bars for last call, cursing my short legs for holding me back.

I burst out of the VIP gates and into the rest of the crowd. A lot of people are already leaving the festival, trying to beat the mass exodus that will occur once Elton is done, and I'm panicking, not seeing him anywhere. It doesn't help that it's dark and few lights are on.

Then I spot him, near the fence, heading with the crowd out the main gates. I fumble through people until I'm out on the main road and can see him heading down it. He's going toward the ocean side, away from where most of the crowd is heading, and I remember that he doesn't know this area at all.

"Lachlan!" I call out, jogging after him.

He doesn't stop, just keeps walking, shoulders raised like he's about to go on a rampage, and my mind is racing, trying to figure out what could be wrong.

"Lachlan," I say again, coming up behind him. "Hey." I reach out and grab his arm. He comes to a dead stop and turns to face me, a weird raging darkness in his eyes that makes me let go.

He takes a deep breath through his nose but doesn't say anything. The wildness in his eyes says enough. From here, the sounds of the concert are muted and deep, and only a few people are walking past in drunken, weaving lines.

"What happened?" I ask carefully.

He shakes his head and looks away, shoulders back, chest out. "Nothing."

Feeling brave, I grab his hand and squeeze it. He stares down at it—his warm, large hand in my small, cold one—but doesn't pull away.

He swallows thickly. "Sorry," he eventually says, his voice like sandpaper. "I...have moments."

"Don't we all?" I say gently, staring up at him and wishing I could just crawl inside his brain and have a look around.

He cocks his head, lips pursed together. "Not like mine."

I offer him a timid smile. I feel like a princess trying to calm a beast, every action made with care. "Try me."

He seems to think that over. Finally he says, "It was the song."

I blink at him. "Someone Saved My Life Tonight?"

He scratches at his beard and looks away. "Yeah."

I squeeze his hand again and take a step toward him, feeling the heat of his personal space. "Did you save someone's life?" I ask quietly.

His eyes flit to mine, shining like green glass. A soft shake of his head. "No," he says. He gives me a sour smile. "I didn't."

I breathe in deeply and know better than to ask any more.

There's movement in the bushes behind us, and Lachlan twists around to look. I look around, expecting to see some drunk person emerge. But the bushes just shake and suddenly two dogs pop out.

Both of them look skinny and mangy. One looks like a pit bull, which I admit makes me a bit scared, and the other is a scruffy mutt with long, matted hair. They look at us with frightened eyes and run off down the road and into the trees, the pit bull limping as he goes.

Lachlan looks back at me. "I have to go," he says.

"Where?"

He nods to where the dogs had gone. "There. The one dog is hurt." He pulls out of my grasp and starts jogging down the road.

I don't know what to say. I watch him go and realize I have two choices—I can go back to the gang and finish the rest of the concert, even though it will probably be over by the time I get back.

Or I can go after Lachlan, who not only seems to be going through something at the moment, but just ran off after two stray dogs.

I take the more exciting option.

Chapter Nine

KAYLA

I run after Lachlan, my boots slapping the concrete with each step. Thankfully he looks over his shoulder and spots me. He comes to a stop, frowning.

"I'm coming with you," I tell him.

"Really?" he asks, studying me. "I'm going after them. Through there." He points into the woods at the tall eucalyptus and pine that stick up like blackened spears into the city-lit sky.

"Then let's go," I tell him.

He rubs his lips together, still watching me close. Then he shrugs, his eyes lighting up. "All right."

"All right."

He turns and starts jogging into the woods of Golden Gate Park and I'm hot on his trail. I pull out my phone, and even though the battery is low, I turn on the flashlight so I don't eat shit. I know it doesn't really help Lachlan see, and from the way he's thundering forward over leaves and brush, I don't think he needs it. If he's a true beast, he can see in the dark.

"I didn't know you were such a dog lover," I tell him, leaping over a fallen log. Then again, I don't know a lot of things about him.

"It's what I do," he says over his shoulder.

"Like a hobby?" I ask, ducking under a branch.

"Like a job," he answers.

I will my legs to lengthen their strides and try to keep up. "I thought you played rugby."

"A man should always do more than one thing," he says, and suddenly we're bolting out of the bushes and onto one of the many paths that crisscross the park. He stops and looks around, eyes scanning the darkness. The only light comes from the faded night sky and my flashlight, and I try not to shine it in his face.

He exhales hard and looks at me. "I run an organization back in Edinburgh," he explains. "I rescue dogs, pit bulls and other bully breeds, but I won't turn down a stray, no matter the breed or the temperament."

I'm completely taken aback by this information. "You run a charity?"

"Aye." He nods, looking around him. "Been running it for a few years now, ever since I had the means and the money to do so."

I can't believe this. "Why didn't you say anything in the interview? This totally ties into what Bram is doing."

"Because that was about Bram. That was for his cause, not mine." Suddenly he gestures for me to be quiet, to stay still. I hold my breath, frozen in place. There is a rustle in the distance, but I don't dare lift my flashlight. Two pairs of eyes glint in the dark.

"Over there," he whispers. "They aren't going to be easy to catch. They're scared."

He slowly starts moving in their direction and I reluctantly follow.

"Aren't they dangerous?"

"We're the dangerous ones," he says. "Until we prove to them otherwise."

"And how do we do that?" I ask.

"With a fuckload of patience, love," he says.

I grin. "Did I ever tell you that I love it when you call me that?" I tell him. I can't help it. "*Love.* It's so...endearing."

He gives me a curious look. "Have I called you that before?"

I nod.

He frowns. "Interesting."

He doesn't elaborate and keeps moving forward through the dark. I follow, matching his movements, even though I wonder how the hell we're going to catch these dogs. They're just going to keep running, it's late at night, and the park is absolutely huge. Unless we corner them somewhere, we could keep running until dawn.

Not that I'm complaining. Even though it's a bit creepy in this park at night, and despite what Lachlan says the dogs could be rabid, I still feel nothing but safe with him.

"Wait here," he says to me. "Turn the flashlight off."

I lift up my phone to do so just in time to see it turn off by itself. As in the battery just died. "Uh, it's not going to come back on. Do you have your phone?"

He doesn't answer me. I blink rapidly, trying to get my eyes to adjust to the dark. Thanks to the light pollution, it doesn't take that long, and I can see him moving forward. The dog's eyes in the distance have faded, and I'm not sure if I'm looking at them or something else.

Lachlan stops walking and kind of shuffles around, leaves crunching on the ground. I can't see him anymore. I hear something crinkle, like he's taking something out of his pocket. He begins talking in low, hushed murmurs and I can't make out what he's saying.

I want to call out after him but I don't dare. I feel like he's part dog whisperer and I have to stay as quiet and still as possible. So I stand there for what feels like an hour, though maybe it's just minutes, while he does his thing.

Finally I hear him walking toward me. He stops a few feet away.

"Now we wait," he whispers. I'm about to ask him what for, but he grabs my hand and leads me to a eucalyptus tree close by.

He sits down on the ground at the base of the tree and pulls me down beside him. For a moment I think he's going to put his arm around me, but he doesn't.

"So we just sit here?" I ask him, my shoulder pressed up against his. It's starting to get cold and my flannel isn't holding up very well. Still, I don't dare complain. I don't want him to think I'm not tough.

"Aye," he says quietly. "They'll come around. Eventually."

"What did you do?"

He turns to face me. "I talked to them in dog speak."

I'm not sure whether to laugh or not. Is he serious? I can't tell in the dark—not that I could tell anyway. He doesn't add anything to that statement, so that doesn't help either.

We lapse into silence for a few moments. I think I can hear the dogs in the distance, eating something maybe, but I can't be sure. The concert is over and though you can see the faint light of the venues through the forest, the music is gone. I really need to text Steph or Nicola and let them know I'm okay. They're probably freaking out.

"Can I use your phone?" I whisper.

"I forgot it," he says.

"Shit," I say. "Mine's dead. They're probably worried about me."

"Did you just take off?"

"Yeah. Well, Bram knew I was going after you. He told me not to bother."

A pause. "I see."

"Obviously I didn't listen."

His face comes closer to mine and I can feel his eyes on me. "And why is that?" he murmurs.

"I don't know, I'm stubborn," I tell him, folding my hands in my lap. "And I don't like listening to Bram."

"Neither do I," Lachlan says lightly. "So that makes two of us."

I try and swallow the butterflies in my throat. "And I was worried about you."

"About me?" he repeats. "Whatever for?"

I shrug, wondering how much to reveal. "I don't know. I just...I wanted to make sure you were okay."

"Well," he says after a beat. "I'm okay."

"Are you?" I ask. I expect him to balk at that, the fact that I'm second-guessing him. He's such a manly man, I don't blame him for taking offense.

But he just sighs. "Yeah. Right now, I'm okay. I'll feel better when we get those dogs. And tomorrow, who knows. I take it one day at a time. That's all you can do."

What happened to you, I want to ask. *What made you this way?*

Can I fix it?

"Are you okay?" he asks me.

"Me? Yeah."

"About the article and everything?"

I sigh and lean back against the tree. I fight the urge to run my hands up and down my arms to keep warm. But even without me saying anything, Lachlan puts his arm around me.

"Are you cold?" he asks softly, his breath sweet on my cheek, his grip strong.

"Yes," I admit. I match his voice, afraid to break the spell. "And no, I'm not okay about the article. Not at all."

I launch into a long, rambling confession about my dashed hopes and dreams, laying out the nitty gritty with absolutely no fear of being judged or second-guessed. It's refreshing.

When I'm done speaking, Lachlan doesn't say anything. He's still holding me close. I turn into him slightly, inhaling his peppery, woodsy smell, and gingerly place my hand on his stomach, sliding it along his waist until I'm holding onto him. His abs are hard, rigid, and well-earned. I bite my lip in want.

"So why don't you get another job?" he asks gently. "Go for what you really want? There's no use wasting your days doing something that doesn't excite you. You only get one life. Well, two lives. The second one starts the moment you realize you only have one."

I look up at him. He's staring off into the distance. "Where did you hear that one?"

He smiles briefly, his eyes twinkling. "I think I saw it scribbled on a bathroom door. People are philosophical when they're taking a shit."

I laugh. "True."

"So, why don't you?" he asks again.

"You're persistent," I tell him, my fingers gripping the soft fabric of his shirt.

"It's only fair," he says. "You got to ask me all the questions earlier. Now I can turn the tables. I want to know more about you." He says the lasts word like they mean everything.

My heart skips, warm, bubbly. "Okay," I say slowly. "Well, the truth is, I'm afraid. I'm afraid that I'll give up something steady and loyal and normal, and trade it in for something I'll fail at. You know?"

He nods. "I know. But if you don't try...can you imagine spending the rest of your life never having that passion? That pull? Never feeling if who you are and what you offer will ever be used the way it should be? You have talent, there's no doubt. And if you believe it and never share it with the world...well what a bloody shame that would be."

He's got this uncanny knack of just reaching inside and knowing what I'm feeling and thinking. As if I don't think about that all the time. The regret that lies ahead of me if I keep going on as I am. One foot in front of the other, never looking up, never looking for a better way.

"But it's not that simple," I tell him, holding his shirt tighter.

"Is it ever simple?"

"No," I say. "It's just that...I don't want my mother to worry about me."

"Your mother?"

I nod. I take a deep breath, summoning strength. "Yeah. She's in her seventies and not doing too well. She hasn't been doing well ever since my father died. That was seven years ago. I'm really the only one in the family that seems to worry about her. That seems to care. My brothers, they're all older and have their own lives—most of them have their own families. She just isn't on their radar. They all assume that I'll take care of her forever, like it's my job. And it's not my job. I do it because I love my mom more than anything—I do it because she took care of us. I do it because she deserves so much more than to be a widower, all alone in that same house." I pause my rambling, remembering to breathe. "She's happy with me, with the job I have. It's steady. It's reliable. I want to be as steady and reliable for her as I can. I'm not sure how much time she has left and the thought of losing her…it only adds to it. It ruins me."

Lachlan doesn't say anything for a moment. Far in the background, there's drunken laughter, but then it disappears. The night grows still again.

"That's commendable," he finally says. "You're a good daughter, Kayla, and she knows that. But I'm sure your mother would want what's best for you. What makes *you* happy."

I feel the question burning on my lips and I do everything I can to hold it back.

But he can sense the change in my body. He cranes his head to look down at me. "What?"

"Nothing," I say.

"You can ask me," he coaxes.

I swallow. "Did you know your mother?" I ask softly, holding my breath, thinking he might blow up at me.

He stares at me, deep into my eyes, and I gaze further into his, barely visible in the dim. He slowly licks his lips, gives a single nod. "My mother gave me up when I was five. She was all I had. I like to believe that she wanted what was best for me. I don't think she realized what it would do to me. What I would become."

What I would become.

The words echo in my head, sharp and potent in the dark, in this isolation.

Who had he become?

Who is this man, this beast, I am holding onto?

More than anything in this world, I want to find out.

I stare up at him, craving so much more than he's given me. He looks away, frowning, almost if he's in pain, head hanging down.

"You know, I've never told anyone that much about what happened," he says gruffly, the depth of his voice making the skin on my arms prickle.

I press my fingers into his skin, relishing the feel of him against me. "Thank you for telling me. I won't tell a soul."

He slowly turns his head to look at me. His eyes are deep, intense pools that pull me in. They welcome me to drown in them, tell me I might even enjoy it.

I'm such a fucking goner.

I was from day one.

"I know you won't," he murmurs. "You're not like the rest of them. I don't think you're like anyone I've ever met."

I raise my brows. "You mean you don't have a slutty, immature, loud friend back at home?"

It's a joke but he doesn't smile.

He puts his hand on my chin, tilting my head up further. "That's not you. That's not what I see."

I want to tell him that it is, that it's all anyone ever sees of me.

But for once in my life, I keep quiet.

He runs his thumb over my bottom lip.

"I'm going to kiss you," he says.

Oh Jesus, is this happening? I'm not going to survive this.

"Please tell me you're not joking," I whisper.

His fingers grip my chin tighter and he lowers those gorgeous lips toward mine, his expression still caught in that frown, as if he can't quite believe it himself.

"I've never been more serious," he says.

Coming from a man like him, I know that's saying a lot.

I close my eyes and there's a delicious, aching second before his lips meet mine. Soft, unbearably soft, and I'm sinking into them, falling down, down, down into a rabbit hole.

The kiss is sweet, slow, gentle. The kiss is like lingering in satin sheets with sun streaming on your skin. The kiss is soothing but it does nothing to soothe me.

It only stirs up those butterflies. It lets loose the birds from the cage. It makes my mouth open against his, suddenly insatiable, hungry, desperate for everything he can possibly give me.

He responds in kind. He groans into my mouth which shoots fire down my spine, incinerating my nerves. His lips are wet and wanting, enveloping mine with softness, with wildness, with desire that I can taste.

His hands bury themselves in my hair, holding me, his body twisting against mine to get closer. I grab him tighter, pulling him toward me, then let my hands roam up and down his sides, feeling the taut muscle underneath. I slip my fingers underneath his shirt, his skin soft and warm beneath my caress.

The tip of his tongue touches mine and I am lost to him. Whatever armor I had over my black, bitter heart is being chipped away with each passionate kiss, each deep, slow pull of my mouth to his.

I feel like I'm being kissed for the first time. This kiss is erasing every single man that has ever crossed my path. It's a restart button being pushed.

It's the best kiss I've ever had.

And it doesn't seem fair that the finest lips to ever grace mine are leaving in a week.

He pulls away, just briefly, his lips sliding away from my open mouth and slowly moving down my jawbone, nipping, sucking, tasting. His rough beard tickles my skin, inflaming my desire. His grip around my head tightens, containing me, and his mouth is hot against my neck as he lets out a ragged breath.

I moan, unable to help myself, pressing against him, wanting him to devour me. There is so much heat, so much built up tension between us, I don't know how I can ever extract myself from him. I've wanted him so badly and now that his lips are kissing my neck and he's holding me, so tight, and I can feel his own lust for me, I'm not sure if I can ever stop.

A rustle sounds from the bushes beside us, bringing me back to a hazy reality.

Lachlan pulls away, breathing hard with my face in his hands, his eyes searching mine. He slowly turns his head and looks to the side of us. I suck in my breath, my lips still throbbing from his kiss, and follow his gaze.

Eyes stare at us from the bushes. I freeze up but Lachlan whispers in a raspy voice, "Shh, shhh, it's okay." He slowly moves into a crouch and I shuffle over to give him room. He turns and faces the eyes in the bushes—which I hope are the dogs—and takes something out of his pocket.

"Did you like that?" he asks them gently. "Here."

He tosses something into the bushes.

The eyes come closer, the wet snap of jowls, eating whatever it was.

"Do you just carry dog food with you everywhere?" I whisper, but he doesn't answer me.

He coos at the dogs, tosses them something again, and slowly moves toward them, keeping his hulking frame as low as possible.

I squint, trying to watch him in the dark. I'm a bit worried that the dogs might attack him. At the same time, I'm cursing them for being cockblockers.

"Easy now," he says, taking off his belt. "Easy."

Is he going to use his belt as a leash? What kind of dog superhero is this guy?

A bunch of shuffling follows, then more hushed, calming words from Lachlan until finally he stands up slowly.

"Okay," he says to me. "I've got one of them."

I get to my feet, dusting off the dirt from my ass, and peer at him. At his side is the shadow of a dog, his belt looped around its neck. Though the dog is tense, straining slightly at the makeshift leash, it amazes me that he's not fighting, not trying to run.

"How did you do that?" I ask in awe.

"Used my belt. It's a little too big for me anyway."

"No," I say, "I mean the whole thing. How did you lure them here?"

He gently taps his cargo pants pocket and the dog looks there. It's then that I notice the other stray slowly coming forward, also drawn by the noise.

Lachlan reaches in and pulls out what looks like beef jerky. "I always carry some sort of food on me, just in case."

"Wherever you go? Just in case you find a stray dog?"

"Aye," he says calmly, as if it's totally normal.

I gesture to the other dog. "What about that one?"

He glances at the scruffy mutt now standing beside the leashed pit bull. He hands both dogs more jerky and they take it, eager and wary at the same time. "This one will follow the alpha."

"Aren't you the alpha?" I ask.

"I will be by the time the night is over."

God, he can alpha me anytime he wants. Even with the dogs here now, I'm having a hard time forgetting that just moments ago my lips were locked with his and I was lost in all he was giving me. I need more of it. That kiss can't be it.

But now he's preoccupied. A cold, wet breeze laced with fog washes over me and I fold my arms across my chest. "The fog is rolling in again."

"We'll get going," he says.

"Where? To the pound?"

"Fuck no," he says sharply. "These dogs will be put down in a few days if I do that."

I obviously have a lot to learn about all of this. "Really, why?"

"Because the pound is overwhelmed with dogs, as are most shelters in any given city. There just isn't any room for them, and these two are shy. Being a pit doesn't help either. They won't get adopted. They won't get rehomed. They'll be killed."

I swallow uneasily. "That's horrible. I'm sorry, I had no idea."

"Most people don't," he says, staring down at the dogs. "So I'm taking them home."

"Home? To Scotland?"

"I'll take them to my flat here first and try to find homes for them this week. If I can't, they'll fly back with me."

Jesus. I'm floored by the size of this man's heart.

"Who are you?" I can't help but whisper.

"Just a man," he replies. "Come on."

He turns and walks off through the darkness, the pit bull pulling on the belt but reluctantly following, limping as he goes. The scruffy dog is right on his tail.

"Is he going to be okay?" I ask.

Lachlan eyes the dog. "Seems minor. I'll get him to a vet tomorrow."

I walk beside Lachlan on the other side, careful not to vibe out the dogs since they seem so taken with him. Hell, I can't blame them. I'd also follow him anywhere, whether he had food or not. I mean, I guess I did just that when he ran off into the forest.

He keeps talking to them in his low voice, and my brain is going wild. It's hard to know what time it is or even what direction we're going along the path now. I wonder how the hell he's going to get home, let alone me. I wonder if I should bring up the fact that we made out, just in case he's already forgotten. Cuz I sure as hell have not.

Finally we see the trees thin out and the rise of buildings and lights. The road, Lincoln Way, cuts along the edge of the park, and there are still a handful of concertgoers straggling along the sidewalk.

"This seems busy enough," Lachlan says as we come to a stop a few yards from the road. "You can hail a cab from here. Do you need any money?"

I stare at him blankly. "No. Where are you going?"

He gestures with his head down the street, where it disappears into the heart of the city. "Cabs don't let you take dogs."

"An Uber might."

He raises his brow. "This Uber thing, you need a phone for that, aye?"

"So you're just going to walk?" I ask, incredulous. "That's like miles and miles from here. That's the whole freaking city. It will take hours."

He shrugs. "That's fine. Will give me time to get to know the dogs better. If the pit's leg gets worse, I'll carry him. If he lets me."

I know I'm staring at him like he's crazy, but I can't help it. "It's not safe to walk the streets this late at night," I tell him.

He rubs at his beard and gives me a small smile. "Listen, love, I can handle it." He gazes down at the dogs. "Plus, I have a pit bull now. I'm sure I'll be given a wide berth."

The fact is, anyone looking for trouble would give him a wide berth anyway. Those mountainous traps and shoulders, those hard, wild eyes, they warn everyone to stay away.

Everyone but me.

"I'll go with you," I tell him.

He shakes his head. "You just said yourself that it's a long walk."

I cross my arms and attempt a commanding stance. "That's true, but you're not getting rid of me that easily."

In the distance, a siren wails. Lachlan looks off, chewing on his lower lip, that lip I'd give anything to chew on again. Finally his eyes slide to mine, amused and kind. "All right," he says. "If that's what you want."

"Yup."

"You really are something aren't you?" He takes a step closer to me. "Stubborn as shit."

I grin at him and my grin widens when he reaches out and grabs my hand, giving it a squeeze.

"Shall we?" he asks.

I squeeze right back, my palm pressed against his, skin on skin, electricity buzzing up my arm. I don't know when I of all people started finding kissing and hand-holding to be insanely erotic, but I did. All because of him.

Hand in hand, we head off across the city.

I talk the entire time.

About my mother.

My brothers.

My father.

My ex-fiancé.

My job.

He listens intently to every single word that comes out of my mouth. It's an amazing feeling to actually be heard. More than that, he seems to *understand*.

We pass sketchy characters, but all Lachlan has to do is look at them and they shrink away. We pass parks where he spots other stray dogs, and it breaks his heart—and mine—that he can't save them all. We walk through blocks and blocks of harsh city life, and Lachlan seems more at ease than ever. He's alert but comfortable, even as we pass the fringes of the dangerous Tenderloin district. And I never feel unsafe.

The dogs stay by our side the whole time, with Lachlan feeding them from another packet of beef jerky that I ran into a 7-11 to get. They seem more comfortable, and Lachlan tells me that he can tell they both had homes at one point, which will make it easier for them to get adopted.

When we get to his apartment building, my feet are burning and the sky seems to be growing lighter in the east, and I hope it's a trick of my eyes because I still have to go to work when day breaks.

I hope the dawn never comes.

I want the night to go on forever.

It's a bit of a struggle to get the scruffy dog inside, especially as we're trying not to attract attention to ourselves—Lachlan's not sure about the building's pet policy. Finally he takes off his Henley shirt and wraps one of the long sleeves around the dog's neck until we get him in the door.

At least I think that's what he does because I'm staring at his shirtless body with my mouth open. I don't even have the decency to look away. I'm tired and sleep-deprived and sore, and the sight of all those muscles, all those tattoos, lifts me up like a tonic.

But if Lachlan can tell I'm staring deliriously at him, he doesn't show it. We eventually get up the elevator, the dogs freaking out now, and into his apartment. He immediately gets a bowl of water for them while they wander around the place sniffing everything. He puts his shirt back on—dammit—and starts rummaging through his kitchen.

"Can I help with anything?" I ask him.

He shakes his head and takes some raw ground beef out of the fridge. "It's lucky I eat a lot of protein," he says, putting the meat into two bowls and setting them down. "This should do."

The dogs sniff it warily then launch into it, devouring it quickly.

I watch Lachlan as he stares down at them, arms folded across his wide chest, a quiet smile on his lips. His eyes are lit up, the corners of them crinkling slightly. The way he looks at the dogs is completely different from the way he looks at anyone else, myself included. There's real love there.

That's a look I'd die to have.

Take it easy, crazy pants, I quickly admonish myself. *One kiss and a night of hand-holding and you'd think you were going to marry the guy.*

I don't even have to remind myself that he's leaving next week.

As if sensing the finality of it all, Lachlan looks at me. "I guess I should call you a cab."

"Oh, okay." I look around for the time and spy the clock on his wall. It's fucking 4:05 a.m. "Holy shit. I have to be up for work in *three* hours."

He looks apologetic and unplugs his cell that was charging on the wall. "Time flies when you're walking across San Francisco."

He makes the call and tells me a cab is on the way.

I gesture to the dogs who are sniffing in the kitchen. "Are you going to be okay with these guys?"

"Aye, we'll be fine. Come, let me walk you downstairs."

He opens the door for me and we head down the hall. Once in the elevator, it's awkward without the dogs there. We aren't speaking and I'm not sure what we should be saying. There's a lot I want to say to him. There's even more that I want to do.

So many, many things.

But as we stand outside the building, I keep my eyes on the street, scanning for the cab. I want to stare at him. I want to take him in like a cool glass of water. It's just that I'm so wired and tired that I'm afraid I'll do something stupid.

"Thank you," he says to me, and at that I finally meet his eyes.

"For what?"

"For being there," he says. "Tonight. It was nice to not have to do it alone." He pauses, licking his lips. "Sometimes... solitude can be blinding."

God. I know this. I feel those words in my soul. My throat closes up with some flash of strange emotion.

He reaches for my face with his hand, grazes my cheekbone with his rough fingers. His brows knit together and his mouth opens like he wants to say something. I hold my breath, waiting, wondering, wanting.

The cab pulls up and honks, making me jump. Lachlan's hand drops away.

I give the cabbie my death stare, sighing in frustration.

Rude.

I look back at Lachlan, wishing I could have those seconds back.

"So..." I say, fumbling for words.

"So," he says. "We should get coffee this week. If you want, that is."

"Coffee would be great," I say.

Dick would be better, though.

He leans forward and kisses me softly on the lips. "See you soon, love."

Fucking. Swoon.

When the cab finally drops me off at home, I stagger over to my bed and collapse on it, remembering at the last moment to set my alarm. I'm going to feel like absolute shit in the morning. I didn't even get laid.

But, god, it was absolutely worth it.

I know I fall asleep with a smile on my face, because when the alarm rings a few hours later, blaring and unwelcoming in the dawn, I'm still smiling.

Chapter Ten

LACHLAN

In the dream I'm five years old again. Walking down Princes Street in Edinburgh, alone and naked in the falling snow. Everything is the same and everything is different. The junkies I pass on the street are my friends. I see Eddie with his fingerless gloves, nails thick and yellow with nicotine. I see Thomas and his sobriety bracelets he never takes off, even though he's too drunk to stand. I see Jenny with her peeling skin and matted hair held back with a plaid headband.

And they see me. But they don't wave, they don't smile. They scream as I pass them, until the noise is too loud, until their screams wrap their hands around my head and squeeze.

"Where's Charlie?" Eddie yells, spit flying out of his decaying mouth. "Where is he? What did you do to him?"

I don't answer. I run through the snow and then I'm back at the old flat.

I'm no longer five.

I'm thirteen. Tall, skinny, underdeveloped. My anger has just started to eat at me, and the world is poison. Mr. Arnold has me cornered in my mother's old bedroom. She's lying on the bed, staring up at the ceiling like I'm not there.

She didn't save me when I was five. She wouldn't save me now.

I face the wall, too afraid, too disgusted to look at my foster parent as he approaches with greedy hands.

"Don't tell Pamela," he says to me, voice dripping with lust. "It's our secret."

His hands close over my throat but I don't turn around.

I cry.

I haven't learned to hit back yet.

When I do learn, he's sent to the hospital.

His wife Pamela says I'm a black seed. That I made her husband do it to me.

And I'm sent away again.

Now I'm at the Hillside Orphanage.

I'm twenty years old.

My bony arms are covered with scratches.

I scratch them some more.

I'm dying on the inside.

My teeth are being ground away, falling out of my mouth like sugar.

In front of me, at the headmaster's desk, sits Charlie.

His back is to me.

He's not twitching.

He is deadly still.

Charlie is never ever still.

"Charlie," I hiss at him. "Charlie, do you have any?"

But Charlie doesn't move.

I step toward him, my limbs jerking, uncontrollable.

Charlie has what I need to make it stop.

The craving.

The ache.

The emptiness.

Everything that resides deep in my bones.

I put my hand—ghostly white and peppered with bruises—on his shoulder and spin him around in the chair.

He stares at me with dead, glassy eyes, blood running from his nose.

It drips onto the stuffed lion he holds in his hand.

In a flash, he moves. Charlie is in my face. Empty eyes. Bared, rotting teeth.

"You're not just going to leave me here," he utters, sounding like a child. "You cannae do that, Lachlan."

The next moment I'm lying in an alley.

Charlie is crumpled beside me. One of the dogs is sniffing his face. Gives him a tentative lick. Charlie doesn't stir.

Charlie is dead.

I close my eyes.

And I am dead too.

...

When I wake up, I'm drenched in sweat and clawing at my sheets. My breathing is shallow, and I'm hungry and desperate for air, as if it could clean out all the dirt inside.

I smell urine. For a moment I think I've pissed myself—how about that for regression—but then I remember the dogs. I remember last night. I remember where I am.

Who I am.

I sit up and try to get a hold of myself. I haven't dreamed like that for months and its return unhinges me.

Inhaling deeply, I swing my feet out of bed and wince when they land in something wet. I groan and look down to see a faint yellow puddle. I wonder which one of them did it.

I'd told Kayla that they must have had homes at some point, but that doesn't mean they are housebroken.

"Hello," I call out softly, walking to the door and peering out into the living room. There's a pile of shit on the carpet and another in the kitchen.

Both dogs are sleeping on the couch, entwined with each other. That sight alone makes up for the fact that I'm going to be in shit myself if I continue to let them destroy the place.

I put on a pot of coffee and absently scratch at my arm, a bad leftover from the dream. I pull my hand away and force my brain into a better place. I saved those dogs last night. There is hope for them, hope that I've given them.

But, of course, that's not the only thing that happened last night.

Kayla.

That tiny sprite.

I kissed her.

I fought and I fought and I fought against it.

But there was nothing I could do.

She's a riptide.

I'm just a man without oars.

And she...bloody hell, she had started to get under my skin far before last night. I've been thinking about her ever since the impromptu rugby match, ever since she left my flat in my clothes, ever since I saw her at the bar. The way she looks at me...it's not just that she wants me, because I know she does. It's that...I feel she might see me, too. Beneath the layers.

Not that she ever could, ever would, see all. But just to have someone scratch the surface—to want to see me for more than me, is enough.

Scary as fuck. But enough.

Then there's the fact that she's this gorgeous wild little thing. Those eyes that implore me to tell her all my secrets, that beg me to have my way with her. Those eyes that promise I'll never forget her, if I just give her a second, give her a chance.

I gave her a chance last night.

But I didn't do it for her.

I did it for me.

Because I fucking needed it. I needed that touch, that comfort.

Hope. Somewhere in there was hope.

I felt it when I put my arm around her, like I was containing it against me.

Hope before death.

It's tattooed on my side.

I got that a few years after Charlie, to remind me of why I cleaned up and how I moved on.

Or, at least, tried to.

Kayla felt like that hope, even though I know how foolish it is to even think like that over a girl I barely know. But just for that moment, it felt good to have even a glimpse of it.

Of course, when that damn song came on, it threw me back into reality. Of who I was and the parts that made me. The events. The battles. The ugly fucking truth.

That didn't mesh very well with the here and now.

I panicked. I got up and left—to escape the song, escape the past that liked to show itself on lonely nights. Which is every night. But it had no place right then, not with her there.

I had no idea she would follow me, and when I first heard her call my name, my stomach did a backflip. And then she was there, by my side, her hair messy from running through the crowds, face beautifully flushed.

She came after me.

She worried about me.

I can't remember the last time someone worried about me. Everyone by now knows not to bother, knows not to ask. Lachlan is a lone soldier, they say. He's *survived*. He'll be fine.

But this girl, this woman with the smiling eyes and the teasing lips, she knew I wasn't *fine*.

And when she wanted to come with me, after the dogs, into the dark woods, well fuck. She wasn't afraid of anything. We share the same tenacity.

And with that same resolve, I could have kissed her all night. Her lips, her mouth, the warmth of her tongue—we fit together like a lock and key. I wanted nothing more than to lay her on her back in the dirt and leaves, explore her body with my hands, my teeth, my tongue, and feel all of her in the dark. Her body promised to take me far away. I wanted to fuck the war out of me.

I had to admit that I wanted Kayla more than anything.

Naturally that didn't happen. I can't say I'm disappointed, because in the end I saved the dogs. And I almost got the girl. The peace. And there's still time. Less than a week now until I'm flying back to Edinburgh, ready to jump into training, ready to shift my whole life to rugby.

There's still time.

Isn't there?

By the time the dogs stir, I've cleaned up their piss and shit and put defrosted ground beef down for them. I have some collars in my dresser—I know Kayla thought it was strange to be so prepared, but I've never not found a stray—so I put them on the dogs and make leashes out of rope.

We go for a quick walk. The pit bull is still headstrong under the leash and seems to shy away from loud noises and quick movements. But with some love and obedience training, he'll be a good pet for someone. I can tell by the eyes. A dog's eyes don't lie. A dog doesn't lie. If you see the good in them, there *is* good in them. Last night when I was cleaning his paw, finding the debris imbedded in a cut, the cause of the limping, he looked at me with thanks. I felt that deep, deep inside.

The smaller mutt, the terrier mix, is more fragile. She clings to the pit bull's side and still doesn't trust me too much. She may in time, but I have a feeling she'll be coming back to Edinbugh with me. I've seen so many dogs like her, which are dogs like me. She needs someone like Lionel to bring her back around. Lionel will show her the ropes; he always does.

I put them back in the flat and then head out to the nearest pet store. It's strangely chilly today, the weather here even worse than Scotland's in the summer, and I shove my hands into my jacket pockets, turning up my collar and keeping my shoulders hunched against the fog as I move through rough neighborhoods.

I never feel fear, or disgust, or pity for these people—the homeless, the addicted, the forgotten. I was them. I know what it's like. I know too well. All I feel is hope and hopelessness, a stunning combination. Hope that they'll one day come to that point, that road, that branch, and decide for themselves to get up, to grow, to live.

But the hopelessness, that lies in myself. Because there's nothing I can do for them. Every decision to better your life has to come from within, not from anyone else.

And then there's that bitter, hard truth that grows in you, in your darkness, like mold. The truth that you'll never be free. You'll never forget that sweet song that pulled you under and brought you to your knees. That once you've seen how far you can sink, you know exactly how far you can fall. That truth tethers you. It lurks behind every thought, every action.

Sometimes, the slide backward into who you once were seems inevitable.

When I return back home, arms crammed with dog food, treats, and leashes, I look up a local vet and make an appointment for them tomorrow. The pit bull needs his paw properly looked at—he's also not neutered, and I'm unsure if the terrier is spayed. Both of those things need to happen before they're given homes.

I settle down on the ground and spend a good hour at their level, just observing them, until my phone rings. I roll the Kong toy I bought them back toward them, the pit going for it with gusto, then I get up to answer it.

It's Bram.

"Aye?" I say into the phone.

"What the hell happened to you last night?" Bram asks. "You just took off and we couldn't find you. We couldn't find Kayla either."

"I went for a walk."

"You're always going for a walk," he says. He's right about that. Jessica—my adopted mother and Bram's aunt—always say I have too much troubled energy and I need to keep walking it off.

"Has Nicola spoken to Kayla?" I ask. I haven't texted her yet. I've been debating it all morning.

"Yes, she's texted her. Kayla said you found some dogs and took them home?"

"Aye. I'm looking at them right now." I clear my throat. "Look, sorry, I left my phone at home and hers died so we couldn't get in contact."

Bram sighs. "Okay. Well…you missed the end of a great concert."

I suppose that was a jab over the VIP ticket. "The day was fantastic. Thank you, mate."

"Don't take this wrong way, Lachlan," he says, "but…"

I exhale heavily. "What?"

"I worry about you. When you do stuff like that. When you just leave."

My jaw tenses at that admission. "What are you worried about, exactly?"

He pauses. "You know," he says quietly. "I feel responsible for you while you're here."

I grip the phone tightly, feeling a burst of anger radiate through me, molten and hot. "I'm fucking thirty-two years old, Bram. I'm here to help your arse, not to be babysat. You might think you bloody know me, but you don't."

"I know, I know," he says quickly. "Sorry. Okay? Sorry."

"That's fine," I mutter. "I better go."

"Wait," he says. "Just reminding you about tonight."

I frown. "Tonight?"

"With Justine."

"Oh, Jesus fucking hell." I press my fist into my forehead. "That's tonight?"

"It's Monday, and it's the only chance we have, Lachlan. Please do not back out. There's no way that Nicola will let me take your place and I'm pretty sure Justine won't want me there either. It's all you."

Kayla. I'm thinking of Kayla. Will she care? Is it even worth mentioning?

"I really don't feel like dealing with people today," I say, even though I know that it's futile. "Especially people like that."

"Lachlan," Bram says. "You're leaving next week. Just go, have a few drinks, meet the father and tell him everything. That's all you can do and it's our last shot."

"What about..." I trail off, wiping at my nose.

"What about what?"

"Nothing," I tell him. "All right, I'll do it. I'll go. But as soon as I think it's done, I'm out of there."

"Good," he says. "We'll be at the Lion so you can come right there afterward."

"Of course you will."

I hang up.

And with that troubled energy, I take the dogs for a walk.

I sit by the Giants' Promenade and watch the boats in the marina, one dog on the bench beside me, the other at my feet. I decide to give them names. The pit bull is Ed. The terrier is Emily. I like giving human names to dogs. It's more respectable that way. It tells them they're one of us and reminds us of the same.

I take my phone out of my jacket many times, look at it many times. I think about contacting Kayla. Asking how she is. If she's okay. I want to mention that I'm going to a function with Justine, that it doesn't mean anything.

But I don't. Because I'm afraid her response will be, "So, you can go out with anyone," or, "It's fine, you don't owe me an explanation" or even the biting, "Why are you telling me this?" I want to do right, I do, but I'm not built for this. I'm not even with Kayla and I'm already acting like I am. Not the right trap to fall into right now. Or at any time.

Eventually the dogs and I head back to the flat. I keep busy. I go for a run. I lift at the gym downstairs. I spend time scouring the internet, trying to find rescue agencies in town that might be able to find a foster for Ed.

And I check on my plans with Justine. They're on. She'll swing by with a Town Car at seven o'clock. So I shower. Trim my beard down to the bare minimum, slick my hair back, put on a black suit and tie. It feels utterly unnatural, and it's only the glimpse of a tattoo at my collarbone—nunquam iterum—that reminds me that I'm still me. A big bad wolf in sheep's clothing.

Thankfully, the evening isn't as horrendous as I envisioned. I'm still out of my element. I hate socializing with these people, the ones who sit at the top and throw stones down below. But I can have a good poker face from time to time. I make nice. With Justine. With her father's cronies. With her father himself. In the suit and tie I look just respectable enough to fool them all, and when I talk about Bram's project, Bram's vision, it's convincing. I'm pulling from in deep and it's working. Because I believe in it, and I want them to believe in it.

It's just after nine when I pull Justine aside and whisper in her ear. "How do you think I did? Be honest."

She just smiles coyly and runs her fingers over my tie, pulling me close to her. "I think you sold him. I wouldn't be surprised if he invests."

I can't help but flash her a smile. "Good."

She doesn't let go of my tie. "Want me to get you a glass of champagne?"

"Nah," I tell her. "I'm good. Actually, I have to get going."

Her bottom lip juts out in a pout. "Why?"

"Dogs," I tell her, tugging at my ear. "I have dogs. If I don't take them for a walk, they're going to shit everywhere."

"When did you get dogs?"

"Yesterday," I tell her. "I rescued two strays."

She makes a face. It's the reaction I thought I'd get. "Strays? You took in two strays and put them in your apartment?"

I shrug. "It's the least I could do."

"They might have fleas. Rabies. Who knows what disease?"

"They needed my help."

She lets go of my tie but tries to look pleasant, giving me a thin smile. "Huh. Well, aren't you just a giving man."

"Someone has to be," I say, an edge creeping into my voice.

"I guess," she says, and steps away from me. "The world needs more people like you."

I raise my brows. "Does it?" I can read the insincerity in her voice. It's the line that people say when they don't really believe it. It's what they say in order to make themselves look like they care.

She takes a sip of her champagne and starts looking around for someone better to talk to. Who knew that just mentioning stray dogs would turn her off? If I'd known that, I would have talked about Lionel and the organization from day one. Then again, it wouldn't have led me here to right now and I still have to do what I can to make sure it goes through.

I give her most charming smile, and from the way she blinks at me, I can tell she's dazzled by it. I rarely use it, and when it's sincere, it's never meant for people like her. "I really want to thank you, Justine," I tell her, grabbing her wrist delicately. "For inviting me here. This means a lot to me, and to Bram, just to have your father want to do good in a world that needs it. His help is really appreciated. And yours has always been."

She softens a little bit, but she's still regarding me with a wariness that wasn't there before. Gone are the days of footsie under the table and eager hands in the back of a cab.

I lift her hand to my lips and kiss the back of it. "Take care," I tell her. "And if you don't mind, I'll have Bram get in touch with your father." With my other hand, I show her the business card her father gave me.

"Sure," she says. "I'll let him know. Take care, Lachlan."

And that's it. Though it was a lot to get through, it's over now. It's not quite time to celebrate, not until Bram and Justine's father talk and work out the kinks, but I have a feeling it's going to work out. The man was sold on what I was selling him.

I quickly exit the ballroom at the hotel and get into a waiting cab. I should go home to the dogs first, but the reality is they've probably already made a mess, so what's the difference? I might as well tell Bram the good news.

It's not long before the cab is dropping me off at the Lion. It's a Monday but it's still surprisingly busy.

I stride into the noisy, dimly-lit bar and immediately get a lot of looks. It takes me a minute to realize I'm wearing a suit and tie and I stick out like a sore thumb here.

"Look at you!" Linden hollers from a booth in the back. He's sitting with Bram, Steph, and that fucker James. "Secret agent man, working for M.I. Six!"

I walk over to them and stand at the end of the table, hands jammed into my pockets. "Do you want to hear the good news?" I say to them, rocking back on my heels.

Bram's eyes widen. "How good?"

I shrug. "Nothing is a done deal. But here." I toss the business card on the table. "That's his info. I had a very lengthy conversation with him. He wants to invest."

"What?!" Bram yells, nearly jumping out of his seat.

I raise my palms. "Don't get excited, mate. As I said, nothing is certain. But he's interested. He heard me out. He wants to help. The ball is in your court now."

Linden looks at his brother. "I think this is a cause to celebrate." He looks back at me questioningly. "You do think we can celebrate, right?"

"If you want," I say. "If we're going on vibes and feelings alone, then I'd say yes."

Bram lets out a whoop of joy and Linden pats him on the back. James gets up and says he's grabbing some drinks so I slide into the booth next to Stephanie. She's being oddly quiet, smiling at Bram and Linden but not quite looking at me.

Of course this in turn makes me want to look at her.

"Where's Nicola?" I ask. "And Kayla?" I add, as if it were an afterthought.

It wasn't.

Stephanie looks at Bram. "Well, Nicola is at home because Ava wasn't feeling well. And Kayla *was* here..." They exchange a loaded look. Finally Stephanie sighs and turns to me. "Look, Linden told me you were on a date with Justine."

My head whips around to look at Linden, who shrinks from my gaze.

"And," Stephanie continues, "I told Kayla that."

Now I'm staring accusingly at Bram. "You know that wasn't a date. You practically forced me to do it."

"I know!" Bram exclaims. "I know. By the time I got here, they'd already told Kayla and she'd left. She was upset."

I groan and place my head in my hands. "It was just to secure the investment. That's all."

"I tried to text her that but she's not answering me," Steph says. "The messages aren't being delivered. She must have turned her phone off." She briefly puts her hand on my shoulder. "I only told her because she asked where you were and I didn't want to lie. I know she likes you...I just didn't think she had it that bad for you." She pauses. "Honestly, she'll kill me for saying this, but you're making her behave like…I think she's head over heels."

Hearing that makes me both warm and cold at the same time.

"Did you and Justine…" she starts. "You know…"

I glare at her and she moves an inch away from me. "No, we didn't. But still." I get up just in time to see James approaching with a bottle of sparkling wine. "Tell me where she lives," I say to Steph.

"What? You're going to go over there?"

"Yes," I say, bringing out my phone. "What's her address?"

She tells me and I enter it into my phone. "Thank you," I tell her, then I turn on my heel and walk off. Bram calls after me but I don't turn around. Let him celebrate. This is his baby, his project. This is his passion.

I need to go fix mine.

Chapter Eleven

KAYLA

I floated through the entire day, as if on cotton candy clouds. It didn't matter that I'd only had a few hours of sleep or that my eyes were rimmed with plum colored circles. I didn't care that it was Monday, that I hate where I work now, that I won't be joining the ranks of the writers on the other side of the office.

I know I should care about all of that. I know that on Sunday morning it was still a big fat splotch on this new future I had somehow built in my head.

But Lachlan, he'd erased everything. He'd taken over everything in me and had replaced all the shit with...well, I don't know what. Something to look forward to. Something to look back on.

Fuck, I needed to see him again. He'd said we could do coffee this week, but I didn't want coffee this week. I wanted him now. I wanted to quit work and just go back to his apartment, show up at his door like they do in the movies, and maul the shit out of him. That kiss was everything and still just the tip of the iceberg. If his lips could leave such an imprint on me, I couldn't wait to see what else they could do.

I checked my phone obsessively throughout the day, wondering if he would text me. Wondering if I should text him. I lamented that the normal Kayla, the one who had no problems chasing after men, was missing in action. I was scared to hear the word "no." I was scared to fuck something up before I even had a chance to have it.

On the other hand, I knew he was leaving soon. Very soon. So there wasn't really anything to fuck up. I just wanted to see him again.

But he didn't text, and I didn't either. Nicola and Steph did though, completely freaking out. When my phone finally charged this morning, I had a billion frantic texts from them all pouring in at once. I didn't want to divulge too much information, so I told them that my phone had died and that we'd rescued some dogs. Neither of them knew what to say to that.

Later, Steph told me to come to the Lion for a drink. And stupid, silly me, I did. Because I thought there might be a chance that Lachlan would be there.

I decided to make myself look extra pretty. Put a few waves in my hair. Contoured up my face. Slicked on liquid liner. I squeezed myself into a snake-print leopard skirt, black high heels, and a black lace top. I looked pretty damn good.

I sashayed my way into the Lion, electric flutters in my stomach, my eyes casing the joint, hoping to see the big, bad Scot somewhere. Steph and Linden were in a booth, but I knew from the moment they spotted me and Steph gave me a hesitant wave that something was off.

I slowed my pace, my fingers anxiously twitching at my side. "Hey," I said.

"Looking good, Kayla," Linden commented, and I eyed him suspiciously, wondering if that was the truth or he was just trying to "be nice" like Steph had told us to.

"Thanks." I looked at Stephanie, but she wasn't meeting my eyes. "What's wrong?" I asked her.

"Well, nothing," she said. She patted the seat beside her. "Sit down. You look pretty. Is there a special occasion?"

I gave her the stinkeye. "Do I normally not look pretty? Why would I need an occasion?" I sat down. "So..." I looked around. "Is Bram here?"

"Not yet," Linden said.

I stared hopefully at Steph, hoping she would read my mind. She looked down at the cider in her hands instead.

I cleared my throat. "How did you guys like the rest of the concert?" I asked. "I missed the last part..."

"It was good, yeah. Good." Linden took a swig of his beer.

I sighed and bit the bullet. "Do you guys know if Lachlan is coming here later?"

"I don't know," Linden said. A little too quickly.

I turned to Stephanie and punched her lightly on the arm. "Hey, what's going on? Why are you guys being all weird?"

Steph exchanged a look with Linden and chewed on her lip before facing me.

"You and Lachlan," she said cautiously. "You guys just kissed last night, right?"

I jerked my head back. "Yeah. What...why does that matter?"

She swallowed thickly and looked at Linden again. "Well, I just wanted to make sure how freaked out you would or wouldn't get. If you just kissed, then you should be fine with it."

"Fine with what? What the hell, Stephanie? Just say it."

"He's on a date with Justine," she said, and then quickly downed the rest of her cider.

My heart lurched. Actually lurched, like it was saying goodbye to my chest and moving on out. "What?"

She shrugged. "Linden told me."

I turned to him, as if it was all his fault. "Bram told me," he said defensively. "Sorry, Kayla. I'm sure it's just for business. It doesn't mean anything."

Ugh. I wanted to be sick. "How do you know that?"

"She doesn't seem like his type."

"Well, neither do I and..." I paused and shook my head. "Fuck. Fuck this shit. I'm such an idiot."

"You're not," Steph said. "It's just a date."

"No, I know that," I told her, rather harshly. "He's leaving soon, so what's the difference, right? I'm just such an idiot for *caring*. Like, Jesus. One kiss and I'm fucking broken-hearted that he's gone on some date. Who is this Kayla? I don't like her."

"Hey," Steph said, putting her hand on my shoulder and shaking me. "It's okay to care, you know. I've never seen you care before. Maybe it's a good thing...to know what you want in the future."

I shrugged away from her. In that moment I didn't want to hear any of that crap. "But what I want is now on a date with some rich bitch he's been on a few dates with before. I just...ugh. Whatever. I'm out of here."

I angrily slid out of the booth and got to my feet. I left the bar in a cloud of defeat and went straight back home. I kept berating myself over and over again for the feelings that were moving through me like a swarm of hornets.

This was exactly what I didn't want. This was why I decided to shun off men. I thought that by avoiding sex I could avoid disappointment, but I hadn't even had the chance to fuck him yet, and here I was, disappointed as hell.

So now I'm in my apartment, curled up on the couch with a few glasses of wine in me. I'm "Netflix and chilling" without having anyone to chill with. The wine is dulling the anger, but not that weird sickly feeling in my chest. I go through nearly an entire season of New Girl, hoping Schmidt and Nick will make me laugh, but finding myself getting sadder. More pathetic.

This is bullshit.

I lie back on the couch and stare at the ceiling. I want to rewind the last few weeks and pretend I never went to the Lion that one night, that I'd never seen Lachlan McGregor because before that, I was doing fucking fine. Then I had to see his goddamn stupid beautiful face and become an obsessive, desperate horndog. How could this man, how could any man, do this to me, render me so bare and vulnerable? That was never part of the plan. I wanted to get under his skin, not the other way around. I was supposed to come out of this game on top, fighting through the challenge of it all and getting what I wanted.

I was supposed to be the player here.

I want to pull up the edges of my black heart and pull it around me like a blanket. From now on, the moment I feel myself being lured by anything other than the physical, I'm out. I'm sticking to my damn vow, and if it ever does break one day, it's for just sex and nothing more. Anything more than sex isn't Kayla friendly.

I start to drift off, feeling better about my new plan, my new resolve. I want the dreams to take me away and tomorrow I'll start a new me. The old me.

The apartment buzzer goes off, making me jolt. I inhale sharply and look at my phone for the time, but I turned it off a while ago, not wanting to be disturbed. It's probably Steph coming to check up on me. I could have used her earlier in the night when I was a ball of rage, ready to bitch and ramble on, but now I am more subdued, sleepy, and kind of drunk, and not in the mood to talk about anything.

I walk over to the buzzer and press the button.

"Steph?"

"Uh, no," says the deep Scottish brogue over the speaker. "It's not."

I freeze. My heart hammers.

Oh shit. Lachlan?

"Hello?" he says again. "Kayla? Can I please speak with you?"

No, no, no. Definitely not. Think of your plan, the new old you, I tell myself.

But I still press the button to let him in.

Fuck.

I look down at what I'm wearing. The fucking t-shirt he lent me and nothing else.

Oh god. I need to change. I need to fix my face, my hair. I need to not let him in.

But seconds later he's knocking at the door.

I breathe in deeply, trying not to let those dumbass, unwanted, unwarranted emotions get the best of me. *Be cool, girl,* I tell myself. *Like ice.*

I slide the chain across and open the door.

Lachlan is standing there. In a fucking suit and tie. Hair slicked back, just enough stubble on that angular jaw. Perma-frown. Towering over me like some well-dressed god.

Oh my god. I am so doomed.

"Just come from a wedding?" I attempt a joke. My mouth is drier than a desert.

"Can I come in?" he asks, his shoulders hunched up. "Please?"

Be cool, be cool.

"Sure," I say, opening the door wider with a shrug, pretending I'm not hurt, not mad, and definitely not wearing just his t-shirt.

He walks past me and all I want to do is breathe in his scent. Well, that's not all I want to do.

I shut the door behind him, resting my forehead briefly on it and gathering courage before turning around to face him.

He's standing in the middle of the room, staring right at me. Jesus. He's so beautiful to look at it almost hurts. It *does* hurt.

"I need to explain something."

I cross my arms. "What?"

"I know what Stephanie told you," he says. "About me and Justine."

I shrug, trying to play it off. "Oh well, that's cool."

His frown deepens. "I heard you were upset."

I give him a tight smile. "I don't get upset," I tell him and walk over to the kitchen to busy myself with something.

"Yes, you do," he says, eyes following me. "I've seen you get upset. I know your voice when you're upset."

I want to challenge him, to tell him that he doesn't know me at all. But I don't want that. I want him to know me. I want him to think he does.

"And so I'm upset now?" I say. "Why?"

He chews on his lower lip for a second and finally looks away. "Because. You want me."

I can't help but let out a shocked laugh. Obviously it's true, but I can't believe he has the audacity to just say it so bluntly.

His eyes slide to me again, feverish and hard. "Don't you?"

Suddenly it's not so funny anymore. I lean against the counter, my hands gripping the edge while my mind tries to think of what to say, how to possibly answer that. Finally I tell the truth. "Yeah," I say quietly. "So?"

"So," he says, voice low, almost delicate, "last night was something I've needed...for a long time. It may have been just a walk in the park and a kiss to you, love, but to me...it was far more. And I want to know if it was more to you."

I can only stare back at him, locked in the intensity of his gaze. He's looking at me like he's peeling back the layers, determined to get to the core.

My throat is dry and my heart pounds with excitement and anxiety. What is he doing? What am I doing? There is so much space between us, and I don't know how to bridge the gap or if I want him to, because if it happens it's going to be so much more than I can handle.

"You're leaving on Sunday," I tell him. "That's less than a week."

"So?" he says. "What does that have to do with anything?"

I cock my head. "It means...well, what can happen between now and then?"

"I can fuck your brains out," he says gruffly. "That's what can happen."

Holy shit.

Did he seriously just say he could fuck my brains out? I stare at him with wide eyes, dumbfounded and turned on in an instant. It's hard to swallow. It's hard to think. "Uh..."

"But before I do," he says, starting to loosen his tie. He takes a step forward. Oh god. "I need you to know that tonight I was helping Bram. Justine was never anything other than a favor, and no, I didn't fuck her. Not even close. Whatever it was though, it's done. And for the next week, the only thing on my radar is you." He takes another step toward me, pulling off his tie and tossing it at my feet. "On this counter, in your bed, against the wall. Whatever way I can."

Oh Jesus.

My legs start to tremble and I tightly grip the edge of the counter. I've wanted this more than anything, and now that it's slowly walking toward me, like *I'm* the prey, I've turned into a mute chicken shit. It was so different when I was chasing him. Now that he wants me, he actually *wants* me...I'm terrified that I won't survive it.

He's only a foot away and I can feel the heat of his presence as he begins to eclipse me. He shrugs off his suit jacket and tosses it on the counter, his eyes never leaving my body. My skin smolders under his gaze as he slowly looks me up and down. "You're wearing my shirt," he says, his voice soft and rough at the same time.

He reaches out, grabbing the end of it, rubbing the fabric between his fingers. He's so close now. I'm still a statue made of throbbing blood and a wildly beating heart, and I can't move an inch. I can't do anything but watch him, every movement, every breath, every look. He's so physical, immense—he's become my world.

His eyes drift lower. He leans down into me, his mouth at my ear, his hands moving down my thighs. "Another no pants party?" he murmurs. I shiver, goosebumps from his breath and the bass of his voice. His large, warm palms trail back up my bare skin, lifting up my shirt and skimming over the lace of my underwear.

"Depends what you mean by *pants*," I manage to say.

His lips close gently around my earlobe, teeth razing my skin, the heat from his breath lighting firecrackers down the expanse of my neck. His fingers curl around the edge of my underwear, pulling them down my hips, lifting me forward slightly so he can get them over my ass. I'm between both of his hot hands and it makes me realize how damned small I am compared to him.

My underwear falls down to my knees, then down to the floor, and I'm naked except for the shirt. He licks his lips and I want to shove those fucking lips down between my legs and hold him there until I come. I swear it won't take long.

His grip on my hips intensifies. He lifts me up effortlessly, placing my bare ass on the cold counter, and moves forward between my legs, my underwear dangling from one foot.

He places his beautiful hands on either side of my face, holding me in place, his nostrils flaring as he breathes in hard. It's as if he's trying to restrain himself, and I want him to let go and unleash it all on me, everything that he has. The furrow between his brows only deepens as he tries to drink me in with his eyes. I'm holding my breath, wanting *so* much, and he keeps searching me, trying to read me.

Just fucking take me, I want to say. *Read this.*

My mouth parts.

His eyes drop to my lips.

His gaze burns.

Carnal.

Predatory.

Unwavering.

It's the flash of light before the bomb hits.

Then it hits.

He pulls my face forward and his lips crash against mine, fevered, crazed and wild. His hands sink into my hair and my hands fumble for the buttons on his shirt. Our mouths are lost to each other in a race, a battle, where both of us win. It's breathless, desperate. This kiss is nothing like the other kiss—it's pure molten heat, wet lips and hard pressure, like we're creating a diamond.

My toes curl.

My heart somersaults.

I'm lost to him.

I'm drowning under the onslaught of his tongue, each hot, torrid stroke inside my mouth making me absolutely drenched.

I wrap my legs around his waist, greedy and eager, and I pull him to me. We both moan into each other's mouths. He's as hard as cement and pressing against me in all the right places. With just the slightest movement, the fabric of his pants brushes over my clit and I almost lose my mind.

One hand makes a fist in my hair, tugging at it and making me shiver, while his lips bruise me, our mouths messy and hard, teeth hitting teeth in our uncontrollable need to devour each another.

I'm absolutely rabid for this beautiful man. With his white shirt unbuttoned, I drag my nails over the hard planes of his chest, over the tuft of hair and the expanse of inked art. I reach down to the waistband of his pants and undo the button, while his mouth goes for my neck again, sucking, biting, and I throw my head back to give him better access.

I deftly undo the button and zip down his fly before sliding my hand over his hardness. Holy fuck. He does go commando. The long, heated length of him pulses beneath my palm and he lets out a low, rough growl that vibrates down my spine.

"Oh fuck," he groans, breathing hard into my neck. "I'm already going to explode."

"That makes two of us," I tell him. He's so fucking huge, and just touching his cock is bringing me to the edge. I don't know how I'll survive it inside of me but I'm dying to try.

I wrap my hands around firmer and free it from his pants. I curl forward, glancing down to see. He grows harder, firmer in my hands, the tip dark, flushed, and gleaming. Oh god, I just want to put it in my mouth, all of it, sucking, tasting every inch of him.

At the same time I want him deep inside of me, as far as I can take him, even though he could break me in two.

What a fucking predicament.

I start stroking him, running the precum over his silky hot ridge, pausing at the round and full tip, before going back down again, one hand going further, down over his balls. Lachlan's got a fair amount of hair on his arms, chest, and treasure trail, so thank god for manscaping. I gently cup his balls in my hand and he shudders against me.

"Oh love," he says, raspy, sucking in his breath. "Don't ruin me just yet."

I bite my lip and smile at the effect I have on him. I want to ruin him and I want him to ruin me. The need, the power, is intoxicating.

He pulls back for a second, watching with a delirious look in his hooded eyes as my hands work him up and down. His scrapes his teeth over his lower lip then slowly looks up at me. "You'll have to stop that or I'm going to come right here and now," he warns.

I pause and grip his gorgeous cock tighter. His eyes roll back in his head, and the muscles in his thick neck are corded, straining. "Make me," I tease.

He grunts and moves back into me, ripping the shirt over my head, causing me to let go. My nipples are as hard as pebbles, and he cups my breast, licking a path to the center. He takes one in his mouth and I'm swept away by the warmth, by the fire-laced nerves that radiate out from me.

"Oh god," I cry out softly.

He makes a noise of agreement against my breast, causing more nerves to incinerate. He slips his hand below, sliding it over my clit which is slick as sin.

"You're fucking soaked" he says huskily before taking my nipple between his teeth and pulling slightly. "I knew you'd have a greedy little pussy."

I moan, trying to tell him that it was pretty obvious that I did, but my words are ripped from my mouth as he pushes one big finger inside of me, the roughness igniting my screamingly sensitive skin. The heavy penetration seems to roll through me and I automatically jerk my hips forward, bringing his finger further inside.

He makes a low, guttural sound and pulls out slowly before adding another finger. I bite my lip to keep from yelling his name as he expertly slides his fingers over the swollen bundle of nerves that threatens to destroy me from the inside out.

"Fuck," I moan, my mouth open and gasping as my senses are nearly blinded.

"That's coming," he says before flicking my nipple with his tongue. "And so are you." He pulls his fingers out and then pushes three in and I'm breathless and shaking. Crazed. His fingers are so thick, it's nearly unbearable. It's the size of an average cock, and from the way he plunges them in and out, he works them like one, too.

His thumb brushes over my clit and I'm seconds from losing my mind, from losing everything.

"Wait," I cry out desperately. "Please. Not yet, not yet. I want to come around your cock. I want you to feel me squeeze you as I come."

He pauses and lifts his thumb away. He takes his mouth away from my breast, his beard wet with moisture as his heavy eyes gaze at me. "I plan on making you come all night long, love."

I'm breathing hard, my hand going to the back of his thick neck that's already damp with sweat. "The first time I want you inside me. As deep and hard and fast as you can go. Fuck me into oblivion. Then make me come again and again and again after that."

"So fucking greedy," he mutters. He shakes his head slightly, a hint of a smile on his glistening lips. "You're going to bring me to my knees, aren't you, gorgeous?"

"I'll be on my knees first," I say, leaning forward and grabbing his lower lip between my teeth and tugging. "I'm going to put your massive, swollen cock in my mouth and suck you off until you don't know your own name."

"Jesus," he curses roughly, the heat in his green eyes growing hotter. "Fucking little dirty talker you are."

I bring my mouth to the soft spot where his jaw meets his neck, the stubble brushing against my bruised lips. "Give me dirty and I'll keep talking."

"You may regret saying that," he says between moans as I suck at his neck. "I've got a lot to give."

It occurs to me that he's talking far more now than he was before. If my strong, silent beast turns into a filthy blabbermouth in the bedroom, there will be no complaints from me.

He pulls back slightly and reaches into his pocket, his pants slung low on his hips, his throbbing cock beating against me in time with his heart. He pulls out a condom. The foil crinkles as he tears it open, and for a moment I wonder if he'd always planned to see me tonight.

I watch eagerly, holding my breath as he slides the sheath on, loving the ease in which he handles himself. His pants fall to his ankles and he positions his tip against my wetness, hesitating, teasing. He grins at me, biting his lip, sly eyes appraising me, as he rubs his engorged head up and down over my swollen skin.

"Stop being a fucking tease," I whimper, my hands going around the hard lines of his waist, grabbing onto his ass. God, it's just how I thought it would feel—firm, hard, round, and filled with power waiting to be unleased. I press my palms against his skin and pull him toward me, his cheeks bunched beneath my hands.

My world opens.

With a hiss, he pushes his cock into me with one sharp, searing movement. If I wasn't so fucking wet, there is no way I'd be able to accommodate him, and even now I feel so deliciously full, I might burst.

"Oh love," he says with a raspy groan. "Fuck."

I can only gasp, feeling my toes curl as he slides in further.

It's better than I imagined.

It's perfect.

He's perfect.

With each thrust, his cock drawing in and out, I move backward across the counter. He puts his palm behind my head, firmly holding me in place, allowing him to go deeper and deeper and deeper.

My mind is shattering, I am shattering, the sensation of having him so *joined* to me, so thick and thorough and all-encompassing, takes over my every thought. I am just feeling and raw, desperate with need. And I want more. So much more.

I'm a greedy, greedy girl.

I grab hold of his biceps, hard as concrete slabs, as he works me in and out. I hold him, still in awe, desperate to hold him close to me. This man, this beast, for now is all mine, and I'm going to have to work hard to be worthy of this.

His mouth joins with mine, moving together in deep, searing kisses in a rhythm that his body matches as he thrusts his hips forward, his cock driving deeper and deeper inside. Every nerve in my body is being pulled inward, swirling into a hard knot, live wires needing the slightest hair trigger to set me free. Each deep shove of his body threatens to undo me.

I run my fingers down his forearms, feeling the ropey muscles as he holds me in place, then I brush my hands back up to his biceps, to the round slabs of his shoulders, down his bare chest, his rippling abs, teasing over the rough hair that leads down to his shaft. I grip him there at the base, wet with my own desire, and he growls unapologetically with wild lust.

I want to make him make those noises until the end of time. Bringing him to his knees once won't be enough for me.

With one hand, he reaches down and takes my hand off of him and rubs my fingers up and down over my clit. I'm so sensitive, so ready, I whimper, knowing I can't hold back anymore.

"You said you wanted to come around me," he whispers throatily into my ear. "You're going to right now. And I want your neighbors to hear."

What he just said is so hot that I don't bother telling him that the neighbors have learned to block out my noises by now.

His hand rubs my fingers faster, harder, into myself, and he pulls his head back to watch me as both our hands stroke myself to the edge of oblivion.

"That's it," he says, his eyes so dark now, his stare deep and measuring, determined to get inside me, determined to get me off. "Kayla." My name sounds like pure heat. "Come for me."

I can't hold myself back. I let go.

Freefall.

It spreads slowly at first, like lighting a fuse, the spark traveling from my core and out through every nerve in my body. Then I implode with a jolt that makes me scream. I've cried out, yelled, moaned, and cursed, but I've never screamed during sex, yet here I am, violence ripping out of me with nowhere else to go.

And it's not over. I'm a rocket blasting off, just shuddering, shaking, quaking in a rolling boil of fire. I can't control my body or my thoughts—I'm just flying through the air, exploding in a wave of stars. My heart fills to the brim then floods over with emotion that nearly brings tears to my eyes.

I have been obliterated. He's completely ruined me, and I'm already dying to have it again and again and again.

"Holy fuck," I cry against him, my head buried into his sweaty neck, holding his hard body against me, as if I would sink into further oblivion if I didn't. "Oh god. Lachlan."

He gives me one of his monosyllabic grunts and pulls his head back, grinning down at me. The lust hasn't left his eyes, and I realize he hasn't come yet.

"That was the appetizer, love," he murmurs, brushing his lips against my gasping mouth. "I'll go all night."

I can't believe *I'm* about to say this. "I need a breather," I tell him, my hands curling around his neck while I rest my forehead against his scruffy chin. "Have mercy on me."

"Oh, I see," he says lightly. "You can walk the walk but you can't talk the talk."

I raise my head and look him in those gorgeous eyes. "I'm still pulsing around you," I tell him frankly, my breath coming under control.

"I know," he says. "It's only making me harder." He puts his hand at my mouth, runs a finger over my lip. "I can't wait to taste you." He pulls himself out of me, kicks off his shoes and his pants, then grips my hips and lifts me up. "Come here," he says, now stark-ass naked. He carries me across the kitchen to the living room where he places me on my back lengthwise on the couch.

He climbs on top of me, his hard, ginormous thighs on either side of my hips, his cock jutting out. I stare at him, wide-eyed, for a beautiful moment as I drink all of him in. I want to lick every single tattoo on his torso, slide my lips over every sculpted ridge. There is something spellbinding, and it's not only just the sight of him, finally naked and in front of me, but the way his eyes are pinning me down, filled with thoughts and desires I wish I could see.

I expect him to push himself inside me next, but he leans over, bracing his elbows on either of my shoulders. He smiles down at me and I'm unnerved at how gentle it is. It softens everything about him. Lines crinkle at the corners of his eyes, and his brow smooths out. He's less of a raging beast but still just as beautiful.

He runs his fingers over my nose, down the hills of my lips, looking at me like he's *seeing* me, and it's so strangely intimate, considering our non-relationship so far, that I want to look away and break the gaze.

Thankfully, he breaks it for me. He licks along the rim of my ear, the sensation causing my skin to prickle. "I want to taste every corner of your body," he murmurs. "Is that all right?"

I swallow hard. "Do you even have to ask?"

"Normally I wouldn't," he says, licking down my neck, causing my back to arch. "But since you needed a breather..."

I put my hand in his hair and make a fist, tugging on his soft strands. "Just fucking eat me already."

He chuckles. "There's my girl."

My girl. His words fist punch me right in the heart.

Dear god.

He continues to bring his lips and tongue down the length of my body, caressing my collarbone, my breasts, sucking hard at my nipples until I'm dizzy, nearly mad with sensation. My fingers dig into the taut muscles of his back, turning into desperate clawing as he continues to move downward.

My stomach shivers under his tongue, and my hips jerk under the tickle of his stubble, the sweep of his soft lips.

Finally his head settles between my legs and I part them wider for him, thirsty with dire anticipation. Naturally, he takes his time. He parts me open, slowly letting the rough pad of his fingertip brush over my sensitive flesh.

I'm already gasping, unable to keep quiet, to contain myself.

Then his tongue snakes out, sliding along my clit and setting off more fireworks that flame the fire inside me. My breath shakes, unstable, my fingers clawing at the sheets. My hips lift up, wanting more of him.

He obliges, putting his mouth and lips into it. And he's watching me. Those wild eyes are watching my every movement as he gives me more and more pleasure, his teeth razing over my clit, his tongue plunging deep inside. His head between my legs is the world's most beautiful sight, and I know I'm looking dumbfounded and crazed as I stare back at him.

It's too much. Too soon.

But fuck if I don't crave it the minute I look away.

So I look back and his heated gaze is still on me, his brows furrowed in epic determination, like a man going off to war, and I'm surprised his look alone doesn't make me come. I can almost feel him in deep, into the hopeless, dark parts of me I never go, like he's willing everything forward and out into the open.

Fuck, this man is driving me more insane now than when he was giving me the cold shoulder.

I can't hold his gaze any longer. I throw my head back and the world becomes warmer, warmer, tighter, as if my universe were built of tiny heated stars. It grows and grows and grows, this impossible force inside me that gathers every single nerve and piece of my body until its wound over and over again.

The slide of his tongue pulls the trigger.

"Holy shit," I cry out, and he murmurs into me, his groans vibrating deep inside and kicking me over the edge. I'm going over, falling into a net of burning stars, and my fingers grab his hair, pulling at him in desperation, trying to hold on even though there's no use. The orgasm never seems to end and I turn into a quivering, boneless body.

It's only while I'm lying here, legs splayed to the side and trying to breathe, that I realize he still hasn't come yet.

I'm going to need another fucking breather.

But before I can voice that, he's at me, on his knees, and grabbing hold of one thigh and lifting it high, positioning himself. He pushes inside, still hard through all of that, and I'm so wet and spent that he slides in easily. He's still as huge and thick as he was in the kitchen. He shoves himself into me with pressing urgency, and I have to give the man credit for keeping it together this long.

"I won't take long, love," he hisses, his accent muddled with lust. He grinds into me, his hips circling, pinning me to the couch as he pistons himself in and out. He is merciless, grunting hard with each thrust, this rough, animalistic noise that gets louder and louder the closer he gets to coming. It's such a fucking beautiful noise that causes the heat to build in my core, coaxing the last bit of flames I have left.

I stare up at him, at his body, at this gorgeous specimen of discipline and pain and good genes. He grips my leg, pushing my thighs back into my stomach so he can thrust in deeper, and it's almost too deep, but he pulls back just in time, groaning hoarsely.

The couch moves, rocking back and forth loudly, and I'm enthralled as he works me, fucking me like an animal, fucking me like a basic, primal being who has been built for this and only this. Faster, harder, deeper. His pace is relentless.

I can see him starting to lose control, dipping over the edge, and I give myself a hand so I can match him. His eyes burn into mine, and then he's in deep, so deep that he's shaking and muttering my name in low, guttural tones before letting loose a string of filthy swears.

It sets me off for the third time tonight, and once again I'm floating, flying, but this time I'm with him, and we're riding it together, our bodies joined inside and out. For this moment, we are one, moving as one, feeling as one.

My heart is huge and filled with bliss.

I'm sated.

I'm happy.

I am so fucking over my head.

Lachlan collapses against me, his hard body sweaty and sliding against mine, and I do something I never do after sex. I wrap my arms around him and hold him close to me, trying to keep him inside me for as long as possible, not wanting the warmth, the connection, to be broken.

And he stays in me for as long as he can, his breath steadying in my ear, his lips brushing my neck briefly, before he rolls over and pulls out. He seems to barely have enough strength to tie the end together before he gets to his feet and pulls me up.

"Bed. Now," he says, completely caveman.

I dutifully follow, my legs shaking beneath me as we walk into my bedroom. We both collapse naked onto the bed, and he pulls me toward him, not quite spooning but not letting go either. I tell myself that I'll eventually have to move, that I can't fall asleep when someone's touching me.

But the world goes dark. My dreams beckon warmly. And I fall asleep in his arms.

Chapter Twelve

LACHLAN

I feel soft fingers at my cheek. I open my eyes, blinking into the dark until I see the shadow of a girl at my side, hazy light coming in from an open window.

Kayla. I swallow, feeling panicked.

"Are you okay?" she whispers.

"Yeah..." I shake my head trying to get my bearings. "Yeah. Why? What...what time is it?"

"Almost morning," she says softly, her fingers trailing down to my jaw. "You were having a bad dream."

Fucking hell. How much of it did she hear?

"I don't, uh, I can't remember," I tell her, trying to but only recalling feeling despair.

"Probably a good thing," she says.

"What was I saying?" I ask hesitantly.

"You were calling out..." she trails off, hands drifting over my chest. "For Lionel."

I breathe out in relief. "Lionel is my dog," I tell her.

She cocks her head at me. "You have another dog?"

"At home, yeah." Though there's no point in telling her that I most likely wasn't calling out for my dog in my dream.

I was dreaming of being a child again, the day my mum gave me away. But lying here in this beautiful woman's bed is no place to bring up tragedies.

"You must be excited to go back home to him," she says, and though she's hiding it, I can hear the trace of disappointment in her voice. Everything is always more clear in the dark.

I reach for her face, pulling her closer to me. "What I am is determined to make these last few days count," I tell her as I kiss her softly at the edge of her mouth. "I'm far from done with you."

If anything, Kayla has unlocked a part of me I rarely, if ever, tap into. It's been months since I last slept with anyone, and back then it was some bird I picked up at the bar. I was drunk and in a bad place—the two are mutual with each other—and feeling sorry for myself. I shagged the chick in the bathroom, and that was that. Before that, I can't remember. Once I'd decided to quit the meaningless one-night stands, sex was put on the back burner.

Now, I am burning, raging like an inferno, and long overdue. When I showed up at her door, I wasn't sure how she was going to take things, but I knew it was time to stop pretending that she hadn't gotten to me, that I didn't want to have her in whatever way I could.

And, bloody hell, she was ready for whatever I gave her. The words that came out of her mouth did my head in, turned me upside down, as if I wasn't already letting the lust run away with me.

I want more. I want her every day, all the time, until I leave.

"I'm not done with you either," she says throatily, and the tone makes my cock stiffen, hot and thick and straining against the sheets. Her lips open against mine, and I slide my tongue in, tasting her sweet, wicked little mouth.

I need to fuck her, messy, hot, and wild. I want her body, her touch, her light to replace all the darkness that creeps into my dreams.

"Oh, you gorgeous thing," I murmur, running the pad of my thumb over her peaked nipple as she arches back, her body begging for more. "I'll go mad if I can't get inside you."

She looks up at me, and in the dim light, I see her coy smile. "I like driving men mad."

"I know you do, love. But have some pity on me. It's been a while."

She jerks her head in surprise. "Really?"

"Really. So have some compassion and spread your fucking legs."

"Oh no," she says, putting her hand on my chest and pushing me back. "You lie back. You spread *your* fucking legs."

I cock a brow. "What?"

"Believe me," she says saucily, pushing me flat on my back. "You want this."

She straddles me, and I wish she was facing the window so I can see those fantastic tits more clearly. "Do you have a condom?" I ask, my voice croaking with need.

"Yes, for later," she says and keeps moving back until she's at my knees. "You won't want one now." She rakes her nails over the hard planes of my stomach, my abs tensing from the abrasion, before she settles in between my legs.

My cock juts straight up, nearly obscuring her from my view. I prop one arm beneath my head, my other hand sinking into her hair, wrapping the silky strands around my fingers.

She takes my length in her hand, and my blood pulses against her palm. The feeling is nearly too much to bear. Her mouth opens, those lush lips sliding over the tip, pushing me into a flurry of lust that sends my eyes back into my skull. Fuck she's good, sliding her tongue over the veins, over every hardened ridge, like she can't get enough, like I'm a fucking ice cream cone on a hot day.

"Fuck," I mutter, eyes pinched shut, pulling on her hair. "Don't fucking stop."

She pulls her mouth off, a wet sucking sound, and I think for a terrible moment that she *is* stopping, and every part of me tenses in frustration. Then her hand comes down over my cock, sliding like silk, pulling back to the base until I think my head might explode. I jerk my hips up, craving release.

But she has more planned. She lowers her head and slowly, gently takes my balls into her mouth, while stroking me off with her hand.

Jesus. Thank you. *Thank you.* Rare is the woman who will suck on your balls like candy. I wonder if I can smuggle Kayla back in my carry-on. She's small enough.

I don't want to come though. I lift my head, trying to speak. My throat is so dry, my thoughts scrambled. Everything is being redirected to primal instinct, the drive to come and come as hard as I can, and it doesn't help that I have this shadowy view of her head between my legs, tongue and lips sucking my thin skin until I don't know my own name.

"I want to be inside you," I manage to say, my tongue feeling heavy.

She shakes her head, the vibrations driving me mad. I grip her hair tighter. I want her to stop and I don't at the same time, but she's the one in control.

"Kayla," I say, before I moan as another wave of pleasure robs me of speech.

She just pumps her fist harder, and I know I'm a goner.

It sneaks up on me, like someone tackling you from behind. I'm thrown into metaphysical space, my balls emptying, shooting my load somewhere, who knows. It doesn't matter because I've gone off like a detonation, light bursting behind my eyes, and the groans out of my throat are loud, hoarse, and deafening.

It takes a few moments for me to catch my breath, for my heart rate to stop galloping like an animal on the run. My thoughts won't gather; I can only lie here while Kayla extracts herself and lies down next to me, her head propped up on her hand, her fingers tracing the tattoos on my chest.

"Hey," she says.

I clear my throat. "Hello." Even so, my voice is rough like sandpaper. "That was..."

"I know," she says, completely confident in the many ways she just undid me. "It was the least I could do for three orgasms last night."

I lick my parched lips and tilt my head to stare at her in the dimness. Her eyes are so wet and dark, and I know I have a bad habit of staring into them for too long, but I can't help it.

I reach over and take a strand of her hair between my fingers and gently brush it off her face. There's something about her that makes me tender from time to time. She tries her hardest not to show it, but I can see it, how vulnerable she is deep down. How badly she fights to cover it up with brevity and cynicism, but I know it's there. It brings out my ever-present protectiveness.

"I guess you should be going soon," she says softly.

I'm taken aback. Like a dog, my hackles go up. "Okay…"

She curls her hand around the back of my neck and leans in closer. "I don't want you to go. But you do have two dogs at your apartment and I have to get up for work soon."

I nod. Right. The dogs. She's right. I'd never planned on staying the night, it just happened that way. Coming inside her was like taking a massive sleeping pill, and the fact that I just came again—all over my stomach—means I'm apt to fall right back asleep.

"Do you have a towel or tissue paper?" I ask her, nodding at my stomach, at the cum that glistens in a pool. I'm lucky I didn't get it in my eye.

She gets out of bed, her sleek, curvy body like a woman's silhouette in a spy film. She tosses me a tissue box from her bookshelf and I quickly mop up the mess.

"Need a shower?" she asks when I'm done. Her voice drops a register, getting all Scarlet Johansson-ish. "I could use one."

It's a tonic to my dick, and I feel it pulse, despite how exhausted it has to be. But I'm not exhausted. I also have no intention of going home right away if I can help it. It's still so early, the dogs should be sleeping. They'll be okay for a little bit before I return. I don't know how many more minutes of Kayla Moore I get in my lifetime.

"Sure," I tell her. She takes my hand in hers and pulls me off the bed. Now that I'm looming over her, she looks so willowy, tiny, and dare I say, helpless, even though I know she's anything but.

She glances down, sees the stirrings of another erection.

"The hell," she says. "How is that even possible?"

I stand there proudly before her. "Anything is possible with me."

"You really are a beast," she comments.

"Funny," I tell her, "that's my nickname on the field."

"And in the bedroom, I guess."

"No," I tell her, putting my hands on the soft small of her waist and pulling her in. "Only with you."

I can tell she's grinning at me. She steps out of my grasp and does a sexy walk, her hips swaying back and forth, all the way to the washroom. She flicks on the light then throws her hand in front of her face, blinking hard.

"It's a bit bright," she says.

"All the better to see you," I tell her, following her in.

Her bathroom is about the size of a shoe box, with a sink, toilet, and glass-encased shower. A large mirror extends along the entire wall, adding depth. I stare at our reflections. I look so giant next to her, the scars, my messy hair, the scores of tattoos. I look like a bruiser, a fighter, a reject. She looks like a princess compared to me, so delicate and soft and pale. I really am the beast here.

Thank god she likes it. She's meeting my eyes in the reflection, and her lips part just enough for me to get a glimpse of her tongue.

"Get in the shower," I tell her. "Lather up."

She frowns, walking over to it and turning it on. "What are you going to do?"

"It's barely big enough for the both of us," I tell her. "I'm going to watch you clean yourself. Then I'm going to bend you over and fuck you silly."

She tilts her head, appraising me with a look of wonder on her sweet face. "Who are you again? The insatiable man?"

"Perfectly paired with the insatiable girl." I give her a half-smile and jerk my head at the shower. "Go."

"All right," she says slowly with a raise of her brows. She steps in the shower and lets the water run over her. Her neck goes back, her back arches, the water streams over her perky breasts, her tight little arse, over every soft and curvy part of her body. It's like watching fucking porn but it's live and in front of me, and for now, for these last hours of morning, she's all mine.

I lean back against the sink, and in no time my cock is rock hard again and hot between my hands. I watch as she squirts body wash on a sponge and runs it all over her body, the white lather dripping between her tits and down the curve of her hips and pelvis.

"Play with yourself," I tell her, my voice coarse with lust.

She smirks at me. "You're really bossy."

"Again, so are you."

Kayla gives me a triumphant look then keeps her eyes locked with mine as her hands and the sponge dip between her legs. At this point, most girls would look away, feeling like they are display, exposed. But she has no problems baring all to me. She stares deep into my eyes until her own pleasure makes her break. Her head goes back, her eyes pinch shut, that gorgeous, fuckable mouth opens as she moans.

Yeah. I can't handle much more.

I walk over to the shower and she shrinks up against the wall to give me room.

"Keep the door open," I tell her. "Brace your hands on the edge."

"The floor will get soaked," she says, but still complies.

"You have towels."

She shrugs, and I see a hint of tension in her brow. It's not quite worry—she just doesn't know what's coming next.

"Should I go get a condom?" she asks.

"It depends," I say. I grab her hair and force her head down so she's bending at the waist, and her slick, soapy arse is pressed against the length of my cock. She fumbles for the handle of the open door, holding on with both hands. The mirror across from us displays us perfectly, though it's slowly getting fogged up.

"Depends on what?" she asks, but I can tell she already knows what I have planned.

I slide my fingers between the cheeks of her arse, up and down, probing at her cunt and then further up. "This okay?" I whisper, tracing my fingers around in circles.

She nods but doesn't say anything. I slowly push a finger in, then take it back out, making sure it gets extra slick and soapy before it goes back in. She clenches around me, and I have to breathe in deep, making sure I don't lose it before my cock even has a chance to slip inside.

I squeeze a dollop of the body wash in my hand, my eyes meeting hers in the mirror as our features gradually fog over. I rub it along my length and then with one hand holding her hips and the other at the base of my cock, I push myself in the tightest space imaginable.

She gasps but pushes back into me to let me know I should keep going. I take it as easy as I can, my movements slow and deliberate.

"This still okay?" I murmur, hoping she's at least getting some thrill out of it, even if it doesn't match mine. Before she has a chance to answer, I let go of her hip and my hand slides between her legs. It's hard to tell if she is wet from the shower or from her own arousal. I like to pretend it's all for me.

She immediately relaxes into my fingers, her feet taking a wide stance on the slick tiles. The muscles along the length of her back smooth out, and her head hangs down limply as she gives herself to me.

"Look at yourself," I whisper to her gruffly. I want her to look at her reflection, at us, at the juxtaposition of our bodies. The darkness and the light. "Look at me."

She carefully raises her head, and I meet her warm eyes, holding them in place. I push in and out, and her arse is so goddamn tight that I don't have much time—I'm lost to her slick grip, the full milky skin of her cheeks. I'm lost to her.

Thankfully I can multitask. My fingers work faster as I pump harder, with as much control as I can muster. I can't seem to get enough air in my lungs, and the lights are starting to flicker, even though it's all in my own head as I try not to break eye contact with her in the mirror.

I know she's close to coming when her face begins to contort, her jaw open and locked, her eyes fluttering, fighting to keep staring at the foggy version of me when all they want to do is close. She comes hard, shaking so violently she almost falls to her knees, and I manage to keep her upright, all her weight on my hand, my arm straining while my fingers extract every last drop of pleasure from her swollen clit.

I don't look away. Not once. I'm going back to Scotland alone, and I need every single memory of her ingrained in my mind.

I come fast. Abrupt. It catches me off-guard, and my cries echo in the washroom and I pour into her. It feels so bloody good, I can barely stand. When I manage to open my eyes again, Kayla's blurry reflection is staring back at me in the mirror.

"You're a dirty boy," she says. "A lucky boy," she adds. "Anal already?"

I can't help the dazed grin on my face. I shrug before slowly pulling out of her. "I'm not missing an opportunity with you around. I wasn't kidding when I said I was spending every spare minute from now until Sunday with you."

"Too bad you can't come to my office in a few hours," she says. "Maybe go down on me under my desk."

I lick my lips. "Just say the word and I'm there."

She grabs a towel and wraps it around her waist, leaving her beautiful tits bare. "Don't tempt me. I'm so close to quitting my job already." She nods at the shower. "Take your time," she says, then walks out of the washroom.

I quickly put some body wash in my hair, not too picky with what goes on my head, and in minutes I'm out and toweling off.

I stride into her bedroom naked. Flaccid, yes, but from the look in her eyes, she's still damn impressed. Somehow she's already dressed for work, and the sun is just starting to rise in the east.

"You're fast," I tell her.

She gives me a quick smile as she puts an earring through her ear. "Might as well get ready." Her eyes trail over my body. "So, the next time I see you, I hope you're ready to finally tell me about your tattoos."

My smile falters. I swallow, not ready to bare myself in that way. "I'll tell you some stories. The rest will bore you to tears."

"Lachlan," she says, and the way she says my name nearly makes me hard again. She saunters over to me and puts her hand at my jaw. "You are the furthest thing from boring."

I grunt, shrugging. She can find me as fascinating as she wants for the time I have with her, but I'm not about to sink into the truth. She's becoming one last, much needed fling before I return to rugby, dogs, my normal life. In this kind of limited arrangement, there is absolutely no room for reality.

I grab her hand and kiss her palm. "When am I seeing you again? Can you come over after work?"

She seems to think about that for a moment. "How about around eight or so?"

I nod. "Sounds perfect."

Her hands trail to my chest, running her fingers over my tattoos again, like she's reading Braille. "Do you want a ride home? You're not far from my work."

Normally I would insist on getting my own ride, but I don't for some reason. I'm starting to squeeze the minutes here. "That would be lovely," I tell her.

It's not long before I'm dressed in the suit from last night, and she's dropping me off at my flat. The sun is shining down on the city and not a hint of fog is in sight. Everything sparkles with new clarity. Everything.

I lean over and put my fingertips under her delicate chin, tilting it toward my lips. I kiss her softly. "Thank you."

She flushes, the pink creeping into her cheeks, and she nods. "I feel like I should be thanking you. A lot."

"For what?"

She smiles. Embarrassed. "For finally succumbing to my charms."

I grin at her and shake my head. "I succumbed to them a while ago, love. I was just waiting for my brain to catch up. I'm glad it did." I kiss her again and give her a wink before getting out of the car. On the sidewalk, I lean over so I can see her in the driver's seat. I raise my palm in a wave. "See you."

"See you," she says before biting her lip and driving off. I watch her go for a moment before I suck in the morning air, the only time the city doesn't feel as dirty. I head into my flat, ready to tackle the dogs and whatever else the day is going to throw at me.

I have to admit, I'm kind of useless the rest of the day. I do what needs to be done—taking the dogs to the vet, following up on a possible adopter for Ed, hitting the gym—but my brain isn't really into it.

It's a change for me, to be so singularly focused on a person for once instead of rugby or the rescues. It feels good, actually, because it keeps unwanted thoughts and urges at bay. Normally, my brain feels scattered, like every neuron is shot through a prism, and instead of light and rainbows, there are different shades of black and grey. Again and again I'm drawn back to the bleak, to somewhere deep and unsettled, and it takes a lot to pull me out, to scatter those thoughts back into the light.

I know what tames that beast on my back, the one that wants me to backslide. But to pay it too much attention is to give it too much power. But with Kayla…I may still be a jittery mess with a raging heart, but at least she's the cause of it all.

I'm out on another walk with the dogs, trying to teach Emily how to heel. It's not easy since she's afraid of every person, car, and object we come across. Sometimes the dogs pick up on my energy when I'm too wound up, for better or worse. I decide to try again some other day. I head back to the flat, when the truth is, I could walk forever and never burn out.

My phone rings. Bram.

"Hello," I answer.

"Well, well, well," Bram says. "Aren't you the man of the hour?"

"That depends what hour."

"Every hour, it seems," he says. "Do you want me to tell you my good news first or do you want to tell me your good news?"

I clear my throat, perplexed. "What's, uh, my good news?"

"Right," Bram says. "Anyway. Mr. Mulligan, Justines's father, and I had a meeting this morning." He pauses and I don't ask him to continue because I know he will. Always so dramatic. "And he's agreed to invest."

I grin, feeling relief on Bram's behalf. "That's excellent, mate."

"I owe you, you know," he says.

I grumble, feeling uncomfortable with him even saying that. "It was nothing."

"It wasn't nothing," he says, sounding serious. "This wouldn't have happened without you." His tone is adding gravitas to everything. I think I like Bram better when he's joking.

"Look," I tell him, running my hand over my chin and pulling the dogs back as we wait at a crosswalk. "I did what I could. You know I like to help out if I can and this happened to work out for me."

"Too bad Justine didn't make it worth your while."

"It's too bad for Justine that I didn't make it worth *her* while," I say.

He chuckles. "Poor girl. Just like all the others, I suppose. You know, I thought you were used to going around and getting pussy where you could."

"People change," I tell him.

"Aye," he says. "They do. Or do they?"

I know what he's getting at. "Well, thanks for letting me know, cousin. It's a relief that it all worked out."

"You know, Lachlan, it will be a shame to see you leave."

"For you? Yeah."

He lets out a laugh that quickly fades. He exhales heavily. "Would have been nice to get to know you a bit better. Honestly. We never really had the chance, you know, back in the day."

"Was a shame," I say. "But I never made it easy on you guys. And then you moved."

"It's just funny that she'll be the one to know you better."

"She?"

"That would be your good news, right? Kayla. I got the investment, you got the girl."

I rub my lips together. "I don't have the girl," I say deliberately. "And what I do have is just for a short time. Just for a few days, that's all."

Bram snorts. "You're getting laid. You could sound a lot happier."

I really don't feel like discussing this with Bram. It's all sorts of weird, anyway, that he and Linden and Stephanie and Nicola sit around and discuss each other's business. My mates back in Edinburgh don't do that.

Then again, I've noticed that Kayla is the odd one out when it comes to them. She's always on the outskirts, even from the first day I saw her at the bar. I pretended she hadn't intrigued me when she had. But it wasn't her personality, or her looks, not then. Who she was wasn't more than a blip on my radar. What I had noticed though, was that she was the one who didn't really belong. That she was with them, but apart.

I recognized it because I understand it. I live it. If there's someone else out there like you, you'll see it. It's a pattern. You recognize it in a look, in a philosophy, in a song. It's this quiet vein of understanding, a connection. I think we're all looking for that in everyone we see, everywhere we go, so when we do find it, we find ourselves. Through a mirror darkly, they say.

But what I saw in Kayla then was far from darkness. It was light.

"Listen, I better go, Bram," I tell him. "I've got some mutts here that need my attention."

"So I heard," he said, and it made me wonder what else he knew. Maybe Kayla did talk a lot. "Listen, I was thinking... now that you're with Kayla—"

"I'm not *with* Kayla," I interject. With time running out, I don't want *us*...whatever we are...to be a bigger thing than we should be.

"Now that you've got a limited time fuck buddy," Bram corrects himself, though that doesn't sound so right either. "I was thinking the six of us should get out of town for the weekend."

"I'm leaving on Sunday," I remind him, glancing down at Ed and Emily who are staring up at me with big eyes. "And I'll have at least one dog until then."

"I know, I know, hear me out. Your flight is not until the afternoon, right?"

"Aye. Three p.m."

"Friday and Saturday night. Napa Valley. You been?"

I sigh, not really wanting anything last minute to mess up my plans to have Kayla all alone and to myself. "No, I haven't."

"It's about an hour and a half from the city," he tells me. "Gorgeous place. I'll book us all hotel rooms, and I know a resort with a vineyard that takes dogs."

"Maybe you should start saving your money now, Bram," I advise him. "Scots should be cheap."

He snorts. "I'm not paying for everyone. You'll do your own room, yeah? But listen, I don't want to step on any toes. Talk it over with Kayla and let me know. I won't say anything to the others." He pauses. "It would just be nice for all of us to see each other before you go, and that way you don't have to be away from her either."

I stare up at the mist rolling in from the west, blowing between the high rises, and sigh. "All right. I'll ask her. But if we do go, don't expect to see us much except for maybe lunch. And even then, I'm not predicting anything."

"Thatta boy," he says before saying goodbye and hanging up.

I shove my phone in my pocket and stare down at the dogs. "Well, so much for trying to lay low." They cock their head as if they're listening. Sometimes I think they are. Thankfully a dog can never try and give you advice. They just listen and watch you come up with your own decisions.

When I see her tonight, I'll ask Kayla if she wants to go. I just hope such a trip doesn't scare her off. Under normal circumstances, I wouldn't dream of going off with a girl I'd just slept with, and I'd assume Kayla would feel the same way. But because I'm leaving, it makes everything a little different. It bends the rules.

I've never much cared for rules anyway.

Chapter Thirteen

KAYLA

I can't walk properly.

My body aches everywhere. Like after the rugby game, but worse and better all at the same time. Because there's friction between my legs, and other places, that reminds me of what we did all night long.

Because…

Oh my god.

Oh my god.

It's like I need to keep pinching myself all day, except my sore body keeps doing it for me. Every move I make I'm reminded of Lachlan. His unbelievable cock. His skilled, possessive hands. His gorgeous lips…*everywhere.* Those eyes, those searing, searching eyes that wouldn't look away, not for a minute. Those eyes touched me, held me, caressed me just as any other part of him did. Last night I felt completely, wonderfully overtaken by this Scottish beast, and I'm still in awe.

It actually happened.

He gave me the best sex of my whole entire life.

How the fuck am I ever going to get over this?

Luckily he wants to see me again. Right away. I would have come over right after work—it makes sense since he lives close to the office. But I need to gather my thoughts and regroup. I need to process what happened before I'm swept away again because that man is a current that I can't fight against. The next week with him will drown me if I don't get my head on straight.

Before the work day is over, I finally answer Steph and Nicola's frantic texts and tell them to meet me at the Lion at six o'clock for girl talk.

Of course, when I actually get to the Lion and see Steph and Nicola at the booth, talking to each other over beers, I freeze up. Everything that happened doesn't seem like something I can communicate, not without sounding like an idiot, not without selling him short.

I breathe in deeply and walk toward them, trying to keep a straight face, even though I feel a smile tugging at my lips.

They both turn to look at me and stop talking.

"My god," Steph says slowly, looking me up and down.

"What?" I look down at what I'm wearing, skinny black jeans and a tie-neck blouse. I put the outfit on in a hurry this morning while Lachlan was taking a shower. My thoughts immediately flit back to his eyes as they watched me soap up, then our reflection as he fucked me from behind. Up the goddamn ass. I'd done that before, but it had never been like *that*. That was *good*. Hot as all hell. And unexpected, especially from Lachlan, but the man he was when he was fucking was a lot different from the one I'd been around before.

"Kayla?" Nicola asks.

I shake my head and look at them. "Yeah, what?"

Steph laughs, eyes wide in disbelief. "Oh my god. You so got fucking laid."

There was no point in denying it. "What makes you say that?"

"You're glowing," Nicola says.

"And you've got a shit-eating grin on your face," Steph adds. "Now sit the fuck down and tell us about it."

I guess I can't really help this smile. I sit down beside Nicola. "Are you working tonight?" I ask her.

"Yeah, soon. Bram has Ava," she says quickly. "But don't change the subject. You owe us. Tell us everything."

"What happened?" Steph asks, leaning forward excitedly, gripping her beer tightly. "He came here looking for you, you know, and—"

"Yeah, you gave him my address."

"Would you rather I hadn't?"

I shake my head. If she hadn't, last night might not have happened.

"You know that he was only with Justine because of Bram," Nicola adds.

"I know, I know," I tell her, trying not to think about it. "He explained."

"And then you fucked," Steph says with a nod.

I eye her. "That we did."

"Well," Nicola says, staring at me with big, eager eyes. "How was it?"

I lean back against the seat. "It's hard to say."

"What?" Steph asks incredulously. "You mean you're not about to wax on about his Hulk penis?"

Old Kayla would have waxed on about any Hulk penis she may have encountered, but this Kayla…this Kayla didn't feel like talking about Lachlan that way.

"I don't want to talk about it," I tell her.

"That bad, huh?" Nicola says sympathetically.

"No," I say quickly. "No, no. It was the opposite of bad. It was..." I shake my head back and forth, trying to think of the right word. "Earth shattering. Life changing. His cock has ruined me for all other cocks on earth."

Nicola and Steph exchange a look.

"Uh," Steph says. "Wow."

"Yeah. I'm so scared." So *screwed.*

A lengthy pause.

"So there *was* a Hulk penis," Steph goes on.

I give her a look. "His dick is ridiculously proportioned to his body, and he's already a huge man. That's all I'm going to say."

"Good thing you've had a lot of practice to loosen you up," Nicola says with a smirk.

"Shut up."

"So now what?" Steph says.

"What do you mean?" I ask carefully.

She shrugs and takes a swig of her beer. "Well, he's leaving."

"Yes, I know."

"So...are you going to see him again before that?"

I fish my phone out of my pocket and glance at it. "I have two hours before I'm meeting him at his apartment. This will be the last time you'll see me until he leaves. Does that answer your question?"

"Got it," Nicola says.

"Kind of a bummer, huh?" Steph muses. "I mean...you've finally got him...and he's going."

I sigh heavily and brush my hair back from my face. "Yeah, thems the breaks though, right? I mean, heaven forbid

I actually get a chance with the first guy I've fallen for ever since Kyle."

Both of them stare at me with open mouths and it takes me a moment to realize what I've said out loud, what I haven't even admitted to myself.

"Oh my god," Steph says. "Are you saying that you're in..."

I eye her sharply. "No." I clear my throat. "No, I'm not. Obviously. I don't know him. It's still just a crush, whatever."

"This is way more than that," Nicola says. "It's okay to admit it, Kayla. It's about time you felt something for someone."

"Is it about time?" I challenge. "Because this is shitty timing. I don't want to feel anything more for him than just seeing him as a vehicle for awesome sex. Really. So let's forget I said anything. I've got one week to have my mind blown and then he'll leave and I'll go back to being me again. Fuck. It's better than nothing."

Nicola's lips scrunch together, looking stupidly sad.

"What now?" I ask, rolling my eyes.

"You're going to get your heart broken."

"What?" I exclaim, slapping my palms on the table.

"Nic," Steph admonishes. "Way to be optimistic."

The blood is rolling in my head so loudly that I can barely hear Nicola. "I'm just saying that if I were you," she explains, "and I finally started to have feelings for a guy, and I only had a week with him, I'd be heartbroken."

"That's because you're a sap," I tell her snidely. "Even though you weren't such a pussy before Bram got his dick in you."

"He was the right dick," she counters. "And this is your right dick."

"Look," Steph interjects. "We've all got the right dick right now. But Kayla and Lachlan are way, way different than Linden and I. Or you and Bram."

Somehow I'm finding a way to take offense to that. "Oh yeah, how so?"

Steph's brows raise to the ceiling. "Well. As you just said, you don't know Lachlan. He doesn't know you."

"True."

"And he's leaving, so you don't even have the time to get to know each other."

"True," I say, dragging the word out.

"And even though you seem a bit softer around the edges these days, you're still you, Kayla. I bet even if he wasn't leaving, you'd find some excuse to pull back and extract yourself. So actually, contrary to what Nicola thinks, I think this relationship, arrangement, whatever it is, is tailor-made for Kayla Moore." She raises her beer in the air and looks me hard in the eye. "You go and screw the hell out of him this week. For those about to fuck, we salute you."

Nicola grumbles something but raises her glass.

I don't have a glass, so I can only nod at them. "Well, all right then. To fucking."

"To fucking," they say in unison.

...

When eight o'clock rolls around, I park in his empty space and sit in the car for a few minutes, just wringing my hands together and working up the nerve to go upstairs. It's not that I'm scared. But I am nervous. I don't even know why, but I am. Since I left the girls at the Lion, I've been thinking about

Lachlan, about what we did. About what we might do again. I feel like I'm pining over a celebrity, someone larger than life, someone who makes me feel completely out of my element. It's surreal.

"Get a fucking hold of yourself," I say out loud and crane my neck to look up at the floor-to-ceiling windows of Lachlan's apartment building, trying to count floors and see which one is his. I anxiously open my compact and dot more lip stain on my lips, wondering how fast it will be rubbed off once I get into his apartment.

Is he going to kiss me right away?

Will this be a Netflix and chill night?

Immediate fucking?

The possibilities have me on edge.

With a deep breath, I get out of the car and walk over to the entrance. My finger hovers at his apartment number. I take a moment to eye myself in the reflection of the glass doors. I sped home from work to change into a strappy black dress, something like the nightgown trend of the nineties, with hot pink platform heels. No bra. No underwear. What's the point?

I press the buzzer and wait a few moments, my pulse pounding in my wrist. Lachlan's distinct voice comes through, slightly drowsy and smooth as butter. "Kayla?"

"Hi," I say. I'm about to say something else, probably something awkward, but he immediately buzzes me through. I exhale loudly, trying to release tension, but I remain a fidgety mess all the way up the elevator. Last time I was in here, we'd just rescued the dogs. He was shirtless. He'd felt so close at that time and yet oh so far away. To think that now, *now*, after I'd had my hands and lips all over him, my need for him was stronger than ever.

I knock on his door, biting my lip in anticipation, until it swings open and I see him leaning casually against it. The dulcet tones of Fiona Apple's "Slow Like Honey" drift in from the room.

"You shouldn't be wearing that," he says, a faint smile on his lips. God, I've missed those lips.

"Why not?" I ask with a raise of my brow. In a second, all my nerves smooth out and I realize how easy it is to talk with him like this.

"You'll make it impossible to get through the appetizer," he answers, moving back and letting me inside. He's back to casual wear—a white thermal shirt that's partially unbuttoned just enough to show a glimpse of tanned skin, chest hair, and tattoos, a necklace with a small wooden cross, green cargo pants. I like him like this just as much as I like him in a suit.

I walk in, my heels echoing on the tiles. "I thought I *was* the appetizer," I tell him, looking around. The two dogs are on the couch, curled up next to each other like sleeping mice. In unison, they both lift their heads to stare at me. The pit bull gives a thump of its tail but the scruffy mutt shivers slightly, showing teeth.

"Don't mind them. They're still adjusting," he says, closing the door then gesturing to the table by the kitchen, where I had done my interview with him last week. "*That's* the appetizer."

On the table is a bottle of red wine, two glasses, and a cheeseboard topped with brie, cheddar, camembert, figs, jam, honey, and crostini.

"Wow," I say softly. "You did all this?"

He shrugs, making a dismissive noise. "It was nothing."

"This is romantic," I tell him. "I didn't peg you as a romantic."

He raises a perfectly arched brow. "Oh yeah? What did you peg me as?" He slowly pours a glass of wine.

I stand there, watching him pour a smaller amount into the other glass. His forearm flexes, the lion tattoo seeming to roar. His forehead is creased with concentration, perhaps in anticipation of my reply. He seems completely at ease with me, but there's always that wildness in his eyes that never seems to go away. The only time I saw peace in them was after he came last night.

"I pegged you as a man who wouldn't give me a second glance."

He gives me a crooked smile and corks the bottle "Well, love, you know that isn't true."

I slowly walk toward him, looking up through my lashes like some kind of femme fatale. "Oh, it's true. You wanted nothing to do with me."

His look softens for a moment before he heads into the kitchen, grabbing two small plates from the glass cupboards. "I want nothing to do with most people. Never take it personal."

"Tell that to old Kayla. She had no idea she'd get the chance to put your gorgeous cock in her mouth."

The plates rattle against the counter. "You do have some mouth on you."

"Exactly."

He comes back into the room with his hulking swagger, setting the plates down. He nods at the pushed out seat. "Here. Sit down, please."

I hook my purse on the corner of the chair and take a seat. Both dogs stare at me from the couch.

"So, how are they?" I ask him.

He looks behind him and I take a moment to appreciate every hardened, strained muscle in his neck and shoulders. "As I said, they're adjusting." He sits down and folds his hands in front of him. "Someone is coming by tomorrow to see about adopting Ed. But I think Emily will be coming home with me."

"Which one is Ed?"

"The pit," he says.

"Funny, I would have thought he'd be harder to find a home for."

"Usually. But Ed is a big sweetie, and people in this city are a little more tolerant of bully breeds than people in the UK. Emily, however, as sweet as she looks," he glances back at the scruffy dog, who immediately bares her teeth at me, "has behavior problems. She'll need work."

"And are you the one who teaches them?" I ask. "Because if so, then you *are* the dog whisperer, which means there's pretty much nothing you can't do."

He looks down at his hands and gives a lazy one-shouldered shrug. "I found Lionel on the streets in Edinburgh. I was able to teach him. Maybe he taught me some things. You never know with dogs. But…it takes a special kind of person to train dogs, especially those who have been through trauma and abuse. I am not that kind of person. I will do whatever I can to save them, but I'm not the person who can school them on obedience."

"Really?"

A quiet, almost uncomfortable smile tugs at his lips. "A dog with behavioral problems shouldn't learn from someone with behavioral problems."

I expect him to laugh, but he doesn't. "Oh," I say, trying to think of the right thing to say. "You just seem like a natural. These two were strays, and now look at them. Just like that."

"I can get the dogs to trust me," he says in a low voice. "Because I trust them. But I can't get them to trust others."

"Because you don't trust people?"

He slowly blinks and then reaches for the stem of his wine glass. "I think I may trust you. Here's to that."

"Here's to that," I say, raising my glass and clinking it against his. I'm more than meeting him in the eyes—I'm diving in the green and grey. They seem darker somehow, moving shadows. Depthless. Behavioral problems? What kind? How much more can I learn about him before he's gone?

I take a gulp of my wine and he barely touches his. Just a small sip, then puts the glass back down and pushes it away from him.

"I've never seen you drink much," I tell him, hoping my tone is easy enough so he won't take offense.

He gives me a long, measured look before he licks his lips and looks away. "No, I don't."

"Because of training," I say, giving him an easy way out.

A slow nod. "Yes."

He's still not meeting my eyes. His focus is on the cheeseboard, and even though he's not frowning like he usually is, his shoulders seem tense.

"What other things do you have to do for training?" I ask. I feel like we've regressed a little bit and I want that sexy, casual banter back.

He drums his fingers along the edge of the table and I lean forward, trying to get some cheese on my plate. "Lot of work in the gym. Lot of work on the pitch. A good diet."

"I assume it doesn't include loads of cheese," I tell him, drizzling the honey on top of my brie.

"Nah, just boring stuff. Chicken breasts, broccoli. It's not a lot of fun, but at my age, you have to do it if you want to keep playing. When I was younger I could have eaten whatever I wanted."

"How old are you?" I ask.

"Thirty-two," he says, and I'm a little bit surprised. I guess because he looks so manly and distinguished—the lines on his forehead, his scruffy beard—I figured he was in his mid to late thirties. Or maybe it's his eyes.

I stare at them, even though they are now staring sharply at the fig as he hacks his way into it, as if the fig has done something personal to him. It's those eyes that trip me up. The eyes of an old soul, of someone who has seen too much, done too much. There's a war behind them at all times, a war I want to help him win.

"Does that surprise you?" he asks, glancing up at me briefly.

I take a delicate bite of the crostini. "Not really. You just seem more mature than that."

He scoops out some of the fig and spreads it over the goat cheese and crostini. "In rugby, being in your thirties is asking for trouble. All those years of being hit, all the injuries, the strain. It takes a toll. I don't know what happened, but when I turned thirty it all started to slip, just a bit." He offers me the rest of the fig and I take it from his hands, my fingers brushing against his. One simple touch and I feel it travel down the length of my arm, straight to my heart.

Bam. A shower of sparks.

I swallow, trying to ignore the feeling. "How long have you been playing?"

He frowns, eyes squinting in thought. "Twenty-two. Yeah." He nods. "Ten years."

I blink, impressed. "That's a long time. Is that normal?"

"I guess," he says, pursing his lips, considering. "I'm good at what I do. They need someone fast, someone who will break everyone in their way. That's my job. But I can't do it forever. After I fucked up my bloody tendon...I know I don't have long."

"You almost make it seem like you're dying."

He briefly sucks in his cheeks. "Rugby saved my life. I'm not sure what I'll do when it's over."

"Coach?" I ask him hopefully.

"Nah," he says, munching on the crostini and leaning back in his chair. When he swallows, he adds, "I'm either in the game, or I'm not. There is no halfway. That's not how I'm built. Once I'm done, I'm done."

And when this is over? I think, *are we done?*

But of course we are...we aren't even a thing.

"Maybe you'll just do charity work...for the dogs."

"Aye," he says. He reaches for his wine and takes a small sip. He almost puts it back down but takes another gulp, finishing the glass. "I'll keep doing that. There's no expiration on helping others. As bloody cheesy as that sounds."

"That's not cheesy," I tell him. "That's selfless and beautiful."

"Come now," he chides me, seeming embarrassed. He looks away, folding his arms across his wide chest, his unreal body stealing my attention again, turning my thoughts back into a sexual whirlwind. Well played, Mr. McGregor, well played.

"What's the lion tattoo for?" I ask him. "What's the story?"

That startles him and I can tell it's a soft spot. "What are you on about?"

I point to his forearm. "There. Lion. See. You said you would tell me some stories. About your tattoos. Why you have them."

He rakes his teeth over his lower lip and looks me dead in the eye. "Did I now?"

"Yes," I tell him impatiently. "Last night…maybe this morning. After some good fucking."

"Ah, yes. That explains it."

"Well, give me something."

"If I give you something, will you give me something?"

I can't help but grin like a fool. "Of course."

"Okay then." He pushes his chair back slightly and takes his shirt off, tossing it to the floor beside him. He spreads his legs and pats the crotch of his pants, his gaze absolutely feral. "Have a seat."

I am lightheaded at the sight of his torso again. I manage to get up, drawn to him like a magnet. I put my hands on the hard breadth of his shoulders and straddle him. We are so close. Our mouths inches away.

He's breathing hard. I'm breathless.

He's a wall of muscle and ink. I'm soft, yielding against him.

"So, ask away," he says, that voice low and rough, yet cashmere cream. That voice I'll hear in my dreams long after he's gone.

His eyes never leave my lips.

I lean back to get a better look at him, even though the distance pulls at me. I decide to leave the lion alone for now, and run my fingers over his shoulder, the taut, hard muscle. A storm rages in muted ink, a masterfully shaded old ship with tall sails spreads onto his chest.

"This one," I say softly. "Why the storm? Why the ship?"

He chews on his lip for a moment, searching my eyes. "I was twenty-four. I backpeddled with life for a bit. I lost my edge in the game. But I pushed through and was better for it. A ship is safe in the harbor, but that's not what ships are built for." He tilts his head as if observing me, though I'm the one watching him. "It helps me when I get scared. To keep going."

"You get scared?" I ask him, unable to picture this strong, powerful man, afraid of anything at all.

"All the time," he says frankly. "How can life be anything except terrifying at times? We're born here. We don't ask for it. And we're expected to somehow get through it, to live each day without dying. We live, and if we don't, we die." He looks away, gives his head a shake. "Nah. We're all scared, every last one of us."

I know I am. Of so many things. My heart melts slightly to know that someone like him could feel the same way as someone like me.

I trail my fingers along the text on his collarbone. "Nunquam iterum," I read out. "Latin, I assume?"

"Yes," he says slowly, looking away. "It means never again."

"Never again, what?"

His mouth quirks up into a sour smile. "Never again to a lot of things."

"Is that all I'm going to get?"

"From that, yes," he says, finally meeting my gaze again. His pupils are so large, they hypnotize me. "You get one more. Then you're giving me something."

I breathe in deeply and look over every inch of him. The lion. "Hope before Death" across his side. A paw print on his inner arm. A flock of ravens swirling into a tribal pattern down one bicep, making a sleeve. A crest with what looks like Latin on the other forearm. Another similar crest on his chest. I press on the one on his chest, with a boar at the center. "Corda. Serrata. Pando," I say, my finger tracing the words.

"I open locked hearts," he says.

I still, watching him close. "What?"

"I open locked hearts," he repeats. "It's the Lockhart crest. I was born a Lockhart. That is the clan's motto."

"Again, that's terribly romantic," I tell him. "That must be where you get it from." I touch his forearm, the other crest. "And I guess this is McGregor?"

"Aye, though it should be MacGregor, or Clan Gregor."

"'*S rioghal mo dhream*," I try to say but stumble over it. "What the hell."

"Royal is my race," he translates. He gives me a dry smile. "But I'm not a McGregor and it's not my race. So that explains a lot."

I run my hand down the side of his cheek and he briefly closes his eyes. "I think I'd rather you a romantic warrior than one with fussy bloodlines."

He leans in, slowly opening his eyes, gazing at me through his lashes. "Who said I was a warrior?"

I lower my voice. "I say you're a warrior."

You're my warrior.

For now.

He lifts his chin. "What else do you say?"

I adjust myself on his hips, my hand slipping down toward his pants. I shift to undo the top button, bracing myself on his shoulder. "I say you need to get your cock out, warrior."

He reaches out and lets his hands drift down over my hair. "Lead you into battle?"

"Something like that." I bite my lip as I tug down his zipper. I can feel him hard, bare, ready beneath me. I'm wet as hell again.

He knows. He puts one hand at the small of my back, the other slipping between my legs, pushing the dress up. My clit screams with pleasure the moment his fingers slide against me, slick and hard.

"Christ," he murmurs, staring at me with shiny eyes. "You're always good to go."

"Only with you," I say, leaning forward and kissing along his neck, taking in his woodsy, spicy scent that throws me into another wave of lust. I could live my whole life with my face buried here, feeling the pulse along his neck, smelling every ounce of this primal man.

"That suits me just fine, love," he says, grabbing my dress and pulling it over my head. "Get this off. I want to suck on those fantastic tits of yours."

Jeez. Even the way he says "tits" is nearly enough to make me come. Then again, the man could read the phonebook in that warm, slightly growly voice of his, and it would be better than the dirtiest erotica.

I raise my arms and the dress is gone, and I'm completely naked now on his lap. Seems to be a common theme here.

But I don't feel any shame, and if I'm vulnerable at all, it's eclipsed by the way he's staring at me, nearly dumbfounded, as if he can't believe his luck. His eyes rake over my body, hot with desire I can feel. He frowns, almost in anger, and mutters something so low I can't hear.

Then he's leaning over, cupping my breast with large, warm hands, and pulling my nipple into his mouth. My body becomes a roman candle, fizzing, burning, begging to go off.

I moan loudly, grinding myself into his cock, desperate for penetration.

"Easy," he murmurs, sending more shivers along my spine, his tongue lapping at my nipple until it nearly hurts. My other breast is practically aching, needing his touch, and when he moves his wet, hot mouth over, my body shakes in relief.

"Fuck," I say with a moan, throwing my head and shoulders back, trying to push myself into him, wild, crazy, and desperate for more. I reach down and around, grasping his cock and pulling it out of his pants.

"Easy," he warns again, pulling his mouth away from me. "You don't know the power you have," he says, gazing up at me.

"I think I do," I tease, gripping him harder.

He pinches his eyes shut, his full, luscious mouth dropping open in a moan. God, his sounds completely undo me, a thread being pulled looser and looser until I'm flayed at the seams.

"Please, love," he begs, cupping my face with his hand while staring feverishly at my lips. "Not yet. Let me at least get a condom out before I lose it." He reaches for his cargo pocket but I put my hand on top of his.

"Let me," I tell him. I reach in and pull it out, tearing the foil open with one hand. He leans in, kissing me lightly, lips brushing lips, until I start unrolling the condom over his thick, wet head. Then the kiss deepens, a slow, hard pull that reaches deep inside me, feeding the hunger. Our mouths, lips, and tongues dance like savages with each other, violent and ravenous and wild.

He suddenly grabs my waist and hoists me up a few inches, positioning his cock just so before lowering me. I gasp at the intrusion, my body so fucking ready yet so unprepared that I have to remember to breathe.

"Fuck me," he mutters against my neck as he deliberately drives his cock upward and into me, my muscles expanding around him as much as they can. "So fucking good, Kayla. You feel so fucking good."

I can't even answer him. I'm sucked under a wave and all I can feel is him pushing, spreading inside me, taking over every thought and feeling. I've never felt so full, so thoroughly complete before.

Because my legs aren't long enough to touch the floor and his thighs are so large to begin with, I can't do much to pump myself up and down. Instead, I'm at Lachlan's mercy, his hands holding onto my waist like I weigh nothing more than a feather. He lifts me up, just an inch, while thrusting upwards, deeper and deeper until I can't control the sounds that are coming out of my mouth.

I'm so close to coming, and so fast, just on his cock alone, when a funny noise makes my eyes snap open.

I stare over Lachlan's shoulder to see the pit bull on the couch, circling around and trying to get comfortable. The smaller dog is staring right at us.

"Uh," I say, clearing my throat.

Lachlan's breathing quickens with each pump inside me—he doesn't seem to hear.

"The dogs," I manage to say, pressing down on his shoulder.

He slows and looks at me, sweat on his creased brow, his eyes hooded and sex drunk. "What?"

"The dogs are staring at us," I whisper.

He frowns then cranes his neck to look behind him. When he looks back at me, his expression is entirely quizzical. "So?"

"It's kind of weird that they're watching," I tell him.

He smirks, the tip of his tongue poking out. "Really? I would have thought you were the exhibitionist type."

"Hey, I am the exhibitionist type. I don't mind *people* watching."

His brow raises, a heated looking coming over him. "Is that so?"

"It is *so*," I retort, mimicking his accent. "But it's weird with dogs."

"All right then," he says. He lifts me up and off his cock and I'm immediately bereft without him inside me. I step off him and onto the floor as he gets up, towering over me, his pants falling to his ankles. "Get in the bedroom," he commands, kicking his pants to the side.

I do what he says, walking naked and still in my high heels, across his living room.

"You're too fucking much," he murmurs, and when I glance coyly over my shoulder at him, he's standing there, completely bare, in a wide-legged stance that shows off every muscle in his thighs, cock in his hands.

No, you're too much, I think.

Once I'm in the bedroom, the small space tidy and smelling of him, I head for the bed, kicking off my shoes. But before I reach it, he's flicking on the lights and grabbing my arm. "Hold up, love," he says, leading me toward the floor-to-ceiling window that covers the entire wall.

He throws back the curtains and I step away from the glass instinctively. We're not only about twenty stories high, but we have a clear view into the populated high rises across the street from us, and a peek of the lit Bay Bridge between them. We're standing at the window, completely naked, with the lights on. Anyone can see us.

And then I realize what Lachlan is doing. Anyone can see us...

I turn around, giving him a shy smile. "Are you sure?"

He bends down and picks me up by the waist, pressing me back against the glass. I suck in my breath, shaking, immediately met with a wave of vertigo. I'm okay with heights, but it's entirely different when a giant man is pressing you against a window pane from a very high place.

I feel like I can fall at any moment.

"I'm sure," he says, pushing himself into me. I wrap my legs around him, extra tight. He feels like a lifeline. "I won't see those neighbors ever again."

Yeah, but I might, I think. Still, there's something incredibly erotic about it all. I can't see the people's faces in the dark, but if they were to look up, I know what they'd see: my ass pressed against the glass, framed by a beast of a man.

I dig my heels into him, holding on tight as he slowly pushes deeper and deeper inside. My hands grab the back of his neck, feeling the strength in his straining muscles, his hot, sweaty skin. He licks up the length of my throat and moans into me as his hands cup my breasts and his cock thrusts in.

"So warm," he whispers hoarsely. "Just like this." He draws out slightly and drives back inside, pushing me harder against the glass. Every single nerve is a live wire singing, and my heart is beating so fast I'm afraid it might shatter me and the glass.

He comes at me again, arching his hips up, his cock so thick and rigid, filling me to the brim. I can feel his ass flex against my legs as he pounds deeper and deeper in intense, animalistic thrusts. His mouth is hungry, wanting, as it devours my neck, and I feel so wonderfully desired, taken, needed.

Lachlan is just a pure fucking machine, made to fuck, to come, to deliver me into star-bursting ecstasy. He's merciless in his lust, and I surrender every part of me. I've never felt like so much of a woman before, with so much of a man.

"How do I feel?" he asks, breath ragged, before he grunts with another long, hard thrust, and I'm forced to moan in kind.

"Unbelievable," I tell him. "I need more."

His hand slips to my clit and he presses his thumb there, rubbing with each thrust. "And now?" He pulls his head back to stare at me, his eyes flashing with every upward pump of his cock. "How does your sweet little cunt feel now?"

Dear god. Just his words, those dirty fucking words in that rough accent from that wet full mouth, is more than I can handle. I grab him tighter as my back hits the glass again and again. Each strike brings fear of breaking through, of falling to my death, while each thrust brings me closer and closer to pure fucking bliss.

"Look at me," he commands, voice raspy and broken. I open my eyes—I hadn't even realized I shut them—and meet his, inches away from mine. "I could watch you come all day," he says.

I bite my lip, swallowing a groan as his cock drives me closer to the edge. "And I could come all day, if you're ever game for that."

"You're fantastic," he murmurs, kissing me quickly, hot, wet, and sweet, his tongue teasing the seam of my mouth. "So bloody fantastic."

Something changes in his eyes, like a switch being flipped, and they look almost menacing in their desire for me. His pace quickens, his hips like pistons, firing again and again, my whole body slamming against the glass until I'm gasping, but I don't know if it's from fear or from pleasure. Maybe they're the same thing right now because being with him, having his cock barreling into me, is as scary as it is amazing. Because the feelings that he's stirring, the threats of hedonistic pleasure, have the power to take over my life.

He's making me crazy. I'm insane for him, every single inch, from the line between his brows to his thick length inside me, and I don't even know who I am anymore. I'm just here, being fucked hard against a thin pane of glass, high above San Francisco, holding onto a man that will eventually have to leave.

My orgasm sneaks up on me. I feel it generate from my core, spreading outward like a supernova, gaining speed in waves and waves and waves of stardust until it lets go, thundering in aftershocks. I yell nonsense, holding him tight, breaking away from his eyes because it's too much for me to see. I can't even contain it. I ride it, muscles jerking, body a ragdoll gone rogue.

He comes with hoarse grunts and powerful thrusts like he's actually going to fuck me out of the window, but it's okay because I'm already falling and falling and falling.

I collapse into his arms, not even able to keep my head up. Every part of me is both soft and translucent and shaking from the strain.

He grabs my waist and pulls me off the glass, spinning me around and laying me on top of the bed. He climbs in beside me, hooking one of his large, long legs around mine, pulling me an inch closer so my face is nestled into the crook of his arm.

I regain my ability to breathe, in and out, trying to come back down to earth, while he trails his fingers over my hair, from crown to shoulder, over and over, this softness, this gentleness that nearly lures me into sleep.

I open my eyes and look at him. His head is propped up on his hand and he's looking me over with a heavy, sated expression. Everything about him in this one moment is soft and diffused. Even the lines on his forehead and the hardness in his eyes have been worn away to a smooth slab.

He clears his throat. "Do you think anyone saw?" he asks gently.

I swallow, my mouth parched, everything in me so exhausted. "I hope so. We would have given them quite the show. Or the scare. I thought I was going to go over the edge."

"I would have gone right with you," he says gently, running his thumb over my lip. I gently kiss it then close my eyes. The world is still spinning, but it's beautiful.

It isn't long until one of the dogs whines from the other room. I snap my eyes open and see Lachlan smiling at me happily. "Well," he says, moving to get up. "At least they let me fuck you like that."

I can't help but grin at him and watch his ass as he strolls—nude, large, and in charge, into the other room. I fight the urge to run after him and take a bite of his ass, like an apple, and instead use the bathroom.

Once inside, I look in the mirror and barely recognize the girl staring back at me. My lips are red and puffy, my face and chest are pink from orgasm. My eyes are large, wet pools, and my hair is an absolute wreck. I look like I've had a few good days of nonstop fucking and that thought alone makes me wonder what I'd look like then.

When I walk out of the bathroom, I'm not really sure what to do. Do I go home? Stay the night? At least stay a bit longer? But Lachlan is at the door, already fully dressed with the dogs on leashes.

"Come on," he says. "Let's go for a walk."

I'm totally naked still. I eye the silky dress on the floor. My heels are in the bedroom. They're clothes for getting fucked in, not for taking dogs for a walk.

He's smiling at me, amused, as I quickly slip my dress over my head then head back into his room to retrieve my heels. I slide them on, and when I come out of the room, he's holding a black leather moto jacket out for me. It's huge and looks like he's had it for decades.

"To keep you warm," he says as he puts it over my shoulders. He eyes me up and down, admiring the look. He nods and makes an agreeable noise. I pull it close around me and breathe in deep. The jacket is a relic, but it smells amazing, like him.

Though the little dog, Emily, is still looking at me like I'm public enemy number one, we get the dogs into the elevator and walk toward the waterfront. I'm amazed at how well they are behaving with him, walking on a leash like its second nature. It seems unlikely that he can't train them.

My mind wants to focus on what he said earlier: *behavioral problems*. But I push the thought away. Even if it's true, the fact that Lachlan has issues doesn't scare me at all. In fact, it's pretty obvious, just from looking into his eyes, that there are some demons deep inside of him. My only problem is the need to find out. My damn curiosity. If he's broken, how and why? Because he was put in an orphanage? I can only imagine growing up like that would provide you with a lifetime of personal demons.

"So," Lachlan drawls out in his thick brogue as we sit down on a bench, the Bay Bridge nearly over us. "I was wondering...how would you like to come away with me on Friday and Saturday night?"

My heart does a flip. "But I thought you leave on Sunday?"

"Aye, I do," he says, twisting the ends of the leash over and over again in his hands. "It's...last minute."

"Where would we go?"

"Napa Valley," he says, stealing a glance at me. "Bram invited us."

"Us?" I repeat.

He nods once. "Yes. One last hurrah or something like that. He and Nicola. Linden and Steph. And...you and me." He pauses. "I haven't told him yes or no. I wanted to ask you first. I know that we don't know each other well and that going away on a trip can be a minefield for relationships. As if relationships aren't minefields by themselves." He looks away and smiles bitterly at some memory, his face shadowed in the streetlights. "I also know that this..." He gestures with his finger between us, "...is different."

"Not a relationship," I fill in, even though something shifts in my chest when I say that.

He squints at me for a moment. "No. So what do you say?"

"Well, of course I want to go," I tell him, putting my hand over his, partly to make a point, and partly to stop his nervous fidgeting. It's almost adorable.

"You don't think it's odd? To go off with me?"

Hell, I'd follow you anywhere. But of course I don't say that.

"It'll be fun," I tell him. "So long as we get more than enough time to ourselves."

"My cousins will have to drag us from our room," he says, and his expression is still so sincere that I know he means it.

He lifts my hand up, flips my palm over, and kisses it, his lips so full, soft. and wet, his gaze never leaving my face. I love that he does that. Not the back of my hand, always the palm, the love lines, where my skin is delicate and my nerves ignite.

After we sit by the water for a bit, watching the cars on the bridge and the reflection of the lights on the silver water of the bay, we head back to the apartment. It's still relatively early and we fall back into his bed, our bodies finding each other again. His hunger for me just doesn't seem to abide, and I don't think I'll ever get my fill. We fuck and fuck again, every way we can, until it's after midnight and I know, I know I have to go home.

Somehow I force myself to leave him. I kiss him goodbye as he stands naked in his doorway, not caring at all who might walk past. His eyes are soft, that beautiful peace he gets from sex, as he watches me go down the hall to the elevator. Not smiling, just watching.

Maybe wishing, just as I wish, that we didn't hear that clock ticking in the back of our minds.

Counting down.

Chapter Fourteen

KAYLA

I am completely obsessed with Lachlan McGregor.

And not in the good way, in the coy, polite, restrained, never giving into my urges kind of way like most proper girls are. Oh no, not me. I'm obsessed in the *can't stop furiously masturbating every moment I get because I can't get him out of my head* way. I can't stop seeing his hips as they drive and drive and drive into me, I can't stop feeling his lips on my skin, the way he refers to my cunt in that overly Scottish way, the way he looks at me sometimes like he can't believe I'm there. I can't stop picturing his beautiful face, his tattoos, and the parts of him they represent, the parts he locks away and rarely shows. I can't stop obsessing over every detail of his existence.

Because it makes me happy. It makes me so fucking happy that I think I might be going insane. My heart is permanently swollen, like a red balloon, and the more it pushes at my chest, as if my body, my soul, isn't big enough to contain it all, the more alive I feel. My head is just this fuzzy, warm, sparkling place, and I'm walking through the moments of the day in a dream. A beautiful dream that doesn't end.

Before today I could hide my obsession. I kept it inside. But now that he's gotten inside me, I can't will it away. It has people in my office asking me if I'm on drugs. It has me smiling, beaming, at strangers on the street. It has me wondering if I should be committed, because feelings like this aren't normal and aren't to be trusted, but I feel too good to even care.

Unfortunately, going mental doesn't mean that I can just forget about my current life. I'm just about to head over to Lachlan's after work for some hot fucking sex, when my mother calls.

It's a hammer to the gut.

She's sounding weak. Tired. Sad. Her voice reaches into my head, my heart, and lets the air out.

As much as I'm addicted to Lachlan, to every single fucking thing about him, I love my mom, and I can't, won't, push her aside for a man, no matter how good the sex is, no matter how infatuated I am.

I tell my mom that I'll come over and make dinner for us. She sounds so relieved that I know I'm doing the right thing.

I text Lachlan to fill him in, hoping he didn't have anything major planned. Last night, even the appetizers and wine surprised me. The last thing I expected from a big, burly, rugby beast was something romantic.

He answers back with an *Okay, no worries*.

And for some reason it absolutely breaks my heart. I have such little time left with him. I stare at my phone, thinking, while the rest of the office empties out. I want him to text back and suggest we meet up after. Then I realize he might be waiting for me to say that.

Fuck, I'm not used to this. I didn't really care about how I came across to all the guys I was seeing and screwing before. If they didn't seem interested anymore, I moved on lickety-split. But Lachlan is a game-changer.

I suck on my lip and bite the bullet.

I ask him what I really want to ask him.

Want to come with me and meet my mom?

I press send and hold my breath, waiting. He's going to say no. He's going to be weirded out. He's going to gracefully untangle himself from my grip. And me, I'm going to pretend it doesn't hurt, tell him that we're different, that there are no rules right now. He's leaving, and that means we can get away with murder until he goes.

I'd love to.

The text across the screen makes my face split in two.

I tell him I'll come by to get him in five minutes. Then I have a mini-debate over telling my mom that I'm bringing a man over, the first man she's ever seen me with since Kyle. I decide to keep it a secret—no use in freaking her out beforehand, especially as she'll get her hopes up that he's something more than he is. You know, like permanent.

On the other hand, she's fairly conservative. She may see all his tattoos and his beard and pass out.

We'll have to play it by ear.

Soon I'm pulling up to Lachlan's apartment and he's striding from the doors to my car. I watch him, my mouth hanging open just a little, totally in awe. He must have gotten changed at the last minute because he's in black dress pants, a black dress shirt, and his hair is slicked to the side, looking utterly presentable. All his tattoos are even covered.

He opens the door and gets in, giving me a quick glance with bright eyes.

"Hi," he says, putting on his seatbelt.

"Hi," I say, rather breathlessly. "You look nice." And by nice, I mean so handsome I want to cry.

He scratches at the back of his neck and side-eyes me through dark lashes. "Wasn't going to let a chance to impress your mother go to waste."

But isn't it going to waste? Still, I bite my lip, totally thrilled that he made the effort. I would have been thrilled either way, since the fact that he agreed to come is fucking crazy in itself.

I stare at him for a moment and he looks right back at me. I mean, he *looks* at me in that way only he can, and time just kind of locks down on us. It's heavy and persistent, and I know I'm wondering if he's going to kiss me. As if that's a thing we do now, as if there's a *we*.

He leans in and I lean in, and it's all slow motion from here on out. All over a kiss.

But it's more than a kiss. Everything seems more when it's with him.

His lips meet mine, mouth opening, sucking on my lower lip for one wet, hot moment before deepening all the way through. I am so amped up and fileted at the same time, one kiss undoing me before we even have a chance to begin.

Somehow I manage to extract myself and drive, though my lips still burn from where he just was, and I'm tempted to run my fingers across them, to keep the friction going.

He adjusts himself in his seat, legs splayed, trying to fit his body in my small front seat, and I'm reminded of after the rugby game, when we were both wet and muddy and coming back to his place for the first time. That feels like ages ago. Of course, back then he wasn't trying to play down an obvious erection in his dress pants.

"Want to hear some good news?" he says lightly after a few minutes.

"Of course."

"Ed got adopted," he says rather proudly.

"Really?"

He nods. "Aye. A local foster-to-adopt program got back to me and said they had someone interested. She and her husband came by to see him this morning and they fell in love. Ed's gone."

"Aww," I tell him, and my heart flutters like a bird in flight. Not just because he was able to home a dog who needed it, but because I can hear the warmth in his voice, like honey, like happiness. "I'm so happy for him. And you."

He shrugs. "I did what I could do. I'm just glad it paid off."

"And Emily?"

"She's at home. Sad little gal, she is. But once I get her to Edinburgh, she'll be good."

"I guess she'll be coming with us to Napa?"

He glances at me, brow creased in concern. "Is that all right?"

"One hundred percent," I tell him emphatically. "I just hopes she learns to trust me at some point."

"She will, love," he says, gazing out the window as we go over the Bay Bridge. "We all come around after a while."

It's not long before we're at my mom's and I'm pulling the car to the curb.

"Lovely place," Lachlan says as he gets out of the car, staring up at the house. It doesn't look like much in the twilight, but he sounds impressed.

"It used to be really nice," I tell him, my voice hushed as I open the low gate into the yard. "When I grew up here, anyway."

"It's still lovely," he says. He reaches down and grabs my hand and holds onto it, giving it a squeeze. Strength feeds into me from his grip, washing away the sadness and the memories of the *after* period.

We walk up the front steps, hand in hand, me and my beast, and before I can knock on the door, it opens and my mother pokes her head out.

She peers at me for only a second before her eyes drift over to Lachlan. They widen. She looks him up and down, and I can't help but mimic her. Because it's got to be cool to have two ladies giving you the eye at once.

Luckily Lachlan is all charm. He smiles politely and gives her the slightest of nods.

"Mom," I say to her.

She nearly glares at me. "This is the man? This is the man you bring home?"

I look back at Lachlan and he meets my eyes, a half smile on his lips, his brows raised.

"Well..." I say to her but she wags her finger at me to shut up. At least she isn't acting as frail as she sounded on the phone.

"This is the man you bring home," she says again, leaving the door and walking over to Lachlan. He lets go of my hand to offer it to her. "And yet you have never brought him before?"

I laugh in relief. "Sorry, Mom. He's kind of new."

"And I'm kind of charmed by you," Lachlan says, kissing the back of her hand, his eyes smiling. Holy shit. I've never seen him be so utterly charismatic before, and from the fullness in my mom's cheeks, I can tell she's just as impressed.

"Oh my," she says, looking at me with a big grin. "Kayla, you have done very, very well."

"I know," I tell her. "But Mom, you're making him uncomfortable."

"Nonsense," Lachlan says, throwing his shoulders back, making him look bigger than big and taller than tall next to my tiny mother. "I have no problem hearing how I've exceeded expectations."

I smirk at him and grab his hand. "Let's go inside before your ego gets too big to fit through the door."

We step in the house and my mother insists on giving Lachlan the grand tour. She takes him by the hand and he follows her, ever gracious, hanging on to her every word, smiling when she smiles. It brings actual tears to my eyes, tears I have to quickly blink away. Even Kyle hadn't been that way, so attentive, so involved, and he was about to marry me.

While they go explore the rest of the house, I take in a deep breath, trying to steady the race in my chest, and head into the kitchen to see what I can make for dinner. I can hear them walking upstairs. Their footsteps, Lachlan's heavy, long strides and my mother's short, quick ones, go down the hall, to my brothers' rooms, then to my bedroom, where I'm sure my mother is filling Lachlan in about all sorts of embarrassing anecdotes about me.

Then they go into my parents' bedroom, and I don't know what my mother is saying to him, but it must be about my dad and suddenly it hurts. It hurts. Sharp pains stab my chest, enough that I have to lean against the fridge and try to breathe for a few minutes.

"Kayla?" I hear Lachlan say, and then he's at my side, fingers running down the sides of my face, hands curling around my forearms. "What happened?"

I shake my head, keeping my eyes shut. "It's fine," I say.

"Kayla," my mother cries out, and I can hear the terror. This is the last thing I want, for her to worry about me when there's nothing wrong, just my own damn worry, my own damn demons creeping up on me.

"I'm fine," I say again, sharper now, taking in another breath through my teeth. "Really. It's just a cramp. A stitch in my side."

"Maybe you should let me cook," my mother says. I open my eyes to see both her and Lachlan peering at me, and it's only this sight, borderline comical, that gives me the strength to push past it all.

"No, no, no," Lachlan says, straightening up but not letting go of my arm. "Mrs. Moore, you go sit down. Kayla, you sit down with your mum. I'll cook."

I stare at him dumbly. "You'd do that?"

"Of course, love," he says, kissing me quickly on the forehead. When he pulls away though, his eyes are sharp and delivering a message. "Go be with your mum," he tells me quietly.

I nod, stupefied by him. "What are you going to make?" I ask him feebly as my mom heads into the living room, looking at me over her shoulder.

"Go and be with your mum," he repeats, and I sense some weird urgency in his voice that makes my heart do a couple more somersaults in the wrong direction. "I've got this, aye?"

I turn and head out into the living room, sitting on the couch as my mom settles down in her armchair, reaching for her knitting needles. She's in good spirits though, stealing glances at me as I flip on the television and scroll through the channels to find something she might like. *The Big Bang Theory* it is.

But she's not paying attention. She's watching me fully. "Are you okay?" she asks me.

"Yes, yes." I wave her away. "Are *you* okay?"

She sighs lightly, looking down at her needles and seeming to be lost in her own little world for a moment. Finally she says, "I was…not feeling well today. Tired. Dizzy."

I swallow a lump in my throat. "Mom. When you feel like that, you know you need to call your doctor."

She shakes her head. "No, it's fine. It's called getting old, Kayla." She looks up at me with knowing eyes. "Why didn't you tell me he was coming?"

Though her voice is low, the kitchen is right there, and I know Lachlan can hear us. Nothing seems to escape him. "It was a last minute decision," I tell her, trying to play it off lightly. "I hope that's okay."

"Of course it's okay, Kayla, sweetheart," she says, grinning from ear to ear, bouncing lightly in her seat. "It's okay because I've never seen you look so happy before."

At that, my eyes flit over to the kitchen. Lachlan is staring at me while he takes pots out of the cupboards. I can't read his expression, but I at least know he heard that I look happy.

I am happy.

I feel my cheeks flush with heat because I can't ignore the truth. I am happy. Deliriously.

Tragically.

I break our gaze and try to concentrate on Penny and Sheldon on the TV. God, I loathe this show.

"So where did you find him?" my mom asks.

"He's cousins with Bram and Linden. You know Stephanie's husband? His cousin."

She nods. "I've always liked Stephanie."

"Yes, Mom, I know. The daughter you never had."

"Oh, I only say that because I know how much she means to you. I was very happy to see her finally settle down. Now that can happen for you."

Oh god. Oh god, no.

I look up, hoping that Lachlan is preoccupied, that he can't hear us at all. But no. That would be asking too much. He's standing right there, mixing something in a bowl, and those gorgeous, inquisitive eyes are peering into mine.

I tear myself away from him. "That's not going to happen," I tell my mom, maybe more harshly than I meant to. "Lachlan is leaving on Sunday."

She frowns, her needles pausing mid *clickety-clack*. "Leaving where?"

"Back to Scotland. If you couldn't tell, he's from there."

"Oh," she says, blinking hard. "Oh dear. That's terrible. Are you going with him?"

I let out a sharp, caustic laugh. Mainly from shock. "Yeah right!" I cry out. "No. No, he's actually a very successful rugby player in Edinburgh. He's got everything waiting for him. And I have, well, I have everything that I have here."

Which was what? Nothing?

No. Not nothing. My mom. My brothers. My floundering career and my happily-coupled friends.

It was something.

But it wasn't the *something* I wanted.

That something was a future filled with hope.

That something was in the kitchen.

That something was unattainable.

That something was burning a hole into me with his eyes. I didn't even have to look to know. I could feel it. I was so good at feeling his eyes on my skin, always wanting more from me than flesh.

"That's a shame," she says. She goes back to her knitting, but her posture loses that verve she had before. Is it possible that my mother would rather me go chasing some beautiful man across the Atlantic Ocean than stay in San Francisco and keep on keeping on? I try not to think about it. In the end, what she wants, hell, what I want, doesn't really have any bearing on the reality: Lachlan is going back.

And I barely know him.

Thankfully she doesn't bring him up anymore, and by the time the show is over, he announces with that deep voice of his that dinner is ready.

My mom and I exchange a curious look and head into the kitchen.

Damn.

Just, damn it.

Lachlan has not only put placemats with place settings out, but there's a nice bottle of red wine in the middle and flickering candles. He moves around like he grew up in this kitchen as I had.

"Sit, please," he says, gesturing to the chairs. He goes beyond gesturing when it comes to my mom and holds out the chair for her before pushing it in. Then he heads for the kitchen counter, and when he comes back, he places a bowl of mashed potatoes and a dish of chicken parmigiana on the table. Not exactly two things that would go together, but it looks absolutely delicious and smells even better.

"How did you learn to do this?" I ask him. It's not that he shouldn't be able to throw a few things together, but it looks so freaking good.

He nods at the plate. "Just try it first and then ask me. I can't make any promises," he says, sitting down between us.

I take a bite of the mashed potatoes. They're better than the ones at Thanksgiving, with just a kick of pepper or some kind of spice. As for the chicken, it melts in your goddamn mouth.

I'm practically glaring at him. "So," I say between bites, pointing my fork at him. "Last night's appetizer wasn't some once in a blue moon thing for you."

He smirks then rubs his fingers across his lips, taking on a serious face. "I like to cook when I can."

"You should cook all the time," my mother says. "This is very, very good."

"And you should take that as a compliment since she barely eats my food," I tell him, kicking him lightly under the table.

"Oh, that's not true," my mother chides me, but it is totally true. I do my best, but the kitchen has never been my strong suit. When it comes to Lachlan though, it's one of his many fucking strong suits. I swear to god there is nothing he can't do.

Why the hell did I have to meet this beast, this superman, who blows my mind in the bedroom, mows down rugby players for a living, rescues helpless animals, looks like a fucking god, and happens to cook, just before he has to leave? Why is life so damn cruel?

"Here I was thinking all you Scots knew how to make was haggis," I tell him, pushing the heaviness out of my chest and trying to focus on what's in front of me.

"Oh, I can make some pretty stellar haggis," he says. "If I had more time here, I'd see what I could do."

I manage a smile. "As much as I wish you had more time, I'm glad I'm missing out on that."

After dinner, my mother insists on dessert and brings out the matcha green tea ice cream, something Lachlan's never had before.

"This is gorgeous," he says between spoonfuls.

"I grew up on the stuff," I tell him. "Do you know my favorite thing to eat as a child was sheets and sheets of nori? You know, dried seaweed."

"It is true," my mom says with a gentle laugh. "I bought them for sushi, but I would always have to hide them from her. When I found the packets later, they were torn into, like some mouse had gotten into them."

"Strange little creature," he comments warmly, sitting back in his chair, studying me. "What else did you get up to as a child?"

"Oh, she was up to everything," my mother says quickly. "No different than she is now. But she had four older brothers to keep her in line. Brian, Nikko, Paul, and Toshio. Kayla was our little angel. She popped up one day when her father and I never thought I could get pregnant. I never thought I would get my little girl. But here she is."

My cheeks grow hot, and I busy myself by swirling the ice cream into green soup.

"Unfortunately," my mom adds, "she was an absolute terror."

I glare at her while Lachlan lets out a laugh. "Mom," I warn her.

"Oh, she was," she says, leaning forward toward Lachlan, her eyes shining. "Even as a little girl, she'd run away from you every chance she got. If it wasn't for her brothers, I'm sure we would have lost her for good one day. They were good for that, being protective."

"Yeah, but then in high school it got a bit annoying," I remind her.

"For you," she says in jest. "But for us, it was a godsend. She was a boy crazy little girl, you see."

"Oh, is that so?" Lachlan asks me with large eyes, clearly enjoying this.

"Yes, very much so," my mom says before I can neither confirm nor deny. "Every day she had a new crush from school. Billy this or Tommy that. She got in trouble once for kissing a boy and making him cry."

I bury my face in my hands and groan.

Lachlan is laughing hard, such a nice sound, even if it's at my expense. "What did you do, Kayla?"

I keep my face buried and don't answer because I know my mom will.

And she does. "The teacher told me that the boy didn't want to kiss her, so she held him down, and when he tried to run, she punched him in the stomach."

"You might have been a natural at rugby after all," he says between laughs.

"So," my mom goes on, "by the time she got to high school, her brothers acted like chaperones. The poor girl couldn't go anywhere without them knowing about it. All the boys were kept at bay."

"Well, I don't blame your brothers for being protective of you," Lachlan says. "You were probably as stunning in high school as you are right now."

Oh god. I look up, and he's staring at me so sincerely it hurts. My face burns even more at the compliment.

"Look, you've made her blush," my mother says, which isn't helping. "You've gotten under her skin."

"Okay," I say quickly, getting to my feet. "I'm going to the bathroom. When I get back, can we all agree not to embarrass me anymore?"

"But I love watching you get embarrassed," Lachlan practically purrs.

I give him the finger, which of course causes my mother to gasp in outrage, and I stride down the hall to the bathroom, shutting myself in. I take a long, deep breath. My heart is racing, and I don't know why. Everything is going so well, but all it does is make me worry. There's this space behind my heart, a little hole, and it's slowly getting bigger.

I run a washcloth under the cold water and dab my face. I'm still blushing, much like the way I look after sex. Perhaps that's why Lachlan wants me to be embarrassed.

When I leave the bathroom, Lachlan is sitting in the living room and my mom is trying to make some tea.

"Here, go sit down," I tell her, taking the kettle from her hands.

She places her hand over mine. For a moment I stare at it—pale, wrinkled beautifully, speckled with age spots. My mother's hands, hands that have seen me through my whole life, are shaking slightly. When did that start to happen? The shakes?

But I don't ask her because she's looking up at me adoringly.

"You shouldn't let him leave," she tells me quietly. Her grip on my hand strengthens, the shakes abating slightly. "He is such the man for you."

I give her a quick smile and gently pull the kettle away from her. "I honestly don't know him well enough to think that." I swallow and look out at the living room where he's watching TV. "I wish I did though."

"Sometimes you don't need to know someone to *know* them," she says. "And when he looks at you, you can tell. He *knows* you." Then she pads her way out of the kitchen to join him. I shiver, suddenly cold, and get the tea ready. We drink cups and cups of it, watching an episode of my mother's other favorite show, NCIS, until it starts getting late, and I know Lachlan has to check on Emily.

For some reason it's hard to say goodbye to my mom this time. Maybe because I've been extra emotional all night. I hug her longer than I normally do and tell her I'll be by next week. Maybe I can drag Toshio with me.

Lachlan bends down and envelops my tiny mother in a bear hug. Every inch of me dissolves at the sight.

I have completely melted.

"Your mother is lovely," Lachlan says to me quietly during the car ride back into the city.

"That she is," I say, glad he was so charmed by her. And equally as glad she was so charmed by him.

"You said before that she was sick," he says, putting his hand behind my neck and rubbing his thumb against my skin. "What's wrong with her?"

My grip on the steering wheel tightens. "I'm not really sure." I lick my lips, trying to remember. "It started after my father died. She was a wreck for a long time. We all were. She was severely depressed, and I guess all that pain inside started making its way outside. Some doctors say its chronic fatigue syndrome, others say it's still depression and anxiety. She doesn't sleep well and her blood pressure is always through the roof. Her muscles ache all the time. I don't know what to think. But it's been going on for years."

And her shaking hands, well I hope that's just because she was overexcited about Lachlan and me being there.

"Do you have good doctors here in America?" he asks.

I shake my head. "No. Well, yeah. If you can pay for them. She never worked, so she doesn't have benefits that a lot of people her age would. But my brothers and I, we pay for it. We try and get the best for her, a whole bunch of different opinions. Honestly," I say, eyeing him briefly. "I think she's still suffering from a broken heart."

He gives me a tight smile. "There are big risks to falling in love."

I nod and look back to the road. "Big risks."

When we get back to his apartment, Lachlan invites me up. I hesitate. I want to go, I want to be with him every way I can. But there's something heavy on my chest, and if I sleep with him tonight, I feel it will get even worse. I need to be alone to process it. I need to build back my strength by myself. For such a strong man, he only makes me weaker.

That night, alone in bed, I stare at the empty pillow beside me and wonder what it would be like to always have someone there.

Then I wonder what it would be like to never have someone there again.

How far can you fall for someone until you have to call it love?

I hope I never find out.

Chapter Fifteen

KAYLA

At work on Friday, the time passes by like molasses. I stare at the clock on my computer monitor, counting down the minutes, the seconds, until I can go home, get my bags, get Lachlan, and head to Napa.

But when the proverbial whistle blows and I'm all ready and waiting outside his apartment, whatever excitement I had all day has been replaced by acute fear. This is the last time I'll be here, picking him up. After Sunday, he's gone.

Even though I didn't sleep with him after my mother's on Wednesday night, yesterday was a different story. I went right over to his apartment after work, strode inside, and fucked his brains out. In his bedroom, of course, away from the judgemental eyes of Emily. Whatever strange melancholy that had gripped me at my mother's house wasn't present. I lost myself to his body in every way that I could, literally screwing him sideways until two in the morning, when I finally pried myself away and went back home to sleep.

But now, now that I'm waiting for him, now that we're about to embark on our last few days together, that melancholy is back, humming in my soul like a tune you can't forget.

It gets a little better though, as things often do, when I finally see Lachlan.

He takes hulking strides toward the car, duffle bag on one shoulder, pet crate in hand. He's wearing his hiking boots, blue jeans with rips in them, a white t-shirt that perfectly showcases those traps, those shoulders, the swirl of tattoos down his arms. My breath hitches, my legs clench, the heat inside burns and burns. His effect on me will never be duplicated.

He opens the back door and puts the crate inside. I look behind me at Emily. Her scruffy little face is at the gate. I'm prepared for her to growl or at least show some teeth, but she just eyes me for a moment before her gaze goes back to Lachlan. It's obvious the dog adores him; she can barely look away. I wonder if that's how I appear.

"Hello, love," he says to me as he gets in the front seat. He leans forward, cups my jaw in his hand, and gives me a long, slow kiss that makes my heart skip a few beats.

I grin at him, wiggling in my seat from excitement, and then jerk my thumb at the back seat. "She seems to be warming up to me."

"I told you she'd come around," he says, putting his large hand on my bare thigh as we drive off.

The journey to Napa is a gorgeous one. I opt for the longer route, heading over the Golden Gate Bridge, purely because it's more scenic and it gives me more time alone with him before I have to share him with everyone else. The temperature climbs as we head inland. Soon, the sun is baking us, our windows are down, and we are blasting down two-lane highways, the smell of vineyards and warmed fields blowing through the car.

"What if we keep driving forever?" I ask him dreamily, the soulful lament of Lana Del Rey's "Honeymoon" pouring from the speakers.

"What if we do?" he asks, playing along.

"Where would we go?"

"Does it matter?" His voice is so beautifully hopeful that I have to look at him. He gives me a quick smile and props his elbow on the open window, running his fingers over his chin and staring off at the dry hills.

No. It wouldn't matter. We could find a field, a cabin, a mountain stream. We could go north or south or east. We could pull down the next country road and set up camp around the car, just him, me, and Emily. We could take time and stretch it between our fingers and spend an eternity in each other's arms.

But reality doesn't work like that. Not that reality has handed us such a bum deal today. When we reach Napa and I pull the car into the massive parking lot of the Meritage Hotel, I'm incredibly grateful that Bram organized this whole thing—a way for him to see his cousin before he goes and a way for me to do the same.

"Well this is bloody nice," Lachlan says quietly as we get out of the car and gather our stuff. The heat blankets us as we cross the lot and enter the hotel lobby. Immediately we see the gang.

"Heeeeeeeeeeey!" Bram yells with a big smile, glass of red wine in his hand, coming over to us. He pulls Lachlan into a hug, slapping him on the back, and then does the same to me.

"My god, Bram, are you drunk already?" I ask as he pulls away.

"We got here early," he says, and gestures to the rest of them. Linden and Steph stroll over, also with wine, while I spot Nicola in the background talking to someone at the front desk.

"Hey you two," Steph says, hugging me as Bram did, though she doesn't do the same to Lachlan. Her eyes wander up and down, almost as if she's intimidated by him. Maybe because Lachlan is frowning at her something fierce. I know that being around a bunch of people has probably put him on edge already, and I reach out for his hand, giving it a squeeze.

He seems to relax before my eyes, and Steph's gaze bounces between us. She gives me a small smile, and Linden steps in to give his cousin one of those handshakes that takes up the whole forearm.

"Glad you came," Linden says before he spots the dog carrier. He drops to a crouch and says, "Aw, who is this?"

Emily immediately starts barking at him which makes Linden jump back and up. "Jesus, Lachlan, he's as surly as you."

"She," Lachlan corrects. "This is Miss Emily."

Linden snorts. "Bit of a pansy name for a dog. And you named her?"

"Aye," Lachlan says, staring Linden down with a hint of crazy eyes.

"Let's get us checked in," I say, pulling on Lachlan's arm and leading him over to the front desk.

"Are you okay?" I whisper.

He grunts in response. I assume that means he's fine. Or that I shouldn't worry about it anyway.

We say hi to Nicola when we check in, and once we get the keys to our room, she tells me to come meet them at the wine cellar on property for a group wine tasting, even though it seems that they've been doing plenty of tasting on their own already.

Our room is on the ground floor and done up in the Mediterranean style. Lachlan lets Emily out of the crate, then sticks her on a leash, opening the door to our patio and leading her outside to pee. I quickly freshen up in the bathroom, stretching my limbs after being cooped up in the car, and then flounce on the king-size bed, testing the firmness of the mattress. It feels like a dream. I could fuck all night on it.

When he comes back in, Emily hops up on the bed beside me, and I realize that fucking the day and night away might be difficult when the dog will be watching our every move again.

Lachlan lies down beside me on his back, putting his thick arm across my stomach. I watch him inhale and exhale, his chest rising and falling.

"Already feel like being antisocial?" I ask him.

"Mmmm," he says, staring at me. "I'd rather be in here with you."

"Well, if you have anything amorous planned, we may have to do it outside. *Miss* Emily here will be watching our every move."

He shrugs. "So we'll put her in the bathroom."

"She'll bark."

He sighs. "Yes, she will."

I turn into him and run my finger over his forehead, smoothing out the creases. "Always so expressive," I tell him, pressing into the notch between his brows. "Always thinking about something."

"I'd pay to have someone turn off my brain, to be honest," he says. I trail my finger down his nose, over the slight bump, then the curve of his lips. He opens them, taking my fingertip between his teeth and biting down gently.

I watch him closely, and I can see those wheels turning. I lower my voice a register. "I know just the thing to make it stop." I take my finger out of his mouth and kiss him softly. He lets out a faint moan that I can feel in my core. I put my hand on his chest and push myself back. "But first, let's go to the wine tasting."

He shuts his eyes and his head flops back onto the pillow. "Do we have to? Why can't we just stay here and you do that thing that turns off my thoughts, and I'll do that thing that makes your cunt wetter than a waterslide."

"Come on," I tell him, throwing his arm off me and getting up. "We're doing this because you want to see your cousins before you go, and they want to see you. Let's just have some wine and disappear."

He grumbles at that, but gets up. We leave Emily with her dinner and some water then head out into the hotel.

The building itself is huge, and we find ourselves strolling through courtyards and past the opulent pool area. It's busy, and everyone seems to have a glass of wine in hand which makes something in my head stutter and pause. Maybe a vineyard wasn't really the best place to bring Lachlan.

I glance up at him as he walks beside me, eyes darting around, never resting in one place. I take in what I know about him. Behavioral problems. Tattoos that hint at a past shadowed with downfall and demons. The fact that he doesn't drink much, if at all, might not just be about the rugby training. It might be about a whole other thing.

But he hasn't said anything to me about it, and because it's so personal, I'm not going to ask. People who are fucking for a week don't need to disclose the nitty gritty, perhaps painful, details of their lives to each other.

The wine cellar is located in the Estate Cave which is set right into the rolling hillside of grape vines that flank the back of the property. Inside it's cool and dim, with the spa entrance to the left of us and the wine tasting bar to the right. Ahead of us are big dark doors that just beg to be pushed open.

I'm in the middle of doing so, peeking my head inside to see a large, empty cavern with curved stone walls and hanging chandeliers, when Lachlan pulls me back and Steph is screeching in my ear.

"Yay, you came!" she says, and when I turn to look at her, she gives me a sloppy kiss on the cheek. I exchange a look with Lachlan. She's even drunker than before.

"Of course we came," I tell her as she beckons us to follow her into the bar. There are a few people lined up along its length, looking over lists and being doted on by wannabe sommeliers, but we follow Steph to the back where they're all sitting around a private table.

They all cheer when they see us, and I give them a quick one-handed wave in response.

"So," I say, looking over their empty, wine-stained glasses. "You've got quite the head start."

"We're just one drink in," Nicola says, gesturing to the two empty seats next to her. Lachlan and I both sit down, and the wine girl appears immediately.

"Hi," she says in an overly bubbly voice. I guess you have to be bubbly if you want to sell expensive crates of vintage. "Let me top you two off. We started off with a light sauvignon blanc blend." She reaches with her bottle, expertly pouring in a mouthful, but when she moves for Lachlan's glass, he puts his hand over it.

"I shouldn't," he says, not meeting anyone's eyes.

I look at Bram curiously to see if this is odd behavior from his cousin or not. Bram in turn is watching Lachlan carefully, though he doesn't seem surprised.

"Would you like another kind of wine?" the girl asks.

"Give him the red," Linden says. "He seems more like a red wine kind of guy. Right? Less sugar in red wine."

Bram gives his brother a conflicted look and opens his mouth to say something when Lachlan shrugs and removes his hand from the glass.

"Sure, red is fine," he concedes.

I feel like everyone around the table has suddenly tensed, making Lachlan the center of attention so I quickly say, "Bram, thank you so much for arranging this."

And then everyone's attention is on Bram with numerous expressions of gratitude. I put my hand on Lachlan's leg, his muscles flexing as he anxiously taps his foot on the floor.

The wine girl, whose name tag reads "Jennifer Rodriguez," comes back and pours Lachlan a hefty dollop of their red grenache blend. She's actually quite attractive in the white teeth, tanned skin, wavy, honey-colored hair, overly obnoxious way. She won't stop making eyes at Lachlan either.

But she doesn't even appear on his radar. While she's giving him all the information on the wine, babbling on, her eyes flitting over his tattoos, the bulk of his arms and shoulders, he doesn't even look at her once. He just takes a sip of the wine and nods.

The rest of us don't get the same amount of attention, although the wine is quite good. Bram asks a million questions about everything we drink, but Jenn's attention is always on Lachlan. At one point she actually touches his bicep and coos over it.

"I love your tattoos. My *ex*-boyfriend used to have a fleur-di-lis on his arm and a quote across his chest. I always thought they were very sexy on men."

I'm so close to telling her to step off but Lachlan folds his hands in front of him and calmly looks up at her. "Just pour the wine, darling."

Jenn immediately looks flustered, her pouty mouth dropping for a moment, but then she steps into professional mode, sparing herself from further humiliation. I feel like giving Lachlan a high-five but keep my small triumph to myself.

We're a few wine glasses in and Bram has started filling out an order form to bring back a crate of his favorite when Lachlan leans into me and whispers, "Meet me outside in a few minutes." He then gets up and strides out of the bar.

I turn around to face everyone else and they're all looking at me expectantly.

"What?" I ask, finishing off my wine.

"What's with him?" Linden asks.

"He's your cousin. You know how he is."

"Yeah," he says, "but at this point, I think you may know him better."

I look at Bram for backup but he just goes back to filling out the order form. "I'm afraid Linden is right, Kayla. You're the expert now."

"He is so sweet on you," Nicola adds, her eyes all warm and gooey.

"So sweet on me?" I repeat. "First of all, we're not in the fucking south, okay? Second of all, that man is not *sweet* on anything. Except maybe dogs."

Well, and he was pretty sweet with my mother the other night.

Steph violently shakes her head. "No, no, no. Then you don't see what we see. He wants you, Kayla."

I roll my eyes. "Well, that's a given at this point."

"No," she says, louder now, and Linden has to shush her. Good lord, they're all getting drunker by the minute. "No, let me say this," she says, pushing her hand against Linden's face and smushing it. "Let me say this, okay? Let me say this."

I stare at her and gesture with open palms. "Okay, drunky. Say it."

She leans forward, eyes wide with urgency. "He wants you. Like...he's in love with you."

That proclamation emits a simultaneous groan from both Linden and Bram.

"Don't get carried away," Bram chides.

"You women think that any man who gets his dick in you is in love with you," Linden says to her.

"Hey," I say sharply, jabbing my finger at him. "Please don't lump *me* into the 'you women' category. And I happen to know for a fact that none of us here think that, especially your little wife who was in love with you loooong before you got your stupid dick in her."

Steph glares at Linden, and I continue. "And for fuck's sake, we barely know each other. We're fucking, so let us fuck and shut the hell up about it." I look at Steph. "And please, the last thing I need is for anyone to get crazy, unrealistic notions inside my head. No one loves anyone. I don't know Lachlan and he doesn't know me, and we're both fine with that. We have to be fine with that because he's leaving in forty-eight hours for a land far, far away. So please, just let us have our time with each other until then. We don't need any complications. We don't need love, or even feelings, because what we do have is hot as hell and fleeting, and I'm going to suck up as much good fucking sex as I can with him. Got it?"

Bram, Nicola, Steph, and Linden are staring at me wide-eyed.

"Jeez," Linden finally says, "I was just joking. Touchy, touchy."

"Well I'm not joking," I tell him, getting out of my seat. "Now if you'll excuse me, I'm going to go find him. When we come back, I hope to god none of you utter the L-word or any other word except for 'goodbye,' okay?"

I turn on my heel and march past the wine bar, half the patrons looking at me as I go, since my outburst was probably a little too loud. Still, that made me angry as hell. Why did people always have to try and complicate shit? Why couldn't people just fuck and that be the end of it? I mean, my friends never even knew the names of any of the men I slept with after Kyle. Why does it have to be so freaking difficult with Lachlan?

Because you do have feelings for him, my inner voice whispers to me. *Because you are falling for him.*

"Argh," I growl to myself, hands on my ears, turning around in circles in the cave's foyer. "I don't want Steph to be right."

"Kayla?" I hear Lachlan's voice.

I stop spinning and look up to see him on the other side of the heavy door, in the dim cave I looked into earlier, staring at me with his usual concern.

"Yeah," I say, feigning normalness. "Hi."

He frowns deeper then gestures with his head to come inside.

I step in through the doors and he carefully closes them behind me. I look around. The cold stone walls are curved with buttresses, making the room take the shape of half a wine barrel. I take a few steps forward and peer down the rest of the empty hall. It looks like the kind of place where you'd have a *Game of Thrones* wedding, complete with alcoves and elaborate candelabras.

"What were you saying out there?" he asks softly, coming up behind me and placing his hands around the small of my waist. His breath smells like wine. "You don't want Steph to be right about what?"

"Don't worry about it," I tell him, closing my eyes and leaning my head against his chest. "Stupid girl nonsense."

"Mmmm. Sorry I took off like that," he murmurs against the top of my head. "There's only so much I can handle."

I'm not sure if he means the wine or the social situations, so I don't say anything except, "I wanted to get out of there too."

"Good," he murmurs, his hand briefly sliding over my hip. I want him to slip it lower, in between my legs, and flip up the hem of my dress, but he takes my hand instead. "Come here."

He leads me down the long, cavernous hall, my sandals echoing as we walk. At the end, there is a large ornate mirror and a hall leading to the left and right. To the left it's blocked by a heavy door, and to the right there is a locked, floor-to-ceiling iron gate between the room and what looks like a hall to a maintenance area. A cart full of towels sits outside an open door, but there doesn't seem to be anyone around.

"I don't think we're supposed to be in this area," I tell him. I turn around but the look in his eyes grows molten and I immediately know what's going on. The hairs on the back of my neck stand up, and a lone shiver slides down my spine.

"I don't think so either, love," he says gruffly, taking a step forward until my back is pushed against the gate. "But there are no dogs here."

I bite my lip and wrap my hand around his neck as he presses against me, the hardness in his jeans digging into my hip. He groans quietly, lips at my neck, pushing me further into the gate. The bars hurt my back, but it's a good kind of hurt. All the pain you get from sex is a fair trade, especially when it's coming from Lachlan McGregor.

He puts his hands on my thighs and slowly skims his palms up, the hem of my dress lifting with them. They leave trails of stardust and heat then pause at my hips. He lets out a heavy exhale against my neck.

"No panties," he murmurs. "Why do I have to leave you again?"

I swallow, my heart pinching. There is no room for anything except sex, especially here, especially now. "Because you're a smart man who is going back to a promising career."

"But how smart am I when I have to leave a woman like you behind?"

I shut my eyes. "New rule," I tell him, my hand slipping to his jeans and undoing his fly. "We are never to mention the fact that you are leaving. From now on."

He pulls back and stares at me, one hand dipping down between my legs, the other cupping my cheek. His lips are wet, parted, so entirely suckable, his eyes fraught with some wild emotion I can't read.

"I'm not sure I can pretend that," he says thickly.

"You don't have to pretend," I tell him, moaning softly as his fingers slide along my wetness. "We just won't bring it up. Live in the now. Always now." My hand finds the stiff, hot length of his cock, and I pull it out of his pants. "By the way, you don't wear underwear either."

He closes his eyes and hisses softly as I wrap my fingers around him. "Just trying to keep up with you," he says, voice rich and raspy.

"I appreciate the effort," I manage to say as he dips a finger inside me. My body seems to exhale from his touch, as if I need him in order to breathe. Everything aches for him, and I clench around his finger greedily, wanting more, needing more.

But this isn't about me. I slide my hand over his cock, dragging the silk of his precum down his rigid, heated length. I want to unravel him. I want to bring him to his knees. I want, more than anything, to undo this man and leave him the way he's leaving me, like a string pulled and a top spinning, over and over again, waiting for the fall.

His head goes back, mouth open. He lets out an elicit moan, the cords of his neck and the thick lines of his shoulders straining. Good god, watching him succumb to pleasure makes me happier and crazier than he would ever know.

Naturally I want to give him more. My hand works him expertly, knowing now just where to grip, where to twist, and judging by his quick breaths, I'm sure he's close to coming.

But he finally raises his head, his eyes unfocused as they roam over my face, fighting through a haze.

"Turn around," he says, his voice so hoarse that it's barely audible. "Please."

I do as he asks. He pushes up my dress so it's bunched up at my waist, and I bend over, grabbing the iron bars for support. It kind of feels like I'm about to be fucked in prison, like some kind of conjugal visit, and my deepest fantasies go wild. It's not hard to imagine when you have a troubled, tatted beast of a man about to take you from behind.

His hands skirt my sides, over my hips, and down my thighs. I feel him crouch behind me, his fingers gripping my ass, and I try and sneak a look over my shoulder. He's down on his knees and I can just see the top of his head beneath me.

I'm about to ask him what he has planned, but then I feel his face sink into me from behind, his hot mouth closing over me, his bottom lip sliding up over my clit.

Jesus. Being eaten out from behind? Yes, please.

He groans into me and I can feel the vibrations in my bones. I swell between his lips and he sucks me in his mouth like ripened fruit. I let out a loud gasp, my hands gripping the bars for dear life. It nearly knocks me off my feet.

"Love," he whispers huskily, pulling back. He licks up the curve of my ass, my body exploding with a shower of sparks. "I don't think I can ever stop tasting you."

My mouth opens to say something but he dives, no, *submerges* his face back into me and I let out a low, guttural noise, like it's being torn from my throat. I push my hips back into his mouth, a wild, uncontrollable need burning through me.

"Deeper," I plead, so desperate for my release, my cheek pressing into the bars.

His tongue snakes inside me, then a finger, then two, and I'm thrusting back into him like a fucking animal. I know I must look like one of those wild, drug-high girls you see at a fuck-fueled sex orgy, but I don't care.

I'm so close to coming.

I'm at the tip, looking over the edge, ready for the freefall.

Then he pulls back and I actually whimper in disappointment.

"You want more?" he asks gruffly, holding onto my ass. "Tell me what you want. To come on my tongue? Or to come on my cock? Both?"

"God, don't make this complicated," I whine, breathless and insatiable.

"All of the above, then." He spreads my legs wider, my sandals scraping along the stone floor, and pushes his face back in, his tongue, fingers, and mouth absolutely everywhere.

I come instantly, my body a hair trigger. I'm a writhing, moaning, bucking mess of scattered nerves, my limbs dissolving like sugar. I'm barely conscious and I don't know how I'm still upright. I feel him get up from behind me and hear the crinkle of a condom foil.

He grips my hips as he positions himself, and with one long, slow push he eases inside me. I'm so wet and ready that he glides right in. But oh, when he pulls back out, that slow drag hitting just the right spot, somehow I'm groaning for him all over again.

"Don't stop," I hiss as he plunges back inside, deeper this time, coaxing another unrestrained noise out of my throat. "Don't you ever stop fucking me."

"Jesus," he swears, gravelly and low. "I'll bury myself in you, if you let me." Then he moves faster, small stabs of his hips pushing deeper and deeper while his skin slaps my skin louder and louder. The smell of sex, sweat, and musk fills the room.

I'm completely overwhelmed. It's too perfect. It's everything, *everything*. I close my eyes and imagine what we look like to someone else, the ropey muscles of his arms as he digs his fingers into my hips, the raw, uninhibited fucking in this cold, dim and empty place, the sight of his thick cock sliding into me from behind, his heavy balls swinging against my inner thighs.

He leans forward, his fingers sliding down and finding the smooth, swollen face of my clit. He always wants me to come with him, so I know he's about to unload at any moment. But for some reason, I hold back, as hard as I can, wanting to pay attention to the way he so beautifully lets go without losing myself at the same time.

Drops of his sweat fall on my back. He continues pounding me, his hips changing the angle until it makes me gasp for air, my back arching. His breathing is shaky and his muscles are trembling from the strain, but he keeps going and going, whimpering now, clawing me in desperation.

There's a moment, a pause, a sharp intake of air, then the room fills with the sounds of his harsh, sharp grunts, the sound of him coming, a sound I love so much that it pushes me over the edge. It's the signal of his undoing, and his fingers press so hard into my skin that I'm afraid I might break in two. I am breaking in two. I am stretched thin, a plate of fragile glass, and I am breaking and breaking and breaking as he pounds me from behind.

I can barely hang onto the bars. I can barely hang onto myself. Wave after wave of emotion slams through me, filling the blank spaces, the cracks, the parts of me that have shattered off into space. I can barely breathe, and the ache, the fucking ache, is no longer between my legs but throughout my entire body.

"Kayla," Lachlan whispers hoarsely, leaning forward against my sweaty back. "Oh, love." He rests his cheek on my shoulder blades and his ragged breaths rise and fall against me.

I close my eyes and will myself not to cry. It's silly. Stupid. It's just sex. It's just fucking sex. But the emotion doesn't go away. It sits on my heart, and I can't tell what it wants from me. Are these happy tears? Sad tears? Why do I have to feel anything at all but release?

My fingers on the bars are beginning to slip, so I readjust my grip, and somehow that breaks the spell. Lachlan lifts himself off of me, and with a hand on my hip, pulls himself out. I take a moment to run my fingers under my eyes before turning around to face him.

He stands there, pants at his ankles, shirt bunched up, showing off his ink and glorious six-pack. He's pulling off the condom and tying it at the end but I'm barely paying attention. It's the look in his eyes that gets me, steals my breath. They don't have the peace, the softness that he usually gets after sex. He looks haunted instead, like I'm a ghost before him.

I swallow, my mouth parched, and try to think of something to say, but words escape me. I stare at him and he stares at me, electricity built of unsaid words and unknown feelings thrumming between us. There's nothing awkward or uncomfortable about it. It's just us, doing what we do, trying to glean something from each other that we don't know ourselves, forever locked in each other's eyes.

Finally he pulls up his pants, comes over to me, and pulls me into a wet, passionate kiss, his lips pressing hard against mine, his tongue tasting like me, like salt, like sweat.

He holds my face with one hand, running his thumb over my lips, gazing at me deeply. "I'm sorry if that was a bit savage."

I smirk. "The more savage the better." And it's true, because anything that could border on the sweet and sensitive, the emotionally-laden sex that is so often called "making love," well, I don't think I could maneuver that very well. After all, as savage as that fuck was, it still unleashed a torrent of emotions that I'm not equipped to handle. I've had a black heart my whole life, and it doesn't know what to do with anything that could turn it whole and pink.

Noises come suddenly from behind the room's locked door, and we quickly exchange a sheepish glance before we hightail it down the corridor, Lachlan flicking the condom in the trash can as we leave.

Once in the foyer, we pause, spotting the group still in the wine bar, laughing about something.

I look up at Lachlan. "We don't have to join them."

"Aye," he says with a nod. "But we should. Come on."

"Do I look like I just got thoroughly fucked?" I whisper to him.

He glances down at me and there's a flash of a wicked smile. "Oh yes."

"There you guys are," Steph says as we approach the table, and it's too late to even smooth down my hair. I know that my face and chest must be flushed. "I'd ask where you've been, but I don't want to know."

I give her a haughty smile and take my seat like a prim and proper lady. "Just getting some fresh air."

Nicola snorts from beside me. "I think I might need to know where you're getting your air."

"Sweetheart, your air is just fine," Bram says to her from across the table.

With the wine tasting over now, everyone is just splitting a couple of bottles. I hesitate to have a glass, already feeling quite woozy from earlier, but Lachlan surprisingly has one so I join him.

Eventually our stomachs start grumbling and we all head to dinner in one of the restaurants. Lachlan quickly stops by the room to get Emily since we learned you can have pets out on the patio, and we spend a few hours drinking more wine and eating as the sun goes down in the distance, casting a glow over the vineyards.

I breathe in deeply, enjoying the heat of the night air and the crickets that fill the silence. Bram and Nicola excuse themselves, Nicola saying she needs to call her mother and speak to Ava before it gets too late. Then eventually Steph and Linden leave too, hanging onto each other like two drunken fools.

"Alone at last," I say to Lachlan who is sitting splay-legged beside me and puffing on a cigar that the waiter hasn't said anything about. In fact, I think they purposely forgot we were all out here.

Lachlan lets out a small grunt, brow creased and deep in thought. I think he's drunk, but it's hard to tell. If anything, he's gotten quieter as the night goes on.

"Are you all right?" I ask.

His eyes flit to mine. His stare is hard, flinty. "I'm just fine," he says giving me a tight smile.

I swallow. "That's such a girl answer."

He blinks, intensity brewing like a thunderstorm. "Excuse me?"

Even Emily raises her head.

I lean back slightly, appraising him. Even though I was kind of provoking him just now, his mood switch is surprising.

Still, I refuse to be intimidated. We've passed too many bodily fluids between each other for that. "I said that's a girl answer. You said fine, like everything isn't fine, and if that's the case, I just want to know what's up."

His dark brows lower, and it's almost like he's glowering at me. Still, he doesn't say anything. He sticks his cigar in his mouth and looks away.

I sigh and put my hand on his shoulder. "Hey. You can tell me."

He closes his eyes, his head leaning back for a moment. "Love," he says, an edge to his voice. "I'm fine. I'm just… processing what's going on."

"And what's going on?"

He shakes his head and leans over the table, pouring himself another glass of wine. I watch as he downs it. When he's done, he wipes his lips with the back of his hand. "What isn't going on?" he says. But there's so much despair and bitterness in his voice that I feel like I've been backhanded.

I get out of my seat and grab his hand, tugging him to me. "Okay, the wine is gone. It's time to go."

He shrugs out of my grasp. "Go back alone then. I'm still smoking my cigar."

He's slurring a bit, so he's obviously a bit drunk. He's turning a bit Mr. Hyde on me.

I cross my arms. "No. I'm not going back without you."

"Your loss," he says, then laughs to himself as if he's said something hilarious.

I swallow the lump in my throat. "It isn't my loss." I sit back down and stare at him imploringly. Ages pass. Finally, he puts out his cigar.

"Fine," he says, none too happy about it. "We can go now."

He gets up, a bit unsteady on his feet, and reaches down for Emily, but the dog is perceptive and growls at him, shying away.

He stares at her for a moment, frowning, like he can't believe it. Then he rubs his lips together, his eyes beady and hard, and nods his head to some imaginary question.

"All right," he says quietly. "All right." He looks to me and seems to understand. "Do you want to take her? I don't think I should."

"Yeah, sure," I say quickly, and grab Emily's leash. She's still staring up at Lachlan in confusion and he's matching her stare. She knows that something has changed in him, and now he knows it, too.

Dogs with behavioral problems shouldn't learn from people with behavioral problems. Now I understand it. Another piece of the puzzle that is Lachlan, carefully fitting into place. Funny enough that it has to be a dog to knock some damn sense into him and not me.

I grab hold of Lachlan's arm but he doesn't pull away. His gait is a bit awkward, but I manage to lead him around the hotel and all the way back to our room.

He goes straight for the bed, flopping over facedown.

I lock the door, turn on the lights, and let Emily off the leash before I go over to him and tap him on the shoulder.

"You can't sleep with your clothes on," I tell him.

He grunts. "Undress me then."

"You weigh a literal ton," I tell him, trying to reach underneath him to pull off his shirt.

"Hyperbole," he mutters.

I smack him on the ass. "Just sit up, please."

With a heavy sigh he somehow rights himself. I quickly manage to pull off his shirt, his chin dipped against his chest, before he falls back to the bed, creating a minor earthquake on the mattress. I roll him on his side and take off his pants, for once something entirely unsexy.

"How did you even manage to get this drunk?" I ask, even though I'm not sure he's listening.

He swallows a few times, eyes still closed, and says, "I don't drink much."

"Right. The rugby," I say.

"No," he says with a slight shake of his head. "I just shouldn't. I like it too much. I need it too much. Like I need a lot of things. Bad things. And then I'm useless. It's ruined me before, you know."

I pause at this information so casually coming out of his mouth, then I pull his pant legs off before untying his boots. "I see," I eventually say.

"You want the truth, that's the truth. I have many truths. That is one of them."

I toss his boots to the ground and place my hand on his shoulder. "Well, thank you for telling me your truth," I say earnestly.

But he doesn't respond, and a loud snore escapes his mouth instead. Strange after everything he just did and said, I can still find him and his lips so damn kissable.

I sigh, getting into my t-shirt, and crawl into bed next to him, my back pressed against his back. "Goodnight," I tell him, pulling the covers over both of us.

He's fast asleep.

There's one more day left.

Chapter Sixteen

LACHLAN

I wake up feeling like absolute arse.

My first thoughts are of regret. Not just because of how I feel but because of what I might have done. I knew being around constant company and constant wine was a dicey gamble on my behalf, but I hadn't wanted to say no. I hadn't wanted it to seem like something I couldn't handle.

But she knew now. She could see it, and when I told her, she hadn't seemed all that surprised. That was both a good thing and a bad thing. A bad thing because I couldn't be sure how obvious I was. A good thing because she acted like she wasn't bothered by it.

Unless she was a good actress. It was hard to tell with Kayla. Part of her wanted to wear her heart on her sleeve, but the other part was always trying to cover it up.

The sound of the patio door sliding open is like a cheese grater to my brain. I open my eyes carefully and see Kayla stepping inside with Emily on the leash.

She sees I'm awake and gives me a soft smile while closing the door.

"Good morning," she says gently, unhooking Emily from the collar. The dog immediately jumps on the bed, licking me on the nose. I want to move my head, but it hurts too much. Shit, I can't remember the last time I was hung over, and my body is making sure I'm up for maximum punishment.

"Hey," I croak, wishing my voice didn't sound so weak.

I also wish she didn't look so bloody beautiful, the light coming through the gauzy curtains, lighting her up from behind like an angel. She walks over to me, dressed in another sundress I want to fuck her out of, her hair pulled back in a ponytail with not a trace of makeup on her glowing, fresh-scrubbed face.

Something inside me bleeds for her. It's a nasty cut in the heart, a slow, deadly leak. It pains me to look at her knowing I'll be leaving. That pain outweighs the one in my head. It's no wonder I drank last night. It wasn't just about the peer pressure. It was about relieving the pressure in my chest, the one that has been slowly building, brick by brick, all week.

I swallow, licking my lips, as she places soft, cool fingers on my cheek. I close my eyes, breathing her in, letting her touch soothe me.

"How are you feeling?" she asks. I open my eyes to see her crouched down at my level, looking at me with those warm dark eyes of hers.

Tomorrow I won't see those eyes of hers again.

How am I feeling?

I'm not fine.

But I couldn't quite tell her that last night, when I was drunk and trying to erase the feelings, feelings I do not know how to handle. It has been years and years since I was with a girl that I remotely cared about, and even that scared me halfway to hell. It didn't end well for either of us. I drank myself into a rehab center and she went screaming the other way.

This, whatever it is between us, wasn't supposed to happen this way. I should be back at my flat, packing, making phone calls to Alan, our coach, making arrangements to meet with my brother Brigs when I get off the plane. I should be getting ready to return to my old life, the one I'd put on hold for six weeks.

Instead I'm lying helplessly in bed, lost in a woman I don't know, wishing I could know her better.

What a bloody mess.

"You don't want to know how I'm feeling," I tell her.

"I thought as much," she says, kissing me on the forehead. It works like a blast to my heart.

She gets up and goes into the washroom while I struggle to sit up. I need to wake the fuck up and push past this bullshit, or my last day with her is going to go to waste. When she comes back out, she hands me a glass of water and two ibuprofen.

"Take those, drink it all," she says, and sits down on the couch across from the bed to watch me.

I do as she says, forcing it down while she looks on in concern.

"Tell me," she says suddenly, pointing to the lion on my arm. "About the lion."

My head jerks back in surprise which only makes the pain pound back in response. One eye scrunches up as I wince through it. "Now?"

She folds her arms. "I had to put you to bed last night. I think I'm owed an explanation."

I frown at her. "I'm not sure my tattoo will answer your question. What *is* your question?"

"The lion," she says. "When did you get it? What does it mean?"

"Why?" I ask her carefully.

"Because you're always looking at it."

My eyes widen and I'm hit with a wave of self-consciousness. "I am?" Fuck, I had never noticed.

"From time to time," she says. "You may not be seeing it for what it is, but it's one of the *many* places your eyes go."

I exhale noisily. She'd sunken into my skin, just like the tattoo. I could open another page for her. I could give her another glimpse inside. She couldn't throw it back in my face if I was leaving. The pages would just flutter to the ground.

"All right," I say, holding out my forearm for her to see better, for me to remember. "This is Lionel. Not my dog. My lion. I got this tattoo when I was sixteen. I'd been living with the McGregors for a while by then, but..." I pause, wondering how I can explain such a thing to someone who has never gone through it. "When you grow up in a boy's home, when you don't have anyone to love you, to care for you, to think of you, then you cling to whatever is lovely in the world. Lionel was my stuffed animal, given to me as a birthday present. The very same day my mother gave me away."

I reluctantly meet her eyes, but I'm surprised not to see any pity in them. She's involved in my words, as if she's living it as I had. I swallow hard and continue. "Lionel was what I truly loved and the only thing that loved me back. It was soft, you know, in a place that was very hard and very cold and very black. The lion gave me hope, even when everything seemed hopeless. Through many foster families who couldn't...handle me. And sometimes, sometimes I couldn't handle them. Finally the McGregors took me in, but..." I lick my lips. "Sometimes the good things have a hell of a time outweighing the bad. Demons follow you everywhere. All the time." I tap the back of my head. "Mine are here, and they are dark and they are always looking for the weakness in me."

You're my weakness. You'll bring them out again.

I close my eyes to those thoughts, pinching them together tight.

Kayla lays her hand on my arm, and I open them, taking in a deep breath.

"You don't have to say any more," she says. "I get it."

I shake my head. "Nah. Nah, you don't, and I'm glad you don't." I exhale sharply. "So, Lionel the Lion reminds me that there is good in the world. There's always something worth holding on to. It's just another word for hope, you know?"

She nods slowly. "I know." She looks away briefly, her eyes awash with sadness. "Shit. Lachlan, you're breaking my heart."

I sit up straighter and put my hand on her chest. "No. There's no breaking this thing."

She looks up at me through her lashes, mouth twisted into a smile. "Let's hope."

Our eyes lock, and before I know what I'm doing, I'm leaning in, pressing her soft lips to mine, letting the feel of her, the taste of her, wash away the grime.

We kiss for a long time, a slow, lazy, desperate meeting of the mouths, and I find everything in my body stiffens, hot and tense.

But she pulls away, her dainty hand on my chest, and quickly runs her thumb over my brow. "I promised everyone we'd have lunch with them. We're going to a winery."

I frown, not wanting to see anyone but her and especially not wanting to go to a winery after last night.

She continues, reading my face. "Don't worry, it's not a wine tasting. Well, it is, but they're already there, I think. I told them we'd meet them at the winery's restaurant for lunch. It's not far, and I heard it's good food. Farm to table and all that."

I groan and eye the alarm clock. It's eleven o'clock. I can't believe I even slept in that long. Usually I'm up at seven and raring to go.

She holds my hand and gives it a squeeze. "After lunch, I'm all yours. They all know. They don't want to take you away from me."

I narrow my eyes suspiciously. "They sound like good friends."

"They know you make me happy."

Her words are a fist to the gut, and they nearly leave me breathless.

I make you happy? I want to ask her, but I can't. I don't. I swallow her words down and pretend that they aren't affecting me like a goddamn shot of vodka.

"Okay," I tell her. "I'll get ready."

It's not long before I'm dressed, Emily's been fed and walked again, and Kayla and I are in her car driving to the winery. I have to admit, the day is absolutely brilliant, and the fresh country air is doing wonders to clear my head. I think the smog of San Francisco has started to clutter it up a little too much, and for a moment, my heart pangs for Edinburgh, with its quiet lanes and stone buildings and the slower pace of life.

I look over at Kayla as she drives, my hand at the back of her neck, my thumb rubbing against her skin. I could sit here for hours, as long as I can keep touching her. I wonder briefly, so briefly, just a flash, what she would think of Edinburgh if she could see it. Would she like Scotland? Would she see the country, the city that I see? Would she understand why its home?

But such thoughts are futile. They get pushed down into a locked box, and I stare out the window, watching sparrows dance in the blue sky and the endless curve of vineyards that stretch over the hills.

Soon we arrive at a winery composed of hay, rustic fences, and sprawling barns. One of the barns holds the restaurant, and we find my cousins and their women already sitting down, toasting each other with wine to something.

It makes me hold onto Kayla tighter. The four of them seem so tight-knit that I can't imagine Kayla with them after I leave. Will she sit there, just happy to be on her own, happy for her friends, but forever the fifth wheel? Will she have someone else by her side, some other guy? One that she's fucking, one that she maybe loves?

The thought of that nearly makes me sick. I have to stop, mid-stride, and throw my shoulders back to take in a deep breath.

"You okay?" Kayla asks, and I quickly nod, glad that no one else saw that.

"Just in time," Bram says from the table, lifting his glass. "We were toasting to hangovers."

"That seems about right," I say, forcing brevity into my voice. I sit down and give them all a tight smile. My glass is filled with wine, but there's also one with water, so I raise that. "Here's to feeling like the dog's bollocks," I say.

"Here, here," they all say. We all tap glasses, and I noticed that Bram is getting that sentimental look in his eyes that I don't think anyone else ever notices except for me. I give him a sharp nod, not wanting to go down the schmaltzy road, then clink my glass with Kayla's, who is also toasting with water.

I look deep in her eyes, the light in the barn bringing out the different shades of mahogany and teak. "Here's to you, love," I say softly, barely audible. "You're quite the hangover cure."

The corner of her mouth lifts in a soft smile and I impulsively lean over to kiss it.

Bram clears his throat, and I reluctantly look back at him. Maybe he can see in my eyes that I'm just daring him to say something, so he looks away, busying himself by picking up a menu. I can't help but smirk at that. For all of Bram's money and affluence, he's still a bit intimidated by his younger cousin.

The lunch ends up going smoothly, and even though Linden was grating on my nerves yesterday, he's more subdued today. Maybe it's the hangover. Everyone has been turned down a few notches. Still, when the waitress comes by to take away our empty plates, I find myself sighing internally with relief. As much as I honestly do care for Bram and Linden, and I don't mind Nicola and Steph, all I want to do is spend my last moments with the woman next to me. Little by little, I can feel that darkness creeping in, snaking black fingers that take hold of your brain, and I want to do what I can to keep them at bay.

Even though they seem to increase when I'm thinking about Kayla, she's also the cure.

We all make tentative plans to meet later on at the bowling alley bar inside the hotel, even though in the back of my head I know I'm not going to show up. I'll say goodbye to them in the morning. That will be enough for me.

The minute they leave and get in their cars, I grab Kayla's hand and lead her along the peeling paint fence toward one of the barns in the background. Unlike the barns used for the restaurant and wine tasting, this one looks neglected.

"Where are you taking me?" she asks as I look around, checking to see if anyone is looking. From this angle there's nothing in sight except hayfields and rows of grapes.

"I know you're not too keen on the dog watching us," I tell her, leading her into the barn, past farm equipment, to the ladder that leads up to the hayloft.

"I'm also not too keen on rolling around in rat poop," she says.

I shoot her a smile and start to climb the ladder. "Wait there. Let me check." I climb and pop my head over the edge. It's not packed with hay, but there are a lot of bales stacked along one side, some of the hay loose and spreading onto the floor. It will be comfortable enough. And no, I don't see any rats.

I step off the ladder and wave her up. "Come on," I say quietly. "The hay is fine."

She purses her lips, thinking it over. I stand at the edge and unzip my cargo pants, bringing my dick out of them, already stiff as a board.

Her eyes widen as I knew they would. My girl is a hungry little creature.

"I'll be right up," she says, her mouth parting sweetly as she clamors up the ladder. When she gets to the top, she stays down on her knees. Her hands grab the back of my thighs, her nails digging in, and she stares up at me with burning eyes.

She doesn't break eye contact with me—I'm starting to think she gets off by watching me get off. I've been with my fair share of women, but none of them were as brazen as she is, not even close. And it's not that I feel like she's lusting over me like a slab of meat. At the beginning, maybe. But now, it's more than that.

At least, I hope it's more.

She takes me in her mouth, working me softly, sweetly, but oh so fucking wild. I close my eyes and throw my head back, both wanting her to continue and wanting her to stop.

When I'm close to coming, I pull back, breathless. She stares at me, soulful, yearning, her perfect mouth open and glistening, practically begging for my cum.

I lick my lips and grab her by the arms, hauling her up beside me. I put one hand behind her head, feeling how small she is, how perfectly she fits in my palm. The urge to protect her or fuck her is a war raged deep inside, all the time. No wonder she's driving me mad.

Wanting her to feel my fire, what's driving me, I pull her to me and kiss her urgently as the need, the lust, the want comes pouring out. I might just devour her. Everything she offers up is so beautiful, but it's never enough. I don't just want to touch her and be with her, I want to fuse with her. I want to sink inside her so deeply that she'll feel bereft without me there. I want to be everything to her, this sly little minx who has turned my world upside down.

She's kissing me back, wild and untamed. She's clawing at me now, nails on my back, digging through my shirt, and I'm gripping her so hard I feel I might break her.

Quickly, I pull her shirt over her head and toss it on the hay. "Come on," I groan against her neck. I gently push her back until she's lying in the straw and shimmying herself out of her denim cut-offs. No knickers, of course. I'll never tire of the sight of her beneath me, so perfect, every swoop and soft curve that my lips and tongue and hands are so ridiculously addicted to. Her cunt is a fucking treasure, and for this moment, for every moment I've spent with her, I feel like it all belongs to me.

It's a startling thought, the idea that she could. It's not just that it feels like she's mine. It's the idea that maybe, in another world, in another life, she could be.

I pinch my eyes shut, willing the feeling away. But it doesn't go. It just morphs, turns, shifts, into raw desire to have her in every way I can, to make her see just how it is.

"Did you bring a condom?" she asks me, breathless.

I shake my head in frustration. I wasn't really thinking with my hangover. "No," I say regretfully. "I didn't."

"I'm on the pill," she says. Her eyes are clouded with lust, but she's still thinking straight. "And I've been tested. Clean."

I nod. "Same." I had more than a few scares when I was younger. I wasn't always with the best people, doing the best things. I've been more than careful ever since.

"Okay," she says softly, and I see it in her eyes, the look that tells me it will be different this time. To feel her skin against skin. To be so completely bare with her.

I have to take a deep breath, steady myself. Without a barrier between us, I don't know how long I'll have before I lose myself inside her.

But who am I kidding? I've already lost myself to her.

I move between her spread legs. It's almost painful, this desire, this need. Seeing my bare cock hard and ready, her cunt open, pink and soft—I feel like I'm dying a beautiful death a million times over.

I tell myself to get over it but words don't matter. Reason and logic, same. In this moment, I want in deep and to never let go.

Slowly, so slowly, I ease myself into her as she raises her hips, pushing toward me herself, wanting that deeper purchase. Her mouth opens wider the further I get, her skin sliding against my skin like endless silk.

I kiss her, melting my mouth into hers, wanting to be as close as possible.

"This won't take long," I nearly whimper against her lips. "I'm sorry."

"Apologize afterward," she tells me, her breath so airy and soft with pleasure that it nearly derails me.

But I know I won't. I'll make sure there's nothing to apologize for.

Our faces are just inches apart as I slowly pull out and ease myself into her. Our gaze never breaks. Hers is full of lust and wonder, as if she's seeing me for the first time. I can only hope she likes what she sees, that I'm enough for her. When our hips meet, it makes me still, and I have to suck in my breath to regain control. There's something about her that makes me want to completely lose it and I've been losing my mind since the day I met her.

She wraps her legs around my waist and rocks her hips backward, each movement pulling me further and further into her. Her hands are at my back and pushing into my muscles. Our skin moves against each other like we are one.

"Fuck, love," I croak out, sucking along her neck, to her breasts. My tongue teases around the hardened peak of her nipple and I pull it into my mouth with one long, hard draw. Her moan is so loud, so uninhibited that I feel like a fucking king. I barely notice that we're in a hayloft, in a barn, somewhere in California. I only notice her and the warmth, that damn, intoxicating warmth of being really, truly inside of her, of feeling her in every way I can.

"Harder," she says, arching her back. "Fuck. Lachlan."

My name on her lips is a tonic. I piston my hips to drive into her deeper, my knees burning from the hay as I pound her again and again and again. Her perfect tits bounce with each thorough thrust, and suddenly there are no thoughts. No pain. No nothing, and yet everything. That feeling of falling, of realizing how good it can fucking be when you actually care about someone.

And I care for her. More than I should, more than I could ever admit.

"Lachlan," she whispers to me but never finishes her sentence. She just repeats my name. Like I'm revered, like I'm her religion.

Again.

And again.

And again.

The flush on her face spreads to her chest and her legs quiver around my waist. She's holding onto me like I'm about to take flight and she doesn't want to be left behind.

I go to slip my hand over her clit, to give her the boost, but she's already there. She cries out loudly, hips jerking upward, body shaking like a minor quake. She's so unbelievable when she's coming, this pulsing, writhing spirit, and I'm the cause of all of it. I'm the one who brings this little creature to her knees, to the edge.

And she does the same to me.

My orgasm sneaks up on me, like being hit from behind. It's devastating. Stunning. I know I'm loud when I come. I know I'm groaning and grunting loudly, but from the way she's gasping for breath and still holding tight, she feels it. I want her to feel it. To feel me.

I collapse against her, sweat dripping off my brow and over my nose. I can hardly breathe but I don't care. I'm shuddering on the inside, completely unraveled.

This woman. This beautiful woman that I've just come inside of, this woman whose gorgeous, elegant neck I'm kissing because it's the only thing to do.

I can't leave her. I just can't.

I stay inside her for as long as possible, until she starts to adjust underneath me. When I pull out of her, the loss is deeper than I thought it would be.

I brush the hair back from her damp forehead. "Hi," I say softly. Because I feel like we're meeting again for the first time.

"Hi," she says lazily, breaking into a smile. Her hands ghost up and down my back, as if she can't quite believe I'm here.

"I rather enjoyed that," I tell her.

Her smile is coy. "So did I."

"I could do that again."

And now, now she looks pained. She swallows, running her fingertips, light and soft, up to my neck. "I could too."

I take a deep breath, throwing all decorum away. "I don't want to say goodbye."

She blinks, as if this idea is something new. After a beat, she says, "Neither do I."

So then what do we do?

The answer is nothing.

But I don't want it to be nothing.

...

"Are you ready?" Kayla asks me, surveying the hotel room one last time.

I nod, though I'm the furthest thing from ready. When we woke up, we spent as much time as possible in bed before we finally had to get going. Now we're running a little bit late, which doesn't bode well for me when I have a plane to catch.

Still, I can't blame myself for dragging my feet. I'm trying to hold onto the seconds and they're just slipping through our hands.

I grab the dog crate, my duffel bag, and we head out to the car. I planned to head back into the hotel to say goodbye to Bram and the others, but the four of them are waiting outside for us, suitcases packed.

"Sorry we couldn't make breakfast," I tell Bram as we come up to them.

"Understood," he says, and I can't see his eyes underneath his Ray-bans, but I'm going to go out on a limb here and assume he has that same sentimental look as he did yesterday during lunch. The last thing I need is for someone to draw attention to the whole going away factor. I fucking hate goodbyes; in fact my whole life I've just ghosted in those situations.

It wouldn't have been right to just leave without saying anything, but even so, we make it quick. I hug my cousins, tell them it was great to see them again, and make sure they know I mean it. I kiss the hands of Steph and Nicola, who still regard me in the same way that people look at a pit bull, untrusting and on edge, and get in the car before anyone has a chance to get sappy on me.

A few minutes later we're pulling onto the highway that leads us back to San Francisco. The sun is shining but the mood in the car is heavy, a cloud hanging over us. We don't talk. No music plays. Somehow the silence is comforting, something that we share.

I keep thinking about the barn. The look in her eyes as she came, the way her hands held me to her, so tight, like she couldn't stand to let go. It undid me in a way I'm not sure I can reverse. I find myself reaching for the back of her neck, holding her there, as if that could keep her close.

She looks over at me, her eyes both sweet and sad. "I think Bram's going to miss you," she says. "He doesn't have a lot of friends out here yet except for Linden."

I nod, not wanting to talk about Bram. I want to talk about us.

"And you," I say. "Will you miss me?"

Her brow softens, and I have the urge to kiss her forehead, to breathe her in, to bury my hands in her silky hair. I know what I want to hear from her. I know what I need to hear from her. I want her to stop the car, to stop time. I want her for just a few seconds more than I'm allowed.

"Of course I'll miss you," she says, and her voice is quiet, strained. It tells me the truth. That this is hard on her too. "I already miss you and you're still here."

I swallow thickly, knowing exactly what she means.

But what the fuck is there to say? We both knew this was coming. We knew very well. I just didn't expect it to be so hard.

It's fucking killing me.

I run my thumb along her neck, and I am filled with foolish thoughts, wants, desires. I don't dare even repeat them to myself. I'm just having a hard time imagining myself next week, back in Edinburgh. Of course, rugby will sweep me away, consume me, as will the organization. But now that I've been consumed by her, I'm not sure it will be enough.

I open my mouth to tell her something that could make it better, but there really isn't anything that can. So that silence falls on us again.

Until Kayla utters, "Fuck, traffic," and I look to see the highway in front of us backed up with cars.

"We have plenty of time," I tell her. All I have to do is get home, grab the two suitcases I packed, and leave. Emily is already in her crate, and I have a sedative to give her for the journey. Bram has an extra key to the flat and said he'd get a maid service to come by after I left.

But half an hour later, the traffic is still ensnarling us.

"Fuck," Kayla says again, wringing her hands on the steering wheel. "Can you check again?"

I open her phone and refresh the traffic app. We're not too far from the Bay Bridge, but the highway is showing up as a thick red line. "Still showing traffic all the way through to the city, but the delay is only supposed to be ten minutes."

"That's what they've been saying, and yet..." She shoots me an anxious glance. "I'm so sorry."

"I'll make the flight," I assure her calmly. "Don't worry. They say you have to be there three hours before an international departure, but really it's ninety minutes. We're good. I'm just running in, grabbing my stuff, and going."

But time is playing a cruel trick on us. First I was cursing it—it seemed like the car ride couldn't be long enough, that I wouldn't get enough time with her. Now the ride threatened to never end.

"You know, I didn't think I'd spend my last moments with you stressing out about this fucking traffic," Kayla says, resting her head on the steering wheel. "What would happen if I just started honking?"

I look around us. There don't seem to be any accidents, but it's like every person in the world is on the road, lanes after lanes converging onto the bridge, the tolls slowing everyone down. "You'd go nowhere fast. And then I'd have to get out of the car and fight someone, I'm sure."

"You'd win at least," she says. "Maybe you could take off your shirt before you do it."

"Always wanting me half-naked," I chide her.

"Excuse me? Fully naked, please."

I can't help but smile at the sincerity in her voice. What the bloody hell am I going to do without her around? No one else brings a smile out of me like an automatic response, a knee-jerk reaction.

An hour in traffic ticks past. Kayla is losing her shit and apologizing profusely, and I'm massaging her shoulders, trying to soothe her and keep her calm. But eventually, I have to face facts.

I'm not going to make my plane.

"I'm so sorry," she says again, and I give her a measured look.

"Once again," I tell her, "it isn't your fault. We didn't know about the traffic. If anything, I should have made sure we were on the road earlier, but…it was just so bloody hard leaving the bed this morning." We hadn't even been screwing. We were entwined with each other, breathing, just being.

"If I could rewind time," she says, and her voice starts to crack. It cuts into me, sharp and deep, but she quickly covers it up, shaking her head.

"I'll call the airline and get on the next flight." I tell her, bringing out my phone. I find my confirmation number through my email, and dial.

"Isn't that going to cost so much extra?" she asks.

"It doesn't matter."

"But—"

"Maybe it's a blessing in disguise. It could give us more time together," I tell her. She blinks slowly, considering that.

By the time we begin our slow, aggravating crawl onto the Bay Bridge, I finally get through to the airline. I apologize to the clerk on the phone, explaining the dilemma.

"Unfortunately, Mr. McGregor," the clerk says, "the next available flight out to Edinburgh isn't until tomorrow, even if we reroute you through Glasgow."

"All right," I say. That doesn't screw up too much. The first team practice isn't until Tuesday. "Let's stay direct. Are there any change fees because I missed it or…?"

"No," she says. "Because you're business class, the fees are waived."

"Is it a full flight?"

"Getting full, though it should be fairly empty in the business class cabin."

That makes me pause.

"How much do those seats cost?" I ask her, but before she can respond, I follow up with, "Never mind, it's not important." I pause and take a deep breath, because I'm started to feel amped by something crazy. "Do you mind if I put you on hold for a moment?"

I don't even hear her response. I move the phone away from my face and look over at Kayla. She's gnawing on her lip, her brow pinched in worry—maybe sorrow. She has a tiny crescent moon scar on her chin, and I realize I never got a chance to ask her about it. I never got a chance to learn a lot of things.

But chances happen all the time. You just need to take them.

"Kayla," I say gently, as if I can't believe it myself because I don't.

She turns her head, shining eyes meeting mine. "What?"

"Come with me to Scotland."

It's more of a demand than a question.

But I've said it.

She stares at me blankly for a moment, blinking, until I smack my palm against the dashboard to draw her attention to the car she's about to rear end. She slams on the brakes and we both jolt forward against the seatbelt.

"What?" she asks delicately, as if she didn't hear me right.

I clear my throat, conjuring up the sheer nerve to say it again.

"Come with me to Scotland. Tomorrow. I can get you a seat on the plane."

Her mouth drops open but she doesn't say anything. She gives me a brief, confused smile. "I don't...are you being serious?"

"When am I not serious?" If she could feel how fast and hard my heart is beating, she wouldn't ask me that. "I'm serious. I'll get you a ticket. Just come with me." *Please.*

She's staring at me, trying to read my face, and I know she's having a hell of a time pulling anything from it. Finally she shakes her head. I can't pretend it doesn't hurt.

"But I can't," she says. "I wish I could. I mean...I would. But...my job."

"Use your vacation days."

"I can't just up and leave them. They wouldn't let me go."

I know it's futile now, but I can't help it. "You can ask. It sounds like they owe you for a lot of things at this point."

Fuck it. I put the phone back to my ear. "Hello, miss? Yes, actually I'd like to buy another seat, business class, since there is room. If there is one next or close to me, that would be brilliant."

"What are you doing?" Kayla asks, panicking.

I put my hand over the mouthpiece. "Don't worry about it."

The clerk asks me for Kayla's name and info.

"Kayla Moore," I tell her, then I have to pause. I don't even know this girl's birthday. Just what the fuck am I doing here?

"Uh, love," I say to Kayla. "Mind supplying me with your birthdate?"

"Lachlan," she says. "Don't."

I give her a long look, trying to read her, what's she's really feeling, really thinking. "Don't what?" I ask her. "You don't want to come?"

She looks so utterly helpless that I almost feel bad for putting her on the spot. But fuck, the hope it brings is worth it.

"I want to come," she says quietly. "I just don't think it's possible. It's so last minute. Do you really want me to come with you?"

I nod quickly. "I'm getting the ticket."

"No."

"No, listen. I'm getting the ticket. The flight leaves tomorrow at three o'clock. I will be on it. If you don't make it happen, then that's the way it goes. But that ticket will be there, in your name."

She's shaking her head. "I can't let you do that. The cost—"

"The cost is worth it in the event that you show up."

"And if I don't? I mean, if I can't make it work?"

I manage to give her a half-smile. "Then at least I tried." I exhale loudly. "Your birthdate, love."

I can see the wheels turning in her head. Spinning around. Going over every scenario. Not sure what the right answer is.

Finally she says, "July first, nineteen eighty-five. And it's Kayla Ann Moore."

I grin at her and get back to the phone. "Pardon me, miss, you still there? I have the information you need."

And just like that, there's hope.

Chapter Seventeen

KAYLA

In a few seconds, everything has changed. Everything. I've gone from feeling deep, aching, crazy despair to thinking of brand new possibilities in the blink of an eye.

Because he asked me to go back with him.

It's everything I have wished for. Hoped for. It's the same scenario that has played out in my head over and over again the last few days. The dream that he would ask me, would actually want me to go. The sign that this, *us*, is something. It has legs, and given the right circumstances, could go on and on.

He ends the call on the phone, his long fingers curling over it, giving it a squeeze, as if he's not quite sure what he's done. He turns his head to me and a half-smile slowly appears. This time his beautiful lips are twisted with something like shyness. It's disarming to see him look so unsure and anxious, though I can't be sure if it's over what he just did or whether I can go or not.

The truth is, I don't know what to say. But I know how I feel. I don't want to say goodbye right now. And suddenly

I have the power to make a change and take a risk and follow him to another land.

It's crazy. I know it is. It's absolutely crazy.

I shouldn't even be considering it.

But I am.

I just don't want to get anyone's hopes up, especially not my own.

"So," he says finally, after a long pause. "You have your seat if you want it."

I let out a small laugh, shaking my head. "I'm just thinking about how crazy this is. This is crazy, right?"

"Aye," he says with a single, determined nod. "It definitely isn't normal. But…why not?"

"Other than the fact that my work might not let me?"

He smiles tightly. "They might, though. Make a case."

I grumble to myself, thinking about what Lucy will say. Then again, Candace would gladly take over my position. She has probably been lying in wait for this kind of opportunity. "Shit, if they let me take my entire vacation, there's a chance I won't have a job when I come back. I would be so easily replaced."

He purses his lips, frowning as he studies me. "You'll only be replaced if you let it happen."

And how hard will I fight when I return? I hate my job. I hated being shown what I could really do with my life and then having it snatched away. I hated that I wasn't taken seriously, that I was told who I could be and it was nowhere near who I wanted to be.

Fuck. If I came back here and my job was hanging by a thread…it's hard to say how far I'd be willing to go to keep it stitched together.

"We'll only have maybe three weeks together," I tell him.

He blinks slowly in agreement. "But they would be a good three weeks."

Good? That would be the understatement of the year. Three more weeks of continuing to have the best sex of my life with a larger than life man I've become utterly, desperately obsessed with? They could be the best three weeks of my entire life.

I exhale, trying to expel the tightness in my chest. "But what about you? What about rugby? Won't I get in the way?"

"No, love, you could never get in the way. If anything, it might get in the way of you. In having you all to myself, day in and day out, with nowhere to go but the bedroom. Or, you know, anywhere else."

"I just don't want to mess up your life, even if it's only for a few weeks," I say feebly.

He twists his broad frame in the seat and puts his hand on my cheek, turning my attention to him. Thankfully the traffic is at a standstill.

"I want you," he says with a gruff tenderness. "I want more of you. And I don't care how I get it."

I search his eyes, greener now than they have ever been. They're bright and burning, and I *know* he wants me. I can feel it in my bones, and the thrill is like a million bombs going off at once. How did this even happen? I'm absolutely spellbound by him.

I clear my throat, but even so my words are quiet. "You have me."

His mouth twitches up, eyes squinting. "Not yet."

We drive the rest of the way in silence, but unlike the silence of before, which was pure melancholy as my brain and heart wrestled each other with the idea of saying good-bye, this silence is humming with energy. Possibility. And fear.

When I drop him off at his apartment, the fear is so great that it's got a chokehold on me. I'm glued to the car seat. He grabs Emily from the backseat, setting the crate on the curb, then comes around to me, opening the door.

"Come on," he says. "Give me a hug."

"What?"

He reaches in and pulls me out of the car so I'm pressed up against him, and I'm suddenly hit with this goddamn wave of terror, the fear that I might not see him again.

He wraps his arms around me, holding me in a vise of muscle, warmth, and his wonderful scent, and kisses the top of my forehead. "Just in case this is it."

I shake my head into him. No, no. This can't be it. Not anymore.

"I'll have to talk to my mom too," I mumble into him, my fingers clawing at his t-shirt. "I don't like the idea of leaving her for three weeks."

"I know," he says.

I raise my head and stare up at him. "If my brothers promise to come by and check on her more often, I think it will be okay. But I don't think I can talk to my boss until the morning. If she says yes, I'll have to be ready to go right away. You said the flight is at three o'clock?"

"That it is."

I'm blinking back tears. "I'm going to plead my case. I'm going to do what I can."

"I know you will," he says. "I have faith in you."

"So then, this isn't it," I tell him. "This can't be it."

He closes his eyes and leans in to plant a terribly soft kiss on my lips. It makes me want to weep. My hands grab him tighter. Something inside me is shaking my foundation.

"Go home," he whispers. "Do what you can. And I'll see you tomorrow."

"And what if you don't."

He smiles sadly. "Then at least I had hope."

Fuck.

I don't know how I manage to break apart from him but I do. I can barely drive back to my apartment. I'm an emotional wreck, a zombie, yet I've never needed to think more clearly in my whole entire life.

I don't know what to do. I know what I want to do and what I should do, but I don't think they are the same thing. What I really need to do is discuss it with my mother—even if my work does let me take my three weeks' vacation completely last minute, she's the reason I'd have trouble going.

But before I can even bring it up with her, I have to know my plan.

I immediately text Steph and Nicola. *When you guys get back, can you get dropped off at my place? This is an emergency. I need to talk to you.*

I ponder leaving it at that, but I'm not sure it will be enough so I add, *Lachlan asked me to go to Scotland with him. Tomorrow.*

They both text immediately with a lot of questions and say they'll have the guys drop them off.

I pour myself a glass of water from the sink and drink it down in five long gulps. Then I take a half empty bottle of red wine out of the cupboard and have a few swigs straight from the bottle. After all the wine over the weekend, I'm still not tired of it. More than that, I need it. I am flipping the fuck out.

When Nicola and Steph buzz me and I let them up, I haven't really come up with any decision. I've been pacing with a mind so overwhelmed that I can't figure out anything.

"Kayla," Steph says as they come inside. "What the hell happened on the ride over here?"

I stop pacing and look at them, flapping my hands like an anxious bird. "Okay. Okay. Well. He missed his flight. The traffic."

"I know, we were just stuck in it," Nicola says. "He seriously missed his flight?"

"Yes. He was able to book the next one going out, but it doesn't leave until tomorrow. And then…and then suddenly he looked at me…"

He looked at me, and it was something I hadn't seen before in him: hope. I could feel it in my marrow, and I knew, I knew, that something had changed for us.

"And?" Steph coaxes, sitting on the couch and folding her legs underneath her.

"And then he asked if I would go to Scotland with him. He said he'd buy me a seat on the plane."

"So you said yes?" Nicola asks.

I shake my head. "No. Yes. Maybe? I mean…I don't know if I can? What if work won't let me? I'm supposed to stroll into my office tomorrow and ask if I can leave right then and not return for three weeks. And then there's my mom. I can't leave her for that long."

Steph studies me. "Right. All valid. So you're not going?"

I sigh and flop down on the couch, legs spread out, all my strength drained. "I don't know. He booked me a seat anyway."

"Oh my god," Nicola says softly. "He did that?"

I swallow and nod.

"I told you he was sweet on you," she says rather smugly.

I'm too frazzled to roll my eyes. "I wasn't expecting it."

"But did you want it?" asks Steph. "When he asked you, what was your first thought?"

I blow a strand of hair off my face, wishing all my nerves didn't feel so wound up. "I thought…please let him be serious. Please don't let this be a cruel joke."

"Well, Kayla," she says, staring at me with knowing eyes. "You have to go."

"But I can't just go. It's not that easy."

"Okay, let's ignore your work and mom situation at the moment. And by the way, your mom will be totally fine. I'll even go check on her if your brothers don't get their act together." I give her a grateful smile. "So ignore all that. Is there anything else that would prevent you from going? And I don't mean externally, like being afraid of jetlag or hating Scottish food or anything like that. I mean inside. Your compass."

I scrape my teeth over my lip. "I don't know him," I say softly. "I met him three weeks ago. I've only been intimate with him for one week. You don't just go off with someone you don't know to another country. On a whim."

"Why the fuck not?" Steph asks, giving me a strange look. "You think he's going to murder you and leave you in a dumpster somewhere?"

"Well, no."

"Do you trust him?"

My mouth opens but nothing comes out. I have to shrug. "I guess. I mean…can you trust someone you've just met?"

"You can do whatever you want," she says. "Do you trust him?"

I take in a deep breath and look over at Nicola who is watching me curiously. "With my heart?"

Steph tilts her head at me. "Is that what you're worried about? That you're going to go there, fall in love, and have to leave him?"

Ouch. One question and my chest feels like a hollowed out tree. "Well, I'm fucking worried about it *now*!" I tell her, sitting up. I exhale loudly and rub my hands over my face. "I'm worried…I'm worried about that, yeah. I fucking am. But I'm also worried that I'll be disappointed. That I'll get to know him and he won't be the person I think he is."

"And who do you think he is?"

I give them a soft smile. "I think he's everything."

Steph nods and gets up off the couch, heading into the kitchen.

Nicola bites her lip, smiling. "No one has ever been your everything, Kayla. You know you have to go. You'll kick yourself if you don't. You don't want to live with regrets, believe me."

Steph comes back with the bottle of wine I was chugging out of earlier and three wine glasses. "We should all be wined out at this point, but I don't care." She pours the rest of the wine into the glasses, really nothing more than a splash, and hands one to me.

"We can't really celebrate anything yet," I remind her, even though I'm raising my glass anyway.

"We're celebrating your decision. It's rare to get a chance like this. You're taking it, regardless of what the outcome is, and that's something." She and Nicola clink their glasses against mine. "Last time we toasted to fucking. This time we're toasting to...well, more of that. But we're toasting to you, Kayla. Follow your heart."

"Cheesy," I mumble before taking a sip of wine. Cheesy but appropriate. "Do you really mean you'll check in on my mom?" I ask her.

She puts her hand on my shoulder for a moment, looking me in the eye. "I promise I will."

"I still don't know how she'll feel about it," I admit.

"She'll be happy if you're happy. That's all moms ever want for us. Well, most of the time. I'm sure my mom wants me to also have a baby soon."

I look at her in surprise. "She's starting on you already? You just got married."

Steph smiles and looks away, tucking her hair behind her ear. "Yeah, well. I can't say I disagree with her. We've already started trying."

I glance at Nicola to see if she knows this, but she looks just as surprised as I feel.

"Really?" Nicola squeaks. "That's amazing. Oh, I'm so happy for you."

I scrunch up my nose. "Really, Steph? You're joining the mom club with Nicola?"

"It's not so bad," Nicola chides me. "You might change your mind one day."

I glare at her. "You know how much I hate it when people say that."

She shoots me an evil grin. "Oh, I know. That's why I like to say it."

"As I said," Steph goes on. "We're trying. Nothing exciting to report except lots of sex, and I know you're all tired of hearing about that. But what's exciting is this. You, Kayla. You better start packing."

It feels like a million bolts of lightning strike me at once. Packing? To go follow Lachlan to Scotland. To live with him for three weeks. To see him play rugby, to watch him with Lionel, to help out with the rescues, to be in another country. To have endless sex for weeks. The prospect is so exciting, so frightening, I feel like I might shatter all across my living room.

"Come on." Steph slaps me on the shoulder. "We'll help while we wait for Linden to pick us up."

My room is a mess, and packing for an impromptu trip across the pond is extremely overwhelming. Is the weather the same as in San Francisco? Is the city casual or upscale? Should I bring any of my vibrators (the answer is yes)?

Luckily Steph and Nicola are here to keep me organized and on track, and every few minutes I feel like jumping up and down for joy. I'm doing this. I'm actually doing this—the wildest, craziest thing I have ever done. And even though the future is uncertain and I don't know what tomorrow will bring, I have this feeling that it's going to happen. That feeling is what scares me the most. Because shit. I know, *I know* if I go with Lachlan, I will fall head over heels in love with him. I'm already halfway there.

When Linden shows up at my door, it's time for them to go, and I'm pretty much fully packed. Our goodbyes are kind of sad because I won't be seeing them for three weeks.

"Say hi to my aunt and uncle," Linden says, pulling me into a hug that actually feels genuine for once.

"Do you think he'll be introducing me to the parents?" I ask.

Linden smiles dryly. "Kayla, if he's invited you to Edinburgh with him, then he's serious. So, yes. You'll meet his parents and everyone else—his brother Brigs too, I'm sure. Damn. I'm really fucking jealous." He looks at Steph. "Want to go to Scotland?"

She shakes her head. "I'm quite happy staying here. But you can live vicariously through Kayla."

He grimaces. "I'm not too sure about that if she's going to be shagging my cousin the entire time."

"You know me," I say with a shrug, and hug Steph and Nicola, saying my goodbyes. Nicola gets all teary-eyed and I have to smack her upside the head and tell her to stop that. Steph is a bit more subdued, more overjoyed for me than anything else.

Once they leave, I pick up my phone with shaking hands and call my mom.

"Hey sweetheart," she says to me. "How was your trip to Napa? Did you have any good wine?"

"All the wine was good," I tell her, leaning against the kitchen counter. For some reason my legs are shaking, and not in the way they were when Lachlan and I first had sex here. God, that was good fucking sex.

"And the hotel?" my mother asks, and I have to shake my head to get those sex thoughts out of my head. "Tell me about the hotel. I remember your father and I used to go to Napa all the time when he first came over from Iceland. We would always stay at the same place right in town. So pretty."

I inhale deeply. Talking about my father isn't making this easy on me. "The hotel was very nice. Had its own vineyard. We'll go one day. A mother-daughter trip."

"That would be very lovely. If I'm feeling better, of course."

Ugh. It's like I have one foot in Scotland already and I'm reminded of why my other foot needs to be here.

"Kayla?" she asks, and I realize I've been silent.

"Yeah." I clear my throat. "Listen, Mom. Something happened…and I need to talk to you about it. I need your advice."

"Oh? What is it?"

"Uh, well. You know Lachlan?"

"Yes, of course. How is he?"

"Good…good. Yeah, he's good. But he's leaving for Scotland tomorrow. Well actually, he was supposed to leave today but he missed his flight because of the traffic."

"Oh no."

"And, well, when he called the airline to book for tomorrow, he kind of booked me a seat on his flight."

There's a long pause. "What?"

"He wants me to go with him."

"And what did you say?" she asks anxiously.

"Well, obviously I told him I'd have to think about it. I've got work and I don't know if they'll let me take a vacation at the last minute. And then there's you."

"Me?"

"I don't feel good about leaving you, Mom."

"Oh, good heavens. Kayla. Be serious."

"I am serious. I know you're not doing well and—"

"I'm fine." She cuts me off and her voice sounds stronger than ever. "Don't you worry about me. You can't just turn down something amazing because you're worried about your mother. That's just nutty talk."

"I know…but—"

"No. No buts. Do you want to go to Scotland? Do you?"

My nerves buzz with energy. "Yes," I say thickly.

"Then go. Go into work and get your vacation, and if they don't let you, then figure out the soonest you can go. I've met Lachlan. You shouldn't let him get away."

"Okay."

"Kayla," she says seriously. "Don't second guess yourself. This is your track. Get on it and go there. Be with him. You never know what love will bring you."

But I don't love him, I want to say. But I don't say it. Because I know I will. It's inevitable and I have to stop fighting it.

"Okay. Are you sure you'll be fine? What if something happens to you?"

She laughs. "Nothing will happen to me. I promise. Please, Kayla. I just want to see you happy, and he makes you happy. Your father would want the same, I know he would. Take a chance and be with him."

I lick my lips. I tell my mother I will see her as soon as I get back, that I'll call her as soon as I get to Edinburgh, whenever that is. Then I phone Toshio and Paul, making both of them agree to see her while I'm gone. I don't have to remind Steph. I know she's good for it.

So I guess this is it.

This is it.

...

I barely sleep all night. I'm tossing and turning, holding onto my pillow and imagining I'm holding onto Lachlan. I cycle through a million feelings like I would cycle through dreams, and when my alarm goes off in the morning, I feel like the real dream is just beginning.

I don't even know how I get ready and hold it all together.

I'm brushing my teeth and then suddenly—

BOOM.

I might be brushing my teeth in Scotland.

I'm drinking coffee and—

BOOM.

I might be drinking coffee in Scotland.

I'm imagining Lachlan's face, open and inquisitive, wanting to hear beautiful things from me and—

BOOM.

I might have that for three wonderful weeks. The idea that I don't have to say goodbye yet, that in a few hours I could be in his strong, warm arms again makes me feel drunk at eight a.m.

But first I have to go to work. I don't seem to have many principles, but even I wouldn't just leave my job like that. I have to throw caution to the wind…cautiously.

I do a last minute tidy-up around the apartment, pretending that I might not see it for a while, then I cram my suitcase into my car and head off to work.

I'm nervous, of course. Scared of what I might do if Lucy says no. I'm scared that those principles I have might be thrown out the window, and then where would that leave me?

Well, at least I'd be on a plane to Scotland.

I arrive at work fifteen minutes early, hoping to catch Lucy before she gets distracted. When she sees me, eyeing my super casual skinny yoga pants, slip-on sneakers, and a t-shirt (you have to be comfy on the plane), she looks surprised, probably doubly so because I'm never early.

"Kayla," she says as I stride into her office. "What's, uh, going on?"

I give her a tight smile. "May I talk with you?"

She takes her hand off her mouse and gives me her full attention. "All right."

"I'll make this short and sweet, but please know that it's really important to me, and it's a great opportunity, and I don't get many like these. And I've worked here for a long time, and I've been pretty good. Great, sometimes. Anyway, I normally don't ask for something like this, so let's just take a moment to both close our eyes and appreciate that."

She raises her brow. "Okay. But I don't know what you're asking me yet."

I take a deep breath, straightening my shoulders. "I know it's last minute, but…can I take my vacation?"

"Sure," she says, looking back to her computer, probably finding my file. "When?"

"Today."

She pauses typing. "What?"

"Yeah. I have a flight at three p.m. to Edinburgh, Scotland."

"Today?" she repeats just as Candace comes into the office, glancing curiously at us.

"Yes."

"That's more than last minute."

"I know, I know," I say, giving her my most pleading look. "Please."

She rubs between her eyes. "Do you want your whole three weeks?"

"Yes, yes, if I can."

"You know we're getting into fall, things are going to get busier."

"I know, but Candace can handle it," I say. I can't believe I'm about to do this, but I stick my head into the office and yell at her. "Candace, if I go away for the next three weeks, do you think you can take over my account?"

She springs to her feet with overjoyed eyes and practically runs over to us. At this moment I know I'm handing my job, what I've worked for all these years, over to her, but it can't be helped. I know that no matter what, this will be worth it.

And thankfully, thanks to Candace's eagerness for the job, she's the one who sells Lucy in the end.

"Fine," Lucy says, giving me a wary smile. "You can go, Kayla."

"What?" I ask, my breath stilling in my chest.

"Go. Go to Scotland. But when you come back, be prepared to work a lot. And make sure you get some kind of data plan over there. We might need to get in touch for this and that."

She goes on about something else but I can't even hear her. I'm smiling, stupidly, my heart this bubble that refuses to burst. That bubble takes me out of the office and I'm floating, high on joy, all the way to the car. I float while I drive, the car and I hovering happily as I cruise down the highway toward the airport. Nick Cave's "Supernaturally" plays from the speakers, something I've been listening to ever since Lachlan said he admired him. Just another thing I've been doing, thinking, feeling, because of Lachlan.

And now, now I'm going off with him.

And so he is mine.

My Lachlan.

My beast.

My big, broken man.

I am coming for him. I am going to give myself to him in every way possible.

My body.

My heart.

My soul.

I'm going to get on that plane and stop being afraid for the first time in my life. I'm going to let him in and pray, hope, he'll let me in too.

I'm so happy I could almost cry. I laugh instead, slowly, the feeling sneaking up on me as realization hits.

I can't believe I'm fucking doing this.

This is so not me.

But maybe it's the me I've always wanted to be.

And when I get to the airport and see Lachlan standing by the Virgin Atlantic ticket counter, where he texted me to meet him this morning, it feels like the sun is just shining through. It illuminates everything, telling me that this is right.

That there never was any other way for us.

I'm meant to be with him.

I stop where I am and take him in like this, his wide back turned to me. I watch him, unseen. Like a ghost. And I have to pinch my fucking self, because even in his cargo pants, hiking boots, and faded black t-shirt, he's too handsome, too wonderful, too much of a man to exist on this earth.

I'm so incredibly lucky he asked me.

He asked *me*.

As if he can sense me, he looks over his shoulder.

Drinks me in.

His eyes crinkle—light, soulful—and he grins at me.

It's so beautiful.

He grins at me because now he knows, he *knows*, I'm his.

"I'm here," I tell him as I slowly walk toward him, my voice barely audible.

He nods. "You're here."

Part Two

Chapter Eighteen

LACHLAN

"Lachlan?"

Like a ray of light into a dark room, Kayla's sweet throaty voice permeates my dreams. I slowly open my eyes, forgetting where I am for a moment. You'd think that would be nearly impossible when you're on an airplane, but the black, sticky quality of my dreams, quickly fading from my consciousness, render me dazed.

When I nodded off, the lights in the cabin were dimmed. Now it's bright, and light shines in through the bottom of the window cover. Daylight.

I lift my head and let out a low grunt, my neck aching from the way I was sleeping. I look beside me to see Kayla smiling softly at me.

She came. I can't believe she came.

"Good morning," she says, rubbing underneath her eyes. "I wanted to let you keep sleeping, but the flight attendant was making it her mission to wake you up. We're landing in twenty minutes."

I try and swallow, my throat so unbearably dry, and shift in my seat to face her. "You're still here," I say, my voice hoarse. I reach out and touch her face, her skin feeling like heaven.

She twists her head to kiss my hand, her coy eyes never leaving mine. "Of course I'm still here. Where would I go? Another seat?"

"I thought it was all a dream," I tell her softly. "And when I woke up, I'd wake up alone."

"Nope," she says, and I brush the hair from her face, rubbing her silky strands between my fingers, as if I need further proof that she's real. "It's not a dream. It feels like it though, doesn't it? I mean…I can't believe this is happening."

I nod slowly. "Did you sleep at all?"

She shakes her head. "Way, way too excited to sleep. I watched a bunch of movies. And then I watched you sleep for a bit, like a total creeper."

I smile, finding that strangely endearing. "Well, I like it when you're a total creeper, love. You'll be doing a lot more of it when we land. I'm afraid I'll rarely let you out of my sight in Edinburgh."

"That should make my stalking much easier."

The flight attendant comes by and tells me to put my seat up and raise the window shade in that scolding way that they all have, and it's not long before the plane is descending. Kayla leans over me to look out the window, even though there's nothing to see but patches of green between grey clouds. I can't help but close my eyes, breathing her in. Even after being on a plane for thirteen hours, she smells incredible. It's not soap, it's not perfume, it's just her. Something that can't be bottled. Something that makes my blood rush to all the right places.

I shift in my seat, trying to ignore the stirrings of an erection. Kayla is so busy looking out the window that she doesn't seem to notice. Which is good because I know she'd go out of her way to make me even stiffer. As soon as I get her in my flat though, I'm not holding back.

My flat. It feels right insane that I'm back here and she's with me. I don't even know how to properly introduce her to Edinburgh when all I want to do is lock her in my bedroom for days.

But I'm returning to a life I left on pause. There are a lot of things to catch up on. I just hope I can integrate her into the process as smoothly as possible. Once I introduce her to Amara and Thierry, I think that will help. And, if I'm brave enough, my parents and my brother Brigs. Rugby and the shelter are going to take up a lot of my time, but I'll gladly have Kayla as involved in those as much as possible—as much as she wants to be, anyway.

The plane jostles, dropping some feet and lilting to the left. A few people in the cabin gasp while Kayla grasps my hand, holding on tight. I give her a squeeze back.

"It's just turbulence," I tell her with what I hope is a reassuring smile.

She nods, though her expression is pained. "I'm not a good flier," she admits, holding tighter as the plane bumps around again, my stomach flipping.

"It's okay," I say, returning her grip. I look out the window to see the ground getting closer, the perimeter fence of the airport quickly approaching. "We're almost there."

And while I can feel her pulse racing against my skin, I know she can feel mine doing the same. But it's not flying that I'm afraid of. It's what happens when we land. It's beyond complicated, feeling so happy that she's here, and at the same time, I'm nervous about what's going to happen next. It's been a very, very long time since I've let anyone into my life, and

I'm about to do that with her. I have no idea what will happen when she has to leave. Worse than that, I have no idea what will happen when and if she discovers the real me. Because I'm tempted to throw the doors wide open and let her in, to show her all the dark and ugliness inside me.

If she runs and never comes back, I'll have no one to blame but myself. I fear the blame, my habit for self-loathing, might be my ruin once again.

The wheels touch down with a screech and the plane blasts forward on the runway for a moment before the brakes come into full effect. Once the plane slows, Kayla loosens her grip, but it turns out mine is stronger.

"I didn't know you were afraid too," she says as I let go.

I only smile at her. I'd much rather trade one fear for another.

It doesn't take long before we've disembarked and are waiting by the luggage carousel. I laugh when I see Kayla's luggage come around on the belt, screaming hot pink.

"What?" she says defensively. "That way I know it's mine."

"Kind of defeats the purpose if it blinds everyone, love," I remind her, reaching over to pick up the suitcase. Then we head over to the oversized luggage area to pick up Emily in her dog crate.

She looks scared and the crate smells something awful, but there's still enough drugs in her system so she's subdued and not panicking. I whisper soothing words to her through the wire gate and she seems to understand that things will only get better.

Originally, when I was arriving alone, I was going to have my brother pick me up, but with Kayla here, and since we were on a different flight, a taxi is a much better option.

We get ourselves into a cab, and Kayla is already marveling at how different it all is.

"I forgot you drive on the other side of the road," she says. "And this cab is crazy with your flip-down seats and everything." She kicks the seat across from her for emphasis, which makes Emily raise her head.

"I think you need some sleep," I say gently, putting my arm around Kayla and holding her against me.

"Sleep is the last thing I need," she says, sliding her hand over my stomach. But five minutes into the drive and she's asleep against me.

My flat is in the Stockbridge area of the city, so it takes a while for us to get there, battling among the morning commuters. By the time we arrive at North East Circus Place I almost don't want to wake Kayla, she's sleeping so deeply.

"Hey," I whisper to her while the cabbie slides open the door and pulls our luggage out. "We're here." I remove my arm and shake her a bit. It takes forever for her to open her eyes, but when she does, she's frowning in confusion. Once she seems to recognize me, she smiles.

"Wow," she says, her voice croaking. "I was deep under."

"As soon as I get you inside, I'll put you to bed," I tell her, unbuckling our seatbelts and helping her out of the cab. She leans against it, unsteady, while I pay the driver, and stares up at the building.

"Is this all yours?" she asks.

I take her arm and pull her away from the cab before it drives away.

"Only the first floor," I tell her. "Although that's what you would call the second floor in America." She doesn't seem to hear me—she's just blinking in awe.

I guess it does look a lot different than what she's used to. The whole row of stone buildings take up a block as one attached complex. Though the false balconies and wrought iron details are similar to the ones I've seen in San Francisco, it's the stone that sets it apart. And the fact that it was built two hundred years ago.

"It used to be one big townhouse back in the day," I tell her, taking our luggage and Emily's crate to the white-painted door. I nod at the garden and apartments set below on either side of the bridge-like walkway. "A nice couple with a baby rents the bottom and ground floor flats. I have the first floor. The top of the building is owned by an older couple, but they're rarely in the city."

"So you can just own different floors of the same house?" she asks.

I nod. "It's common here."

She looks behind her at the green trees of the park across the street, their leaves shining with morning dew.

"That's Circus Place," I point out. "One of the places I take Lionel or whichever dog I'm fostering at the moment. A couple of blocks down is the Queen Street Gardens. The neighborhood is very dog friendly and it's close to Princes Street, the castle, and anywhere else you'll want to go in the city."

"Is Lionel upstairs?" she asks as I stick the key in the door.

I shake my head. "Amara has him. She'll bring him by later. But first, let's deal with you."

"Oh, I'm fine," she says, stifling a yawn.

I leave the luggage at the bottom of the stairs and take Emily's crate and Kayla up to the first floor.

"I can't believe this would have been one big house," she says, admiring the royal blue carpet on the stairs and the teak wood trim on the walls.

"People had a lot of money back in the day," I tell her, bringing her to the front door on the landing. "And people with money had servants to house. Probably a mistress and a bastard child too."

She raises her brows. "So where do you keep your mistress?"

"You're the mistress, the wife, the girlfriend, the everything." It takes me a moment to realize I've said something that was probably a bit much, but the prettiest pink flush spreads to her cheeks. I can't open the door fast enough.

I place Emily in the hall, closing the door behind us, and grab Kayla's hand. "Quick tour while I get Emily some water and food."

The hallway off the stairs has doors leading to the front and rear of the flat. At the rear is the kitchen and the dining room with shuttered floor to ceiling windows that look out onto the private walled garden that I share with the other residents.

"Holy shit." Kayla whirls around, taking it all in. "This room is huge. These are the highest ceilings I've ever seen."

I quickly duck into the kitchen to fill a dog dish with water, and I add a small amount of dog kibble into another bowl. Lionel usually eats raw food, but it's best to start Emily off with something easy.

I come back out to see Kayla roaming around the room, running her hand over the dark oak table in the middle, marveling at everything. Because the room is so large, I've got a computer workstation set up in the corner and a long white leather couch along one wall.

"It's more than enough space for me, that's for sure," I tell her, and she follows me back into the hall where I set the bowls down and open Emily's crate. I crouch down and try to coax her out, but she shrinks back.

"We'll give her some time," I tell Kayla and step away. "Come, let me show you the rest of the flat." I nod at a door across from us. "The bathroom is accessed through there. I wish it were an ensuite, but what can you do?"

I open the door to the drawing room, the natural morning light flooding from the windows. "This is the drawing room, which is just a living room in your American speak."

"Only it's not just *any* kind of room," Kayla says, impressed again as we walk in, eyeing the comfy couches, the rows of bookshelves, the high hanging chandelier. Funny how sometimes you have to look at something through someone else's eyes to really see it. I knew I'd lucked out when I bought the flat five years ago. I'd finally had enough money to invest it into something worthwhile (a few years after that I bought a tiny flat in London, but that I always lease out). From the hardwood floors to the decorative cornice work to the white marble fireplace, it's always been just a little too good for a bloke like me. But my adopted father, Donald, always taught me to invest, and buying this place was one of the smartest things I'd ever done.

I quickly show Kayla through the double doors to the bedroom, which is long and narrow but looks out onto the street and park. Lionel's dog bed is usually in the corner, though Amara has it now and he rarely uses it anyway, preferring to sleep in my bed, sneaking up in the middle of the night.

"Now," I tell her, taking her by the shoulders and sitting her down on the bed, "you rest. I'll get the luggage and get Emily settled."

"No, no," she says, attempting to stand up but I keep her pinned in place.

"I won't let you sleep all day," I assure her. "I don't want your jetlag to get worse. But a two-hour nap isn't going to kill you, all right, love?"

She puts her hands on either side of my face, and the softness of her touch causes my eyes to fall closed. "Come to bed with me," she says softly, leaning forward and brushing her lips against mine. My whole body relaxes—I hadn't noticed how tense I've been since we landed—and suddenly all I want, *need*, is to crawl onto the sheets beside her. Let her bring me into the here and now.

Somehow I find the will to pull away. "I will," I tell her, my voice low and rough from even the idea of sex. "Let me just deal with all of this first."

She nods and slowly lies back against the sheet, her dark hair spilling around the white pillow like some hypnotic inkblot. I'll have to avoid this room and the sight of her if I'm going to get any work done.

I close the doors and get started. It doesn't actually take too long to get everything in order, though I suspect it's because I'm racing through things. My pulse just won't slow down, and I feel positively charged with excitement and anxiety. I take the luggage up and stack it in the hall, putting away what I can, trying to make the place more homey. Then I text Amara and let her know to come by with Lionel whenever she can, probably in the afternoon since she'll be at the shelter for most of the day. After that, I clean up Emily's crate and take her outside, doing a loop around Circus Place until she seems a bit more comfortable with me again.

Though it's still quite early, a few neighbors are out and about. They raise their hand in greeting when they see me but they don't approach me, asking where I've been, why I haven't been around. They know enough by now that I'm not the talkative type, and while I've always been cordial, I don't care to get close to them. That said, you need your neighbors on your side when you own a pit bull or any kind of bully breed in the U.K. If you piss off the wrong person, they could try and get your dog taken away from you. It's happened before, and Lionel would be killed if it happened again.

Emily looks up at me with knowing eyes, as if she can sense what I'm thinking. I give her a quick smile. "S'all right," I tell her. "You're safe. And we'll find you someone worthy of Miss Emily, yeah?"

I go around the building, hooking left on Circus Lane to check on my Range Rover. The Freelander is still sitting there, looking no worse for wear other than rain spots on the black finish. If it wasn't for rugby practice tomorrow I'd pile Kayla and the dogs into it and take us far away from the city, out to Dunnottar Castle, maybe even to the start of the Highlands. But I'm already missing today's practice, the first of the season as it is.

The thought of it makes knots twist in my stomach. I know that I should be there, especially after missing so much at the end of last season, but I'm not about to leave Kayla to her own devices on her first day here. The poor girl is jet-lagged and in a city where she doesn't know anyone. Besides, I'm truly selfish. Even though we'd just landed, I can feel time sliding past us, and sooner rather than later, she'll be gone. I need to spend as much time with her as possible, like soaking up the sun after an everlasting winter.

With that thought, I head back into the flat. I let Emily off the leash and keep all the doors open so she can explore the flat in its entirety. She seems to take her time in each spot, and I know she can smell Lionel. Hopefully when he comes back later today, the two of them will hit it off okay. I've had some dogs not get along with him, but as long as I kept them in separate parts of the house, we've been able to make it work.

While she's busy sniffing the couch, I go into the bedroom, shutting myself inside.

The sight of Kayla on my bed is a hit to the gut. I have to just stand there and take her in. She's taken off her shoes, socks, and jeans, and is just lying there on her back in a white t-shirt and a pair of knickers. Lacey. Hot pink.

Fucking hell.

The sun is streaming in through the window, bathing her skin in a diffused glow, and her face is absolutely gorgeous. Peaceful and vibrant all at the same time. She's unreal, and just staring at her in my own bloody bed makes me feel crazy. She moves something deep inside of me, something I don't think I can ever move back.

"Kayla," I whisper to her, and she stirs slightly, letting out a soft moan from her lips that makes me unbelievably hard. I want to bring out deeper, hungrier noises from her. I want to make her come in my home. I've never brought a woman here before; in the past we had always gone to her place.

I'm not normally such a wishful thinker, but still, I take off my clothes, casually discarding them on the floor and hope that Kayla is up for some jetlagged sex.

I slowly climb onto the bed, the mattress moving beneath my weight. She stirs again as I straddle her, my thighs on either side of hers, my erection thick and hard, bobbing above her stomach. I lean down, bracketing her shoulders between my arms, and slowly run my lips down her forehead, over her nose, until I place them flush on her mouth.

"Mmm," she says softly. "Where am I?"

"With me," I murmur, nibbling on her bottom lip before leaving a trail of kisses from the corner of her mouth to her jaw.

She raises her arms, lacing her fingers behind my neck. "In Scotland?" she asks, her voice drowsy.

"Very much so," I tell her, pressing myself down against her skin.

She lets out a soft gasp. "Are you naked?"

"Aye." I suck the soft skin on her neck, my head swimming from her raw taste. "And very, very hard."

"Then I'm glad you woke me up," she coos, reaching down between us and stroking the tip of my cock. I don't even have to raise my head to know she's got a devilish twist to her lips.

A moan falls out of my mouth as her fingers get a better grip, the weight of my body against hers adding crucial pressure. I close my eyes, succumbing to the feeling as I work my mouth down her milky white neck, and start rocking my body gently against hers. The friction on her stomach is incredible, my precum adding just enough slickness.

Before I can get as carried away as a teenager, I pull back and kiss and suck my way down her body. From her shoulder, across to the soft hollow of her throat, down between her breasts, my hand cupping them perfectly, one at a time. I love teasing around her nipples, love how she always arches her back, pushing her breasts up, so ravenous for my lips, for my touch. I like to prolong it as long as possible, doing long, circular laps with my tongue and then blowing lightly. I watch her skin erupt in shivers, her nipple becoming harder, pinker, and it's torture not to put it between my teeth and give it a sharp tug.

"Oh god," Kayla whimpers, her hands running through my hair and tugging on the ends.

"Tell me what you want, love," I tell her, my voice rough with lust. "Tell me what you want and I'll give you what I have."

She grabs my head and places my lips on her nipple. "There. Give me pain."

I smile at how bossy she always is and do as she wishes, nipping the hardened end and giving it a long, hard suck into my mouth. She yelps, then settles into a low, throaty groan, her vibrations rattling me to my very bones. The rigid ache of my cock is almost unbearable now, and all my thoughts are being stolen, directed to my very need to be inside of her.

With borderline desperation, I quickly push her panties to the side. She's so hot and slick beneath the satin. I grab the base of my cock and straighten up, gripping her hips. Sitting back on my knees, I thrust into her, barely able to control myself.

She feels so good. Always so good. A silky, tight fist that won't let go.

She cries out, her eyes widening, but I can't help it. There's no time to do this gently. There is a fire raging inside me and she's the only way out of the flames.

I take a firm grip of her thighs, my hands sinking into her soft, smooth flesh, and hold her legs back while I pull out then push myself in again. She's watching my cock slide in and out of her, and I'm watching too, crazed by the raw, primal sight of our bodies giving each other pleasure and how we fit so perfectly. The giant, quiet man and the wild, tiny girl. Who would have thought that this moment, this us, could have ever happened?

"Please don't stop," she says. Her voice is raspy, quiet, and so disarmingly beautiful when I'm turning her on. I could do this until my dying day, just this endless give and take, this exquisite pleasure I get from seeing her features soften, her body respond to me like she's lucid in a dream. She wants me, all of me, always, and when I give her what I have, what I am, she only wants more.

I don't stop, but I need to change it up if I want to keep going.

"Lift up, love," I whisper to her, briefly pulling out and putting my hand beneath her left cheek, rolling her until she's on her side. I grab her leg, admiring the way her thigh muscles stand out and the flexibility in her joints as she limberly straightens her leg against my body. With my grip on her thigh, I slowly push myself in and out of her, sliding in even deeper than before. I'm hitting a sweet spot, and her mouth is falling open while her eyes pinch closed. She's soft and aimless as my thrusts become quicker, and I'm reveling in the look of her beneath me.

I slip my hand down to her clit, so swollen, pink, and wet, and begging for my touch. Her body tenses and she lets out a shaking breath as I rub my finger around in taunting, teasing circles, light as air.

She begins to buck into me, wanting more pressure, wanting so badly to come on my dick and my hand. I give in because I'm bloody delirious for her pleasure and because my own thrusts are becoming sharper, quicker, my hips slamming into her at a rate that will make me expire sooner than later.

I can tell she's close to coming. Her body is shaky with strain, her breaths short and quick. She gets this thing where her lower lip starts to tremble and she has to bite it, almost to the point of bleeding. I like to think it's because she's so overwhelmed and trying hard not to let go.

"Over," I tell her, pulling out again and flipping her over on her stomach. "Hips up." I scoop her arms underneath her stomach and pull her up until her firm, perky little ass is right in front of me. I wrap my hand around her waist, loving the sight of how small she looks against me, and position myself.

"This is one hell of a way to go through jet lag," she says softly, her head down and her dark hair spilling forward over her face. I don't want to let her hide. I reach forward and make a fist in her hair, pulling it back so her neck is arched, her face exposed.

"It's the only cure," I tell her, tugging back sharply.

She cries out in a breathy burst of pain and then moans. "Your cock is the cure for everything."

With one hand pulling on her hair, I lean forward until my damp chest is pressed against her back, my dick so deep inside that we both suck in our breath. I slide one hand over her throat. I tighten my hold, choking her lightly, and put my lips to her ear. "How do I feel?" I whisper, licking up the rim.

Shivers erupt beneath me and I feel her throat moving against the palm of my hand. "Heaven sent," she manages to say. "You feel heaven sent." She swallows and I let up the pressure. "Now fuck me. Fuck me and make me come."

I moan, never tiring of how direct she is, addicted to her own feverish hunger. I circle my hips, my fingers tightening around her neck and hair while my chest slides up and down against her skin. In turn she thrusts her arse back at me, and all thought and reason and sense of self are obscured by her satiny feel, the tight clench around my cock that threatens to take me to another world.

I am but an animal. I piston myself into her, over and over again, the headboard slamming against the wall. I can almost see us from above, me fucking her raw, deep from behind, my muscles flexing as I push in, fast, hard, our skin blistering from such wild need. She's coming, and her pulse is racing into my palm, wild and delicate. The frenzied, high-pitched cries like she's being obliterated in the most perverse way completely do me in.

I'm clutching her throat, her hair, and I'm coming. It's like a sunrise deep inside. It shines right through you and leaves you hot, dizzy, and spent.

Jesus. I don't even know where I am.

I collapse against her, gasping for breath, burying my face in hair that I already feel holds all my whispered words.

Fuck. She holds every fucking part of me in that little body and big red heart of hers.

I can't swallow properly and my breath is slow to return. There's always a moment of clarity after you come, and this one holds an earth-shattering truth.

This woman will own me in the end.

And I'm not sure if I'll own enough of her to make her stay.

"Fuck," she says breathlessly after a minute or two of our bodies being fused together, the sweat cooling between us.

"What?" I manage to ask, ever hopeful that she's going to give me some indication of how she feels about me.

Tell me that you don't ever want to leave.

Tell me that you'll stay long enough to let me learn everything there is to know about you.

Tell me that you're mine.

I'm nearly sick with how needy I sound to myself and I have to dig deep and push it away. Why can't I just be satisfied that she's here at all? If it weren't for the balls I had to ask her to come in the first place, we would already be apart and moving on with our lives separately. That was what was supposed to happen.

But it didn't. And if she's greedy, I'm greedier. I'll never get enough of her.

"You sure know how to welcome me into your home," she says, turning her head to look at me, her eyes lazy with satisfaction.

"You know it's the least I can do," I tell her. I kiss the back of her neck, tasting her skin. Though I had fallen asleep on the plane, it wasn't the best sleep. I'm so tempted to keep lying here with her, though I know that both of us will be asleep in no time, which will then fuck up the day I have planned for tomorrow.

Somehow I get both of us out of bed and into the shower. I've still got just a towel wrapped around my waist when the buzzer goes off. It's Amara.

"Come on up," I tell her. Kayla is staring at me nervously in just stretch pants and a tank top. She's not wearing makeup, and her hair is wet and down around her shoulders.

"She's already here?" she squeaks. "I'm not even properly dressed."

I give her a soothing look. "Neither am I. She's bringing Lionel and she's an old friend. Believe me, you look fine."

"Yeah but you look fucking hot in a towel."

"Listen," I tell her, not exactly proud of this. "I've had my shirt off around her before." Her eyes widen and I quickly add, "Not in that way. But it comes with rugby, all right?"

She nods just as the knock comes at the door.

I open it and barely notice Amara standing on the other side of the door. All I can see is Lionel, jumping up on me, absolutely losing his mind with delight.

"Hey, mate!" I cry out, grabbing him and bringing him up to my level. He's wriggling so fast that he's nearly impossible to grip, like holding onto a wet seal.

I've never been away from Lionel this long and some sorry part of me was afraid he wouldn't remember me when I came back, but at least I know it's not true. He's already dropped a gallon of drool on me in terms of licks and kisses.

Kayla clears her throat from beside me and I'm brought back to reality.

"Kayla, this is Lionel," I tell her, trying to push his face away from mine.

"Yeah, I get that. How about introducing me to the human?" she says smartly.

Right. That.

I give them both a chagrined smile and set Lionel on the floor. He's about to jump up again when he spots Emily poking her head around the corner and immediately sets out after her.

"Sorry, sorry, my manners," I say, knowing Amara totally understands. She's used to it. "Kayla, this is my mate Amara. She works for me at the shelter. I'd be nowhere without her. Amara, this is Kayla. She's..." And suddenly I draw a blank because I don't know what she is. We haven't really discussed anything within the terms of us yet.

"I'm staying with Lachlan," Kayla finishes smoothly, shaking Amara's hand. I eye Kayla carefully, wondering if she's going to give Amara the side-eye. I won't be surprised, nor will I be all that upset if she has a jealous streak, but even though Amara is striking with her Roman nose, fiery red hair, and freckles, Kayla is nothing but warm and genuine.

"Nice to meet you," Amara says, looking briefly at me. Her face is composed, but I can stell she's confused and shocked. I hadn't exactly mentioned Kayla and in no way told Amara that a girl would be coming back with me. Luckily she takes it all in stride.

"So how was he, any trouble?" I ask, steering the conversation over.

"He really hates the muzzle," she says, shrugging her shoulders. "At least when I put it on him."

Kayla jumps back a bit, looking around for Lionel who is trotting back and forth across the drawing room, sniffing Emily. "He needs a muzzle?" she asks.

I shake my head, feeling a burst of anger flare up. "No. He doesn't need one. He's never bitten anyone, nor would he without a muzzle. But the U.K. sees pit bulls as an inferior breed. A bad one. A banned one. It's tricky to own one—you have to prove first that yours isn't dangerous, and even then, they all have to wear a muzzle. Even if they are old and have never hurt a soul. Sometimes I walk Lionel around here without one, but the neighbors know me. In other places though, you can't be too sure who will see you."

"That's fucking stupid," Kayla says, reaching for the hand that I've balled into a fist. She uncurls it and lets her fingers slip inside. My heartbeat slows.

"It is fucking stupid," Amara says, nodding and angrily shoving a piece of hair behind her ear. "The law was introduced in the seventies when dog fighting was a problem. It needs to be bloody updated, but the government is a bunch of ignorant cunts. We're working on it though, trying to educate that it's the people who do that kind of shite that should be banned, not the breed."

I exhale harshly through my nose. "Let's not discuss this too much today. I need to stay in good spirits," I tell them honestly.

Kayla gives my hand a squeeze and nods. She looks to Amara. "What are you doing now? Did you want to go out for a late lunch or dinner with us?"

We hadn't even discussed a late lunch, so the fact that Kayla is already opening up to Amara and inviting her in warms my heart like a tonic.

"Thanks," Amara says. "I'm good though. Going to head back to work. Maybe tomorrow, Lachlan. You can bring her by and show her what we do."

"Aye," I agree. "Before practice. That would be perfect."

She waves goodbye and hurries off. I know that she doesn't have to go back to work until later, so I get the impression that she's trying to give us some alone time. I guess I am in just a towel.

I peer down at Kayla. "So about that lunch," I say. "What other plans do you have in store for us?"

She gives me a grin and a saucy tilt to her head. "Not telling," she says. "I like to keep you on your toes."

She sashays her way into the drawing room and I watch her go.

Though she's trying to look seductive, shaking that delectable peach-shaped bottom of hers, it only lasts about two seconds before Lionel comes bounding out of nowhere, jumping up on her legs, and enveloping her in a flurry of kisses.

She yelps, and if she was ever fearful, it's faded into laughter. Lionel is merciless in his love and need for affection, and Kayla shrieks playfully as he chases her around the room, tongue hanging out if his mouth, wanting nothing from her but attention.

I know how you feel, old friend, I think to myself before following suit and joining the chase.

Chapter Nineteen

KAYLA

I'm dreaming. I'm drowning. Everything is wet.

My face is wet.

Smelly.

Dog breath.

I flinch, fully coming awake just in time to see a long pink tongue slide over my face, leaving a trail of drool behind.

"Oy, Lionel," Lachlan mumbles, throwing his arm out and pulling the dog away from my face and back in between us. "Have some manners."

I slowly sit up, running my hand over my cheek and wiping the dog drool off of me. I look down at Lachlan who's holding Lionel in a hug and grinning sheepishly up at me.

"Sorry about that," he says. "He likes to wake you up with kisses."

I raise my brow, totally fucking charmed by the sight of Lachlan and his tattoos and muscles, holding the sweetest, drooling dog against him, nestled in the white sheets. "I'm not complaining, but I would rather you wake me up with kisses instead."

He grins at me, looking absolutely adorable, a lock of bed-mussed hair flopping over his forehead. "That can be arranged."

I already arranged it last night. Though somehow I was able to make it through the day and most of the evening, when we turned in at eleven o'clock after taking Emily and Lionel for their last walk around the quaint neighborhood, I was absolutely exhausted. Despite that, I woke up at three a.m., wide-eyed and ready to go. It probably hadn't been such a good idea to take that nap, but I don't regret the sex it led to after. And, of course, when it's the middle of the night and you have a Scottish sex god in bed with you, you wake him up with a blow job.

Thankfully Lionel wasn't in bed with us at the time. He must have snuck in when we were both sated and passed out.

Emily barks from the other room, and that steals Lionel's full attention. His ears perk up and his forehead wrinkles in the exact same way that his master's often does, and he jumps off the bed, burning it into the living room.

"You can never sleep in with dogs," Lachlan says, his voice still sleepy in that very sexy way of his. "Which was fine until you came into the picture. Now I think lying in bed with you in the mornings is the best part of the day."

"Can't argue with that," I say softly. I take the opportunity to lie back down, pulling the soft covers over me and settling into my favorite spot, the nook between his arm and his side. I place my fingers on his broad chest, trailing them over his tattoos. I feel like I'll forever be marveling at what a perfect specimen of a man he is. Every second that ticks past, I'm looking at him differently. Deeper. And now that I'm here, with him in his home, I don't think there's any hope for me.

Yesterday, when I woke up from my jet-lagged nap and found him crawling on top of me with that look in his eyes that wasn't just about lust but something more profound, more real, what followed went beyond any fuck I've had before. It was raw and I was ravaged. I could feel his urgency with every touch of his hands, feel his heart beating like a wild beast. There was breathtaking honesty in the way he stared at me, as if I were gold dust, precious and able to blow away at a moment's notice.

We made love. There was no other word for it, and while it used to make me cringe and laugh when other people used that term so casually, so cheesily, I finally got it. I understood it. It was lust and passion and burning desire for each other's bodies, for the pleasure, but it was also feverish want for the person inside.

I didn't just want Lachlan's muscles, his lips, his endless skills beneath the sheets. I wanted him, every part of him. The dark bits that were hidden away and only hinted at by tattoos. I desired all of him, like a dying man desires one more breath.

I'd wanted to bring Lachlan to his knees, and while I could feel him yearning and yielding to me, I was going to my knees first. I had no idea how I was going to pick myself up in three weeks. No idea at all.

"What are you thinking about?" he whispers into the top of my head, his fingers playing with my hair.

That you're the first for everything, I think to myself. "Nothing," I say.

"Ah," he says. "I see."

"I guess I'm just trying to get my head on straight."

He squeezes his arm against me. I love it when he does that. I feel absolutely protected.

"If you're anything like me, it's going to take you a few days to adjust to the new time zone. I remember when I first traveled abroad to Australia for the Rugby World Cup, I was an absolute wreck. Couldn't even tie my own laces. No wonder we lost."

I smile against him, then turn it into a kiss, my lips brushing the side of his chest. "I have a hard time believing you could lose at anything."

He grunts. "Then I shant ruin the pedestal you've placed me on, darling."

I close my eyes and listen to his heartbeat, his rhythmic stroking of my hair. I'm almost falling asleep again, dreams coming at me in dark flashes, wanting to bring me under, when his alarm goes off.

"Can't we ignore it?" I mutter.

"We can ignore the alarm," he says. He adjusts himself just as Lionel jumps on the bed, shuffling his way between us. "But we can't ignore him."

"I just want to sleep," I say, seconds before I get a paw to the face.

"Aye," he says, "but we have a big day."

My tired brain jogs over the plans we've made. Or plans that he has made for me. He has rugby practice at two, and he wanted to bring me to the shelter beforehand and introduce me to the people that work there. I guess he feels bad about leaving me in the apartment with the dogs all day, though I honestly wouldn't mind. Lionel is just a big suck and Emily is warming up to me more and more.

Plus Lachlan's apartment is absolutely stunning. I never pegged him as someone who would live in such a gorgeous, airy, historical place, but even after glancing out the front window and gazing at all the other stone houses on the street, it's obvious everyone here lives somewhat like this. It's kind of like living in a sexier episode of *Downton Abbey*.

But Amara, who I met briefly yesterday, seems nice enough, albeit a little quiet, and I know Lachlan wants me to feel important and involved. The last thing I want is for him to worry.

Somehow the two of us manage to remove ourselves from bed. Lionel is running around the living room like a crazed beast, mouth open in a permanent, gummy smile. While Lachlan slips on running shoes, loose black drawstring pants, a white t-shirt, and a baseball cap, to take Lionel and Emily out for a quick walk, I putter around his sparse, elegant kitchen trying to figure out how to make a pot of coffee. I find a cupboard overflowing with stashes of tea, a small bag of coffee, and finally, a French press.

I sigh loudly in relief, putting the kettle on and taking a moment to take it all in. There's usually so much you can tell about a person judging by where they live, but Lachlan's apartment doesn't give me much. He told me he's been living here for about five years now, but to be honest, it's not that much different in terms of personal touches than the short-term rental he had in San Francisco. There's some art on the walls, vintage concert posters framed extravagantly in the living room, and subdued modern art in the dining room, but none of that really seems to reflect his personality. The same goes for his furniture. While it's all very nice, the only thing that seems to have any reflection of him is the wood dining table, with its knots and grains and imperfections.

The bookshelves hold mainly hardcover non-fiction books ranging from memoirs to travel, but there are just a few items and photos held on the shelves and on top of the fireplace mantel. The photos are of him and Edinburgh Rugby, one of him and Lionel, and then one of him and, who I'm guessing are his adopted parents after a game, his hair matted, barely smiling in his uniform. If this was my house, I would have my shit cluttered all over the place. All you need to do is walk inside, look around, and you immediately know that Kayla Moore lives there.

If I'd met Lachlan on the street, and by some good fortune strolled on home with him here, I'm not sure I could glean anything from his home that I didn't already know. That said, his flat does have a nice feel to it, just as he does. I'm sure over time it will become more and more comfortable. I'll adapt to it and it will adapt to me.

When he comes back from his walk, I hear him in the hallway talking to the dogs in a happy, playful tone. The coffee is ready, so I lean against the counter, slowly sipping from the cup while he walks into the kitchen.

"Wow," he says when he sees me, stopping by the door to look me up and down, shaking his head slightly.

"What?" I ask, wanting to know why he's staring at me with such awe.

He runs his hand over his chin. "You. Here. In my kitchen. In nothing but your knickers."

I raise my coffee cup. "And with coffee."

"Dream woman, that's what you are," he says, sauntering over to me with that ever present swagger. While he may be wowed by the sight of me, I'm equally wowed by him, particularly by the way his drawstring pants hang so low on his waist, showing that perfect V and giving me one hell of a dick imprint. I'm glad I can continue to wow him in every way possible.

He comes over, bracketing me in between his large hands, his body pressed up against mine. He gazes down at me through his lashes, eyes roaming my face, the smallest smirk on his lips. "I think I can get used to this," he says, voice low and husky and reaching inside me. My spine liquefies at the sound of it, my skin dancing with anticipation because I know, I *know*, he's going to touch me and my body is in constant need.

"What time do we have to head on out?" I ask him, closing my eyes as he leans down and kisses my neck.

He groans, sending shivers through me. "Where do I have to go again?"

"To practice," I remind him. "And you're taking me somewhere first. To your work. Though I suppose we could do that another day," I add hopefully.

He sighs. "No." He pulls back and peers at my face. "I wish, but if I don't go back, I'll be in big trouble."

He doesn't have to tell me. I know rugby is his career, and I know how important it is to him. The last thing I want is for him to feel guilty about it.

I decide to lighten the mood. I run my hands down his taut waist and gaze up at him sweetly. "What happens when you get in big trouble? Do the other boys pull down your shorts and give you a spanking?"

He raises his brow. "Filthy, filthy creature," he murmurs.

I run my thumb under the waistband of his pants, feeling his warm, soft skin. "Well, don't spoil my fantasy now."

"Right. Well, yes, of course we pull down each other's shorts and take turns beating each other with sticks. Sometimes we rub butter all over each other and have one big tackle." He pauses. "Actually, that happened once, but I think we all had a bit too much to drink. It's not easy to tackle a naked, oily man. Was good practice though."

I study him, unable to figure out if he's serious or not. "Rugby is a very weird sport."

He reaches around me for the mug I set out for him. "You'll come to practice sooner or later and see for yourself."

"I can do that?" I ask, suddenly excited at the prospect of seeing him in action. I step to the side to let him pour the coffee.

"If you'd like," he says. "I can't say whether I'd be playing or at my full capacity, but I'll arrange it. Hopefully on a good day. I don't want you to start thinking I'm not the player you thought I was."

"Oh, I never thought you were a player," I tease him. "Gay, maybe."

There's just the slightest roll of his eyes. "Right, well that rubbing butter over our naked bodies didn't really help now, did it?" He takes a sip of his coffee and closes his eyes. "By the way, love, this is bloody good. If you can make me coffee every morning for the rest of my life, I will die a happy man."

There's brevity in his eyes, but his words still hit me hard. God, could that even be possible? My thoughts trip and suddenly I'm imagining myself right here, in this kitchen, weeks from now, months from now, years from now. What would that be like? To be with someone like him for that long? Contrary to how I used to think, at least with Kyle, that thought doesn't scare me anymore. Instead, it makes my heart warm, skipping a beat.

"Only thing is," he continues, as if he hasn't just put the most wonderful imagery in the world inside my head, "I wish you could actually be here to see me in action. Our first game starts the week you leave, and I highly doubt I'll be put on the pitch."

My heart may have been skipping a beat but now it's sinking.

I swallow hard and grip the edge of his shirt. "New rule. Neither of us are to mention the fact that I'm leaving in three weeks."

His eyes narrow and he nods. "All right. That's fair. What about when you book your flight back?"

"Leave that to me," I tell him, knowing he's already offered to pay for my return. "I'll take care of it when I do."

"Or maybe you could not, and just stay here indefinitely," he says, focused on his coffee cup until he briefly looks up at me. He shrugs one shoulder. "It might be an option."

This man is tempting me at every turn. First it was coming here, now it's the idea of never leaving.

"We both know I can't do that," I tell him. Then I playfully punch his rock hard shoulder. "And hey, what did I say about that? We don't mention it, okay? Let's just…enjoy this."

"For as long as we can?" he says, and damn if I don't see sorrow in the way he scrunches up his brow.

"For as long as we can."

…

A couple of hours later, after a quick breakfast of sausage and eggs, courtesy of Lachlan (and no, that's not an innuendo), we leave the dogs behind and pile into his car. I've never been inside a Range Rover before, but damn if it's not a perfect car for him—big, tough, and rugged. But instead of taking it out into the wilderness, we cruise through the busy city streets, heading to his organization which is across town.

I can't help but ogle out the window at everything we pass. The buildings are so different, so old, so charming and full of character you can't duplicate. They bleed history, and I find myself getting antsy over exploring the city. Already it feels like there's not enough time to do everything, and even though I want to soak up as much Lachlan as I can, I want to take in as much of Edinburgh as possible. It's probably because of my present company, but it already feels like the city is leaving a stamp on my heart.

We pull up to a stone building near what seems like the outskirts of downtown. I get out of the car, remembering to look right before I'm run over by a car and stare up at the sign above the dark wood door.

"Ruff Love Animal Shelter?" I repeat. I look at him in awe. "That is absolutely adorable."

"Aye. It is. People were surprised how saccharine it was, considering it came from me. But most of these animals can use a sweet bit of PR. Having people view them as cute and adorable is what helps get them adopted."

Agh. Once again, this man has found another way to sweep me off my feet. I look down the building, back up at the sign, then over to him, standing there on the street in black boots, black jeans, and a grey t-shirt, looking about as rough and rowdy as they come, and yet from the goodness of his heart he's managed to do all of this.

"Shall we?" he asks, holding out his arm.

I eagerly latch on to it and let him lead me inside.

It's not as chaotic as I would have thought. There's a reception area where I spot Amara on the phone, giving us a quick wave, then a small row of prison-like cells. I know Lachlan is doing a wonderful thing, but I can't help but cringe painfully, knowing how many animals spend their lives here.

"It's all right," he whispers to me, grabbing my hand and squeezing hard. "The dogs here are the dogs with a fighting chance. Most of them get adopted and go on to live full and happy lives."

He takes me down the aisle, and even though my heart is breaking a little bit at the sight, he points out the good things the dogs have going for them. For one, they all get dog beds and toys in their kennel so they don't have to sleep on concrete. They have more room than most shelter dogs do and the ones that are social can easily share with another. He tells me that thanks to their volunteers, and Amara, all the dogs are walked three times a day, four times for the high energy, and one of those walks is an hour long excursion to a nearby park. Sometimes they go in packs, sometimes they go alone where training is implemented.

We stop by an older pit bull named Jo, who loves to give sloppy kisses through the bars. She's been there the longest because a lot of people don't like to adopt senior dogs, even though she's in good health and is easy going. He's hopeful that she'll be adopted soon.

"Sometimes I sneak her home," he admits to me, while Jo stares adoringly up at him, tail swishing on the floor. "She's spent a lot of weekends with me and Lionel, watching TV."

"So why don't you adopt her?" I ask him.

"If she doesn't go at some point, I will do just that," he says. "But the point of all this is to share the love. If someone adopts her and then discovers what a joy she is as a banned breed and as a senior dog, the odds of them doing it again, or at least encouraging others to do so, is very high. We have repeat customers here, you know, who adopt one dog and then realize how easy it is to make a difference. So they adopt another. Or they donate." He pulls a dog treat out of his pocket and gives it to Jo, smiling at her as she happily eats. "Once people realize how easy it is to make a difference, they're forever changed."

He takes me past the rest of the dogs and I have a hard time keeping up with their names, though I'm falling in love with their beautiful faces. One dog, steel grey with a wide white chest, cowers in the corner until Lachlan crouches near the bars, casting the occasional glance his way. He speaks in low, furtive tones until, eventually, the dog comes over. He shies away when Lachlan reaches out to put a treat through the bars, but then hunger gets the best of him and he quickly gobbles it up.

"That's Bubsy," he says. "I found him, abused, beaten, hanging by a thread in a London alley. Someone had bashed his head in, his fur halfway gone from who knows what. I didn't think he'd make it, but he pulled through. He's terrified of people, obviously. The fuckers who did this to him ruined his trust in humans. And they say he's a dangerous dog, just because of his breed. It's those kind of people who should be banned, not the breed. People are cruel, so sick, far worse than any animal." He sighs angrily, running his hand over his face. "To be honest, we didn't think Bubsy would ever be integrated or adopted. We've had a few dogs that we've put our bloody hearts into and just..." He rubs his lips together, shaking his head. "It's a fucking shame. But Bubsy is getting better, with time. With the right owner, someone patient and kind and strong, he'll have a chance."

My eyes are hot with tears that I'm managing to hold back. "I don't know how you do it," I tell him. "How can you be around all of this, all the time, and not be fucking gutted?"

He tilts his head, eyes wide in consideration. "To be honest, I am fucking gutted most of the time. But I understand these dogs. I know what it's like to be cast aside, to feel unwanted, to believe you have no one to fight for you. I've been there. Time and time again. It hurts like hell, but if I don't fight for them, who will?"

I stare into his eyes, completely enveloped by everything he is, and…*shit*.

This man.

I am so fucking in love with this man.

Then I'm hit with an aftershock, because holy shit.

Did I just admit that to myself? Did I just think that?

I did.

Luckily he's looking back at Bubsy, that wonderful, reckless kind of hope in his eyes, another look that does me in, while I'm feeling lightheaded, breathless, unruly with the realization of my feelings.

Maybe it's just that he's this manly man standing in front of you, talking about how much he loves rescuing dogs, I think.

But of course it's that. It's many things. It's everything.

And I'm completely head over heels in love with him.

His eyes flit to me and he frowns slightly. "There is almost always a happily ever after," he says, and I have to blink at him to get back on track and understand what he means. "And unless we take the risk and bring them in, even if failure will break our bloody hearts, it's worth it."

Oh god, please don't let him be talking in a metaphor for our own hearts.

He smiles at me and I have to look away because I can't stand to lose my footing.

"Want to take a few for a walk? I'll get Amara to join us."

I nod, my tongue feeling thick, my brain stupid. Meanwhile my heart is fucking breakdancing in my chest because it's finally discovered what love is.

The most wonderful, most terrifying feeling that life has ever had to offer.

I'm kind of in a daze when we go and get Amara. I hope I'm speaking to her correctly and making sense, because all I can really think about is Lachlan and love and that dire hope that maybe, somehow, love is something that you can turn off like a switch. Maybe this is just all lust wrapped up in a very sexy, soulful tatted bow. Maybe this is just adrenaline, the thrill of being overseas for the first time, the excitement of taking risks. Maybe it's a lot of things.

But it doesn't stop that feeling.

It's a feeling you can't even question.

Because it's real, and it's beating in a rhythm you never knew you could dance to, and it's there. It is so fucking there and present and taking up every cell in my body.

I have to talk to Steph and Nicola. I have to get their advice. Coming to Scotland for hot passionate sex is one thing, but coming here and realizing you're in love, on day one, is something else. It's dangerous and futile and one more risk I have to take.

I can't even snap out of it, so lost in my own thoughts, until Lachlan realizes he should head off to practice sooner rather than later. He tells me that Amara will take care of me and drop me off at his flat later. I have his spare key in my purse, just in case I'm home before him.

"See you later, love," he says, pulling me to him, oh so gently, and leaving a lingering kiss on my lips.

I sigh against his mouth, my chest fluttering. "Okay," I say breathlessly. "Good luck."

He nods and leaves the shelter, and I'm just standing there like a fucking puddle of Kayla goo.

"So, who do you want?" Amara asks me, handing me a leash.

I gingerly take one in my hands, but have to shake my head to knock some sense into me. "Um, what?"

She smiles at me. She has a giant Madonna-sized gap between her front teeth that gives her this strangely sexy edge. "The dogs," she says. "Which dog do you want to walk?"

"Oh," I say. "Whichever one needs it most."

"How about whatever dog is easier? Jo it is," she says, heading over to Jo's cage and opening the door. She waddles over to me, fat belly swinging from side to side, and immediately stares up at me like I'm going to take her home and never let her go. Even black hearts don't stand a chance here.

"She's Lachlan's favorite," Amara says, snapping the leash on Jo and giving me a knowing look. "Though I think you might be Lachlan's favorite too."

I look away and hope that the heat on my cheeks isn't translating into blushing.

"Hey," Amara says, going over to another cage. "You're all right, yeah? It's good. I've never seen him this way around anyone before. Not that there have been any anyones if you know what I mean."

As she brings two dogs out of a communal cage, I give her a look. "Let me guess, you're going to warn me about how brooding and difficult and quiet he is. Believe me, I know. I heard that same shit from his cousins."

"Oh, well that's a given," she says lightly. "But I wouldn't say he's necessarily brooding—he's just a thinker. And he's not difficult either, he's just honest and he knows what he'll do and what he won't do. Personally, I've always found something very noble about Lachlan, like a breed of man that doesn't really exist anymore. I'm glad, really, to see him with someone that makes him light up. It's about time. You meet his parents yet?"

I shake my head.

"I'm sure you will," she says as we head out of the shelter. She stops and locks the door while the dogs all start pulling against their leashes in excitement. "They're lovely people. They'll just love you and the fact that you're here."

I give her a steady look. "Just how much do you know about why I'm here?"

She tightens the ponytail at the back of her head. "I know that he's not the type to meet a girl and fly her over here. That says a lot about him. And the fact that you came, that says a lot about you."

She's a real straight shooter, this one.

"What can I say? I, uh, really like him."

She doesn't need to know what an understatement that is.

Her eyes squint into a smile. "I know. Ah, before we forget." She unhooks three muzzles hanging along the wall with an array of leashes. "If the dogs aren't muzzled, we can get in some real shite."

She passes me the muzzle and I stare down at Jo's beautiful, open face, the hopeful eyes and the big smile. "Seems kind of wrong to be doing this," I tell her, fixing the muzzle on her snout, which Jo accepts without a fuss. "This is only going to make people more afraid of them. I'm pretty sure Jo wouldn't harm a fly."

Amara sighs as she slips them onto the others. "Yeah, well. Tell that to the government. It's either we muzzle them or we don't get them at all. Most people in the U.K. have preconceived notions about these dogs and the muzzles only make it worse. If only they could see them, how they can really smile, they wouldn't be so afraid. It's that stigma, you know, that we're trying to work through. People want to believe the rubbish they hear about these dogs, and it's really hard to get them to do anything but argue with you."

"It's the same in the States," I tell her. "The more I've been with Lachlan, the more I've been paying attention to the media bias. If a Labrador attacks a child—which is, like, way more common than you think—it rarely makes the news, and if it does they sweep it under the rug as a 'dog attack.' But if it's a pit bull, all the news stations report it with screaming headlines." I give Amara an embarrassed smile. "I confess, the media had me totally fooled until I met Lachlan."

She nods, putting her hands on her hips. "He might not say too much, unless you really know him of course, but if you get him talking about the dogs, he won't shut up. He's done so much good here. He's very, very persuasive."

She jerks her head toward the door and I follow her out into the streets. The dogs look terrible with the muzzles on, but at least their tails are wagging, their noses full of fresh smells.

"So how is the place doing?" I ask her curiously. "I mean, in terms of funding and all that?"

She tilts her head back and forth, thinking, as we stop to let the dogs sniff a patch of grass. "It's okay. I get paid no matter what, and that's thanks to Lachlan's own money. If it weren't for the fact that he's made a lot of smart money over the years, I think my position would be strictly volunteer."

"And the volunteers?"

"They come and go, but we have four of them who are really committed. One used to play rugby with Lachlan years ago. Rennie." Her eyes brighten as she says his name. "He's away at the moment, but he's always a big help."

"Has Lachlan done any fundraising recently?" I ask.

"Well, he's been away, but at the start of the rugby season there's a gala...will you be here for that? It's in a few weeks."

My jaw clenches uneasily. "I'm not sure..."

"I was left in charge so I'm not sure if it will be as up to par as it normally is. Thankfully I had Lachlan's mother, Jessica, to help. She's usually the one planning these kinds of events. Lachlan would be lost without her when it comes to parties and mingling with the rich and famous."

"What about, like, a rugby calendar?" I remember what Neil told me about the French ones.

She smirks at me. "Like have him pose nude to save the animals?"

I grin at the thought. "That wasn't really what I had in mind, but hey, if I saw a calendar with *him* naked in it, I'd buy it. I wouldn't care what the cause is. Women are really fucking simple."

"That doesn't weird you out, to have the world looking at your boyfriend's goods?"

A thrill runs through me at the mere fact that she called him my boyfriend. Is he my boyfriend? I have no idea. But I'm not about to correct her. I like the sound of it.

"I wouldn't have a problem with it. More reason to brag," I add with a laugh.

We spend two hours taking various dogs for walks around the block and then some, until it's time to clean up. Amara says that she'll be back around eight p.m. with Charlotte, one of the other volunteers, to take the dogs for their last walk. I have to say, even though it seems hopeless in many ways for these dogs, they're obviously taken care of very well. I shudder to think of how animals in other shelters are, especially the overcrowded ones back home with the high-kill rates.

When Amara drops me off at Lachlan's, I let myself into his apartment, expecting to see a big mess inside. But both dogs have been well-behaved and Lionel jumps off the couch where he was snuggling with Emily, running over to me with big eyes and a wagging tail.

I crouch down and scratch behind his ears, unable to escape being licked all over my face.

"I'll take you out in a few minutes," I tell him, careful not to say the "W" word around him. He just stares at me with those big eyes, and I have to look away. If he was my dog, he would be so damn spoiled. Now I understand why Paris Hilton dragged that ugly Chihuahua everywhere.

I walk into the bedroom, taking off my shirt and putting on something new and fresh. I pick a black tank top cut low enough to show the top of my lacy push-up bra. My boobs have to look their best for him. The fact that right now, he's at rugby practice, getting all hot and sweaty and manly, running other big men over with his sheer determination and brute strength, well, I'm half-tempted to bring my vibrator out of my half unpacked suitcase and get busy.

But instead, I decide to save what I have for him and start making myself at home. I open up his closet to see how much room he has, though it quickly turns into me snooping through his clothes.

His wardrobe is pretty much the same as I've seen so far, just more of it. Still, for all his money, you never really see any of it in excess. Maybe a Land Rover is pricey, and this flat sure wasn't cheap, not in the way it's so stunningly done up, but Lachlan pretty much lives like everyone else. He's got a few suits, all obviously tailored to fit his extra broad shoulders, but they aren't designer labels. His shirts and jeans are mostly from H&M or some shop I don't recognize. I like that about him, how unpretentious he is.

Since I'm in snooping mode and apparently don't feel all that guilty about it, I move on to the rest of the room. At first it seems like he keeps everything neat and tidy, but then you realize it's just that he doesn't have a lot of stuff.

I move on to the bathroom, out past the hall, the walls painted a vivid blue. I know, I know it's wrong to creep on people, and it's especially wrong to want to check out their medicine cabinet. But there are just some things that have me curious. Sometimes it's the ticks that he has, the ones he probably doesn't even notice—the clenching of his jaw, the scratching of his arms, that wild widening of his eyes like he's about to beat down on someone, the little sounds of frustration he makes at any odd time. We all have things like this, but with him...I just want to know more in any way I can.

And to be honest, I want to know more about what I'm getting myself into. I'm just here for three weeks, but I want to know Lachlan as deeply as possible. He seems to have been through so much...but how much more is there? And how deeply do his demons have a hold on him? Are things going to change now that we're on his turf, or was the Lachlan I saw in San Francisco the one I'm going to get?

I take in a deep breath, nervously peering over my shoulder, as if Lionel is watching and ready to tell on me, and then open the cabinet.

There's a bar of glycerin soap still in the package. A razor blade, a beard trimmer, one of those old-fashioned looking shaving brushes. Toothbrush, mouthwash, toothpaste. Hydrocortisone cream, anti-bacterial cream, arnica cream. A packet of allergy pills, a packet of muscle relaxers. Ibuprofen. Aspirin.

Then three bottles of prescription pills.

One only has a quarter left in the bottle: Ativan.

I know that one well. It's for anxiety. That doesn't surprise me. A lot of people I know are on it, and Lachlan isn't exactly the calmest dude around. I mean, when he's intense, he owns it. It nearly takes your breath away.

The second bottle is Percocet. Pain killers. Must be for the tendon injury because the bottle is almost empty.

Then there is Fluoxetine, which I know is Prozac. My mom took hers for a long time, but this bottle has barely been touched. That's either a good thing or a bad thing. I've seen how my mom is on and off the drug, and I've heard her complain about how it dulls not just the pain but all the joy in life too. Then again, there were times when she really needed it to get through the day.

I carefully shut the cabinet door, holding my breath, afraid that he's going to appear in the mirror behind me, like in a thriller movie. But he doesn't. I'm alone in the bathroom, and Lionel is whining outside the door.

It's none of my business to ask why he might need antidepressants, and lord knows that, given his history, or at least what little I know of it, he has more than enough reasons to warrant it. But even so, I'm terribly curious. I want to know and I want to know on his own terms. I want him to trust me enough to open up to me, to let me in and show me around. Show me his fears and the demons on his back. I want to lose myself in his beautiful darkness.

I want my love to be the thing to bring him light.

But in these passing days, in the situation we're in, I'm not sure that's possible. I'm not even sure if I'll ever tell him how I truly feel, because who trusts those words from someone you barely know? It doesn't matter how much I know it. It doesn't matter that people fall hopelessly in love all the time, every day. I don't know if he'll ever see, really see, just how I feel. And the complicated part is, it's only going to get worse as the days go on and I fall more and more under his spell.

That evening, I make myself some tea and settle down on the couch, with the comfiest, over-sized cushions ever, Lionel and Emily lying beside me. I flip aimlessly through cable channels, trying to soak up as much local Scotland flavor as I can.

When Lachlan comes home, I realize that I should have gotten off with my vibrator earlier when I had the chance. The poor man is absolutely wrecked, and even though he's not limping, he's walking with extra care, as if he's been hit by a truck.

He tells me not to worry, that he probably gave too much trying to prove himself, and that he'll be fine. But I enjoy playing nurse anyway. I run a hot bath for him, dumping in some of my body wash for bubbles, and make him soak the aches away.

"Call me if you need anything," I say to him from the bathroom doorway, enjoying the sight of his hulking, inked body among all the frothy water.

But the way he looks at me makes my blood still in my veins.

It pins me in place.

It's a look that says he needs me and only me.

Or maybe that's just wishful thinking.

Chapter Twenty

LACHLAN

I have the same dream three nights in a row.

For the first few nights Kayla's been in Edinburgh, my dreams have been unmemorable. I've been sleeping deep, solid, and the night, unlike a lifetime of nights, have passed by in the snap of one's fingers. I close my eyes, Kayla at my side, and then I'm opening my eyes, and she's still here.

But by night number four, I'm swept into a wave of terror that resurfaces again and again, pounding me out of slumber and into reality.

Sometimes I wake up gasping for air, which in turn only makes Kayla worry. She questions me with her eyes, imploring me to talk to her, to explain. But I can't, not yet. Not until I have to. Not until I know she won't look the other way. The thought of losing face in front of her, the idea of losing her affection, that sweet, hopeful, hungry look in her eyes, is painful.

It's a dream I've had before, and to share it would mean she'd see all the dark in me, the horrible, pathetic person that I once was.

It's the day that Charlie died.

Of course, in a dream, it's all skewed and a bit off. Just enough to fuck with you. But it's the same alley, ironically not too far from the housing projects I grew up in. It's the same Charlie. It's the same Rascal, the stray that I would call my own dog until that very day that I never saw him again. It's like Charlie's death scared sense into the both of us.

In the dream though, it's snowing. And unlike reality, we are never alone. There are people lined up along the alley walls in black and red rugby colors. Some of them wave flags that say McGregor number eleven on them. They are completely silent, and that's the scariest part. They are rooting for me, for us, for our demise, with open, flapping mouths and judgemental eyes, and the only thing I can hear is the falling of snow and Charlie's raspy breath.

It was only his second time doing heroin. I had been there for his first, but I hadn't approved, not that first time. I didn't have a logical, coherent part of my brain left, and yet somehow I knew that heroin was one step too far. As if it weren't that much worse than meth.

But the second time, well, I got the drugs for him. The first time had gone so well, and he'd been a different man for a while. And isn't that how it always bloody goes? One won't hurt you. One makes it all better. Two will be fine.

But it isn't fine. I get up off the ground, and even in my dream I can't feel my frozen legs. I limp over to the line of rugby fans and I ask each one if I can score some smack. No one responds. They just scream at me, soundlessly. Men, women, young and old, their faces forever in silent torment. I beg, I plead for some, just a little bit, but nothing. No one hears me, no one cares. I might as well be invisible.

Charlie, though, he's anything but invisible. He always was larger than life. He's yelling at me to hurry up, to help him—he's telling me I'm a terrible friend and hasn't he done so much for me already?

Charlie is probably the only friend I've ever had, so of course I do what I can to keep him happy. I keep trying, even though the people's expressions are changing, becoming more distorted, more demonic. The presence of pure evil is everywhere, that black oily shadow that clings to your back, influencing your thoughts and soul. Even after all these years, it's still there, waiting for me to fuck up. It's only when I reach the last person in the alley, and see that it's myself at five years old, skinny and bruised and not so much different than the way I am in my dream, that I have a chance.

Five-year-old Lachlan hands me Lionel the lion. He nods at it, hinting at something more. I tear the lion open, splitting the seams along the gut, and the heroin pours out like white sand. It doesn't stop filling the space around my feet, rising, rising, rising. Hands grab my ankles, pulling me down—my mouth, nose, and ears filling with the grains, my head exploding in fireworks.

Charlie stands above me, waving goodbye, blood running down from his nose and eyes.

"See you soon, mate," he says with a bloody smile. "One-way ticket straight to hell."

The drugs drown me and the world goes black.

No wonder I wake up with my heart racing erratically, my lungs feeling devoid of any air.

"Another dream?" Kayla asks softly, and in the low light I can see the gleam in her eyes. She's propped up on both elbows, watching me closely, trying to downplay it all, but I can see how scared she is.

My mouth is parched. "Aye," I say roughly, taking in a deep breath.

"Have you had them before?"

I nod, just once. "I need some water."

I get out of bed, Lionel sleeping so soundly at the foot that he doesn't even stir when I crawl over him.

Once in the bathroom, I splash cold water on my face and stare at my reflection. Dark circles tinge the inner corners of my eyes. How is it possible to feel so bloody happy and look so much like shite at the same time? I open the medicine cabinet and eye my prescriptions. I'd purposely left the Percocet at home when I went to the States. The pain had subsided and I didn't need the temptation. The anti-depressants only fuck me up, and not in a good way. The Ativan works most of the time.

I fill the glass by the sink with water and down the Percocet and Ativan together. If that doesn't help me get back to sleep, then at least it will carry me through to the morning. Maybe even into the evening, when I think I'll need it most.

That's when I'm bringing Kayla around to see my parents, Jessica and Donald, the real McGregors. I wish I could say I haven't been worrying about it ever since the plans were made, but that would be an outright lie.

The thing is, I'm not even sure why I'm nervous. Is it because I'm afraid my past will be brought up? It seems pretty unlikely. My parents respect me enough to never talk about it. Is it because I'm afraid Kayla won't measure up to their expectations? That's unlikely too. They're the least judgemental people you could meet, regardless of their status in society. Kayla would only charm them.

Or is it that bringing her to meet my parents—when I've never brought anyone to meet them—says far more about the way I feel about her, about us, than I ever could?

I have a feeling the last one is the right answer.

I close the cabinet and lean my forehead against the cool mirror, closing my eyes.

"Lachlan?" I hear Kayla's soft voice from outside the bathroom door. "Are you okay?"

I grunt in response, clearing my throat. "Just a minute."

I take a quick piss, and when I get back to bed, she's under the covers, watching me.

"I'm fine," I tell her, climbing in beside her. "Come here." I wrap my arm around her shoulders and tug her up against me. I brush my fingers along her hairline, feeling the silk of her hair and skin sooth me into a drug-induced sleep.

...

Jessica and Donald live about an hour outside of Edinburgh, their house just a few shrub-lined blocks from the Firth of Moray and a fabulous fish and chip shop I used to spend much of my allowance on.

About twenty minutes away, I pull the Range Rover in beside Robbie's Bar and put it in park.

"What are we here?" Kayla asks. "Do they live in a pub?"

"Nah," I tell her. "But I used to frequent this place a lot growing up. When I was fifteen I hit my growth spurt and didn't even need to use a fake I.D. It's not as dodgy as it looks. Come on, let's have a beer."

She frowns at me, so I flash her a smile. "Don't tell me it's not fancy enough for you," I add, knowing that will egg her on.

"Hey," she says, raising her palm at me, "don't talk to me about fancy. The most interesting people are found at dive bars."

"Well, this is a dive pub, so it's a step above. Just don't order any of the food."

"Don't want to spoil my appetite."

"You don't want to get sick." I get out of the car and grab her hand.

To be honest, I haven't been in here since high school, but it smells just the same. Grease and salt from the fryer, fish batter, stale beer that owns the red and green carpet. The memories come flashing back, not all of them horrible.

It's just after five o'clock, and the pub is fairly full of regular blokes off from work. We snag a high-top table by the door and I ask Kayla what she wants to drink.

"Surprise me," she says, though there's an air of caution in her voice, as if I'm going to get her a beer called the Haggis Surprise.

"Done." I saunter over to the overworked bartender, who's wearing a grey shirt with sweat stains down the sides. I'm pretty sure he's the same guy who worked here fifteen years ago.

I lean against the bar and wait until he notices me, and when he does his eyes go wide. But there's no way I look the same as I did back in the day, growth spurt or not.

"Well, I'll be," the man says, wiping his forehead with the back of his arm. "Lachlan McGregor." I squint at him, trying to figure it out when he continues, "You're the best part of

Edinburgh rugby. Tell me you're fully healed now? The team has been playing the dog's bollocks since you left us."

That's not exactly true. The end of last season wasn't particularly good, but that might have happened whether I was on the team or not.

"I'm back," I tell him.

"Brilliant. Practice going well? Ready for the big game?"

"Aye," I tell him, not wanting to get into it. "Could I get a pint of ale and a pint of cider for the lady over there?" I gesture to Kayla. She's sitting at the table, taking it all in.

"No worries. It's on the house, mate," he says, and promptly pulls out the pint glasses.

"Well, cheers then," I say as he hands me the drinks. I take a moment to stare at the amber liquid, my thirst suddenly rampant. I could down it all in a second, just two gulps, and the relief would be immediate. Instead, I bring both drinks over to her, my hands shaking slightly.

"Here you go," I tell her.

"Did the guy know you?"

I shrug. "Not really. More like he knew who I was."

She beams at me, sliding the cider toward her. "That's awesome. You're famous."

I grunt, holding the beer up to my lips. "It happens rarely."

"Nooooo," she says. "The other day when we were walking on, what was it, Princes Street, there were a lot of people looking at you."

"They were looking at you," I tell her warmly. "My beautiful girl." I hold out my beer and knock it against her glass. "Here's to..."

"Meeting your folks," she says.

I nod. "Yes. That." I drink my beer, half of it gone immediately.

She takes forever to finish hers, so when my glass is empty, she nudges her cider toward me. "Here, I can't finish this."

I hesitate. Just for a moment. Just enough to maybe rein myself in. The glass is about half full and I'm already feeling swimmy. If I finish it, I know it will lead me to that place where every guilty thought I've ever had will magically disappear.

I want to be in that place, especially now, especially with this gorgeous, wonderful woman who I am so terribly unworthy of.

But I won't. With effort, I shake my head, declining the drink. I get us out to the car and on our way. The wind is picking up now, pushing grey clouds in from the coast and coating everything with a fine mist. Everything is blindingly green because of it.

Jessica and Donald's house is about three hundred years old and looks it. The stone fence outside is crumbling, a few of the larger rocks having toppled over no thanks to me and my predisposition for running along it when I was younger. The rest of the house has ivy growing up the sides, though Jessica's garden is manicured as always, the sunflowers along the south side already waist high.

"Oh my god," Kayla says, her hand to her chest as we pause by the iron gate. "This is like something from a movie. Is this where you grew up?"

"Aye," I tell her. "Hasn't changed much."

"It's like a fairytale."

Something in my chest clenches. While the pub held mostly pleasantly memories, maybe because I was always in there with my mates, the house held a world of others. It was both my first real home since I had been given up for adoption, and it was also the place I felt most unworthy of. It also held the time where my life began to go tits up for no reason other than my own doing.

Christ. I should have had that cider after all.

Before I can dwell on it anymore, the front door, forever painted bright red, opens, and Jessica and Donald step out, giving us a wave.

"Lachlan," Jessica calls to me in that sing-songy voice of hers. She's wearing all black, believing it to be slimming even though she's always been quite thin. Her grey hair is straight and shiny, and she's wearing just a few sparkly jewels and what looks like little makeup. Donald looks just as dashing in his usual vest, his hands shoved down into his pockets, wearing glasses that complement his sharp eyes. My adopted parents are some of the classiest, smartest people you'll ever meet. I often wonder how they found it in their hearts to take me in at all.

I make the introductions quickly, giving them both a hug hello before proudly showing them Kayla. "Jessica, Donald, this is Kayla," I tell them. Even though I mentioned on the phone a few days ago that I was bringing a girl over, I don't think they've quite gotten over the shock because they both look taken aback.

Finally, Jessica shakes her head. "Oh, she's darling," she says, and brings Kayla into a light hug. When she pulls away, she holds her by the shoulders at arm's length and peers at her. "Where ever did you find such a lovely girl? And one that would want to come all the way here with the likes of you?" she adds, taking the piss out of me like she often does.

Kayla is blushing. I love how she's so confident at times yet always takes compliments with a sense of disbelief, as if she's never heard how beautiful she is, as if she's hearing it for the first time. It makes me want to say it again and again and again, until she believes it. If only she didn't look so bloody brilliant when flushed.

"It's really nice to meet you," Kayla says. "I've heard so much about you."

I raise my brows. Actually, I've rarely talked about them, but it seems to be the right thing to say because Jessica looks pleased as punch.

"Is that so?" she asks, sending me a questioning look. "Good things, I hope."

"Always," I say just as Donald comes forward, offering his hand.

"Glad to have you here," he says to her. "How are you enjoying Scotland so far?"

"I love everything about it," she says. "It's going to be hard to go home."

If I was numb, those words wouldn't hurt the way they do. She seems to still a bit after saying it, the smile frozen on her lips, almost hyperaware. She'd told me a few days ago that we weren't to mention that she was leaving, and we'd been sticking to it, living in a dream of sex and soul, pretending the days were endless and time was only for other people but not us.

"Well, you just stay here for as long as you like," Donald says smoothly, putting his arm around her shoulder and leading her into the house. "We have a nice cuppa ready for you."

As he leads her inside, Jessica grabs my arm and pulls me down toward her.

"I just wanted to say," she says quietly, her eyes bright, "that I didn't know what to expect when you told us you were bringing over a girl. I don't want to make this a bigger deal than it is. I know you very well, Lachlan." I frown at her and she continues, "You've never been one for sentiment. But I just wanted to tell you that I'm so happy for you. She seems lovely, and she's beautiful."

I swallow uneasily. "Thank you," I say gruffly, but I don't add anything else.

"She treats you well?"

I give her a quick smile. "Yes. She does."

She pats my back, satisfied, and we go inside to the sitting room where Donald is pouring Kayla a cup of tea. I sit in my usual seat, a vintage upholstered chair that Jessica always wanted to throw away because it was threadbare in places, but I'd convinced her to hold onto it. They've always been very wealthy and love to show that off in subtle ways. Jessica's aesthetic for the house is cozy but not enough for ragged furniture. The chair was the only thing I could really relate to though, as daft as that sounds. When you're an orphan, you look for comfort anywhere you can find it.

While Jessica putters about, getting shortbread and scones for us and placing them on the table with her finest white and pink china, Donald asks Kayla if she's from San Francisco, which then gets them talking about the city. Donald worked in finance from an early age and a lot of his career had him traveling around the globe. Born to a poor family, he is a completely self-made man and it's one reason why I admire him so much, other than the fact that he took me in when he did and ruled with an iron fist when he had to.

"And your job?" Donald asks, biting into his shortbread which leads to a shower of crumbs on the carpet. Jessica makes a good-hearted tsking noise and sits down, sliding the plate toward him so it won't happen again.

This is where I see Kayla stutter. She rubs her lips together, and I know she's trying to think of the right response. Finally she says, "I work for a weekly newspaper. The Bay Area Weekly. I'm in advertising."

"Ah," Donald says, adjusting his glasses. "That must be very interesting."

Kayla glances at me and then says, "No. It's not really." She lets out a dry laugh, shrugging. "I've always wanted to be a journalist, to actually write the articles, but it seems no matter how much I try, I can't get there."

I clear my throat. "Well actually, Kayla wrote a brilliant article about me and Bram about the work he's doing over there for lower-income housing."

"I did," Kayla said with a slow nod. "Unfortunately, I don't think I'll ever get that chance again. I didn't even get credited with the article. Someone else did."

"That's bollocks," Donald says, slapping his knee lightly and trying to talk without spitting crumbs everywhere. Jessica has all the elegance in this relationship. "What did you do?"

"Nothing. I mean, I complained, but the editor doesn't listen to me. Or anyone."

"Have you ever thought about writing on the side then, maybe for free for a while?" he says, peering at her over his glasses. "Build up a portfolio and a reputation, hone your craft. Then start looking for a job that will actually pay you to write?"

I often wish I were Donald's actual son, least not that he could have passed those brains down to me. Being born of crackhead blood is never to your advantage.

"Yes, Donald," Jessica says. "That's a great idea. Why not start with travel writing? You're here, maybe Lachlan could show you some of the hidden spots of our country, the places no one writes about." She gestures at me with her cup of tea. "Or another article on the organization. Even the gala next week. You could help each other out."

Kayla and I exchange a glance. I hadn't thought of that, and clearly neither had she.

"I wouldn't know who to write for," she says.

Jessica dismisses that idea with a wave. "Oh, don't you worry about that. I know a lot of people. So does Donald. It wouldn't be for pay, but like Donald said, just to get your foot in the door and build up your brand. At the same time, Lachlan and the dogs would benefit. What do you say? If I could make this happen, would you be interested?"

Kayla blinks for a moment, then straightens up. "Yes. Yes, of course! That would be great. When is the gala again?"

"On Friday," Jessica says, and gives me a hard, discerning look. "If I know Lachlan, he's completely dropped the ball on this one. Wouldn't be the first time. One year he showed up in his rugby uniform because he came straight after practice."

I clear my throat. The fucking gala is a fundraiser for the shelter. Jessica hosts it every year, and I just kind of show up, sign autographs, meet people, and put out some good PR for the organization. I usually bring Lionel to the event with me, and he wins people over far better than I can.

"It slipped my mind," I tell them. "I've been...busy."

Kayla smiles knowingly at that. "It's okay. Amara told me already. I just wasn't sure when it was."

"Always at the start of the season. People are excited for rugby again, and usually I can get a few of my teammates to come show some support." I pause, very aware of the way Donald and Jessica are staring at me. "I would love it if you would be my date, so long as you don't mind sharing me with Lionel."

"You know I don't."

"He's a good one, isn't he?" Jessica says warmly.

"Who, Lachlan or the dog?"

I let out a small laugh. "Oh, love, please don't choose."

My words bring out a look between Donald and Jessica which I do my best to ignore.

The doorbell rings and Jessica gets up. "That must be Brigs."

Brigs is my brother, and I immediately feel bad that I haven't gotten in touch with him upon getting back. We've had a pretty good relationship, though I put him—and Jessica and Donald—through hell when I was younger. It's only recently that he's pulled away more than I have. His wife and child died three years ago in a horrible car crash, and he hasn't been the same ever since. I understand him, though I can't say I understand his exact grief—nor would I want to. But I get why he's distancing himself from everyone around him. It's not just the pain of loss. He blames himself for the accident since they had a fight beforehand. I never learned what the fight was about, but according to Brigs, it was enough to make him think it was all his fault. Sometimes I want to reach out to him, to tell him I know what guilt is, but I don't have the courage to even bring up that shit with myself.

"Hey, Mum," Brigs says, kissing Jessica on both cheeks. Though I call them my parents, I've never been able to call them Mum and Dad. I'm not sure if that's a defense mechanism or what.

Brigs walks in the house and eyes the rest of us in surprise. You can see my cousins in Brigs, and vice versa. He's tall and athletic, though looking quite thin as of late, with vivid blue eyes that I can't describe as anything other than haunted. His cheekbones are thanks to Jessica, sharp and angular. When he's feeling particularly angry, you definitely want to clear the room. I can silence someone with my fists, but he can silence a room with one look.

"Lachlan," he says, and there's a gaiety to his voice that wasn't there before.

I get out of my chair and give him a hug, the old slap on the back.

"Good to see you, brother," he says, looking me dead in the eye.

"Same to you."

He looks over my shoulder and raises a brow when he sees Kayla. "And who is this, then?"

I can't help but beam proudly at her. I probably look quite the fool, but I don't care.

"This is Kayla. She's from San Francisco."

"Is that so?" he asks, and gives her a nod. "First time in Scotland, yeah?"

"It sure is," Kayla says.

"And you have this ape as your tour guide? I should show you around, yeah? Show you the real Scotland not seen through the eyes of a hothead rugby player," he says with a big grin. It takes him from sinister to jokester in a flash, and I can see Kayla's shoulders relax.

"Brigs," Jessica warns. "Be nice."

"Nice is a four letter word," Brigs says, and luckily everyone laughs. It's nice to see him happy, and for a moment I realize it's probably nice for everyone to see me happy too.

Soon we gather around the dining room table while Jessica goes about preparing the dinner, a succulent roast duck that Donald says he shot in the Highlands last weekend on a hunting expedition. The wine comes out. It takes a lot out of me, but I decline and have a glass of mineral water instead.

The conversation then moves on to normal topics. Donald discusses his work with the Lions Club, Kayla talks about housing in San Francisco, and I say a few things about rugby practice. Brigs is ever quiet, more so than me, until Jessica starts dishing out the sides and brings up the fact that he's got a new job.

I don't make too big of a deal about it because that's just the way that Brigs is. He lost his job as a teacher after the accident, and has been looking for work ever since. I was never worried—he's a shrewd guy and a hard worker, he was just going through a lot. But Jessica is bursting with pride. I can tell it makes him uncomfortable.

"Congratulations," I tell him. "It's about time. Here's to that."

And maybe I've said the wrong thing because his eyes narrow sharply and he raises his glass. "Here's to me? No, no. Here's to you, Lachlan."

I frown and he continues, completely sincere. "I'm serious. Really, I'm serious. I don't think we've ever really toasted to Lachlan and the person he's become."

There's a worm of unease in my chest.

Brigs looks at his parents. "Really, I don't think we have. I think we just opened our arms up to Lachlan and brought him back in, but I don't think we've ever really told him how proud we were that he was able to beat his addiction."

The globe stops spinning on its axis, just long enough to make me feel sick.

"Brigs," Jessica warns, in barely above a whisper.

But Brigs isn't picking up on how still I've gotten, on how my hands have curled into tight fists, on how Donald and Jessica are sending him warning looks, and Kayla is staring at me with open confusion. He doesn't pick up on any of that because he's looking into his glass of beer like it's telling him what to say.

"We really thought you were gone, Brother. Meth, heroin. Not many can pull themselves off the streets, pull themselves off the drugs, and actually do something with their lives, but you. You. You've done everything you set out to do." Finally he raises his head to look at me, completely earnest, not noticing my wide, wild eyes. "Here's to you, Brother. I'm glad you're back. I'm glad you're here. And I'm glad she's here too."

The most awkward silence imaginable blankets the room. Everyone eyes each other then slowly reaches for their glass. I can't even bother reaching for mine. I'm utterly paralyzed. Not just from humiliation, because when you've lived for years on the street, you learn to have no shame. None at all. But it's the fear that grips me, like a vise around my heart, because Kayla didn't know any of that, and I wasn't sure I could ever bring it up with her.

But there it is, out in the open, for her to reflect on, to judge, to fear.

I can't even look at her. I quickly excuse myself from the table and walk through the kitchen to the bathroom, passing by the fridge where I swiftly grab a bottle of beer and head right on in, locking the door behind me. I lean against the sink, breathing in and out, willing the pain to stop, for the regret to subside, but it doesn't. So I slam the top of the beer against the sink, the cap snapping off, and down it in five seconds.

I burp. I wait. Wanting it all to go away, for my pulse to stop fighting my veins.

The longer I stay in the bathroom though, the worse it will get. I put the beer in the rubbish bin then head back out to the dining room. I swear, this moment is scarier than any moment I've ever had on a rugby pitch.

Thankfully, luckily, they're all talking about Obama, of all people, so my return to the table isn't overly noticed.

Except by Kayla, of course, because she notices everything. And there is absolutely no way that I'll be able to let this sleeping dog lie.

I decide to wrap the evening up early, just after dessert, telling everyone that I have to return home to the dogs, especially Emily who isn't used to being left alone yet. We say goodbye to everyone, though I know we'll see Donald and Jessica at the gala. When Brigs hugs me goodbye, he pulls me tight and whispers in my ear.

"If she still loves you, she's a keeper."

I want to smash his fucking face in for that and can only mutter an angry syllable in return.

The car ride back to Edinburgh is as choked with silence as one can imagine. I try to concentrate on the road, on the white lines slipping underneath the car, at the black highway rolling toward the headlights. There's something so dreamy about the moment, that after-dinner, late night drive, but the gravity of the situation brings me back.

Finally, I can't stand it anymore. I clear my throat, keeping my eyes ahead, my grip stiff on the wheel. "Do you want to talk about it?" I ask, voice low and dripping with unease.

It takes her a moment. "About what exactly?"

I really don't want to spell it out for her, but I will if I must. "About what Brigs said. His toast to me. About the person I used to be."

She sighs noisily. "Right. The person you used to be. Tell me about him, then."

"Do you really want to know?" I glance at her to see her nodding, her eyes focused out the window and into the darkness.

"Yes," she says. "I want to know everything about you. Especially the events that made you who you are."

"And who am I?" I ask softly, heart pleading. "Who am I to you?"

She turns her face to me, skin lit up by the pale dashboard lights. "You're Lachlan McGregor. And you're mine."

Another gut punch, but sweeter this time, dipped in honey.

"Please don't hold anything back from me," she says. "You don't owe me anything, but I...I want to understand. I want to be there for you, I want to know every inch, not just your body, but your mind and your heart and your soul. You can trust me, you know. I'm not going anywhere."

But that's a lie. In a few weeks you won't be here at all. Then you'll have my heart and all my secrets, too.

I swallow that down and nod.

"I'll keep it short and not so sweet because..." I exhale, my hands sweaty on the wheel. "You need to understand that this isn't easy for me to talk about. I haven't talked about this with anyone, and I rarely even think about this myself. There are a lot of things that just need to stay in the past, and the person I was is one of those things. But I need you to know that it's all over and done with. Everything that happened is over. You have to trust me on that. Do you trust me?"

"I trust you," she whispers.

"Okay," I say with a slow nod. "Okay. Well, uh…when I was first brought into Jessica and Donald's home, well it all felt too good to be true. You've met them now, you've seen how they are. They are nice people. Good people. They took me in, a scrawny, damaged young boy with no potential for anything, and they worked around the clock to prove to me that the world wasn't out to get me, and that not all people were bad. But…when it was all I had ever known, time and time again, it wasn't an easy thing to believe."

I blink hard, trying to compose my words. "They gave me everything I could ever want, including honest, real love. But I never felt worthy. I went through high school, I got my degree, and I tried to live a normal life. The problem was…people knew them, knew I wasn't their son, and even though that was rarely an issue, unless some wanker made it one, it was something large and heavy in my own mind. I guess I never really trusted them or their intentions. I never even unpacked my bag—I kept it by the door, always, just in case, because too many times I'd either be thrown out of foster care or I'd have to escape. And those horrors, the horrible, sick things that lurk out there in the minds of some people, waiting to prey on you, they're always out there. I wanted to trust Donald and Jessica, even Brigs, but I couldn't. My last year of high school I started to backslide. It's the same old story. I hung out with the wrong people. I stole cars and drank moonshine and shot guns into the sky. Then the drugs came into play, and I was spending weekends in Glasgow, scoring chicks, scoring drugs, being the person I knew how to be. Unworthy, you know? I didn't deserve shit."

I glance at her to see if she's listening, and she's staring at me with so much interest, so much concern that I feel like she's actually there with me, in the past, holding my hand.

I go on, my throat getting drier. "It was the unsexiest drug that did me in. You'd think it would be coke, but I'm not that classy. Never was. It was crystal meth. Alcohol, too. Coke on occasion, maybe some painkillers if someone could get their hands on them. That was at first anyway. At first you're always picky. Then you get to the point where you'll steal nutmeg from your adopted mother's kitchen because you think it will get you high. Maybe you'll pawn her jewelry and her fur coats. Maybe you'll steal every single bit of their life, their life that they gave to you, to rescue you—maybe you'll just throw that all out the window. Because you're a selfish fucking coward. With no balls. Because all you care about is making this whole damn world and every cell of your existence disappear. That's all there is. Your life becomes all about erasing life, like a memory card wiped clean. I did drugs and I stole and I lied and I hurt and hurt and hurt until that card was blank, and there was nothing new to hurt me anymore."

I was nearly breathless from all that. The only sound in the car was from my own lungs, sucking in air, trying to come to terms with what I had just purged. I'd just told Kayla the worst possible thing that anyone could admit. I just told her, the only woman I've ever cared for, that I've ever fallen deeply, madly for, that I used to be a drug addict. There was no way her opinion of me wouldn't be forever altered. The truth didn't make me feel good at all because it's the type of truth that should never come to light.

Moments pass. Heavy, weighted. The blood wooshes loudly in my head and I have to adjust my grip on the steering wheel. I keep my eyes on the road, too afraid to look at her but also too afraid of the silence.

"Brigs said you were on the streets," she says quietly, and I can't tell if she's disgusted or if she's in shock.

"Aye," I say with a nod. "When you pawn your adopted parents' shit for drugs, their patience for you grows real thin. They did what they could. I put them through literal hell before I put myself through literal hell. There were fights, always. I would scream and cry. I was such a fucking wanker it was unbelievable. Just a pathetic piece of shit. I can't...I can't even tell you how much I hate myself, that me, that person I was, and all that I did. They did the right thing, you know. They gave me an ultimatum. This is how you repay us for taking you in? Then get clean or get out. And I chose to get out. That's what I always deserved, anyway. The mean streets. And that's where I lived for a few years."

"A few years?" she says with a gasp.

I can't even swallow down the shame. "Yes. Sometimes in shelters, sometimes on the streets. Me and the strays, you know, we were the same. But a dog is just trying to live, trying to survive. I wasn't trying to live. I was trying to die."

And I almost did die. Charlie happened. Charlie died. It could have been me. It should have been me. But I can't even bear to utter his name.

"Fuck," she swears, and she surprises me by putting her hand on my arm and giving it a squeeze. "I had no idea. I knew you had issues, I mean, even just from being given up for adoption. But this? This...I can't," she trails off and shakes her head. "You're just so fucking strong."

I glance at her, frowning. "Strong?"

"Yes," she says emphatically. "You're strong. You're brave. And maybe magic. How the fuck did you get from there to here, to right now? With your career and your Range Rover? How did that happen?"

I tilt my head. "It happened. It wasn't overnight." But it was overnight. One horrible night. "One day I just showed up at Jessica and Donald's and told them I needed help. I begged them. On my knees I pleaded for them to save my life, to take me back. It was then that I finally realized I didn't want to die. I wanted to live. And if they were any other sort of people, they would have turned me away. I was never their son and they didn't owe me anything. But they didn't. They took me in. I went to rehab to get off of meth and other drugs. I focused my life on the physical. It happens a lot, you know, when you've abused your body so much that you want to make up for it. I became a fitness and health fanatic, and eventually joined a local rugby team. Rugby became my new obsession, you know? I had the speed, the strength, and that anger that I now know will never go away, and all of that combined was like a super fuel. I became really good, really fast. The rest is history."

"Some history," she says. "I had no idea. And I'm sorry that I didn't."

"I never wanted to tell you, obviously. I could have murdered Brigs for bringing it up like he did, even if his heart was in the right place."

"I can see why you'd want to keep it all inside, but...isn't that tiring? Doesn't that hurt you, to keep so much of who you are hidden from the world?"

I shrug with one shoulder. "Maybe."

"I'm glad you told me," she says, shifting in her seat and running her hand through my hair. "I don't want you to ever be afraid to be honest with me."

"Even when it means you might run the other way?"

"I will never, ever run from you, Lachlan. I'll only run toward you. Always."

God, what I would give for that to be true.

When we finally get back to the city, I'm exhausted and emotionally drained. Kayla tells me to get in bed, that she'll walk the dogs. I want to protest, but I can see in her eyes that she wants to do this for me, such a simple thing that means so much. She fucking cares about me. She's not running away. I don't even know how to process any of it.

I get into bed and force myself awake long enough for her to get back from the walk. I can hear her talking to the dogs in the other room as they settle down on the couch to sleep before they later move onto the dog bed or our bed. There's something so comforting, so peaceful, about hearing her in there, shutting it all down and preparing for the night. In another world, a merciful world, it wouldn't be the first time and it wouldn't be the last. All these nights would stretch on and on and on, and she would fall asleep in my arms with all my darkness and all my demons and all my ugliness stored safely in her heart. In a perfect world, she would hold it there, away from me, so she could understand me better, so I would never be harmed again.

She would willingly harbor my truth inside her.

I would willingly let her try.

But the world isn't perfect.

I just don't know what kind of world we have now.

Chapter Twenty-One

KAYLA

"So are you sure no one is going to pull down your pants?" I ask Lachlan as we get out of the Range Rover. I have to admit, I'm nervous as fuck about seeing him play, though he doesn't have to know that. Actually, I'm anxious about a lot of things, but he doesn't have to know that either.

"No promises," he says, and jerks his chin toward the massive stadium in front of us. "There she is. Home of Edinburgh Rugby."

I have to admit, I was surprised this morning when Lachlan asked me to watch him practice. After the night we had last night, the dinner at his adopted family's, and the stark confession in the car, I expected him to pull away from me, to put up barriers and increase the distance.

But that didn't happen at all. He was hungry for me and extremely affectionate in the morning, and even though morning wood wasn't uncommon in the last seven days that I'd been in Edinburgh, this time there was something different. I felt he wanted not to just possess my body but everything that came with it. The way his gaze burned me was akin to the greatest thirst.

Obviously, I had no complaints. After what happened last night, I needed to feel closer to him myself.

I can't lie. What he said scared me, and while I thought I had him figured out at least a little bit, the whole being addicted to meth and living on the streets completely took me for a ride. It was far, far worse than I ever could have imagined, and my heart broke with every single heartfelt, raw word that came out of his mouth. No wonder he was so intense, so broken, so misunderstood. The man had gone through hell and back, and even though he rose like a phoenix from the ashes to become the man he is, that smoke still clings to him. I can smell it.

And that's what scares me. It's the fear that it's not all over. Because how can it be over? How can a person go through all of that and just brush it off? You can't. Not even with the best therapy and the best medication can you ever get over being abandoned, adopted, on drugs, homeless. It's one terrible thing after another, and just the fact that he's alive and well has me completely dumbfounded.

But I don't want to live in fear for him, and I don't want to believe that he could slip up at any moment, even though I'm not naïve enough to ignore certain things, like his relationship with alcohol. I want him to keep being strong, powerful, noble. A proud beast. I want him to not be ashamed of who he was because it's only made him the amazing person that he is. Though I know he thinks the opposite, learning the truth about Lachlan made my respect for him go through the roof.

And now, now I really understand his passion for the dogs, for rescuing the "bad dogs" who are cast aside and forgotten. He literally was just like them, depending on the kindness of strangers.

Yet here is, and here I am, about to head into the stadium where I'll witness just how he pulled himself out of the rubble.

"Now I must warn you," he says to me as he slides a key card into one of the back entrances. "You might fall asleep. We're not going all out quite yet. I'll be working on my sidestepping today, especially since I have a tendency to just plow through people."

"Oh, I know," I say brightly. "I read it on your Wikipedia page."

He groans. "I have one of those?"

"That only means you've made it."

"Bloody hell. Anyway, I can't really run people over anymore without risking injury to myself, so that's where the sidestepping comes in handy."

"Will I at least see you in a scrum?" I ask as we walk down a dank, cement tunnel toward the lit green field at the end.

"Nah. As the wing you just watch the scrum. Wait and see what happens." He gives me a wry look, pursing those lush lips together. "Don't you remember any of that rugby I taught you?"

I laugh sharply. "Let's be honest. I was just trying to flirt with you, maybe get a good feel of your ass."

"If I recall correctly, you were definitely flirting with me."

I roll my eyes. "Well, you didn't seem to know it at the time."

He stops and pulls me to him. "I knew it at the time, love. Just had to work up the courage to do something about it." He kisses me on the forehead, and we continue on our way.

We're a bit early so he leads me up into the stands where he selects a good seat for me. "You're close enough to hear Alan, our coach, yelling at us, and at me especially, and you'll be able to see everyone. I better go check in on the locker room."

I anxiously grab his arm. "What, you're leaving already?"

"I'll be right back. Down there." He points to the field. "Try and stay awake."

He trots off down the stairs and I watch the muscles in his ass bounce as he goes. After a few minutes, when I realize it might be a while before it all starts, I bring out my phone and start emailing people. I email Steph and Nicola, wanting so bad to tell them what Lachlan told me, but knowing it isn't their place to know or even understand. It's Lachlan's past that he entrusted me with, and I cling to that with reverence.

I email my mom too. The last email I got from her was a few days ago. She said she misses me, which hurt like hell, but that she was fine and that Toshio and Sean had been over. She hadn't mentioned my other brothers, Nikko, Paul or Brian, at all, so I also drop an email to Toshio to see if he can remind them. After everything that Lachlan told me, I feel strangely weak and shaky inside, and my need to know that everyone will be okay is stronger than ever. I wish there was a teleporting machine so I could go back, just for a moment, and give my mother a long hug. Those kind of hugs fix everything.

But that doesn't exist, and instead I'm on the bleachers of an empty stadium waiting for a man that I've grown hopelessly, helplessly in love with. I hate that I can't have everything, and I hate that it's human nature to want more when you finally have it.

Finally there's shouting from below, and I stop emailing to crane my neck down to see a bunch of big burly men in tight shirts and shorts heading out onto the field. Lachlan is at the back of the pack, talking to a shorter man in a windbreaker that's nearly as wide as he is. I assume that's Alan, the coach.

I can't deny that my heart does a double back flip at the sight of Lachlan on the field, in those clothes that show off every thick, sinewy inch of his muscles. He's a fucking god and a god I'm fucking. I have to pinch myself, even though my own pulse is threatening to step out of bounds.

Though he walks with a familiar swagger, he holds himself differently here. Proud. He's beyond confident. He acts like he owns the field, owns the very game. If I was a girl living here, I'd be at every single game watching him. In fact, I wouldn't be surprised if that's what half the stadium consists of—girls wanting to get their Lachlan McGregor on.

The practice itself isn't very interesting. There's about a dozen or so people on the field, and the coach alternates between having them play each other full on for a few minutes, then pairing players off to work on exercises. Just as Lachlan said, he spends a lot of time running with the ball, dodging players coming at him. He sidesteps them, sometimes causing the other player to fall flat on their face, sometimes spinning off a tackle. Sometimes he doesn't sidestep at all and just goes for the opponent's shoulder. I can tell he pulls back at the last second and doesn't hit with all his strength. If it were an actual game and that wasn't his teammate he was slamming into, I bet he wouldn't hold back at all. He really is a beast.

And he's fucking fast. Though he's not used all the time and often spends a lot of the game hanging at the edges of the team, when he is passed the ball, he takes off down that field like he's about to take flight. It's amazing how a man of his stature can run so damn fast, those muscular legs pumping like a machine.

I could literally sit here for hours watching him. I can't take my eyes away. He's so into the game that he only looks up in the stands a few times. But when he sees me, he gives me a nod, and I find myself waving shyly like a school girl.

It's hard to even imagine him skinny and scrawny on the streets, doing drugs and feeling so hopeless. What a different man he is on the field.

Eventually practice ends, and as everyone heads back under the bleachers and to the locker rooms, he runs up the stairs toward me, tireless and taking the steps two at a time.

"How you doing?" he asks, sweat glistening on his scrunched brow as he stands over me.

"Good," I tell him. "You're like…a rugby machine."

He looks over at the field, wincing while he wipes his arm across his forehead. "Yeah? Didn't feel like it."

"Well, you *look* like it. I'm…lucky. I'm lucky. You're amazing. You've impressed the pants off of me."

He looks at me, the corner of his mouth lifting up. "Is that so?"

"I've never wanted to screw you more," I tell him honestly.

He chuckles. "All right. Well that can be arranged. You don't mind if I have a shower first?"

I frown. "Are you actually serious about having sex with me?"

"Love, I am always serious about having sex with you. And yeah. Maybe a locker room shag has always been a fantasy of mine."

Fuck. Sign me up. As if I wasn't already turned on watching him get all sweaty on the field, asserting his dominance, now he's staring at me with a gaze that can only be described as molten.

"What about your teammates? I'm not *that* much of an exhibitionist."

"Glad to hear that," he says. "There's another room for the opposing team. It's probably open." He reaches down and grabs my arm, pulling me to my feet. "By the way, tonight, Thierry, my good mate on the team, invited us to a pub. He wants to meet you. That all right?"

I'm totally flattered that his teammates even know about me. "Sure."

"Good," he says, kissing me softly on the lips and letting out an agreeable noise. "I want to show you off to everyone I've ever known and ever met," he whispers against my mouth.

I practically melt and kiss him back eagerly, our lips and tongues hot, wanting him to feel just how he makes me feel. I'm not even sure how to describe just how he does me in.

He leads me down the stairs and across the field, toward the tunnel on the opposite end. I pause in the middle, looking around me, imagining what it would be like to be Lachlan, to step out here among thousands of fans staring down at me, cheering me on. I don't know how he does it, he must get into some kind of zone.

I think he does that with me sometimes. It's like he sees me and nothing else, like I'm his whole world, the only thing in his existence.

Even now, the way he's glancing at me as he takes me into the darkened tunnel, I feel enslaved by his intensity. Fuck it. I'm enslaved by everything about him. His beauty, his darkness. His cock. Definitely his cock.

And definitely now.

He takes me toward a door and tries the knob but it won't budge. He pushes me back a bit, looks both ways up and down the tunnel, then kicks the door in.

"Wow, are you sure this –" I start to say but the look in his eyes shuts me up and he practically throws me in the room. He closes the door behind him and flicks on the lights.

It looks pretty much like any locker room I've ever seen. Lockers, benches, showers at the end. And, thankfully, empty. I look back at Lachlan and he's already peeling off his sweaty shirt and tossing it to the cement floor. His shoes, socks, shorts go next. Totally commando.

"I, uh, thought you always wore your underwear when you played," I say to him, my eyes drawn to his massive erection that he's holding in his fist, stroking it slowly, up and down and burning into me with dangerous eyes. "You know. Because of the shorts being pulled down thing..."

But my words are trailing off because the sight of him in the locker room, his rugby kit discarded on the floor beside him, all his gorgeous tattoos and primed muscles on full display, makes me stupid. God, the fact that I just saw all that his body can do on the field, and now he's going to show me all he can do to *me* in here...I'm practically panting for it, and I know I'm wet as sin already.

"I like to mix it up," he says unapologetically.

I unbutton my jeans, sliding them down my hips in front of him, about to step out.

"No," he says hoarsely, a gleam in his eyes. "Leave them around your ankles."

I tilt my head and blink at him. Just what does he have in mind?

His strides past me, cock in hand and goes all the way to the showers. He turns one of them on and steps in, letting the water stream over his massive body. His stroking increases and I watch, tantalized, as his fist slides from the thick base to his purple, swollen tip.

"Just watch," he says through a groan, his head back, the beads of water pouring down his throat, down between the hard mounds of his chest, following the carved path of his stomach. "I want you to beg for it."

"I *am* begging for it," I tell him, feeling slightly ridiculous that I'm standing here, with my jeans and underwear around my feet, watching him jerk off in the shower. I want more than anything to get down on my knees, put that delicious dick in my mouth, let the water cascade over me. I don't care if I get wet. I want to make him *come*. Preferably in my mouth, but I'll take what I can get.

"Get on the bench, right there," he commands, opening his eyes as the water runs over his head, flattening his hair, his mouth open with that puffy bottom lip just asking for trouble. The look on his face is absolutely hedonistic.

I do as he says, getting on my knees. It's such a fucking turn-on when he's bossy. This whole scenario is like a porno waiting to happen.

"Turn around," he says, turning off the shower. "Face the other way."

"I'd rather look at you," I tell him. "Have you seen you?"

A slight smirk tugs at his lips. "Do as I say."

I glare at him. "Can't we both win?"

"Aye. You'll win. Now turn around." He storms toward me, his dick bobbing with each stride, menace in his eyes.

I obey but only because I know it will pay off.

I wait, ass in the air, the top half of me still clothed, balancing precariously on the bench.

I hear him come up behind me, feel his presence. His shadows looms over me and I instinctively grip the edges.

Seconds pass and I'm dying from the anticipation. I feel like I'm blindfolded, every part of me on alert and waiting for what sinful thing is going to come.

I open my mouth to beg when suddenly –

CRACK

– his large, strong, wet hand spanks my ass with so much force I nearly fall off the bench.

I yelp, loudly.

It *stings.*

Oh god, it stings and my eyes are watering.

But then the pain starts to fade as quickly as it came on and I'm breathing hard, chest heaving, waiting for more.

"Did you like that?" he asks, voice so gruff and low, it relays every single dirty thought he has in his head.

I catch my breath. "Yes."

CRACK.

He spanks me again, the other cheek.

My back arches and I cry out. "Fuck!" My head feels hot, like it's going to burst and my ass is tingling from the strikes, but I've never felt more dirty, more sexed up in all my life. This doesn't feel like playing, this feels excitingly real.

He places his hand on my hip and flinch from his touch, expecting more. He holds onto me, then I feel the head of his cock slide over my sensitive, raw skin where he spanked me, still damp from the shower.

If he's trying to soothe me with his penis though, it's not working. This just riles me up. I want him deep, deep inside until I can't see straight.

I tell him so and it brings out a thick grunt from his throat.

He steps back from me and smacks my ass again, harder than before.

"Holy shit!" I scream but then before I can even process the pain, his tongue is on my ass, licking over every welt, with soft, smooth strokes. He moans into me and I'm so fucking gone. The push pull of pain and pleasure is making it hard to control myself and I jerk my hips up and back, wanting him in.

He gets the right idea.

He grips my waist with both his hands, nearly reaching all the way around, that's how large he is compared to me.

I'm so damn wet that all he has to do is inch forward and he slips inside.

It feels.

Too.

Fucking.

Good.

The angle is everything. He pushes himself in to the hilt and I feel myself expand around his thickness, his cock dragging over every wild nerve inside me.

A long, aching groan pours out of my mouth.

"You like that too, aye," he growls. "Your greedy little noises and your greedy little cunt."

I gasp, gripping the edges of the bench harder but my hands are so sweaty that I can barely hang on. If he lets go of my waist, I will go flying because my limbs are loose and I'm so full from him inside me, stretched like silk, that nothing else matters to me now except coming fast and coming hard.

He slams into me, his hips circling quickly, hitting the right spot every time and the feeling in my core grows and builds and tightens until I feel like I might pass out. Our skin slaps loudly against each other, a frenzied soundtrack to our animalistic fucking.

With one smooth movement he pulls my hips up higher, angling himself down in a long, powerful thrust and he's hitting my G-spot with the perfect hot grind.

All the tension snaps, a wire pulled too taught.

I cry out, unraveling and unraveling until I fear there's nothing left of me but hot blood and instinct.

He moans as I pulse around him and his pace quickens. He's driving himself inside me, so hard and thorough and punishing, as if he's punishing me again and again. And I'm still riding my orgasm, each brutal thrust keeping me going on the wave, like I'll keep coming for as long as he's in deep. I'm up so high, high, high and I can't come down, even if I tried.

It's pure, primal bliss.

"You fucking ruin me, love," he growls, so savage and frantic in his rhythm, and then he slows with one, heavy push. His fingers dig into my skin, hard enough to leave bruises and his loud, wild groan fill the room, tangling with my own.

"Fuck," he gasps roughly. "You ruin me."

He stills against me, drops of sweat falling on my back, our heavy breathing in unison, and it feels like he has to pry his fingers away from my hips, he was gripping them so hard.

Eventually he pulls out and I feel his cum spill down my leg. He puts his hand up my thigh, wiping it away and then leans forward, placing soft kisses down my spine.

"Thank you," he says softly, voice beyond husky, as if he drank a gallon of gasoline. "I won't forget this."

Getting spanked and fucked in the locker room of a rugby star? Yeah. I'm not going to forget this either.

...

I'm excited for the first real pub night with Lachlan and his friends, even though I'm a bit on edge with what Lachlan revealed last night. I won't bring it up because I don't want him to think I'm watching him, and I also know what he told me in Napa, about his relationship with alcohol. I just have to trust that he knows what he's doing. He'd told me that it was all over and done with, that he wouldn't backslide, and I just have to have faith that he's right.

I spend some time trying to select the outfit that's just right for the girlfriend of a rugby star. Not that I'm his girlfriend but…fuck. I'm not sure what else I'm supposed to be.

"Are you ready?" Lachlan asks while I try on a white lace tank top for the millionth time. I settle on skinny jeans and high heels, but I still feel it's not enough.

"Ugh," I say, making a face at myself in the mirror. "I don't know." I turn to face him as he leans against the bathroom door. "Do I look okay?"

He raises a brow. "Are you taking the piss?"

"No, I am not *taking the piss*, though I'm still not sure what that means."

He shakes his head, walking over to me. He studies my face, blinking in almost disbelief, before brushing my hair off my shoulders. My eyes close, surrendering briefly to his touch.

"It means you're insane if you think you don't look okay," he says in a growly voice. "And that I'll never think you're anything other than beautiful."

"You know how to say all the right things," I tell him, and he plants a few kisses down my neck, making me shiver.

"Because I'm with the right girl," he says against my skin.

I swallow at that, trying to find the courage to speak. "About that," I say softly. "Am I your girl?"

He pauses and pulls back to observe me, brows pinched together. "What are you on about?"

"Am I your girl? I mean, we've never really discussed our actual relationship, what we are with each other, and so...I don't want to be presumptuous and assume I'm more to you than I am. So I just wanted to know, so I could be clear, you know...how you feel."

Oh god. I'm a rambling fool.

He stares at me for a long moment, which only makes me wince. Finally he says, "I invited you to come to Scotland with me. I bought you a plane ticket just on the *hope* that you would come. Kayla...you're my girl. You're my beautiful world. And I'm whatever you want me to be, just as long as you know that I have never, ever, felt this way about someone in my entire life." He lowers his face, eyes focused intently on my lips. "I'm losing myself in you. Every day. And it's the most wonderful, terrifying feeling in the world. If I'm being honest here, you're starting to drive me a bit mad in my affections for you. I don't know if I will ever be of right mind again."

Jesus. My heart is near combustion. His words are like sunshine, banishing everything scary and dark. It's everything I want to hear.

I clear my throat, trying to act cool. "So, am I your girlfriend or what?"

He grins at me. "You're my girlfriend. My girl. My woman. And I'm all yours."

"My man," I say, kissing the stubble on his cheek. "My beast." I pause. "My sex slave."

"Bloody right I am," he says before kissing me so deeply that it steals my breath away.

Satisfied that I look okay, at least to him, I snatch up my purse and we head on out for the night. Lachlan calls a taxi, and it's only about ten minutes before we're on Grassmarket, heading for the pub. This one in particular is underground, though it's done up with lots of teak wood and orange and green plaid seatbacks.

Lachlan nods at a table near the middle of the room where his teammates are sitting. I recognize them both from earlier, even though I was watching from far away.

"Hello, hello," says one with a crooked nose and a mop of reddish brown hair. The other one, olive-skinned and darkly handsome, just nods with a shy smile.

"John," Lachlan says to the ginger, then nods at the other one. "Thierry." He pronounces his name like "tea-erry," which sounds terribly French to me. "This is Kayla."

"Ah," Thierry says, and low and behold, he was a terribly French accent. "Nice to finally meet you. You must be the reason Lachlan's been fumbling at practice."

Lachlan gives him the stink-eye which would make any another man shrink in his seat, but Thierry only gives us a slow smile, pleased with himself.

"Oy," John says, elbowing Thierry in the side. "You better watch your mouth, mate, or I'll tell Lachlan all about your latest escapades over the summer."

"Latest escapades?" Lachlan repeats, clearly interested. He sits down across from them and motions for me to do the same. "What did I miss?"

Thierry rolls his eyes but says nothing. He folds his arms across his wide chest and looks away.

"You see here," John says, leaning forward with a goofy grin. "And I only found this out a few minutes ago, so you can't blame it for being fresh in my mind, but it turns out Thierry met a girl back in Paris over the summer. She broke his bloody heart, though if we know our Thierry well, he probably broke hers. Always playing the victim, eh, Thierry? On the pitch and off."

Lachlan is grinning at this and gives me a conspiratorial glance. "Thierry is what we call a manwhore, so even the idea that someone could have broken his heart is nearly joyous news."

I look at Thierry and can immediately see why he'd be breaking hearts. He's not as tall or as built as Lachlan, and he only has a few tattoos on one bicep, but with his warm dark eyes, honey skin, smooth lips, and thick black hair, he's pretty arresting. If I wasn't attached to the most gorgeous, giving man on the planet, I could see myself throwing some flirts his way. He definitely looks like he's built for speed and agility.

"So," Lachlan says to him with a nod. "Do you want to talk about it?"

Thierry gives him a dry look. "Right. To you, of all people."

Lachlan shrugs. "Fair enough."

"Though I have to say I'm surprised you dared to bring this beautiful woman to meet us," Thierry says. He gives me an apologetic smile. "Rugby players aren't known for being very classy."

"Only French rugby players," John jokes. "You should see him when he makes a try. He practically ballroom dances across the line, like a fucking pansy-footed waltz."

"Well, I'm not very classy either," I tell them. "Which is probably why I get on with Lachlan so well."

"Get on?" John repeats. "You're sounding like him, too."

"I'm going to get you a drink," Lachlan says and quickly leaves the table. I don't miss the warning look he shoots his teammates.

They, of course, ignore it.

"So where on earth did you meet Lach?" John asks. "Don't tell me they play rugby in America."

"Actually, they do. He joined a pick-up league for a bit," I tell them.

Thierry laughs. "That I would love to see. What a one-sided game that must have been."

"He was trying to downplay his skills, but I don't think it worked." I turn to John. "I met him through friends. My two best friends are with his cousins."

"Huh," John says. "Seems I need to go to America to meet a good woman."

"No," Thierry points at him with his beer. "You need to go to France."

He shakes his head. "They sound like heartbreakers over there, no thank you. As you can tell, Kayla, deep down inside, we're all a bunch of softies looking for love in all the wrong places."

I shrug. "Aren't we all?"

They both exchange a questioning look. Thierry cocks his head at me. "Do you think you're looking in the wrong place?"

I'm not sure what to do with that question because it's oddly serious for what we were just talking about.

"I hope not," I tell them just as Lachlan comes back, putting two big pints of dark beer on the table, foam spilling over the sides.

"Sorry, love," he says to me. "They're out of cider and their house wine is rubbish."

"That's okay," I tell him, actually preferring the dark Scotch ales over the stuff at home.

"Hopefully they weren't giving you a hard time," he says, eyeing them both cautiously.

"Them?" I say. "They're nothing but pussycats." I raise my glass. "Here's to you, softies."

We all clink glasses, and as if on cue, the music in the pub gets louder.

More people come in.

The sky goes dark beyond the narrow basement windows.

By the time I'm done with my giant beer, Lachlan is on his third, as are Thierry and John.

They're all drunk and I'm struggling to catch up. The thing is, it's loud in here and there are a bunch of girls giving Lachlan and Thierry the eye, and the music is grating and I'm feeling left out of the drunken conversation. They try to bring me in but their accents get thicker and thicker until I can barely understand what they are saying. I just want to drink more so that everything stops annoying me. But the beer is so strong and thick that it takes forever to get through another glass.

The atmosphere in the pub has completely changed. People keep banging into the table and spilling our drinks. I've seen Lachlan curl and uncurl his fists a few times, his face going red, that wild, piercing look coming into his eyes.

But Thierry and John are too drunk to notice or care, singing along to some screeching tune.

I lean into Lachlan and still have to shout to be heard. "Want to go and sit somewhere else? It's so loud here and people keep bumping into us."

I can't hear what he says in return, but it sounds more like a grumble.

I don't know. I'm getting a weird feeling. He's gone from relaxed at the start of the night to tense and edgy. I don't want to blame it on four Scotch ales, but I don't see what else it could be. I know he doesn't like to be around people in particular, especially when there's a bunch of them acting like idiots, so adding alcohol to the mix probably isn't the best idea. If we could just go back home, we could settle down on the couch and watch TV, or just find each other in the sheets of our bed.

Finally some girl with mangy blonde hair, orange skin, and tits pushed up to her chin totters on over in her heels and drapes herself over Lachlan.

"You're Lachlan McGregor!" she yells at him in a twangy English accent, her heavy, false eyelashes making it hard for her to keep her eyes open. "I've seen pictures of your cock."

My eyes widen, my skin immediately growing hot. Did she just say what I think she said?

She looks at me briefly, enough to give me the up and down glare, then looks over at Thierry. "I've seen your cock, too. Both very impressive. My name is Polly, by the way. You want to buy me a drink?"

I'm really waiting for someone to fill me in on this. I'm staring at Lachlan, open-mouthed, but he's not looking at me. To be fair, he hasn't even glanced at her, either. He's just staring at his half-drunk beer like he wants to smash the glass over someone's head.

It's John who explains things to me. "They both did a nude rugby calendar a few years ago," he says loudly. "I, of course, didn't get the call. I think it's because red pubes don't photograph very well, even in black and white."

So the nude rugby calendar really is a thing. When Neil, and even Amara brought it up, I thought it was a joke. I guess not.

And with that, I calm down a little bit. If she's seen his dick via calendar, probably everyone has seen his dick, and there's not much I can do about it except be proud that his dick belongs to me.

And even though I don't like this bitch touching my man, I'm not going to say or do anything. Don't get me wrong, back in San Francisco I have no problem getting in someone's face. I remember once having to step in when some chick was threatening to beat up Stephanie over some guy, I don't even remember who. I had to get all crazy Asian chick in her face, and luckily it didn't come to anything more than that. But I have a feeling Scottish, or English chicks as this girl is, aren't to be fucked with. I keep my mouth closed and ignore it.

Until it becomes impossible.

Because now the tawdry slut is standing behind Lachlan and running both her hands down his arms and whispering something in his ear.

"Um, excuse me, *Polly,* is it?" I say with my finger raised in the air. "I don't think you want to do that."

She gives me a glare with one closed eye. She looks like a drunken pirate hooker.

"Mind your own business," she says, slurring her words.

I'm staring at Lachlan now, wondering why he's not moving, not reacting. I don't even know if he knows what's going on at all—it's like he's in some sort of trance, which doesn't help me at all.

Fine. I can take care of it myself. I lean in closer and put my hand on her arm. It's sticky and cold. "Polly, I'm not sure if you realize this, but this man is my boyfriend which means he *is* my business. Now if you'll kindly remove your arms, there are plenty of available men in this bar that I'm sure would love a night with the likes of you."

She sneers at me. "Oh fuck off, you slag."

My head jerks back. I don't even know what a "slag" is, but I'm guessing it isn't good. I'm about to look to John and Thierry for some support, since Lachlan has gone catatonic, when suddenly there's a looming shadow over our table.

"What the fuck is going on here, huh?" A voice booms, and I look up to see a big bruiser of a dude with a bald head and beady eyes standing behind the slaggy chick. He's staring at the girl and the way she's hanging on Lachlan like he's got laser beams for eyes and is trying to burn a hole through the both of them.

"Hey!" the guy yells, grabbing the girl by the arm and throwing her off of Lachlan. "What the fuck you doing with my girl, you cunt?"

I wince. Oh no. Oh no.

Wrong thing to say, buddy.

I'm frozen in my seat, watching Lachlan closely, my breath in my throat. I can feel Thierry and John doing the same thing. In fact, the whole bar seems to quiet, though it could just be my imagination. It's as if everything stills, holding its breath.

Lachlan doesn't turn around, just cocks his head as if he's finally listening. He has that mad dog stare going on, a volcano about to erupt. His shoulders and neck tense, like someone has wound him up as far as he will go, and he's about to spring.

"What?" Lachlan says, voice so stiff, so low, I can barely hear him.

"Are you fucking deaf?" the guy says, leaning closer so his face is practically shouting in Lachlan's ear. "I said stay the fuck away from my girl, faggot."

Lachlan swallows slowly. I watch his fists curl so tight his skin goes white. His eyes sharpen, pupils growing tiny, mean, and hard as hell. I want nothing more than to grab him and lead him out of here. I should have done that a long time ago.

The guy doesn't back off. He might have muscles but he's a fucking idiot. Instead, he smiles at Lachlan, showing misshapen teeth. "You rugby players think you're the cock of the walk, don't you? Like your shit don't stink. Like you can do anything you fucking want. Wel,l you can't. I know all about you, you pathetic little fuck. You want it all and you don't deserve any of it, not like the rest of us." He looks over Lachlan's head at me, and there's so much disgust in his eyes that it nearly makes me sick. "Why don't you go take care of your *chink* girlfriend and leave mine alone?"

I feel like I've been slapped in the face. It takes me a minute to register that he just called me a fucking chink, one of the oldest, most-outdated racist terms in the book. I can't even think or breathe or react, other than to stare dumbly at him, like I'm not even sure who I am for a second. But holy hell does that make me feel like garbage.

Lachlan's reaction, unlike mine, is immediate.

He explodes up from the table with a terrifying roar that silences the whole pub, then he whirls around and punches the guy square in the face. It's hard enough that blood flies out of his mouth, hard enough for the sound of bone crunching to settle somewhere inside me.

The man flies back but doesn't fall. He grabs his face, still smiling, though I swear a tooth falls out of his mouth. But in his eyes he's taunting Lachlan.

There is no time for that. Lachlan storms toward him, fists out, shoulders raised, eyes as crazed as I've ever seen them. He's like a whole new person, and if the guy had any brains at all he would get the fuck out of here because I don't think Lachlan can be stopped.

But he doesn't. The guy tries to get in a punch and it catches Lachlan in the jaw, but he doesn't even try to duck or move—he just takes the hit and keeps coming like nothing has happened. And when he comes again, he's coming with both fists, and the guy goes flying back through chairs and onto someone's table.

Lachlan pins him down and punches him in the nose.

The cheek.

The chin.

Again.

And again.

Over and over and over like a wild, feral animal.

I hear the same sound of smashed bone and spilled blood, like someone thudding two pieces of raw meat together, echoing through the bar.

This is a nightmare.

"Stop it, stop it!" the girl cries out, trying to pull Lachlan off.

It makes him pause enough to push her off with one arm and yell, "Shut the fuck up, you cunt!" Thierry and John finally snap out of it, jumping out of their chairs, and run over, trying to pull him back.

"Fuck off!" Lachlan yells, throwing another punch. The guy is now on the table, groaning helplessly and barely moving. His face is just blood. Lachlan reaches for a bottle of beer, smashing it over the edge of the table and holding it up to the guy's throat.

"You fucking apologize to her," Lachlan seethes, his own face splattered with the guy's blood.

But the guy can't even talk. Finally John and Thierry work in unison, and with one hard pull, they get Lachlan off the guy.

Lachlan just stands there, staring at the guy while everyone in the pub is dead silent. Even the music turns off. The only noise is the spitting sound as the guy tries to move his broken, bloodied mouth, and Lachlan's heavy, raspy breathing.

Suddenly Thierry is handing me my purse, whispering to me. "You both have to go now, right *now*." He jerks his head subtly at the bartender who is making a phone call. "The police are being called. You have to get him out of here."

I nod dumbly, the feeling slowly coming back into my limbs.

I hate to admit it, but I'm scared when I reach out to grab Lachlan's hand. It's not that I think he'll hurt me, but I'm not sure he even knows where he is or who I am at the moment.

He flinches at my touch but slowly turns his head to look at me. I pull my hand away, my fingers now red and sticky.

"We have to go," I tell him, my voice squeaking. "Please?"

He stares at me for a moment until it's like he actually recognizes me. Then he nods and turns, storming out of the bar, shoving chairs out of the way.

"I'll take care of it all," Thierry says to me, putting his hand on my back and pushing me towards the door. "Just get him home."

I lick my lips and run after Lachlan, catching up to him on the street. He's walking fast, so fast, that I have to stay at a jog.

"Lachlan, Lachlan, talk to me," I plead.

He doesn't say anything. Finally I see a cab heading our way, and I flag it. As it slows, I quickly take a cardigan out of my purse and wipe the blood from his face. If he looks too messed up, the cabby might not take us.

He lets me do this, completely docile, though he's not looking at me—he's just staring off into space with disbelieving eyes. I know my cardigan is now covered in someone else's blood, but at least Lachlan looks human again. Back in the pub, he was anything but. I'd seen bar fights many times, but never like that.

That was raw, that was feral. And absolutely dangerous.

The cab stops beside us and I open the door, pushing Lachlan in. I'm relieved to see him not resisting. The driver glances at us in the rearview mirror, but I play up the fact that I'm American and sober.

"Number Four, North East Circus Place," I tell him promptly. He stares at me and Lachlan and nods.

"Aye," he says. "Rough night?"

"You could say that," I say under my breath.

"Welcome to Scotland, lass," he says with a tight smile, and we take off down the road.

Lachlan slumps against my shoulder, all his weight on me, and I put my arm around him, holding him close. I'm not sure if I'm trying to comfort him or comfort myself. We're both in shock.

"I'm so sorry," he mumbles against me, his tone high-pitched, nearly whimpering. "I'm so sorry, love."

"Shhhh," I tell him quietly, squeezing his shoulder. "It's okay."

He shakes his head. "No," he says. "I'm never okay." But he doesn't say anything else after that.

When we get to his flat, I tip the cabby with the wads of American dollars I have in the bottom of my purse and help Lachlan out of the cab. He can stand, but just barely. I lead him to the door and fumble through his jean pockets for the key. Any other day and at any other time, I would have made a joke about feeling him up, but there is no joking tonight. I don't see how we can joke about anything anytime soon.

I get the door open and walk him up the stairs. Once inside his flat, Lionel and Emily come to say hello, desperate for a walk. But once they see Lachlan, they get a bit standoffish. It's as if they're unsure who this man is, if he's really their master.

I take Lachlan straight to bed where he collapses on top of it. I roll him onto his side then attach Emily and Lionel to their leashes. Because it's so late, I don't bother with a muzzle for Lionel and do a quick pee trip around the park.

The dogs seem to loosen up with me, but I know I'm tightly wound. I have no idea how I'll sleep at all tonight. I want to talk to someone about this, but I'm afraid to. Lachlan is such a private, personal guy, and it wouldn't be fair to him to tell someone else what he's been like. Even if it was someone like Stephanie, who I tell a lot of things to, who wouldn't judge me or him.

I decide to bottle it up for now and think that maybe one day I can talk to Thierry about it. He and John didn't seem all that surprised over what was happening. Maybe beating the shit out of someone is a normal thing in Scottish culture. It's possible, though the fact that we both had to hightail it out of there because of the police was a whole other thing altogether.

Then again, I don't have much time left here. Even though earlier today we proclaimed ourselves a genuine couple, and even though I find myself falling more in love with him each and every day, I'm just not sure where we can possibly go next. If I leave, then what happens? Do long distance? Does that even work?

And if I stay, if that's even remotely possible somehow, can I handle him and all his demons? Is this just a one-off thing, or is this the start of something more? He said his past is behind him and I need to believe that, but I can't pretend it's not possible for him to fall prey to his darkness. If this is just a hint of things to come, am I strong enough to get through to him? To survive it? It's just so much for a new relationship to survive.

I have to remind myself that I might be jumping the gun. That tonight, as scary and horrible as it was to see that anger unleash from him, might have just been it and we can still have a beautiful love story together.

It's fucked up. It's all over the place. I'm all over the place. Why can't anything be simple? Why can't I just love him and why can't he love me, and why can't love be the only thing to juggle? Instead, the past is holding onto him and our relationship has an expiration date.

I love a broken, damaged man who might run the both of us into the ground.

I have no idea how this is going to end well.

Later that night I crawl into bed, and I'm doing everything to keep my hardened heart from opening again. I want to pull away, I want to shut him out. I've talked myself out of everything that is open and beautiful.

But then he rolls over and grabs my hand and he holds onto it so tight.

So tight.

His eyes are pinched shut, and when he speaks it's barely audible.

"Kayla," he says hoarsely. "I love you."

I burst into tears.

He falls back asleep.

Chapter Twenty-Two

LACHLAN

I have a dreamless sleep. No nightmares, no nothing. In some ways it's worse, because when I do wake up and slowly realize where I am and what happened last night—what I became, well, I think a nightmare would have been preferable. At least I know that's not real.

But this *is* real.

My head is throbbing with a sickly ache, and my mouth tastes putrid, sour, like I can taste my own bloody heart. My knuckles burn where they hit and hit and hit that man again and again.

I'm beyond disgusted with myself.

That feeling hurts most of all.

And I'm terrified to open my eyes.

If I keep them closed, I'll never have to face up to anything.

But the images come slamming back into me, reminding me that this side of me is never going away. What's done is done and I did it in front of the woman I love.

"Hey." I hear her voice and it sounds like an angel, pure and light and the opposite of me. "Hey," she says again, her soft hand on my arm, shaking me. "I would let you sleep, but I know you have practice in an hour."

Fuck.

Fuck.

Practice.

God, I am such a fucking wanker.

I slowly open my eyes, the light causing mini explosions deep inside my head. I see Kayla peering at me. Her eyes are puffy and she looks tired. Beautiful still, but it hurts to know that I'm probably the cause of a restless night, of terror and sorrow.

I lick my lips and try to speak, but I can't. No words come.

"Hey," she says again, gently touching my cheekbone. Somehow she's staring at me like she still likes me. I don't see how that's possible. She's finally seen what I'm like. I'm surprised she's even here at all.

I attempt to clear my throat. "I'm sorry," I croak, staring at her imploringly, wishing I could open up my chest so she could see how sorry I am. My heart feels damp, waterlogged.

"It's fine. I get it," she says.

I shake my head, even though it makes my brain feel like it's caving in. "You shouldn't get it. There's no excuse. I'm just…I'm sorry. I don't know what happened."

"Well, you were drunk," she says.

I close my eyes, rubbing at my forehead. The goddamn shame is like an anvil on my chest, and I can't shake it. And I shouldn't. "I was drunk, I know, and I shouldn't have been."

"But that guy was being an asshole. He was asking for it. He wanted you to fight him."

"I know. I know and I was trying not to." I give her a pained look. "But then he called you that name, and I just…I couldn't let it slide. I'm sorry, but my tolerance for racist fuckheads is lower than my tolerance for men who disrespect my woman. I snapped." I suck in my breath. "I just fucking *snapped*."

"I know," she says soothingly, but I don't want her to be soothing. Because it's not okay. It's never okay. I don't deserve to be soothed right now.

I close my eyes for a moment. "And I shouldn't have snapped. I should have walked away. I should have never been there to begin with. I don't know what happened. It was all fine one moment, and the next...I was punching a bag of blood."

She grimaces at that and I immediately regret my words.

"Sorry," I tell her quickly. "I'm just...it won't happen again."

"Has it happened before?" she asks cautiously. "Because Thierry made it seem like you'd been in trouble with the police before."

"Well yeah, I have," I tell her. "But not for that. I mean, I've been in a lot of fights. It's Edinburgh. It happens. And I'm a rugby player. Everyone wants to prove their worth against someone like me. And I've been in trouble in the past. On the streets. You know...back then. But I've never been arrested, I can promise you that."

I sigh and prop myself up on my elbows, the blanket falling down to my waist. I look her dead in the eye. "When I first got Lionel, some wanker complained about him. For no reason at all. Lionel has always been nothing but sweet. But someone had it in for me, and hate is a poison. Lionel was taken away from me briefly under the Banned Breed Act. I didn't see Lionel for weeks while they assessed his behavior. Thankfully, he passed all their supposed tests with flying colors. But they weren't so sure about me. Somehow though, the judge gave him back to me, and that was that. As long as he was muzzled, I was allowed to have him." I pause. "But if I ever get in trouble with the police, I'm terrified they could link the two, and Lionel might be taken away for good. Ultimately destroyed, as that's what they do. I need to be on my best behavior."

"I'm sorry to say this," she says, "but last night was not your best behavior." She stares down at her hands, a strand of hair falling over her face. "And I hate to tell you this, but… you scared me. A lot."

Fuck. It's like a bullet to the chest to hear that from her.

She goes on. "Not because I felt I was in jeopardy. I just didn't know who you were. I didn't know what you would do. You're…please just take it easy from now on. I don't want to see you get hurt." She finally looks at me, her eyes wet with tears, and it pushes that bullet further in, breaking my fucking heart into a million pieces. "I care so much about you. You don't even know, Lachlan. You don't even know."

I reach for her, cupping her cheek, completely overwhelmed with every emotion possible. But on the forefront, racing first, is hope.

A memory floods back to me, hazy, but the feeling is bloody clear.

"Last night," I say gruffly, searching deep in her warm eyes, "I told you that I loved you. Did that happen? Or was it a dream?"

She smiles crookedly. "You told me you loved me."

I grunt, looking away, nodding quickly. "Okay. What did you say?"

"You passed out before I could say anything," she says.

I eye her, suddenly afraid for her to go on. "What would you have said?" I ask her, wishing my voice didn't sound so thin and reedy.

She stares at me for so long that I'm almost lost to the fear, to the rejection, to the fact that I've been nothing but a sad, pathetic fool.

"You know what?" I say quickly, my breath hurting my lungs. "I don't want to know. Forget it. It doesn't matter."

She leans in quickly and kisses me flush on the mouth. Soft, yielding, always beautiful. She rests her forehead against mine, our mouths inches away. "I would have told you that I love you too. That I'm desperately, foolishly in love with you."

I close my eyes, trying to keep a sob from rising out of my chest. "And now?" I whisper. "In the light of day?"

"In the light of day I love you even more."

I can't even handle it. My whole system of being wants to break down.

"In the light of day," she says to me, "I can see all your cracks and your darkness and your flaws, and I fall in love with it all. And I hope you can fall in love with everything that I am, all that lurks in my dark, all that shines in my light. I want you to love every little piece of me, because it all belongs to you."

At first her words hurt—they *hurt* because I'm feeling them so deep down, like a knife plunged straight into my chest. But it's not pain. It's joy so acute that I can't even process it. And the knife, the knife is red-hot, then warm, and it's spreading across me, better than the sweetest, most merciless drug.

I want to cry. Yell. Shout. I'm not made for this, and I'm a bottle rocket full of energy with nowhere to go.

I can only whisper, "I love you," even though my voice is broken, even though I feel painfully whole. "I love you," I tell her and kiss her simultaneously.

"I love you," I say again.

I kiss her cheek.

"I love you."

I kiss her neck.

"I love you."

I kiss the swell of her breasts.

And then my hands are sliding down her body and I'm moving on top of her, and I'm ravenous and starved for every bit of love I can possibly get.

We move in slow motion, through honey, and it's slow and sweet. I pull down her underwear and push inside of her and she opens up to me like she's letting me in for the first time. Her legs wrap around my waist like she's never going to let go.

And I want to believe that she won't let go.

That she's not leaving me in two weeks.

I'm not sure the human heart is built to be so capable. How can it handle the joy of finally loving someone and the ecstasy of finally receiving love, while still being so fearful of the pain that's yet to come?

Because that pain is coming.

How much longer can we ignore it?

"Stay with me," I whisper to her as I thrust in deep.

"I'm not going anywhere," she says breathlessly, neck arched, head back. Such a bloody goddess.

But that's not what I mean.

It doesn't take me long to come, and when I do, our eyes are locked and I feel myself slipping more and more and more.

Into the past. Into the future. I'm losing myself completely, and I just don't know which way I'll end up, if I'll even be whole in the end.

I rest my weight on my elbows, my head down against the pillow while she gently touches my back.

"Stay with me," I say again, voice rough with exertion. "Don't go home."

She tenses up beside me, her hands stilling at my shoulders. "Don't go home?"

"Quit your job. Move here. Be with me."

I can't believe I'm even saying this to her, but it's too late now. She wants all of me, so she'll have all of me.

"Lachlan," she says warily. "I can't just do that."

I pull my head back to look at her. "Why not?"

She frowns. "Because! I…I worked hard for the job I have."

"You hate your job."

"But it's still my job. What would I do here? I can't get a job."

"You can do whatever you want."

"Yeah, but that's easy for you to say. I've spent my whole life working for what I have, aren't I supposed to stick with it? It's crazy to give all that up."

"That's not what's crazy. Crazy is never branching out, crazy is never living up to your potential, never discovering what it is in life that makes your heart beat just a bit faster. Kayla, who you are and who you think you should be are two very different things."

She looks at me pleadingly. "Then who am I?"

"You're you, love. And you know what you want to do. Jessica said she would help you with the writing."

"Yeah," she says. "For free. Writing for free. How do I live until my portfolio or whatever gets big enough to even get me a job?"

"I could—"

She pushes her finger against my mouth. "And don't tell me that you could support me. I know you can, and you would, but I wouldn't accept it. That's not how I'm built. I do things on my own."

I shake my head at her stubbornness. "I could help you get employed. You could work at the shelter, like Amara."

"Amara says that you can barely afford to pay her," she tells me, and that makes me grimace, because I know it's true. "You couldn't afford me, too."

"I could," I tell her. "I would sell my flat in London if I had to."

"No. No way. No way would I let you do that for me."

"Why not?"

"Because I'm…you barely know me. I'm not worth it."

I sigh, my eyes pinching shut. "Please don't say that. Don't say that I don't know you when I feel like I've known you my whole bloody life. Don't give me that, and don't tell me you're not worth it. That's for me to decide, isn't it?"

She looks away, blinking. "I don't want you to do anything for me."

"Well, that's tough luck ain't it, love, because if you want to stay with me, I will do whatever I bloody can to make sure you can stay here. So just give me the word. Give me the damn word and you can stay here for as long as you like."

"It would be crazy," she says quietly.

"And love makes you do crazy things. Or so they say, but I'm starting to think every fucking cliché about it is true. So just own up to it. Embrace it. Be crazy and do those things that are just a little bit nuts."

"I...I can't, Lachlan."

I groan, my hands gripping the pillow. I know I'm being completely fucking selfish asking her to give up everything to stay here with me. I know it.

"If I could move to San Francisco," I say slowly.

"No way," she says.

"You really don't want to be around me, do you?"

She grabs my chin and makes me look at her. "Listen to me," she says, her eyes flashing. "You're right in that I don't have a lot to give up at home."

"I never said that."

"It's true," she says. "I do have a job I don't like that I fantasize about quitting. And while I do have my friends I would miss dearly, and my family who I love more than anything...I don't know if the fear of being away from them is enough to keep me from leaving. But in no way, shape, or form are you to even consider coming to California. You have your career here, an actual goddamn career, and you have your dogs and your charity, and you have so many good things lined up. If anything at all, I'll be the one to find a way to stay here."

My chest aches at the possibility. "Just say the words, please. Tell me that you want to stay, that you'll try, and I promise you, I promise you, I will make it work out."

She searches my eyes for a moment, thinking about it. I can almost see the wheels turning, weighing over each option, much like she did in the car when I invited her here in the first place. That feels like a lifetime ago.

"I need to think about it," she says. "Give me another week and I'll know for sure."

I rub my lips together and nod. "All right," I tell her, kissing her on the forehead. "Thank you."

"Now," she says, smacking me on the ass. "Get out of bed and get to practice. It's already going to suck that you're hungover. I don't want your coach calling me and complaining."

I nod, that shame from last night creeping up my throat again like bile. I quickly get ready and head out the door in the nick of time. I have to stop at a corner store to get a bottle of Gatorade, some Ibuprofen, and spend a few minutes trying to compose myself before I show up at practice.

I'm expecting for everyone to know what went down. Not that the team would really care, but Alan usually lays into us for any misconduct off the pitch. But everyone is acting normal, except for Thierry and John of course, who regard me with concern, and no one seems to notice my banged up knuckles or the faint bruise on my jaw from where the guy's first—and only—punch was thrown.

That has to mean the guy is alive and well. Still, I go to Thierry during break and pull him aside.

"Hey, thank you for last night," I tell him quickly, looking around us, keeping my voice low.

He glares at me, shaking his head in disapproval. "You owe me one," he says in his French accent. "The police showed up and John and I had to make a big elaborate story about how some guy came to our table wanting to fight."

"You told them it was me?"

"No, I did not," he says indignantly. "John gladly took the blame. He's always looking for more street cred. You're lucky you're a local hero, you know that? All the witnesses blanked out, agreeing with him. Ugly fucker comes looking for trouble, John beats the shit out of him. End of story."

I swallow, feeling sick. "How is the guy?"

He shrugs, taking a sip of water. "I don't know. I wasn't holding his hand. But he left the bar on his own two feet and before the police showed up, if that makes you feel any better. I think you got away with near murder on this one. What the hell were you thinking?"

I give him a sharp look. "I obviously wasn't thinking."

"I know, just...take it easy, man. I should have known better than to bring you to a bar. I thought you were doing better. You were the last time."

"That was months ago," I remind him. "And I'm fine," I add quickly. "I just have a lot going on right now. It's tripping me up."

"The girl," he muses.

"It's not her fault," I say harshly. "She has nothing to do with this."

"But she's what's on your mind, what's tripping you up. No?"

I wiggle my jaw back and forth, trying to relieve the tension. "I'm going through some things. It won't happen again."

"It better not, Lach," he says to me, putting his hand on my shoulder. "Because that girl is in love with you. Believe me, you do not want to fuck that up."

I squint my eyes at him. "So what really happened in Paris?"

But he just smiles at me and walks away.

I sigh and return to the game.

Being on the rugby pitch has always been the one place where I can put everything behind me—all my past and my future and just live in the present.

But for the rest of practice, I'm as useless as tits on a bull. Maybe it's the hang over, but it's most likely everything else. The great highs of this morning in bed with Kayla, hearing her say she loves me, having her tell me she might stay, combined with the lows of last night, the shame over my violent behaviur, the way that I must have made her feel. How quickly I went from "one drink will put me at ease" to not having a limit at all.

"McGregor," Alan yells at me as I'm leaving the pitch. "Smarten up next time. We need you sharp."

I nod, grunting, and head into the locker room to shower.

I needed to smarten up, and fast. For the sake of everything.

Chapter Twenty-Three

KAYLA

"Please stay with me."

I hear his words over and over again, and each time my mind replays it, each time it brings up that look on his face, desperate and needing, my heart is torn in so many directions. How is it possible to feel so alive, so full, at knowing he wants me to stay, at even considering it, while I also want to crumble and weep because it just seems so impossible?

I mean, how could I stay here? Is this something I really want to do?

I know the answer to the last question, but the first one needs a lot of work.

"You going to be all right?" Lachlan asks me. His voice is so low, so quiet, that I turn away from the drawing room window and look back at him.

He's got his duffel bag full of rugby gear slung over his shoulder, brow furrowed in concern. After he told me that he wants me to stay, he's been acting different around me. Like he's afraid to say anything more, as if it will set me off and running.

I raise my cup of coffee at him. "I've got this. I'll be good."

"Weather isn't very nice," he says, and I look back out the window at the rain streaming down.

I shrug. "Perfect day to stay indoors. I'm sad I won't see you getting all muddy in the field though."

"Actually we're conditioning at the track today," he says. "You're welcome to come."

I'm not sure that I am, not after the other night. Sometimes I worry that it was me being around his field, around his teammates, that set him off. I shake my head and give him a small smile. "That's okay. I have a whole day to lounge around here with the dogs and watch *The Vicar of Dibley*. Besides, I have to get ready for your gala hoopla, and I'll need a lot of time to get gorgeous."

His eyes trail up and down my body, at my lacy shorts and thin tank top. "You can just wear that. I wouldn't mind."

"I'm not sure this outfit would help Ruff Love's reputation. When will you be back?"

"Half past three, I'm sure." He licks his lips, seeming like he's going to say something. Then he just nods at me. "I'll see you later, love."

"Bye," I say softly, watching him leave.

Once the door shuts, I settle down on the couch, pulling a blanket over me, even though it's not that cold. I just want the comfort.

After a few episodes of watching Dawn French, I decide to pull out my laptop. I log on to my work email, which I admit I haven't checked since I got here, and scroll through.

To my surprise, they've all been dealt with by Candace. I guess Lucy gave her my login info. Nothing is private when you work for someone else, and she seems to have taken over the first week of my absence with ease.

I look at some of her replies, and it's quite obvious that she's doing my job far better than I ever could have. Probably better than I ever will.

And that makes me sad. Like, really sad. And regretful. Not that she's doing a better job per se, but because the work was so uninteresting to me that I could never build up enough passion, enough feeling, to care. And if I stay in this job, like I always expected I would, I would never reach that point where I was giving it my all. Because in the end, it didn't really matter to me. I looked for joy and purpose outside of it.

Now I've found Lachlan. And while he's not my purpose in life, he's bringing me so much joy, love, every fucking emotion possible that I feel like I'm living in color instead of shades of black and white. What if I find a job where I could feel a similar kind of joy for the daily work that I do? What if I could find purpose in the things I did every day, find passion that rivaled the passion I feel for Lachlan? Who says that only one aspect of your life can be fucking fantastic?

The more I stare at the emails, the more I realize that Candace, for whatever reason, loves doing her job and even more than that, loves doing *my* job. And I don't love anything about my job whatsoever. Now that I know what love is, I don't want to be stuck where it's absent.

I take in a shaky breath as the realization hits me. I need to find my purpose and my passion. I need to leave my job and take a risk.

I need to stay here, with him, and start again.

But knowing that doesn't make it happen or make it easier.

The fear will always hold you in check.

I check my phone and calculate the time back in San Francisco. Everyone is still asleep. I can't talk to my mom and ask her what she'd think of me moving here, even though the thought of bringing it up pains me. I can't talk to Stephanie and Nicola and tell them that I'm in love with Lachlan and that he's in love with me, and that even though he's messed up, I still want to chance it and be with him permanently.

So I make myself a cup of tea, cuddle up with the dogs, and stare out the rain-pattered window, as one does when they're feeling all pensive and moody.

I guess at some point I fall asleep, because I wake up to Lachlan coming in the room and planting a kiss on my forehead.

"Tough day?" he asks lightly.

I glance up at him, his face flushed from running. He looks like the picture of health. It's hard to imagine just a few days ago he was hung over and burdened by his own shame.

"Yeah, exhausting," I tell him, stifling a yawn. "Is it already half past three?"

He nods. "Aye, but we don't have to be at the gala until seven. You can keep napping if you want."

My body does want to nap forever, but I'm not missing an opportunity to dress up for Lachlan's main event. I even went shopping with Amara on Princes Street the other day, looking for the perfect gown. I mean, when else would I ever be able to wear such a thing? Every girl gets a Cinderella moment once in her life, and this one was mine. I'm going to exploit it for everything that I can.

I get ready slowly, enjoying each moment. The dress I picked wasn't that expensive but it looks like it is. It's floor-length and black, with a high neckline and an open back almost to my ass. There are slits up either side to show off my shoes, and I've decided on my hot pink platforms so I don't seem *too* serious about it all.

Once it's on, I step out of the bedroom and into the drawing room where Lachlan is already dressed and waiting for me. He stands up, and we both take a long moment to take each other in. I thought he would have opted for a tux, but he's in a navy blue three-piece suit.

With a kilt.

Dear lord in heaven.

"Oh my god," I say. He looks like a fucking Highlander ready for a ball before the battle.

"You look stunning," he says to me, coming over and taking my hand in his, making me twirl around. "Jesus, bloody hell. I don't even think I can let you out of the house."

"You're not bad yourself," I tell him, gesturing for him to turn around. "Let's see all of you."

He obliges. "Never seen a man in a kilt before?"

"Not other than the bagpipers on the street, and I wouldn't dream of doing this to them." I reach down and stroke his warm, strong quads, my fingers flipping up the hem of his kilt and going up, up, up.

I grin. "No underwear, huh," I say, softly teasing him. He hardens under my touch. "It's risky to get an erection in this. You'll be tent-poling it."

"Tell me about it," he says gruffly. "And if you don't stop manhandling me, we're going to be very, very late for this thing. I'll make sure of that."

It's always tempting, especially when he feels so deliciously hot, long, and thick under my hand.

"I'll make it quick," I tell him, dropping to my knees and flipping the kilt over my head.

"Bloody hell," he says with a throaty moan, his fingers curling into my hair as I take as much of him as I can into my mouth. The salty hit of him against my tongue spurs me on, and I want to make his eyes roll back into his head. He's such a big, masculine man made up of so many dark and damaged parts, but the fact that I can ruin him with my tongue, mouth, and hands is addicting beyond anything else.

It doesn't take long to make him come, and it shoots nearly straight down the back of my throat.

"Fuck," he mutters, voice straining. "Love, you undo me."

"Good," I say, wiping my mouth with the back of my hand and peering out from beneath the kilt. He's staring at me with those lazy, hooded eyes, and I know I've done a good job. His mood has changed from being slightly on edge to at peace. Maybe if I just keep fucking him throughout the event, everything will go smoothly.

"I'm ready to go," I tell him, standing up. "Told you I'd be quick."

He shakes his head at me and then impulsively kisses me. I love that he doesn't care if I've just sucked him off or not.

I ask him if he's going to call a cab for us, but since we're taking Lionel, Amara comes to pick us up in her car. She also looks beautiful in a simple green cocktail dress, her red hair piled high on her head.

"Well, aren't you three the belles of the ball," she says as we climb in. Even Lionel has a dark leather leash and a tartan bowtie that matches Lachlan's kilt.

"You don't look so bad yourself," I tell her, proud that I'm the one who suggested her dress to her when we went shopping.

The gala is being held at a hotel near the Royal Mile, so it doesn't take too long for us to get there, though Amara says she'll drop us off first and find herself parking after. When I see all the fancy people outside, lining up to get in, I'm nervous. I mean, there's even a person with a camera taking pictures of everyone as they enter the hotel.

"Is that the paparazzi?" I ask Lachlan.

He looks out the window and grunts, shrugging. Guess he doesn't know, but it does remind me that I told Jessica I'd try and write an article about the event. I bring my phone out of my clutch and check the battery power, making sure there's enough juice left for me to take some notes about the event. Just that alone makes the situation easier to handle.

I glance at Lachlan, studying his handsome face. He doesn't necessarily seem nervous, but that mellowness in his eyes is gone and he's observing the world with a level of hardness.

"Hey," I say softly, feeling nothing but love for him. I grab his hand. "Thank you for inviting me."

He regards me like I have two heads. "Of course I would invite you. That's pretty much a given now, isn't it? Where you go, I go."

But his words hang in the air for a moment because we both know that's not exactly true. I wonder, if I asked him to come to San Francisco to be with me, would he do it? Would he give up everything for me? Why can't we both be in a relationship where neither of us has to sacrifice anything?

The world just doesn't work that way, I guess. I'm not an expert on love, but from the love I've seen around me, it's not always easy. Nicola had a hell of a time finding a guy—the right guy—before she found Bram, and even then there were some uncomfortable truths she had to come to terms with. Stephanie and Linden were friends forever before they made their stupid pact, and then Linden majorly fucked it all up, separating them for a long time before they both realized they needed each other. And then there was my mother and father. They seemed to have an epic, fairytale kind of love story, but in the end, death pulled them apart. The greatest obstacle of them all, something no relationship can ever overcome.

There is no reason why the road for us should be easy. I just don't understand why it has to be so hard. I always thought if I ever met someone I loved with my heart and soul, it would at least run smoothly at first, before the hard obstacles were thrown in the way.

But there is no time for pity and doubt. Not now. I'd been with Kyle for years and years after a long, slow courtship, and I had never ever felt for him what I feel for Lachlan. That alone has made it all worth it.

"Come on, love," he says to me as Amara puts the car in park. Already the photographer turns his flashbulbs on us.

I freeze, but Lachlan puts his hand on the small of my back and leans in to me, whispering, "It's all right. Just smile. I don't like it either, but it's just for tonight, and it's all for a good cause. Think of the dogs."

I think of Lionel as I step onto the sidewalk, Lachlan pulling me to his side, his arm around my waist, staring stoically at the cameras. Lionel sidles up between us, and at the lightest command from Lachlan, sits down, hamming it up for the flashbulbs.

I have to admit, it's hard not to smile when you're on the arm of this man, especially when people are yelling his name. I know that being the centre of attention is the last thing that Lachlan wants, but he handles it with so much ease it surprises me.

He doesn't waste too much time before he whisks me inside the hotel, Lionel trotting proudly beside him.

It's crazy inside. There are fancy-dressed people everywhere, and even though I know I look the part, I sure don't feel it. This is part of some society that I've never belonged to, and it's only Lachlan's viselike grip on my hand that keeps me sane. He only lets go when he has to shake a hand or two, but other than that, he's holding on to me.

I can't remember anyone's names. I spot Thierry, John, and a few other rugby players in different parts of the venue, and later we see Amara, Jessica, and Donald. Everyone else blurs into one. It's pretty obvious right away that a lot of them don't really care about the animals, or about Lachlan in particular. They just want to be *seen* doing the right thing in front of the right people. But charity for the wrong reasons is still charity, and whatever can help the dogs is always a good thing.

I have to say, I'm completely smitten by the way Lachlan treats me. I was really worried about this event, more so than I admitted to myself. But he hasn't had a thing to drink, and while I swill champagne and feel guilty about it, he drinks sparkling water with lime. He's approached by people again and again and again, and he always introduces me first as his girlfriend. He pulls me into conversations, never leaving me out of them, and always has his hand in mine or around my waist. He makes me a part of his world as much as possible, as if I'm a permanent fixture, as if I always have been.

And I can't help but stare at him with big, googly eyes. If I were a cartoon, I would have hearts in them, and I would be constantly sighing, and I'm sure I would look no different to someone watching me from afar. I am smitten, hanging on to his succinct words in that elegant brogue, and the way he focuses on each and every person with those magnetic eyes of his, holding them in his stare. I know that he's doing this because he has to, that he's not usually so personable, but he's just so damn good at it that he fools even me.

Throughout the night I fall more in love with him. I swear if you look close enough, you'll see my heart beneath my ribcage, bursting at the seams. I can't stop smiling. I don't want to ever stop smiling.

At some point a band starts playing and Lachlan hands Lionel over to Amara, pulling me onto the dance floor.

"You dance?" I ask him as he wraps his arms around me, Lana Del Rey's "Young and Beautiful" starting to play.

"Not a bit," he admits with a smile I feel down in my toes. "But I can fake it for a few steps."

Okay, well maybe dancing isn't one of Lachlan's hidden talents. The man can't be good at everything. But he does a decent job of faking it, and at least he doesn't step on my toes.

We stay on the dance floor for more than a few songs. I'm in no hurry to return to schmoozing and I assume Lachlan isn't either.

"I just wanted you to myself," he says, burying his face in my hair. It's like he has read my mind.

"How much longer does this gala go for? I mean, when do you usually leave?" I ask him, staring at the other elegant partygoers gliding past us.

"I'm usually the last one standing," he says. "I don't want to be that guy who throws a party, asks for money, and then leaves."

"No, that's not you. Then we'll stay till the end."

"Till the very end," he says.

The Beatles "All My Loving" comes on, and he holds me tighter to him, his hands brushing down the length of my bare back and holding the small of my waist. He very faintly sings the lyrics in my ears and I close my eyes, letting the words sink deep, letting the moment last for as long as it possibly can. Everyone else drifts away, and it's me and him and a world built for two.

"I'm so in love with you," he whispers, the roughness of his cheek pressed against mine. "So in love. There is no bottom. I just keep falling."

I'm falling too. But my heart has grown wings. It threatens to carry me forever, and each time I'm dropped, careening toward the abyss, it will pick me up again.

I never thought it could be like this.

I never want it to be any other way.

"I love *you*," I say softly, my voice choking as all that emotion climbs up my throat, almost overtaking me. "I can't leave you. I won't leave you. I want to stay."

The words are unplanned and take me by surprise, but that doesn't mean they aren't true.

His upper body stiffens, his steps becoming slower. He pulls his head back and eyes me carefully. "Are you being serious?"

I swallow and nod. "Yes," I tell him, staring deep into his eyes. "Yes, yes. I want to stay. I can't bear the thought of losing you, of leaving you. I can't go back to the life I had, not after this life here, as brief as it has been. I know what I want, and I want you."

He stops moving and cups my face in his hands. I can feel his strength seep into my skin. "You have no idea how happy you've made me," he says, shaking his head. "No idea. No idea." He kisses me hard and passionately, his fingers sinking into my hair, his forehead resting against mine. "I will give you everything you need. I will be everything you need me to be. I'll take care of you."

I'm about to protest that I don't need a man to take care of me, but I clamp my mouth shut and don't say a word. Because I do need Lachlan, at least in terms of my heart, and I also know how much it matters sometimes to just feel needed. I want him to feel that, to know that I need him as much as he needs me.

"I know you will," I eventually say. "You're my man."

He breathes heavily into my neck, almost a gasp. "I'm going to make you so happy."

"You do make me happy," I tell him truthfully. "Sometimes I don't think it can possibly get better, but then it turns out there is more room in my heart than I thought."

He sighs blissfully, holding me closer for a few moments. Then he whispers, "We need to find a room." His voice is back to that warm, growly tone that makes my panties wet in a second. Hell yes, we need to find a room. All these proclamations of love need somewhere to go.

He takes my arm and strides across the dance floor, shoulders back, taking long, wide steps, like he's the king of everything. My eyes are peeled for a cloakroom as we dodge people here and there, especially avoiding Jessica because she doesn't need to know what we're about to do. We disappear around the corner, past the hotel reception, and find the washroom. It's the best we can do.

He pulls me into it, looks back and forth down the hall to make sure no one saw us, then locks the door.

I'm backed up against the sink, my hands resting on the edges, waiting for his onslaught.

But he doesn't attack me, at least not right away. He just stares at me, our eyes locked in a gaze. "What?" I whisper to him, afraid to break the spell.

He tilts his head to the side, observing me, frowning, as if I am some riddle he's trying to solve.

"Did you mean it?" he asks. "When you said you would stay?"

It nearly hurts that he sounds so doubtful. "Of course I did. I meant every word."

"Do you promise?" he asks, stepping toward me, leaning forward with both hands on the edge of the sink.

I hold out my pinky finger. "I pinky swear."

He dismisses it with a glance. "Nah, that's rubbish. Your word is more than enough." He brushes my hair behind my ears. "I want to make you feel as incredible as you make me feel."

He grabs my hips and hoists me up so that I'm balanced on the edge of the sink, my hands gripping the sides to keep me steady. He tugs my dress up and over my ass, then crouches down, his head between my legs.

I barely have time to compose myself, to prepare. He's at me like he's starving, his fingers sliding me apart, his tongue and mouth so soft and warm. I feel every sensation like a hammer, each stroke a hit, radiating outward.

I want so much from him. I want him deep inside, all of him. But among his satisfied groans and his hungry sounds, I know he just wants to devour me. He wants me to have as much pleasure as he can bring me, because he isn't sure that he's doing enough, making me feel enough.

But he is. He so is.

His mouth is savage. He's tireless. His tongue plunges deep inside me before licking up my clit and sucking me into his mouth. I nearly scream, my body at the height of all awareness, on the verge of overload. He reaches down with one hand, and two long, beautiful fingers thrust deep inside, curling against me. The heat builds deeper, and my nerves are a million champagne bottles about to burst. It's the slow, twisting anticipation that makes my mouth drop open and my neck arch back until my head meets the mirror.

I'm both hypersensitive and barely aware. My legs clench around his face, driving his lips and tongue and fingers against me, inside me, harder, deeper, and he responds by acting as if I'm all he needs to live his life, like he'd die without me.

With impatient hands, he pulls me toward him, his tongue hard and urgent, and the world begins to tip on its axis. This world built for two.

I want to feel him, feel him, *feel* him. My hips rock into him hard. He drags his tongue back over my clit, flicking it so fast, back and forth, over and over, and I can't breathe anymore.

He moans against me.

And then I let go.

I just fucking let go.

I'm in the freefall, coming onto his mouth, nearly falling off the sink. His hands grip my waist, holding me up, while he finishes me up with the hard suck of his lips, ripping a cry out of my throat.

I'm loud. I know I am. I always am. And I don't mind if someone is outside the washroom, overhearing my cries, because everyone in the whole fucking world needs to know what kind of a lover he is. He loves with every inch of himself and gives with every part of himself.

When my orgasm subsides against his lips, he straightens up, staring at me with feverish eyes. His eyes that say he knows me, knows what I like, and will never stop giving it to me.

But I'm completely selfish. I grab his head and kiss him, long and soft, the taste of me on his tongue reinvigorating me.

He moans into my mouth, and it's a sound straight from his gut, making my blood run even hotter. "You see how good you taste," he whispers, his lips moving to my neck. "I'll never get enough."

I fumble under his kilt for his cock, grasping his stiff length in my palm, so hot and pulsing against my skin. He moves forward and I guide him in, so wet and ready for him that he slides in like silk, our bodies accustomed to each other with a beautiful kind of ease.

I wrap my legs around his waist, my heels digging into his firm ass as he starts rocking into me, each slow, slick glide igniting my nerves once again.

I whimper as we find our rhythm, like we always find our rhythm, and this time, this time, I know it doesn't have to be the end. My body aches from wanting him so intensely, and without saying anything, his body responds, always giving me more than I need.

"Oh, Kayla," he groans against me, breathless, as a bead of sweat falls off his brow and onto my collarbone. I nearly expect steam to rise. He thrusts in harder and deeper, and it feels like the air is being pushed out of my lungs and I'm clinging to his body as his pace quickens.

I press my nails into his back, hanging onto the ride. Our skin slaps together in a violent, thick sound that echoes off the walls. Each push is long and hard, and he grunts with effort until his cock hits me in just the perfect place.

I go off like an atom bomb.

His hips pound against me, brutal, punishing, and he's gone in a flurry of groans, my name whispered over and over as he claws at my hips, releasing every inch of himself inside me, shooting as far and as deep as he can go.

It's so fucking beautiful.

When we've both caught our breath, when our hearts have slowed their schizophrenic pace, he pulls out of me and I hop down from the sink, my ass completely numb.

We don't know what to say to each other. I don't think we need to say anything. We give each other lazy, knowing smiles. He gets a few pieces of tissue paper and wipes it up the inside of my leg, making sure I'm dry. Then he holds his arm out for me like a gentleman.

Like a lady, I take it, and we make our way out into the rest of the night.

Chapter Twenty-Four

KAYLA

The next few days pass by in some hazy kind of bliss. Ever since I told Lachlan I would stay in Scotland, I've just been luxuriating in the idea. And luxuriating for the both of us means a lot of hot, happy sex. We're reveling in the fact that our relationship has been given an extension, that the finite amount of days we were initially granted have been stretched out into infinity.

What I'm really doing though, is avoiding all the tough decisions. The hard calls. I don't want to call my mother and tell her I might not come home. I don't want to email Stephanie and Nicola and tell them that I'm risking it all on Lachlan. I don't want to contact my work and tell them I'm putting in my zero-week notice—from afar.

Lachlan brings up the fact that I could just go home, sort out my affairs from there, and then come back. But there's something about that that makes me nervous. I know it's probably the right thing to do, but I also feel it could make things harder. If I saw my mom again, if she looked more frail than before or sounded so painfully sad, I don't think I could leave her. And then where would I be? The last thing my mother would ever want from me is to feel like I resent her, and though I never could, I know I'd spend the rest of my life nursing a broken heart and wondering what could have been.

So I eschew being a responsible and reasonable adult. I blame my foggy head on an excess of love and hormones. Just a few more days of putting off the hard part, of having to say goodbye, of having to justify my decision. Lachlan and I plan instead, about my future here, about what it all entails.

I mentioned all the hot fucking sex, didn't I? And with Jessica promising her help in terms of the article, it means concentrating on building my portfolio. The next day after the gala, even in a slightly hungover state, I wrote up a few paragraphs in the style of something you'd see in one of the gossip magazines, just a short column piece. I emailed it to Jessica who made a few corrections and said she was passing it on to someone she knows.

I still haven't heard back, but I'm just happy that she wants to help me, that she thinks she can. Lachlan seems to believe it as well, and is adamant that I could work at the organization with Amara.

I want to try and get a job on my own two feet and on my own terms, but I also know that it's not exactly easy when you're living in Scotland as a somewhat illegal immigrant. I'm legally allowed to be here for a certain amount of time, but I'm never allowed to work without a visa. Lachlan says it would be easy for him to sponsor me, and that my only other way is to work under the table at a bar, but that doesn't sound so bad at all.

In fact, there's something romantic about it. If I were back at home, I'd hate the idea of working at a bar. I mean, Nicola works at The Burgundy Lion, but it's only temporary and she's got people skills in spades. And I hate everyone. The idea of serving them day in and out, and alcohol of all things, does my head in.

But here, in Scotland, I could totally be a barmaid. Here, I can be anyone I want to be. That's the beauty of travel, of throwing everything you know aside and starting over.

That said, I don't want to start seriously looking until everything is official. That means as soon as I've officially resigned from my job, as soon as I've filled in my friends and family, well that's when the work begins.

I just wish, wish there wasn't this tiny, niggling feeling in the back of my chest that's telling me things aren't going to work out the way I want them to. That it won't be this easy. That there is a lot of heartache coming my way.

When Monday morning rolls around, I get up with the intention that when everyone else in the world rises, when Monday hits on Pacific Time, then I'll make the phone calls. Maybe that notion makes me already a bit irritable to begin with, I don't know. But Lachlan wakes up on the wrong side of the bed, too. Even Emily is a bit snappish, though Lionel is about as chill as can be, regarding us all warily.

I guess I'm leaving it down to the wire here. Technically I only have a few days left here, and if I had been proactive and already booked my flight, I'd be leaving at the end of the week. Maybe that's also adding to the prickly stew, the sense of the unknown.

But if I know anything, it's that coffee solves *everything*. I head into the kitchen to make a whole bunch of it while grumpypants Lachlan takes his monosyllabic caveman speak to the washroom.

After one cup I'm feeling better, the cobwebs clearing, and Lachlan strides into the kitchen with a towel around his waist, hair damp from the shower. I always make time to check him out—I can't help it. Living with him is like living in some girl's Tumblr account filled with tall, muscular, tattooed men. And by "some girl," I totally mean my account from a few years ago.

"I made coffee," I say to him rather dumbly. Coffee doesn't give me a new brain until the second cup.

He opens the fridge and pulls out a carton of eggs. "Thanks," he says but doesn't look at me.

"Rough night?" I ask him. We'd both gone to bed at a decent hour, and it still took me a few hours to fall asleep, my mind going over every big thing that I needed to do.

He shrugs and finally looks at me. His eyes are a bit wired looking, bloodshot. I'm guessing he didn't sleep well either.

"I'm fine," he says, getting out a frying pan to make some eggs. "So today you're going to talk to work, yeah?"

Right. So this is weighing on him.

I nod, hoping my smile hides how unsure I am. Again, not about moving here, it's just...well, nothing is for certain, and all my fears keep sneaking up on me. "As soon as it rolls around to nine a.m. over there, I'm making the call."

He studies me sharply. "You're actually going to quit your job?"

Jesus. Did he have to voice it so plainly? My fear multiplies.

"Like we said."

"Good," he says, and turns back to busying himself with breakfast.

"Are you all right?" I ask him, coming over and placing my hand on the hard, sinewy muscles of his back.

He pauses, his chin dipping down for a moment. "Yeah. No. Sorry. Sorry, love." He gives me a tight smile. "One of those mornings when you wake up with a monkey on your back. You know?"

"Of course," I tell him, reaching for a cup and pouring him some coffee. "But coffee is the cure for everything. We know this."

"Thanks," he says softly, taking it from me. "I'm just... holding my breath, I guess." He takes a sip before putting it down and getting back to the eggs. "And the first game is coming up, against Glasgow, and I want to play, and I also don't. I want to prove myself, that I'm back, but I don't want to risk going out there and fucking it all up. Or fucking myself up."

"I think you know your body better than anything," I tell him, hoping I make sense. The last thing I want is for him to stress even more. "And your body knows exactly what to do to win a game. Granted, I haven't seen you practice much, but I would be totally lying if I told you I haven't been watching Youtube video after Youtube video of you playing, running people over, scoring tries, and just fucking owning it. You're going to be fine."

"And us?" he asks, glancing at me. "What about us?"

"You should never worry about us," I tell him, and in the moment I say it, I believe it completely.

...

While Lachlan goes off to rugby practice, I stay in the flat thinking about all the phone calls I have to make. While I know it's the right thing to do, and what I want to do, I'm not sure how responsible it is. Okay, I know how responsible it *isn't*. That's what's making me hesitate when I stare at the phone, turning it over and over in my hands, counting down to when I have to pull the trigger.

What if it doesn't work out between us? What if I give up everything to stay here, to be with him, and our relationship isn't strong enough to survive whatever will be thrown our way? We're so new at this, not just in terms of knowing each other, but in terms of love. We both haven't had a lot of experience, at least I know I haven't. Not like this. And what if moving here is harder than it looks, that once the honeymoon period wears off I start resenting Lachlan for never having to make any sacrifices himself?

I don't want that to happen. But if I don't take the risk, I'll never know. It's the honest truth. I love him so much that it's consuming me. My first encounter with him planted a seed and I had no idea how fast and lush it would grow inside of me. I'm tangled in love, hopelessly, as it grows over me like a beautiful weed, ruthless to the root.

Part of me wants to bring out the weed killer and spray the shit out of myself, because I've never been the kind of girl to feel this way, to do the insane things I'm about to do. The other part wants to revel in the wildness, to embrace it, to grow crazy and merciless and unchecked.

Around four p.m., Lachlan hasn't arrived back from practice yet and I decide to make the call. I choose my mother because she always has to come first, even before my job.

The phone rings and rings and rings. It's early at home but she's always gotten up at the crack of dawn anyway. I sigh and hang up, feeling a strange sense of relief that I don't have to break the news to her just yet.

I'm about to call Stephanie, just to feel like I've done something, when I hear Lachlan's keys in the door. I also hear voices.

I crane my neck from the couch to see him come inside the hall with Brigs. Lionel and Emily jump off the couch from beside me, Lionel wagging his tail at Lachlan's brother, Emily barking at him.

"Oy, shut up," Lachlan says to her, and it's the first time I've heard him yell at a dog. It puts a sour taste in my mouth.

I cautiously get off the couch and come over to them.

Lachlan is different. The change in him is immediate. His head is lower, shoulders hunched up, a cagey tightness in his eyes. He's out of his uniform and in jeans and a v-neck t-shirt, but I don't think he showered after practice. A patch of mud clings to his arm.

"Hi," I say to Brigs, moving my eyes over to him. "Nice to see you again. If I knew you were coming, I would have made myself look more presentable."

"Oh, please," Brigs says to me, displaying a charming smile and very white, straight teeth that no doubt were created by an orthodontist. "You look lovely."

Lachlan stalks off into the dining room, heading for the kitchen. I watch him go then look back to Brigs expectantly.

"Did something happen?" I ask quickly, lowering my voice.

He purses his lips, eyes darting to the dining room. "I had time today, so I went by to watch his practice. I told him a few days ago I might stop by, so he knew. I always try and see a few games, kind of tradition, aye? Well, I only caught the last half of practice cuz I was running late, and I got there just in time to see him completely plow into Denny. Denny's his teammate. Lachlan didn't pull back at all, and I know he normally does. Now Denny's fucking injured, who knows how bad? Might have dislocated his shoulder."

My mouth drops open. "Shit. Is Lachlan in trouble?"

Brigs frowns, his blue, blue eyes becoming positively icy. "Hard to say. I don't think so. Lachlan is a hard-hitter and sometimes he doesn't know his own strength. The coach knows that. Fuck, he encourages it from him. But even if the team isn't concerned, Lachlan is to blame if Denny isn't better by the first game."

I'm not even sure how to process that. The last thing Lachlan needs is blame.

I'm fumbling for words, wanting to hear from Brigs that everything is going to be all right, but Lachlan comes out of the kitchen, eyes on the ground, brushing past us to the door.

"Where you going?" Brigs asks him.

"For a walk," Lachlan mumbles, shutting the door behind him.

"I should go after him," I tell Brigs, but he puts his hand on my shoulder.

"Give him space," he says, giving me an imploring look. "Believe me."

"He must feel so horrible." I cross my arms across my chest, feeling cold all of a sudden. I don't want Lachlan to go for a walk, alone, lost to his inner torment. He needs me to be there, to pull him out of the dark.

"I reckon he felt something horrible to start with," Brigs says. "Otherwise he wouldn't have hit so hard." He gives me a steady look, placing his hands in his pockets. "Listen, I don't profess to know about your relationship with Lachlan. I barely know my own relationship with him sometimes. I was just leaving school when we brought him into the family. I'd grown up with a lot of foster brothers and sisters coming in and out of the house, but for some reason Lachlan stuck, even though he was nearly impossible to get to know. My mum saw something in him and didn't want to give up. I suppose he saw the same in us. But it was a rough ride. And I was so angry at him, at this young fuck who acted like we hadn't done anything for him. I just didn't understand his demons." He pauses, looking away, his expression pained. "I do know, though. I know what it's like to live in guilt, to believe you have no worth at all. I do."

He clears his throat and looks at the floor. "I've been going through some stuff, to put it mildly. And I'm sorry that I wasn't there for Lachlan, a long time ago, when he needed it. But I'll be there for him now. You can bet on that. The thing is..." He glances at me. "He's reverting. Slowly but surely. I don't know why, but I can only guess. It's never not going to be an issue though. He's never going to shed his past because his past made him who he is. People with addictions...it's naïve to think they'll one day be cured. That's not how it works. It's an ongoing illness, you see? An illness for which there is no real cure, just a way to manage it. And he can't manage it alone. He needs people around him who are supportive. You understand?"

His tone makes me a bit defensive. "I understand. I *am* there for him."

"I know. You care a lot about him."

I stand up straighter. "I love him," I say, my voice soft but my words strong.

"That's even better," he says. "But sometimes love is not enough. You have to know that he's going to hurt you again and again and again, and you're going to have to learn to love him even when you hate him. That's the reality. Those are the facts. You need to know that if you truly love Lachlan and want to be there for him, and want to see him out of this hell, you're going to be put through the ringer and spat out. And it will keep on happening. It's the ugly truth, and not many people are built for that kind of responsibility."

He's watching me closely for my response, but I'm still feeling so defensive that I barely let the words sink in. He doesn't know the kind of person that I am and what I've gone through in my own life.

Also, I refuse to believe that love isn't enough. How can it not be enough when it feels like it can change the whole entire world, if not just every fiber of my being? It *has* to be more than enough.

"I'm built for more than you might think," I finally say.

"I'm glad to hear that," he says. "He's a good guy, you know. Really good. Heart of an angel, a warrior, whatever you want to call it. It's just such a bloody shame this whole thing. So strong on the outside, a scared, abandoned little boy on the inside."

"He's not a hopeless case," I tell him, knowing my words mean little from someone like me, someone new to his life.

"No, I suppose not," he says with a heavy sigh. "But it sure does feel like it sometimes." He brings out his phone and checks the time. "Do you want me to stay with you until he gets back? He, uh, might not be sober when he returns from his walk."

I blink at him. "Might not be sober?"

"He's most likely at the pub down the street right now."

I feel like the rug has been pulled out from under me. "He's drinking? Well, why the hell didn't you let me go after him? I could have prevented that!"

He shakes his head slowly. "No, you couldn't have. You can't. You think you can convince him not to drink when you tell him he shouldn't? When you set rules? That's not how it works."

"He listens to me!"

"What did I just say about love not being enough? He's not going to listen to you, Kayla. This is all up to him, and when he's in a certain frame of mind, it's like you don't even exist."

My throat feels like it's closing up. It's impossible to swallow. "Please. Please, can we go get him from the pub? You don't know he won't listen. To me or you. I can't just let him drink himself silly. He might hurt himself. He might get into a fight, hurt someone else. What if he stays out all night? Fuck, you just said that he's feeling horrible for what he did at practice. I can't..."

I can't just stay here and do nothing.

I turn around, grabbing my purse and keys from the shelf. "I'm going to find him. What pub is it?"

"Kayla," he warns, stepping in front of the door.

Even though Brigs is a tall, strong man, he moves easily when I shove him to the side. "Don't tell me, then. I'll check every single pub around." I give him a level stare. "I love your brother, okay? I'm not going to let him do this to himself."

He looks up, contemplating. "Fine," he says. "I'm coming with you."

Brigs and I head out into the streets, the sun behind the houses, coloring the sky in a hazy gold. People are out walking their dogs, laughing, and it's hard to believe that we're out looking for Lachlan, a man enraptured with darkness, who can't see the sun at all. My heart feels sick, beating erratically while I keep imagining all the worst case scenarios. I know it hasn't been long at all since he left, and maybe, just maybe he's in the frame of mind to listen.

If we can even find him.

Because he's not at the first pub Brigs brings me to.

Nor is he at the second or third.

He's not answering any of our texts or phone calls.

And now I can see that Brigs is really getting worried, the lines at the corners of his eyes deepening. Edinburgh is a big city, full of many pubs and people looking for trouble. Even so, we search through various neighborhoods for hours before we decide to turn around, heading back from the Old Town, up Dundas Street. The sun is long gone, and the darkness is everywhere.

This whole time I can barely feel anything except a sinking feeling in my chest, my lips dry and chewed up from biting them so anxiously. I keep telling myself that Lachlan is his own man, that he knows what he's doing. He's probably fine, and I keep repeating it to myself over and over. Finally I'm just devoid of thought. I'm just coasting along on my panic.

"Maybe he's back at the flat," I say to Brigs as we turn onto our street.

He doesn't say anything to that.

But when we get upstairs to the front door, it's already unlocked.

"Hello?" I ask, pushing it open slightly. I expect the dogs to come running but they don't. Brigs steps in front of me just in case we're ambushed by a robber or something.

"Lachlan?" he says, and we hear movement from the kitchen.

The both of us go in, through the dining room, and peer around the corner. Lachlan is sitting at the kitchen table, head down, eyes closed, his fist around a bottle of Scotch. At his feet, under the table, are Lionel and Emily, staring up at us with big eyes. Lionel gives one soft thump of his tail.

"Hey," Brigs says quietly, walking in beside him and pulling out a chair. He leans forward, trying to get into his face, to get his attention. "We were looking for you."

Lachlan grunts something and his fist around the bottle tightens. He still doesn't open his eyes.

Brigs looks to me, a questioning look on his face. I'm not sure he knows what to do. I'm not sure either, but as he's shooting me these looks, Lachlan raises his chin, just an inch, and stares right at me.

His eyes are frightening. Bloodshot and so fucking hard and flinty, they might as well be made of iron.

I try and soften my features, to let him know I'm worried about him, to tell him everything is okay, even though it isn't.

It doesn't seem to work. He fixes his hard glare on Brigs for a moment, and I swear he's going to break the bottle in two. Then he looks back down, nostrils flaring, and closes his eyes.

Eventually Brigs gets up and comes over to me, leaning in close to my ear. Lachlan is staring at us again. I don't recognize him as my boyfriend. It's the beast from the other night, but far, far worse.

"Do you want me to stay?" Brigs whispers to me.

I'm not afraid of Lachlan. I refuse to be. I can handle him when it's the two of us. I have a feeling that maybe it's the presence of Brigs that's making Lachlan tense up and go to the dark side.

"I'm fine," I tell Brigs. I quickly add, "thank you."

He nods and pats me on the shoulder before leaving the room.

"Take care of her, Lachlan," he says, and the longest, heaviest moments pass until I hear that front door shut.

I exhale like I've been holding my breath this whole time. Now it's just me and him. I'm standing near the kitchen door, and he's sitting at the table. His knuckles are still white from where he's gripping the bottle. I can't tell if he's a lot drunk or a little drunk. He seems to be completely lucid, and if it weren't for the half empty bottle, I wouldn't think he's been drinking at all. His eyes, as hard as they are, seem to take everything in with a frightening amount of clarity.

I walk to the table and sit down across from him, placing my hand palm up, desperate for his touch, for a kind kiss from his lips.

"Talk to me," I tell him.

He holds my eyes, and I can't read anything in them.

"Please," I plead. "Lachlan. Brigs told me what happened at practice. I'm so sorry. It wasn't your—"

"Brigs told you," he says thickly, and that's when I can hear the alcohol in his voice.

"Yes. He explained. He's worried."

He nods, a cruel twist to his lips. "I see."

"And we were worried about you when you just took off like that."

He raises his brows, one eye lazy. "Oh, really? Why?"

Oh god, how to say this delicately. "Remember the other night at the bar? I didn't want *that* to happen again."

He glares at me so hard I shrink back. "You don't understand a fucking thing, do you?"

A fist squeezes my heart. "I'm trying," I say quietly.

"Oh, you're trying," he says, getting out of his seat and turning around, placing his hands on his head. He tilts slightly to the left, nearly toppling over, but he holds steady. Jesus he's drunk. "You're trying. Is this how you try?"

It's like the kitchen fills with quicksand and slowly everything starts to spin toward the center, sinking. I felt helpless, hopeless before, walking the streets, looking for him in vain. But now, having him here, having him safe, the feeling is just as strong.

I don't know what to say or what to do. It's like he's talking about something that happened to someone else, not me.

"Have I done something wrong?" I ask him.

Suddenly he whips around, picking up the bottle and throwing it against the adjacent wall, screaming, "Fuck! Would you fucking listen to yourself?"

The dogs run out from under the table, the glass scattering across the floor. I hear a jackhammer going off somewhere, but realize it's just my heart in my ears. I watch the Scotch run down the wall, and behind my shock a part of me is glad that he can't drink the rest of it.

I'm speechless. Frozen. I can only stare at him, wishing this was all a bad dream, wishing he were somebody else. I want the man I love back.

"Got nothing to say now, do you?" he yells at me, spit flying out of his mouth, his face red up to his temples. "Bet you had plenty to say to him."

I shake my head dumbly. "Him?"

"My brother," he sneers.

My brain stumbles over itself, trying to make sense of him. "Brigs? What about him?"

"Sure, sure," he says, heading to the fridge and yanking the door open. Beer bottles that weren't there earlier rattle, and he grabs one, opening it with an angry twist. "That's what they always say. Always the lies, the fucking lies," he slurs. "I thought you were better than that."

"Lachlan," I raise my voice. "I have no idea what you're talking about."

"You think I don't know the lies he was spreading about me?" He's slurring so bad I can barely understand him. He sits down and slams half the beer back down his throat.

"Please," I tell him helplessly. "Just calm down and we can talk about this like rational adults. Just explain to me what you mean."

He shakes his head angrily, taunting me with a sour smile. "You're just like all the others. Waiting for someone to fuck up so you can cast them aside, so you can move on to someone fucking else. I know it. I know you, and I know him, and I never got your fucking love to begin with, from either one of you."

Is he suggesting what I think he is?

It's mad if he is. He's mad.

"You think something happened with…me and your brother?" I ask, almost laughing because it has to be a fucking joke. "Just now?"

"I've been waiting here for you for fucking hours!" he says, pounding his fist on the table, making the foam rise to the top of his beer.

"What?" I cry out, my blood boiling. "We went looking for you! You just left!"

"I said, I told you, I was going for a walk." He shakes his head, repeating himself. "I told you I was going for a walk."

"You went to the goddamn pub, that's where you fucking went, to drown your sorrows and revel in your anger!"

"You," he says sharply, eyes like daggers, his finger pointed at me, "you know shit about me, okay? Yeah? You understand that? That you don't know anything, so don't you fucking sit there on your fucking high horse and judge me."

"I'm not judging you!" I yell at him. "I'm pointing out the truth. You went to get fucking drunk. Brigs and I—"

"Don't even say his name," he says through clenched teeth.

"*Brigs*," I say loudly, "and I, went looking for you. To stop you."

His head jerks back like he's been slapped. "To stop me? Stop me from going to a pub, stop me from getting a few fucking beers? Who the fuck are you?"

"Lachlan," I plead, feeling this is getting out of control.

"No!" he yells, getting to his feet, his chair scraping noisily against the hardwood floor. "No! Who. The. Fuck. Are. You?!"

"I'm someone who loves you!"

He laughs. He actually laughs, head thrown back, and it's the saddest, most bitter sound I've ever heard. "Love? You don't fucking love me."

Tears are springing to my eyes. I shake my head slowly, that quicksand pulling me under. "Please, please just listen to yourself. I love you."

"If you did love me, I'd feel nothing but pity for you."

"Don't do this, please. Let's not go down this road."

"I would pity you for loving a sad sack of shit like me. Get some fucking respect, huh?"

"You're not making sense."

"I'm making perfect sense. You're just some stupid girl who came all the way over here because she thought she was falling in love. I bet it hurts to fall out of it."

I can't breathe. I just can't. I feel like someone has filled me with water, and it's quickly freezing over, and every organ inside is halted in this one horrible moment.

"You need help," I manage to say, and the words float in the air between us. "You need help, Lachlan. This isn't you."

Another vile chuckle. "This is me. Wake the fuck up. I warned you. I warned you what I was like. It's not my fault you're a fucking idiot."

My stomach twists in so much pain that I have to close my eyes. My fists ball at my sides. I try to take a steady breath in, to calm the hurt, but I can't.

"I knew I shouldn't have come here," I whisper to myself.

"No one to blame but yourself, darling."

My eyes flash open, bile rising up my throat. "How dare you speak to me like that?"

I'm begging, pleading, praying that something in his eyes will change, that he'll realize what he's saying, that he'll realize who he's yelling at. What I am to him. It happens in the movies. When the drunken hero sees the error of his ways and he sobers up and he snaps out of it, feeling nothing but remorse for the woman he's wronged. I'd take that if I could get it, if he could just see what he's doing to me.

But this isn't a movie. In real life, in this real life, he doesn't soften. His eyes are still mean, dark, full of so much hate that I can feel it in every inch of my soul.

I should have asked Brigs to stay. I should have been prepared. I should have known it could be this bad, that he could be this bad.

But I didn't. I'm a fucking idiot after all.

"Well?" Lachlan says. "Finally speechless? Nothing else important to add?" He squints at me as he finishes the rest of his beer. "No protest about this beer, huh?"

I make one last attempt. One last hope in hell.

"Lachlan," I say, my voice trembling. "I love you. No matter what you say or what you believe, I do. And I swear you believed me, you felt it, up until hours ago. Please, don't forget that. I don't regret coming here, no matter what's going on with you. But you have to work with me, please. You have to understand that you're drunk."

"Oh, fuck off."

"You're *drunk*," I repeat loudly, trying not to scream until he gets it, until he sees. "You have a problem, and it's nothing to be ashamed of, but it is going to kill us and kill you, if you don't stop. Please. If you can't help yourself, please let me help you."

He watches me for a few beats then cocks a brow. "Is that all?"

"No," I say, the frustration choking me. "No. It's not all. It's everything." I pause, closing my eyes because I'm afraid to see the truth. "Don't you love me?"

Time is stretched thin. Too many moments pass and my heart is thudding so loudly that I'm afraid I wouldn't hear his answer anyway.

Finally he says, quiet and gruff, "How could I ever love anyone who could love me?"

Fuck.

That does it.

My eyes snap open, the anger hitting me all at once. "You know what?" I snap at him. "I'm getting really sick and tired of your woe is me bullshit!"

But he just shrugs at that, looking away. "You know where the door is."

"Unbelievable," I say. "Do you hear yourself?"

"Do you want me to show you the door?" he asks, looking back at me, like he's completely fucking earnest.

"Are you seriously threatening to kick me out of here?"

"Do I have to threaten you?"

Whoosh. All the air is sucked from my lungs.

"No," I tell him, the tears starting to flow. "No you don't have to threaten me, asshole. I'll show myself to the door." I walk past him and pause briefly at his side, staring down at him with so much rage that it might just rival his own. "I don't know who you are, or what you did with Lachlan. But I do know that *this* you, I don't love. I have nothing but *hate* for this you."

He doesn't say anything. But it doesn't matter.

I storm past him and out into the hall. I can barely see through my tears. I don't even know where I'm going, but I have my purse on me, and for some reason I think that's all I'll need, that I'll be okay.

Lionel is sitting by the door, whining to go out, looking scared and pitiful. If I don't take them, no one will. Lachlan is a lost cause.

So, so, lost.

I grab their leashes, hook Lionel up to one, and then find Emily, who is shaking under the coffee table. I leave the flat quickly, almost running down the stairs, and then head out into the night. I run down the street, the dogs running beside me, nervous, frightened, not sure what's going on.

I don't know what's going on either.

I just keep going and going and going.

Because I have nowhere to go.

Eventually I collapse onto a bench, on a park by the Leith Waterway. It's dark, and probably very dangerous, maybe even with two dogs. But at the moment, I'm not scare of anything except the demons who have taken hold of the man that I love.

I put my head in my hands and break down, wild sobs ripping out of my throat. I cry because I feel nothing but hopelessness, I cry because I love him so much that I don't know where he ends and I begin. I cry because he doesn't deserve any of this, because he never asked for the life that was handed to him.

My broken beast.

How you can both love and hate someone at the same time is a merciless trick of the heart.

I don't know how long I stay on that bench for, but eventually the dogs get restless and want to go back. I don't really have a choice but to return. The dogs belong with their owner, and I belong with him too, if not just for one more night. I honestly don't know what tomorrow will bring.

I start to head back. I'm scared that he's going to still be up, still be angry, still be that horrible person I hate. The things he said echo in my head, the foreign, heartless look in his eyes. Each recall hits me like an ice pick, cold, sharp, and deep.

But thankfully when I get into the flat, there's no sign of him until I look into the bedroom. He's asleep, sprawled on the bed and snoring loudly. Normally I'd bring him some water and Ibuprofen for his hangover, but tonight, well tonight he can go fuck himself. If he wakes up feeling like shit, then good, he deserves that and so much worse.

I can't imagine sharing a bed with the thing he's become, so I change into my nightgown and settle down on the couch. Lionel curls up at my feet, Emily on the rug beneath me. Their presence is comforting, but not enough.

I try not to cry again, but it's pretty much impossible for me to turn off my emotions at this point. That black heart of mine is long gone, and this new one is beating in agony. The only good thing about crying your eyes out is that it works as good as a sleeping pill, and it's not long before I fall asleep.

I wake up briefly though, in the dark, maybe the middle of the night, to see Lachlan's shadow at the foot of the couch.

I hold my breath, waiting.

He places a thick blanket over me, tucking me in.

Then he turns and stumbles back to the bedroom.

I pull the cover up over my shoulders and close my eyes.

Chapter Twenty-Five

LACHLAN

Guilt isn't an emotion.

It's a living, breathing organism. It's another man living deep inside of you, screaming so loud sometimes that you wish you could tear off your skin and let him escape.

But you can't.

And there's nothing you can do to silence him.

Nothing at all.

There are things that you think will help you.

Wicked, beautiful things.

Sex.

Narcotics.

Alcohol.

They all sing their sweet siren songs to you, hoping you don't recognize the evil underneath. They are a temptress, promising to alleviate your pain, promising you a soft, warm hug. They promise you the world.

And they deliver. They always keep their promise. Maybe for a moment, maybe for a few hours, they let you be taken by the undertow.

That's why you keep going back. Because they don't lie.

And because the next day the guilt has multiplied. You're an even worse person than you were before, as if that were even possible. As if the hate inside you for yourself could ever deepen.

But it does.

Again and again.

Day in and day out.

And there's only one way to get through it.

To dull the pain.

Mask the sorrow.

Numb the hate.

You do it to yourself again.

Until it's the rest of your life.

But I don't want it to be the rest of my life.

Because there is someone in my life that makes it worth living. That makes me want to be a better man. That makes me want to fight against all the things I've given in to, time and time again.

The irony is, I think I've already lost her.

I don't even have to open my eyes to know she's not with me.

Her absence hits me harder than the pain inside my head, the sour, rolling swell in my gut. When Kayla isn't in bed beside me, I feel utterly adrift.

Alone.

Somehow I push aside the self-pity, the loathing, and the hate, and try to formulate a plan. My brain is sluggish and keeps re-circuiting into old patterns. It's painful to reroute it, to concentrate, to figure out what to do to fix this before it's too late.

If it's not already too late.

I open my eyes and the sunlight streaming in through the window nearly blinds me. I blink at it, gathering courage, pushing past the sick agony that's rushing inside me.

I don't remember much from yesterday, and that's a problem.

It didn't use to be a problem. The blackouts. There was something so neat and tidy about them. Whatever happened in the spaces I didn't remember never happened. Even if someone told me that I fought someone or said something horrible or vomited all over the bar, or whatever it was, I couldn't conjure up the memory for the life of me. So it became like make believe, and I just pretended that it was some other guy who did all of that because me, *me*, well, I would know exactly what *I* had done.

But now, I had no idea what I'd done, and I could no longer pretend it happened to someone else. Now Kayla was involved, and I cared more about her than anything.

I remember practice. I remember...well, I remember before practice. Going to a pub up the street, having two pints of ale. I hadn't eaten anything that morning except for eggs, and in my strange rationale, I thought the two beers would be better than nothing.

But that was just an excuse I was making to myself. I knew that. I had woken up sick and worried about what Kayla's decision was going to be. Even though she told me she was going to stay, it wasn't real until she told someone else *other* than me. I was so used to people telling me what they thought that I wanted to hear and I wanted to see it—to know it.

I wanted to take the edge off. I wanted to not care.

But that's not how your temptress always works.

She riled me up instead.

She added fuel to a bonfire.

Denny had already pissed me off earlier in practice, and for whatever reason, I wanted to hurt him. Really hurt him. As if that would make it all better, my anger having some place to go.

So I hurt him. I slammed into him as he came at me, wanting the ball, and for that moment I thought, "*No way, mate. You won't stop me.*"

And so I stopped him. I barely felt the impact myself.

Alan was pissed. Everyone was. And Brigs, I saw him up in the stands, watching me, and I could feel his disappointment from all the way up there.

I fucked up.

In one of the worst ways possible.

I hurt one of my own, which means I hurt my teammate, which means I hurt myself.

But that was the point, wasn't it?

Everything after that was a blur.

I left the stadium and went up the street to the same pub I was at earlier. Drank a pint. Brigs came by and tried to talk to me, but he's the last person I want to hear from sometimes. Sometimes he's my brother. Sometimes he's just a reminder that I don't really belong. That my family isn't my blood. And that my blood thought I wasn't worth keeping around.

I remember coming back to the flat, but feeling so ashamed of what had happened, so angry that I couldn't even stand to be there. I didn't want Kayla to see me. I couldn't even talk to her or look her in the eye.

Then my memory blanks out.

What I do remember is the feeling. The putrid, black tar of my heart and soul, where the darkness had gotten in and spread like a cancer. I remember anger and rage and paranoia and jealousy, and everything else that hurts and cuts and kicks you to the core.

I know all of that must have been directed at her.

I'm beyond praying for miracles. I know she got the brunt of it.

I swallow painfully, my mouth like it's filled with sawdust, and slowly ease myself out of bed.

I walk unsteadily to the door, the room tilting as I go. I pull open the double doors and peer inside the drawing room. There's no one there except Lionel and Emily on the couch, on top of the extra comforter I usually keep at the end of the bed.

A flash comes into my mind, a fragment of a memory.

I remember getting up in the middle of the night, taking the blanket to her asleep on the couch, and putting it over her.

I remember that.

The memory breaks me.

I have to suck in a long hard breath to keep a sob from escaping.

She wouldn't even sleep with me last night.

And now she is nowhere to be seen.

I make my way into the hall, the bathroom, the kitchen.

It's just me and the dogs.

Like it usually is.

Like it probably always will be.

Lionel follows me wherever I go as I look for her, showing me his loyalty. He only loves me because I love him, but that's all that I can get and it's all that I can take. He's a constant. He'll never leave, even when he's seen me at my worst too many times to count.

Emily is too new. She stays put, watching me warily. She doesn't know me in and out yet. In many ways she's like Kayla. Thinking she can trust me, hoping for the best. But this isn't me at my best, this is me at my worst, and what trust she had in me is shattering slowly. I think Emily will come around, because I rescued her, saved her, because she is, in the end, just a dog.

But Kayla is infinitely more complicated. She's a beautiful, caring, sexy as hell, multifaceted human being, and I know I have hurt her in ways that are probably irreparable. She can't be taught by conditioning, by rewards. Her loyalty isn't infinite. She doesn't provide love unconditionally because I've taken her in and offered her kind words. She's someone I'll have to spend my whole life trying to win over, to prove myself to, to constantly give my heart and soul to. There are no guarantees with love or life, and her love is something I can never take for granted, if I'm even lucky enough to still have it.

I search around the flat for signs of her. Her purse is gone, but her suitcase and everything else is still here.

I have no idea where she's disappeared to. I contemplate calling Brigs, or even Amara, but I'm not sure how to explain myself. Of course I call her a few times, but I'm put right through to voicemail. Even the sound of her cheerily sardonic message feels like a dagger to the heart, and I'm bleeding all over again.

What if I have fucked up beyond repair?

What if I've really, truly lost her?

Bloody hell.

What did I do last night?

So I wait. I sit down on the couch and I wait and I wait until it becomes less about waiting and more about fighting. Because it's guilt again, and it's hate and it's shame and they're coming around, trying to pull me under and smother me until I can't take another breath.

And out there on the street, in the nearest store or pub, there's something that can take me far away from all of this pain. It's even singing from the bathroom medicine cabinet. I can't pretend that I've not been popping a few of those every single day, too.

I put up a good fight, though. I hold my ground, even though I know it would make the physical pain go away. I can't count the amount of times I've thrown up already this morning.

Even as noon nears though, she hasn't returned and I have no choice but to go to practice. It's the last thing I want, the last thing I need. I don't want to see the accusing looks of my teammates, I don't want to feel guilty all over again, I don't want to move a fucking muscle because of how sick I feel.

But I can't fuck up absolutely everything in my life.

I slowly get ready then leave Kayla a note on the hallway table in my chicken scratch handwriting.

I've gone to practice. Coming home straight after. Please don't leave. I love you. We can work through this. Please stay and wait for me.

I stare at it for a moment, and the words sound so soulless and futile, as if they could ever convince a woman like Kayla once she's made up her mind. But I leave it there anyway because it's all I can do.

...

Practice was unbearable. If it wasn't for people like John and Thierry and my coach who seem to believe in me no matter what I do, even when I fuck up, I would have turned around the moment I stepped on the pitch. I would have just walked away. I've been through so much, but everyone has a breaking point, and today would have been mine if I hadn't had a few supportive faces there.

The good news is that Denny will be fine. I guess being a bit drunk before the game helped in my favor because when I bowled into him, it wasn't a direct hit against the joints. He wasn't at practice though, which was a good thing because I'm not sure if I could have handled that. Alan says he'll return in a few days, ready for the big game. I don't know what I would have done if it turned out one of our star players couldn't play. As it is, I'm not playing in the first game, so we really would have been fucked going against Glasgow.

The drive from the stadium to my flat seems to go on forever. I'm kneading the steering wheel the whole time, knuckles white, afraid that Kayla won't be there when I return. Is it possible that she just left and caught the next plane out? Maybe sticking around for her bags wasn't worth it. Maybe fleeing me, the scene of our destroyed relationship, was the only way out for her. If she had her passport in her purse, it's all she would have needed to vanish.

I can't blame her. For all I know my hope that I'll walk in my flat and see her beautiful face might be in vain.. Right now she might be somewhere over the Atlantic. Right now she might be heading back to her new life without a backward glance over her shoulder. Maybe that's why my calls aren't going through and my texts aren't being delivered. She's in airplane mode, heading far, far away.

The last time I was around her I didn't even look her way. What if that was the last time I'll ever see her again? What if my last memory of her is of me feeling too shameful to even glance in her direction? If I had known that would be the end, I would have grabbed her and held on to her with every ounce of strength I had. I would have stared at her so deeply that I wouldn't know where I end and she begins.

I would have done everything differently.

I would have never given her an excuse to leave.

I have to pull the car over, motorists honking and swerving past me. I don't care. I can't even *be* right now. The thought of losing her so soon, without even a goodbye, is debilitating.

I stay like that, trying to breathe, my head resting on the steering wheel, parked illegally. I stay like that until I find the courage to keep on going and face my truth, whatever that truth may be.

I find parking around the corner from my flat and head on up. Outside the door I wait and listen, hoping to hear some kind of movement inside that will put an immediate end to my suffering, at least on one level. If she's still here, I still have a chance to right things.

I quickly unlock the door and step inside. Lionel comes running over, begging for me to scratch him behind the ear. I crouch down, absently petting him, listening for any sort of sound.

There. From the kitchen. The fridge door closing.

Hope sings from somewhere deep within me.

I head straight on over there and see her standing with a glass of juice in her hand. She's staring at me like she's been waiting, her hair stringy and hanging around her face. Her eyes are red and puffy, and I can feel every ounce of pain that's radiating from her like poisonous sunbeams.

"I thought you were gone," I manage to say, dropping my bag to the floor.

She watches me for a moment, her face contorting momentarily. "I tried to."

I lick my lips, unable to say the right thing. The only thing I can say is, "Kayla, I'm sorry," and it comes out in a harsh whisper.

She raises her chin, trying to keep it from trembling, and all I want to do is stride across the room and hold her in my arms and promise her that everything will be okay.

But I stay in my place. Because I know to hold her right now would be hopeless.

"What are you sorry for?" she asks flatly.

"For what happened?"

"And what happened? Do you remember?"

Guilt has one foot on my lungs, slowly pushing down. I shake my head. "No."

Her face pinches together. "Then why are you sorry?"

"Because," I cry out hoarsely. "Because I know I got drunk, and I know I was in a mood, and I know I did something very, very wrong. I don't know what but…I can feel it. I can feel what you must have gone through. It's sticking in me, like knives, and I can't shake them loose." I pause, trying to breathe. "I know I hurt you. And you can't know how sorry I am for that. For everything wrong I've done."

"But you don't even know," she says breathlessly, as if in disbelief. The look in her eyes is another kick to the gut. "You don't even know what you've done, what you said. You don't know the person that you became."

"I have an idea."

She gives me a bitter smile. "Oh no, I don't think you have any fucking idea. You are nothing like this man here. You're not you. You're someone else, someone I hate."

Hate.

"You're the fucking devil, that's all I know. Mean. Horrible. You stare at me like you don't even recognize me, you talk to me like I'm someone else, and no matter what I say, how I reason with you, nothing works. It's like I cease to exist to you. How can I handle that you? How can you promise I won't see that side of you ever again?"

I want to promise. In my desperation I want to promise her everything. But I know I can't. Because if I promise it and it happens again, I won't get another chance.

"Listen, love, please. I am going to do whatever I can to make sure that doesn't happen again."

"You said your addict days were behind you. They aren't. And you know it."

But the thing is, I didn't know it until now. I've been making too many excuses, too many justifications for years. As long as I kept my career, as long as I wasn't on the streets, as long as I seemed okay to everyone else, then it wasn't backsliding. I wasn't like the junkie anymore. I wasn't powerless and enslaved to something beyond my control. I wasn't Lachlan Lockhart.

Sometimes it takes years to realize the truth. Sometimes it takes a moment.

My truth is this and it's immediate: I'll always be Lachlan Lockhart.

And I'll always be fighting a very bloody war.

"You're going to break my heart," she whimpers, tears streaming down her face that she wipes angrily away.

"No," I tell her, shaking my head. I stride up to her, grabbing her by the shoulders desperately. "No, no, no."

"Yes," she cries out, avoiding my gaze. Up close her heartbreak is terrifying. "Yes. If this continues, yes. You will break me. Or I'll break myself first."

"Please," I beg her, the tightness in my chest suffocating me. "We can work through this. I promise you we can."

"No," she says, shaking her head quickly, her lips pinched together. "We can't. We aren't strong enough. I'm not strong enough."

"Yes you are," I tell her. "You're the strongest person that I know, Kayla, and I know it's a lot of pressure I'm putting on you, just asking you to even put up with me, let alone move here, but please. I love you. I love you so much that I can't see straight, and it's destroying me. You're ruining me to the very ground, can't you see? But there's nothing else I want more than to be at your feet."

I collapse to my knees, holding her around her legs. "I can't lose you. Don't walk away from me. Don't leave me. I've finally found you. *You*. I don't want to go through the rest of this life without you at my side. I don't even think I can."

She's rigid in my arms and I sob onto her thighs, holding her so tightly because I feel if I don't let go, she can never leave. I'm just a ravaged mess of a man at the feet of the woman I love, begging for her to stay.

When her hands find their way into my hair, her fingers touching tenderly along my scalp, I nearly cry with relief. Her touch, her affection, soothes me like a bandage on a wound, and I melt against her.

"Please," I mutter against her legs. "I've never been more serious. I'll do whatever it takes."

"Rehab," she whispers. "Or counseling. Something, Lachlan. You need something, and it has to be more than what I can give you."

"Yes," I tell her, even though the idea of going back to rehab for alcohol, more than a decade after going to rehab for meth, is embarrassing and shameful. Even though there will be no secrets if I go, that the world will find out and know just what kind of person I am. But I will do it for her. "I'll go."

"You have to want to go," she says.

I stare up at her, resting my chin on her thighs. "I want to go," I tell her.

"But you can't do it for me," she says.

But I would be doing it for her. I'd do anything for her, anything at all.

"I don't want to be like this anymore," I admit, voice choked with pain. "I don't want to be the man you hate, only the man you love."

She sighs heavily, and I can feel how heavy her heart is. I hate that I've done this to her, my beautiful, happy girl. "I just don't know..." she trails off. "This relationship is just so new...shouldn't it be easier than this?"

I swallow hard. I have no answer. Because even though loving her scares me, not loving her scares me even more. How can love be easier? How can it not be anything but absolutely terrifying?

"Loving you is what's easy," I tell her after a beat. "That's the only thing I know."

She glances down at me, her brow softening, even though I can see the battle behind her eyes. I haven't won her back yet, not fully.

"I have to go to the bathroom," she whispers to me, and I let go of her legs, getting to my feet. She shoots me a small smile as I'm back to looming over her. I pull out the chair and sit down, head in my hands, waiting in anticipation for some clear sign that everything is going to be okay. But there's never a sign for that, is there?

All I know is that things have to change. And as much as it hurts, as scary as it is, I will make the changes. I'll face everything head on, I'll work through anything just as long as she'll stay with me. The thought of her leaving is this big black hole in my chest, promising nothing but emptiness.

Her phone on the table rings, startling me, and I glance at it. She doesn't get many phone calls, and the number says Toshio, her brother. Normally I would just let it ring, but in her emotional state, I figure she may need to talk to him. Who knows, maybe she'd already called him, wanting to come home.

I answer it. "Hello, Lachlan speaking."

There's a pause. Then, "Lachlan. Is Kayla there?"

Something about his voice puts me on edge. "She's in the bathroom. She should be out any minute. Do you mind holding?"

"Sure," he says so softly that it's almost an afterthought.

I get up and take the phone over to the bathroom, knocking on the door.

"Kayla?" I ask, and she opens it, stepping out into the hall. I show her the phone. "It's your brother, Toshio."

She frowns. "Okay, thanks." She puts the phone to her ear, turning away from me slightly. She clears her throat. "Hey

Toshio." A long pause. "Um, no," she says to something and her voice warbles slightly. She looks at me, but she's not really seeing me. Her eyes are slowly growing wild.

She gasps loudly, mouth dropping open. "What?! When did…" Her hand flies to her chest and I'm right next to her, peering at her, trying to figure out what's happening. Her lip trembles and she starts to shake. "No. Oh, no. No. Oh my god," she whimpers. Her eyes pinch shut, and I put my hand at her waist to support her. Something absolutely terrible has happened, far more terrible than what happened last night.

Now she's nodding, staring ahead with pained, glassy eyes, trying to breathe. "Okay," she says quickly. "Okay, I'll be there. I'm coming. Just…" She pushes her fist against her forehead and yells, "Oh god. Oh god!"

The phone drops out of her hands, skittering across the floor.

I quickly bend down to pick it up, trying to hand it back to her, but the call has already ended. She turns away from me, fingers pressed over her eyes, her mouth open, and I have to pull her back by the arm before she walks into a wall.

"What happened?' I ask gravely, prying her fingers from her eyes. "Kayla?"

She stares at me in a new kind of horror. Her lips open and close. Eventually she says, "My mother. She had a stroke, they think. They don't know. Oh god. They…they found her. Toshio found her a few hours ago in the house, and…and…" She swallows loudly, licking her lips. "She's in a coma. The doctors had to put her in a coma to protect her brain. Oh god," she gasps and nearly falls over. I quickly wrap my arms around her, holding her up. She starts shaking in my arms. "I have to go home. I have to go home right now. I never should have left her. I never should have left her."

"It's not your fault," I try and tell her, but I know my words fall on deaf ears. My good friend guilt has a way of blocking everything else out.

"I have to go home," she repeats, her face frozen in this state of blank fright. "I have to get on the next plane out of here."

I bury the crushing fear deep inside. "Of course," I tell her. "Let me handle that, okay? Just go and pack. We'll get you back to your mother. Everything is going to be fine. Okay, love? Everything is going to be fine."

She nods and turns in a daze, heading over to the bedroom.

I feel like I've been hit by a truck. If her mother doesn't pull out of this, Kayla will be beyond devastated. More than that, she'll be an orphan, just as I was. And though she grew up with two loving parents, when I only had one for a short time, I know what it's like to feel utterly alone in this world.

This is going to destroy her.

I lean against the wall, trying to breathe. Our relationship is hanging on by a thread. I'm probably the person she trusts the least at the moment, and now she has to go back home. I can't even go with her because of rugby, even if she wanted me there.

Still, I have to make sure. I could try.

I head to the bedroom to see her shoving everything in her suitcase, a blank expression on her face.

"Do you want me to go with you?" I ask her.

She barely looks at me. "You can't go. You have rugby."

"I know I do, but this is important."

She shakes her head, grabbing a pair of jeans out of the laundry basket. It's all happening so soon. She's leaving.

It would be completely selfish to fear that she might not ever come back.

"You stay here," she says. "This is…I have to go be with my brothers. We have to figure out what to do."

"I know," I say softly. "But I could make something work. If you need me, you know. For support." The truth is, I probably couldn't make anything work. Not right now, before our first game. But if she needed me to be there, if she wanted me there, I would do whatever I could.

"You stay here," she says again.

I nod. "Okay. I just wanted to make sure."

I go to my computer and quickly book her a ticket on the next flight out of Edinburgh. There's one that leaves tonight, stopping over in Newark and then LA, but at least she'll get to leave as soon as possible.

And just like that, both our worlds completely change for the second time today. We're both silent and reeling on the drive over to the airport, with Lionel and Miss Emily in the back seat to keep me company on what I know will be a very lonely drive back home.

Everything is happening so fast, my heart and mind can barely catch up. One minute I'm begging her to stay, to give me a second chance. The next minute she's leaving and it's out of our hands. She's leaving, and what we are as a couple, who we are to each other, is being left completely unresolved. But that's the least of our problems right now, and right now I don't think I deserve to dwell on anything that remotely resembles myself.

It's about Kayla. And that's where my heart breaks all over again. Because I know how much she loves her mom, how much responsibility she feels for her. I just want to be with her, by her side through all of this. I want to be the rock she so desperately needs. I want to be the hand she reaches for at night, the chest that she cries into.

And skip, skip, skip goes time.

I'm getting whiplash.

We're now at the security gate, and she's already said a teary goodbye to Lionel and Emily in the car, and she's all checked in, and now we're standing a few feet apart and the short distance between us feels a continent wide already.

"I know I'm going to regret this moment," she says quietly, her tone still flat, in shock.

"What do you mean?" I ask, reaching for her hand. It's cold and limp in mine.

She blinks a few times then studies my face, her eyes pausing at my nose, my lips. "I know that in the future, when things settle down, in whatever way they will, I'm going to look back at this moment and regret that I didn't take it all in. That I didn't see who was standing in front of me. That I'm going to wish I could recall your face." She shakes her head, and a single tear spills down her cheek. "None of this is sinking in. That I'm leaving. I don't know what's going to happen. With her. With us."

I raise her hand, flipping her palm up and kissing it. "Your mother is going to be fine. You'll get there and she's going to be fine. She'll know you're there. She'll pull through, okay? And us. We'll be fine, too. You'll come back to Scotland when she's better, love."

But as soon as I say the words, I see the look in her eyes. The look that says she doesn't know. The look that says that maybe she was planning on leaving anyway.

Sorrow carves a path through my chest.

She was never planning on staying.

It takes all my strength to stop from collapsing to the ground, right there in the airport.

"I'm sorry," she says to me.

I try to smile. I fail. "Don't be."

"I love you, you know."

My vision blurs. "I love you too." But my voice cracks, and it's all too obvious that I'm being decimated from the inside out.

This is probably the last time I'll ever see her.

And now I know I'll regret this moment too.

For not forcing myself on her plane.

For messing everything up and preventing us from having a chance.

For letting her go.

I can't let her go.

With tears in my eyes, I grab her face and kiss her hard on the lips, letting all my love, all my cares, all my pain melt into her, as if she could take all of me with her.

I let out a soft sob against her mouth, my hands starting to shake.

This is the end.

We're both so blindsided.

She pulls away from me first, sniffing hard, mascara underneath her eyes. "I have to go," she whispers.

Then she turns away.

Walks away.

Disappears behind the security partition.

And I'm lost in the distance between us.

Chapter Twenty-Six

KAYLA

The flight attendant is telling me to buckle my seat belt but I barely hear her. I can barely move my fingers, they are so cold. I feel like a block of ice, numb to the marrow, but I think it's keeping me alive, keeping me from losing my mind to worry and grief. So I welcome the way I move, slow motion, underwater. I hope it wraps around me for everything to come.

If I try and think about any of it, it creates cracks down my middle and I am trying so hard to hold it all together. On one hand there is my mother, in a coma, on the threshold of life and death, and none of that would have happened if I had been there. It's my fault through and through that this happened and I have no one to blame but myself.

On the other hand, there is Lachlan, the man I love, the man with demons I can't fight, that fight me back, and I left him. I left him in Scotland, and I left our relationship broken with no chance of repair. I might never see him again, and that too, even for all his faults and his self-ruin and his terrible addictions, feels like a death as well.

Shut it down, I think to myself. *Bring up that big black heart and shut it all down.*

It's a shame. But it's the only way I'm going to get through this in one piece, even though I know I've already left a vital part of me behind in Scotland.

When my plane finally lands in San Francisco, I'm a walking statue. The only thing that gets me through is seeing my brother Nikko, along with Stephanie, waiting in arrivals.

"Oh, honey," Stephanie says softly when she sees me, running toward me with open arms. She holds on to me tight, sniffing into me, and it takes so much to not break down and lose it. I have to stay strong though, because if just seeing her makes me cry, I'm not going to get through the next few days.

"I'm so sorry," she whispers, pulling back. Her eyes are swollen from tears. "Toshio called and told me what happened, said Nikko was going to pick you up. I had to come along." She looks around me. "Lachlan couldn't come?"

I shake my head. I can't even explain.

She winces. "It's okay. I'm here. We're all here for you. Nicola, Bram, Linden. We'll get you through this."

I nod, appreciating it more than anything. I look over at Nikko and give him a soft smile.

Nikko is the second oldest, a really smart software engineer with a wife and a toddler. He's always been the quiet one, the calm one, the old soul, and I'm glad he's the one who came to get me. Nikko always provides the right amount of comfort.

"Kayla," he says, embracing me. "I should have been there. We should have done more."

I shake my head. "No. I was wrong to leave."

"No," he says adamantly, pulling back. He stares intently at me. "Kayla, you have done so much for her. So much. Her sons just haven't been there, and we should have been. We should have never let you take on so much by yourself."

Oh god. Now his eyes are watering. I can't do this.

I turn away. "Let's just go. Please. I need to see her."

The drive to the hospital feels surreal. It just doesn't seem like anything other than a bad dream. Then again, the last twenty-four hours have been a nightmare, with Lachlan starting it all. My eyes pinch shut at the image of him dropping to his knees, holding on to me for dear life as he sobbed his apologies. I know he meant it all. I know he did. But the damage was already done.

My beautiful beast. I don't think I'll ever see him again.

I lean forward, curling over the pain, and Stephanie reaches forward from the back seat, rubbing my arm, telling me it will be all right. She doesn't even know the half of it.

Once at the hospital, we go upstairs, and I'm hit by the painful wails, the sterile smells, that heaviness in the air. Each step we take down the hall seems longer than the first, and there's a part of me that starts to panic, wondering if it will all be too late by the time I get there.

Eventually we get to the ICU and see Paul and Brian in a small waiting room, talking to the doctors. I give them quick hugs as they tell me Toshio is on his way, that he had to drop off Sean somewhere.

The doctor, a tall blonde woman with a no-nonsense face, proceeds to tell me everything as Steph holds my hand.

My mother appeared to have a major stroke, a blood clot in the brain.

Toshio came over to the house, found her unresponsive on the kitchen floor, and called an ambulance.

They'd said the damage so far points to her being on that floor for a very long time.

In the back of my head I think about when I rang her to tell her my news.

And she never answered.

Could that have already been it? Could I have been so selfish in my desire to stay with Lachlan that I was calling her up to tell her this while she was suffering from a fucking stroke?

Loathing myself has reached another level.

The doctor then tells us that she's been put into a medically induced coma in hopes of keeping the swelling down. The coma shuts down everything in the brain so that in extreme cases such as this one, it has a chance to recover.

"And what are the chances of recovery?" I ask quietly. I glance around at my brothers' faces and I'm hit with how grim they look. They already know. Of course they already know. The chances aren't good.

The doctor gives me a tight smile. "We can't say for sure yet. It depends. If the swelling recedes, then we can try and lighten up the coma and see if she can come back and what her level of function is."

"*If* she can come back?" I ask incredulously.

"Our goal is to get her out of the coma as quickly as we can. We don't want to have her under for any longer than we should. But it's still a risk to put her there. We never know if the patient will come out of it, even if we lessen it. But sometimes it's the only chance we have." She tilts her head sympathetically. "When we decide to put a patient into a coma, we're already talking about extremes. Your mother has a very tough time ahead of her. You're all going to need to be very strong."

I almost faint. Steph tightens her grip on my arms, keeping me upright. "Can I see her?" I whisper.

The doctor nods. "Of course. Follow me."

We go into the nearest room and she pulls a curtain aside.

There is my mother.

But it's not my mother.

My mother was tiny, but she's never this tiny. Not this old.

This is a small, dying woman, skin greying, almost translucent, painfully thin, and hooked up to a million machines. They beep, monitoring her, the only sign that she's not dead at all. I watch her heart beat on the monitor for a moment, then look back at her, trying to connect the two images, the proof that she's alive.

"That's not her," I whisper, my hands at my mouth, waiting for someone to agree with me, to tell me that this is all a big joke. But no one says anything. The amount of pain between us all is staggering. I can't even comprehend it, and my brain shuts down all over again. Switch by switch.

But still, I pick up her hand, her papery skin so weak and thin, and I hold it, willing strength into her, screaming inside my head for her to please, *please* pull through.

There's no response. I don't know why I thought there would be. They have to wait to bring her out of the coma anyway. But even so, I thought that maybe, maybe just me being there, having all her children around, would let her know that she has a lot left to fight for.

I'm terrified, terrified, that wherever she is, she can see my father and he's reaching out for her, that she's going to take his hand. She's going to let him pull her away because that's all she's ever wanted since the day he died.

I can't stop the tears from rolling down my face. Even I can't shut down completely.

Steph holds me, and I'm so glad she's here, and I'm so glad my brothers are here, but I know who I really need, whose arms I want to crawl into tonight.

With everything that's happened, everyone I'm losing, I'm amazed I can still feel my heart in my chest at all. I would have thought there was nothing left.

...

The next few days ghost by. Somehow I go back to work, though after one day of moving through the motions like a robot, Lucy tells me to take more time off. I know it's also because Candace has effectively taken over my job now, but I don't care one bit. I don't care about anything at all.

So I'm at the hospital most of the time. I sit by my mother's side, I hold her hand, and I talk. I just talk. About everything. Happy things. Old memories between us, the good old days. Things were so beautiful, so simple then. Everything that seemed to happen before this seems to shine in remembrance. Nothing will ever be the same again. I know this.

Steph comes by when she can. Sometimes with Linden. Sometimes it's Nicola and Bram. Usually one of my brothers is here. They all have the same apology to me, that they should have never let me be the one to handle everything to do with my mother, that I needed their support, that they should have been less selfish, that they weren't raised to be that way.

But it really doesn't matter what they say. I don't blame any of them. I just blame myself for not being there. If I hadn't left for Scotland, maybe this would have never happened. I don't know what the signs were leading up to it, but I'm sure if I could have gotten her to a hospital, I know I could have made a difference.

The funny thing is, I'm starting to understand Lachlan more and more. It's grief and guilt of a different kind, but in the end, the emotion eats at you the same way. When I'm at home, I find myself drinking a few glasses of wine just to take me to a fuzzy place where I don't have to think, if not to just pass the hell out and find sleep.

I haven't talked to him much. He texts me, always, asking how I am, how my mother is. I never answer him back with more than a few sentences. It seems easier that way, even though I care about him. Even though I want to know he's okay, that he's getting help. I want to know how his rugby game went. It's enough that I look it up on the internet instead of asking him. He didn't play that first game against Glasgow, but they won and that brings the smallest, saddest smile to my face.

After it's been about a week since she had her stroke, we're told by the doctors that the swelling has lessened a bit and they're optimistic about bringing her out of it.

We all gather at the hospital, just my brothers and me, anxiously standing around while it happens behind closed doors. This could be it. We could walk in there and she might be smiling at us, groggy, but she could be our mother again. She could tell us about the dreams she had about our father, and we'd laugh and cry and thank her for coming back to us, her children who need her more than we've ever been able to say.

But when the doctor comes out, we immediately know it's bad news.

She exhales heavily and looks us all in the eyes. "We weren't successful."

The floor drops out from underneath me.

"She's alive, but…we can't take her off life support. She wasn't able to come back."

"So she's still in a coma?" Paul asks, sounding irate. That's always been my oldest brother's job. To get angry.

The doctor nods. "As I said, putting her in a medically-induced coma is a last resort for anyone, especially someone her age. It is, and always has been, a leap of faith."

"Well, what do we do now?" Toshio says, panicking. "What…what can we do for her?"

"We've weaned her off the barbiturates that essentially turn off her brain to begin with. But sometimes the brain doesn't switch back on. It's impossible at this stage to know how much damage was done because of the stroke and how much was done because of the coma. If she had a good chance to begin with, she should wake up. But she hasn't. We'll give it a few more days, but, I'm so sorry, I don't think she's going to come out of it. The only thing you can do is wait. Pray if you must."

"Pray?" Paul says with a sneer.

Nikko elbows him to shut up then says to the doctor, "Look, how long can she be in the coma? She's in one of her body's own doing, correct? Well, people wake up from comas all the time. I don't even think we should be discussing any alternatives until we give her all the time that she needs."

Toshio is nodding, wiping away a tear. "Yeah. Sometimes people wake up after years and they're fine."

Yeah, I think sadly to myself. *But those people are young. Our mother is not.*

I glance at the doctor and I know she's thinking the same thing. It's the truth, and one I've spent my whole life trying to come to terms with, knowing I'll have to see my own mother die and probably while I'm still a young woman.

But the doctor doesn't say that. Instead she says, "We will keep her on life support until you, as a family, tell us not to."

I close my eyes and feel Nikko's arm around me.

I want to believe we will never have to make such a horrible decision.

I want to believe that my mother will still come out of it.

I want to believe in a lot of things.

But I'm not sure how much belief I have left anymore.

Chapter Twenty-Seven

LACHLAN

For days after Kayla left, the only people I see are my teammates and Amara. That's all my world has whittled down to. Without Kayla, everything just shrinks. When she was here, the world was wide and infinite. Now, it's back to sleepwalking, just as I had been all those years before she came into my life.

So while I've been ignoring calls from my family, from even Bram in the States, I'm not too surprised to find Brigs buzzing my doorbell and throwing stones at my window late one afternoon.

I poke my head out the window, glaring down at him. "You know I have a buzzer," I yell.

"Would you answer your buzzer?" he asks.

"No more than I'd answer some bugger pelting my window with rocks." I sigh and take the key out of my pocket, dropping it down for him.

To be honest, I'm nervous about seeing him. The last time I saw him was the day everything ended between Kayla and me, and I still can't quite recall what happened. But he was there, at least for part of it.

He comes in the door, shutting it behind him. "Hey." He slides his hands in the pockets of his sharp suit and saunters over, watching his shoes on the hardwood floor before glancing up at me. "I saw the game. Congrats."

"Thanks. You know I had nothing to do with it though," I tell him, sitting on the couch, Lionel flopping over on my lap, begging for his stomach to be scratched. He knows when I'm anxious, and this is more for me than him.

"Ah, I'm sure everyone is playing better because they know you'll be joining them soon." He pauses, squinting at me. "How is Denny? He seemed in fine form."

I nod, trying to ignore the spread of shame. "Yeah, he's all right. I guess it helped that I was a bit drunk during that practice. I wasn't able to do as much damage."

I look at him for a reaction.

He only raises his brow. "I see. I thought as much. You know, Lachlan, this isn't exactly a friendly visit from me."

I lean back in the chair and stare down at Lionel, running my hand over his stomach. "I guess that would be asking too much from my brother."

"Oh, now I'm your brother," he says. "I see. Only when you're sober then."

"I'm sorry," I tell him, angry at how weak my voice sounds. Pitiful.

"I know you're sorry," he says. "But I don't think you're sorry enough. Lachlan, I know you pretty well, I think. I don't claim to know everything about you, but that's only because you keep your cards close to your chest. And for good reason. But I think, even though we aren't technically related, we handle things in a similar way. We drown in decay. Because when the pain gets too great, it becomes a comfort. You can fall in love with your sadness and your shame. I know I did." He bites his lip and looks up at the ceiling, as if reasoning with God. "I did. And only now do I feel strong enough to crawl away. But you have to hit that point. You hit yours a decade ago, when your friend died and you were too fucked up to save him. But you and me. People. Everyone. We all have many points during our lives. There is always more than one bottom. This is your other one. You have to crawl out of it. I'm telling you this as your brother, your friend, someone that loves you and knows you. You have to crawl out of it now."

I stare straight ahead, letting the weight rest on me. "It's not that easy," I tell him, and I regret it the moment I say it. I eye him warily and see so much indignation and pain on his face that it shames me.

"Don't tell me it's not that easy," he says softly, his voice shaking. "I lost my wife and my son. At the same time. They were taken from me and I have no one to blame but myself for that. Do you know what the last words I said to her were?" I shake my head, not wanting to know. "They were 'please forgive me.' I was begging for her forgiveness because I fucked up something in a major way. And she never got a chance to forgive me. She took Hamish with her, and she fled from me. She drove fast and the roads were wet, and then I didn't have a family anymore. The irony is that I was on the verge of losing them anyway. So, don't tell me it's not easy. It's the hardest fucking thing to do, to come out of that black dark hole and into the light where you can clearly see what a piece of shit you are. And I'm still climbing out of it, but at least now I know that I'm going to make it through." He closes his eyes and gives his head a quick shake. "I have to. I can't live the rest of my life hating myself. That's not a life at all."

I don't have a rebuttal to that.

He quickly sits down across from me, leaning forward, elbows on his knees. "I'm not telling you all this to discount all you've gone through. This isn't a competition to find out whose life went more tits up. Yeah? This is about me reaching out to you and trying to give you help. Will you let me help you? I know Kayla wanted to, but she's not here anymore and I'm not going anywhere."

I want to tell him that it's not Kayla's fault that she left, but I think we both know it's my fault anyway.

"What kind of help?" I ask thickly.

He reaches into his front pocket and pulls out a piece of folded up paper, holding it out between two fingers. "This is the number of my psychologist." I stare at it blankly until he shakes it. "Take it. Call him. Make an appointment. Please."

I hesitate. My pride is begging me to turn it away. "Brigs..."

"No," he says. "Do you want gravity to take you back to the bottom? Do you want what happened with Kayla to happen with someone else? Do you want to lose your organization, your career, because I guarantee all of those things will happen if you don't do something right *now*."

"This is some sort of intervention," I mumble to myself, but I take the paper from him.

"Yes it is," he says to me. "Our parents don't need to know about it, so it's between you and me. But I need to know that you'll call him. I'd watch you do it right now but I'm not your bloody babysitter. I trust you, aye?"

He gets to his feet. "I also hope you'll check into rehab. There's a great facility for sports players. They're discreet. And you know it's nothing to be ashamed of anymore. Don't make me sing you an Amy Winehouse song." He nods at me. "I'll be in touch. Make the coach put you back on the pitch. You need it."

And just like that he leaves, leaving me reeling on the couch.

"What do you think about that, Lionel?" I ask him, holding out the paper. He sniffs it then deems it uninteresting and goes back to sleeping.

I've been to rehab before, but a psychologist is a totally different thing. My prescriptions so far have been filled by the team doctors. Tell me your problems, here is something to fix it, boom, you're done.

But a psychologist will bring up every single ugly detail of my life. I don't think I'm strong enough to relive it. I relive it enough in my nightmares as it is.

I don't discount it though. I respect Brigs too much for that. I get up and post it on the fridge door, underneath a magnet, so it will look me in the eye every day until I finally get the courage to do something.

...

Game number two is tomorrow, and I know Alan will be putting me in. I'm nervous but relieved all at the same time. I don't want to fuck up, but I'm so glad the waiting period is over. With Kayla gone, there's just this ghost of her everywhere I look, haunting my bones, and I need something else to keep me going, to push me along the right track.

Still, I need to hear her voice. Just for a moment. All my texts and calls to her either go unanswered or they just get something generic, and I need, want, so much more from her.

And I need to be there for her. I can't imagine what she's going through right now.

I call her. It's around dinnertime here so I know it has to be morning for her.

As usual though, it rings and rings and rings.

I'm just about to hang up when she answers.

"Hello?"

The sound of her voice nearly breaks me.

"Kayla?" I say. "It's me. It's Lachlan."

"I know," she says flatly. She sniffs and I wonder if she's been crying.

"Are you okay?" I ask her. "How is your mum?"

"She's...she's still in a coma."

"Shit, love. I'm sorry. I've been trying to call you..."

"I know. I'm in the hospital a lot. They don't really want you using your phones."

"That's okay, I understand." I pause, pressing my fist into my forehead, closing my eyes. "It's just...you don't know how good it feels to hear your voice. I miss you. So much."

So much that my chest is burning with the words.

I hear her swallow. "Yeah. I miss you, too." Her voice sounds so fragile, like glass, as if she doesn't really believe what she's saying. But still, I cling to it. She misses me.

"I...I think about you all the time. You know I love you," I whisper.

But there is only silence stretching an ocean between us.

I go on, unable to handle it. "I know I really fucked up, love, but..."

"Lachlan," she says tiredly. "It doesn't matter."

"Yes it does. It matters. You matter. I'm changing, I swear. I know I have a problem."

She grunts angrily. "Yes, you have problems. But I have problems too. My mother is in a fucking coma. Forgive me if I don't care to hear your sob story right now."

Ouch.

No blow in rugby has hurt quite like that.

"Okay," I say raggedly. "I'm sorry."

"I know," she says. "Look, I have to go, I'm heading back to the hospital now. I'm just…this is my life now, you know? Just waiting for the other shoe to drop."

"I could come over there," I tell her. "I can help."

"No, you can't help." she says quickly. "You can't even help yourself. You stay where you belong. Okay. Look, I just can't deal with you, with what we were, right now. Please, just…don't call me again. Don't text me either. I can only handle one heartbreak at a time."

I feel the last shred of hope inside me crumple into a ball, blown away by some cold wind, never to return.

"Bye, Lachlan," she says.

I can't even move my lips to answer her back. She hangs up, and everything I had with her is immediately severed. I can feel it, cutting so deep.

I've truly lost her.

My love.

I get up, grab my wallet and keys, and leave out into the night.

I go to the closest shop, pick up a bottle of Scotch, then go and sit in the park across from my flat. I sit there for hours.

I nearly drink the whole damn bottle.

When I wake up, I'm on the bench still and some man is trying to steal my shoes. I kick at him, catching him in the face, and he runs off across the grass, jumping over a fence.

I stumble to my feet, leaving the bottle behind, and somehow manage to get inside my flat.

When I wake up again I'm on my stomach in the hallway.

A puddle of vomit lies beside me.

My vomit.

A few piles of shit and piss are near me too.

Thankfully those aren't mine. Just poor Lionel and Emily's, since I never took them out last night.

No, instead I did a noble thing and got absolutely wasted by myself, chasing the sorrow Kayla left me with in an unending flood of Scotch.

I can't do this anymore.

Brigs is right. I won't get Kayla back this way, and I probably won't get her back any way, but one day, if I ever get a chance again, I can't fuck it up.

I can't fuck up my life anymore.

I have these dogs. I have my friends. My brother. My family.

I have all these beautiful, lovely aspects of my life, and when I started out as a wee lad, I had nothing at all but a stuffed lion.

I started with nothing and was given everything.

And look where I am, drinking, feeling sorry for myself, trying to give it all away.

I slowly pick myself up off the floor.

I clean up the mess.

I take the dogs for a very, very long walk, practically to the shore and back.

I talk their ears off, apologizing, drawing looks from passerby as I usually do when I'm talking to the dogs, but I don't care. They need to hear it all. I need to get it off my chest.

When I get back, I go straight for the medicine cabinet, and for a brief moment I feel the guilt smash into me, threatening to drag me under again. The Percocet calls my name, offering a rope, just as Scotch handed me a rope last night.

But it turns out the rope is no different from a noose.

I take the pills, and though there aren't many left, I empty them into the toilet and flush them.

Then I head over to the kitchen, snatch the phone number from the fridge, and before I can second guess myself, I make an appointment. The receptionist is also nice enough to suggest a short-term rehab clinic I can check into on the weekend, so it won't interfere with the games.

I have some people I need to talk to. Jessica and Donald. Alan. Amara and Thierry. I need to be honest with them, as honest as Brigs was with me. They need to know what's going on in my life. They need to know I'm not well and I'm not doing okay and I need as much love and support from them as I can possibly get. I want to do this for myself, but I can't do it alone. I've been doing it alone for too long. And it's not enough.

I know now who I want to be.

Still me.

Just better.

Chapter Twenty-Eight

KAYLA

It's been three weeks.

She's been in a coma, unreachable, for three fucking weeks.

My life has become a living hell, but I can't even imagine what she's going through, where she possibly is in this world in such a hopeless, dead state. I can only hope that somewhere, somehow, in whatever limbo she is in, that my father has her hand. I know the stronger he holds on to her, the less likely she'll return to us. But at the same time, I can't bear the thought of her being alone, lost inside herself.

Because I'm lost too.

So lost.

And throughout all the pain, I keep thinking back to Lachlan, to the way I treated him on the phone. I told him to leave me alone and to never call me again, but in truth, that was a lie. I just didn't know it at the time. I pushed him away, punished him for caring about me, making him feel worse about himself than I'm sure he already does.

I just want to take it back. I want to hear his voice, for him hold me in his strong arms and tell me everything is going to be okay, even though we both know it won't be. But just to hear it from him—he used to make me feel like it was us against the world and that he could protect me from everything.

He just couldn't protect me from himself.

Then again, he couldn't protect himself from that either.

I wasn't lying when I said I miss him. Because I do. All the time. Constantly. This dull, throbbing ache in my heart that won't go away. It's a different kind of pain than the one I feel for my mom, but they are both so terribly unbearable.

And when he told me that he loved me…I remembered for one blissful second what it was like to so freely have his love and so eagerly give him mine, and it feels like another time, like we were just these young kids in love, and the world was this sunny, endless place. Our playground. I crave those days so badly that it makes my gut twist, hungry for something I'll probably never have again.

It's a Friday when Paul calls me at work and asks me to meet them all at the hospital around lunchtime. I don't even have to ask Lucy if I can leave, I just go. I have a feeling that they're just waiting to fire me when the time is right, that they just don't want to be total dicks and lay off a long-term employee whose mother is dying. But really, I do nothing all day because Candace has taken over everything, and even when I try and am in the right frame of mind, it's a half-hearted attempt. There's just too much on my plate, and I'm not going to fight for a job that I wanted to leave in the first place.

I decide to pick up Toshio on the way to the hospital, needing support to even make it through the drive. We all know what this is about, what it's come to.

In three weeks there has been no improvement at all.

It's time to decide how long we can do this to her.

And, let's face it, how long we can keep doing this to us.

Though her stroke has brought us closer together, unlike ever before, all five of us are gaunt and ashen, just shadows of our former selves. This is not what our mother would have wanted for us.

"So you think this is it?" Toshio asks, and the pain is fresh on his face.

I swallow, nodding. "Yes. I think we're going to have to make a decision. Together."

He stares at his nails for a moment and then says, "Sean broke up with me."

I'm flabbergasted, not expecting that at all. "He what?"

"Yeah. Fucking dick, right?" He tries to smile but a tear slips down his cheek instead. "Sorry, I'm just…I'm so fucking angry. So angry. I mean, I've stuck with him through so much. His last break-up, his cat dying, his STD scare. Then he lost his job and I had to support him, remember that? And then…and then he says he can't be around me anymore, that I've changed too much. I'm too sad. Sad! Of course I'm fucking sad!" He hits the dashboard with his fist. "I'm sad and I'm fucking pissed off. Why couldn't he love me through that?"

I make a little growling noise. "I can't believe it. Who dumps someone when they're going through a hard time? I mean, I know my work probably wants to get rid of me, but they're holding off out of courtesy."

"Well, I got no courtesy from him. Normally I wouldn't even want that, but fuck, honey, just fucking fake it until I'm better."

I'm absolutely livid on his behalf. Toshio has been with Sean for at least a year. "I'm going to kill him."

"I'll kill him first," he says, narrowing his eyes out the window. "You can just help me bury the body."

We lapse into silence. I can't believe that asshole would break my brother's heart like that when it's already breaking. I can't imagine the strain on him.

But then again, I can. I'm living it. Only it's my own fault, not Lachlan's. Lachlan, who was reaching out for me every day, all the time. Lachlan, who loved me with all his heart, even when there was no chance of him loving himself. Lachlan, who would never leave because I was hurting, grieving. He would only offer me his arms and kiss me until the pain was a memory.

He gave me everything he could, every part, even the dirty, cold, terrible parts. He was fucked up entirely, a slave to demons he never asked for. And yet in the end, I was the one who couldn't handle him. I'm the one who left him emotionally. I had the best thing and I lost it, and lost myself in the process too. Even though it would never be easy and it would always be a struggle to help him be free from his shackles, to keep the dragons at bay, that didn't mean it wasn't a good thing. Love is always good, no matter who is giving it to you.

Once we get to the hospital, we have to wait around for Brian to show up since his work isn't always so lenient. So we stand around, eyeing each other, arms hugged across our chests, stepping from foot to foot. No one wants to speak until we are complete.

Then Brian comes and Paul launches into it.

"I've spoken to the doctor as well as the neurologist here, and..." He closes his eyes, shaking his head. "We can't let this go on anymore. She doesn't have a hope in hell. I wish she did, we all do, but…I think we have to think about what she would want."

"She wouldn't want us to give up," Toshio says, his heart extra soft now. "I don't want this to be the end. Not yet. I'm not ready."

"None of us will be ready," Nikko says. "I wasn't ready to say goodbye to Dad either. I'm still not, you know. Sometimes I see him in my dreams and I'm so relieved that he's not dead, like it was all some bad joke. But…we can't keep her like this. Paul, the doctors, they're right. She's in limbo, between us and Dad. It's selfish to keep her here for us."

"It's *for* her," Toshio says angrily, his hands curling into fists. "What if she could come back to us? What if she has a chance? If we end her life, we'll kill her."

"She's already gone," Brian says quietly. "She was gone the day this happened to her. We've just been kidding ourselves."

"Oh, sure," Toshio spits out. "Throw salt in the wound, make us all seem like idiots for wanting her to live. If we never give her a chance, we'd regret it. We'd hate ourselves."

"After a while there are no more chances," Paul snaps. "Don't you see that? This is the end for her. For us. We have to let her go. It's the right thing to do, even if it hurts us."

Toshio walks around the room, kicking the chairs. "I can't…I can't accept that."

"Well, you have to because we need to make this decision together. We need you to agree, Toshio. You'll resent us our whole lives if you don't, and we're already so broken as a family. We won't survive that."

"Well, what does Kayla think?" Toshio asks, pausing to shoot me a look. "She's the one closest to Mom. She should decide."

The rest of my brothers' heads swivel toward me with curious looks.

I shake my head. "No. Please don't put this on me."

"She's right. She's done enough," Nikko says. "She stepped up when no one else would. But…still, Kayla, we need to know how you feel."

"How I feel?" I repeat. "How do you think I feel?" I press my palm into my chest. "Sometimes I'm surprised I'm alive, that I even have a heart. The last three weeks I've been in a fog. I can't see clearly no matter how I try. You know…I think about how I left it with Mom and…I should have known something was wrong. Her hands, her hands were shaking, you see, and I should have said something, done something. I should have never gone to Scotland. I should have never left her."

"She was shaking before that," Toshio says quickly. "Her hands, her legs when she walked. It's been going on for a while, Kayla. I figured you knew that."

I close my eyes, trying to think, but all my memories are blurred now. Now I just see her lying in the hospital bed, barely hanging on to life. "I didn't notice," I say quietly, feeling so much shame. And I thought we were so close.

"You can't always notice things like that when you see the person all the time," Paul says. "This isn't anyone's fault. Sometimes it's just life and it does what it wants with you." He sighs, running his hand through his thinning hair. "But us, the five of us here, we're in charge of what happens next. Kayla, please. We think it's time to cut her off from life support. We think it's time to say goodbye, to let go. What do you think?"

My chin trembles and I have to blink back tears. Such a terrible burden on one's soul. I'm not God, and I would only want to play God if I could bring her back.

But I know, I know in the deepest part of me, I know she's not ever coming back.

That she's made her choice to leave us. And that she's waiting somewhere. On a boat in the middle of a river. Us on one side, the love of her life on the other.

I cry softly, but I don't wipe the tears away. I just nod. "Okay," I choke out. "Let's say goodbye. But…twenty-four hours from now. To give us all time alone with her. And for Toshio, just in case she comes back." He gives me a grateful smile, but I can't return it.

I walk away from the waiting room and down the corridor, heading outside. There's a fine mist in the air above the parking lot, and even though it chills me, it feels better than being inside there for another minute.

I sit down on the curb and put my head in my hands and try to breathe. I can't believe what I just said. I can't believe what's happening. In twenty-four hours, if she doesn't wake up, I will cease to have a mother. I'll never see her smiling face again, just as I'll never see my father's.

I'll be an orphan.

An *orphan*.

A quiet sob rips through me, and I start to shake. There's too much loss in my life for me to even stay contained.

My hands are shaking now like my mother's once were, and I take out my phone, ready to call Stephanie to tell her what's going on.

But she's not who I want to talk to. Not right now.

I dial Lachlan's number, and while it rings, I calm my heart by trying to figure out what time it is over there. It has to be the evening. God, I hope he's around, that he still cares for me, that he hasn't found anyone else, though I know, I know from the intensity of his love, neither of those things seem likely.

When he answers with, "Kayla?" I breathe in so sharply that it makes me cough. "Kayla, is that you?"

"Yes," I manage to say. "I just...I wanted to talk to you."

"Alright," he says in that beautiful brogue of his, deep, warm, and silky. I close my eyes, imagining it wrapping around me. "I'm so glad you called me."

"Me too," I whisper. "I'm sorry I was so mean last time."

"No, listen," he says. "I more than deserved it for the horrible way I've been."

"You're not horrible."

"Oh, love, you know I can be."

"But that's not you. It's not the you that I know, and I should have been more understanding. I didn't want to end things like we did."

"I know, but you had no choice. You had to go." He pauses. "How...how is she?"

I let out a little whimper. "We're pulling her from life support tomorrow. I have to figure out how to say goodbye in the next twenty-four hours."

He groans softly. "I am so sorry, my love. I can't...if there is anything I can do for you, please, just tell me. I wish I could take all your pain and carry it for you. I'd do anything to help you through this."

"I know you would. I guess that's why it hurts even more. Because I could have had you here. I mean, if rugby wasn't a factor. How…how have your games been?" I ask, trying to switch the topic.

"Good," he says slowly. "Lost a few, won some more. Kayla…just tell me what you need me to do."

I need him to be here. But I know he can't be.

"Do you…do you still love me?" I ask rather bravely.

He sounds breathless at that. "I've never stopped loving you. Please. Please believe that. You're the only way I see the sun."

My heart swells, the feeling so strange and unaccustomed as of late.

"Then please keep loving me. I need it. And if I can't have you here, then I need your love. As cheesy as that sounds, I need it. I need the strength in it."

"You have it. All of it. All of me." He pauses. "What hospital are you at? Are the doctors being nice? Has she been taken care of well?"

"I'm at UCSF," I tell him. "And yeah. They're some of the best. They've been doing what they can and they're very patient. They want what's best for her just as we all do."

"That's good. Good," he says softly. "That means she's had the best people looking after her. It's all you can do, Kayla. You've done all you can do."

"And now I have to say goodbye."

"I'm so sorry."

I can barely exhale. I get to my feet and stare up at the building, knowing I'm going to be spending the weekend here. I'm not leaving until the very end.

"Thank you," I tell him.

"For what?"

"For picking up the phone."

"I'll always pick up the phone when you call. You know this."

How wonderful it is that it's the truth.

"I better go," I say softly.

"I love you."

"I love you, too." I hang up the phone. It feels like all my bravery goes with it.

But even so, through all of this, his words have bought me a little bit of strength.

I slip the phone back in my pocket and head back into the hospital.

...

I don't know how I get through the night, sleeping on the chairs in the waiting room for maybe an hour at a time. We all spend our time with her throughout the night, though Nikko is the first to really say goodbye and leave, heading back to his family. We hug and cry, and it's so unbelievably horrible that we all have to go through the same thing.

When I'm with her, I just talk. I'm saving the best for last, letting her know how I feel at the very end. I don't want to pretend she's dead until she's gone. So I talk with her as I have been these last few weeks. About everything I can.

Finally, when the birds start chirping somewhere in the sky and I can feel dawn about to break, I know the end is near. For us. For a mother and her daughter.

I take her hand, squeezing it, rubbing my thumb on her skin and thinking that she's nothing more than a husk. That the real her, the way she used to do a little dance when she was eating a good piece of chocolate, the way my father used to make her laugh so hard she'd almost fall out of her chair, is somewhere else. I remember the look of concentration in her eyes while these same hands pruned her roses. She took so much joy in them. She took so much joy in everything. She loved life so much. I just think she loved my dad that much more.

I cry, my head on her arm, holding on to her like a baby. I'm still her baby. I don't know how I'm going to get through the rest of my life without her. She's just always been here, always been watching me, loving me. Even when I do something to upset her, she could never hold a grudge. Her heart and arms were always open.

"I hope I've learned so much from you," I cry out, the sobs shaking me. "I hope you'll be proud of me. I love you so much, Mom. I don't think I ever said it enough, but I hope you know now. You're my best friend. I don't know how I'm supposed to live the rest of my life without you."

I'm crying so hard that the bed is shaking and her arm is soaked. I'm dying for her to wake up, dying for anything other than the beep of the machines. But she doesn't. She's gone, and I'm left all alone without the one person in my life who loved me unconditionally.

It's losing my father all over again, but so much worse, because I know the absence of both of them together is something that will sever me for the rest of my life.

I don't know how long I cry for. I know at some point someone opens the door and looks in, one of my brothers, maybe a doctor, but they leave me alone in my violent grief. This is pure agony and it consumes me. The tears just never seem to abate, and my face hurts sharply from the pressure behind my nose and eyes. My lungs are burning, raw.

And still she doesn't wake up.

Now I know she never will.

Eventually I'm worn down to nothing. I feel flattened out, weak, my heart too heavy now to even extract itself. The tears stop and I'm a numb, painful mess.

I take in a deep breath, looking my mother over, hoping, wishing, praying. But it's a lost cause.

"You know, Mom," I say softly, my mouth so dry it hurts. I take her hand again and hold it between both of mine. "I fell in love. Just as you said I would. With Lachlan." Just saying his name to her makes my lips want to smile. "It was impossible not to. I guess I knew it from the start, but you know me. I refused to believe in that kind of thing...love at first sight, true love, crazy love that consumes you until there's nothing left in you *but* love. The kind of love that you and Dad had. I always thought it sounded horrible." I let out a dry laugh. "And in some ways it is, because it's a disease and it takes over your whole life and every cell in your body. It was like everything I did somehow related to Lachlan. He became my everything and my always. But...I guess even fairytale love has a dark side. There isn't always a happily ever after. The prince can seem more like the villain at times, but...then again, so can the princess. Maybe that makes them right for each other. I don't know. But I did love him, Mom. I still do. I got to experience it fully. And then I got to lose it too, and that was always my greatest fear. Losing that wild, beautiful love, the same love you had for Dad. But now...now you'll be with him again. And I know how happy you're going to be."

I raise her hand to my mouth and kiss it softly. "I'll see you again too, one day. And I'll tell you all these things all over again. But I'll make sure I have something good to add."

A single tear rolls down my face and I wipe it away before standing up and giving her hand another squeeze. "I love you."

I turn and leave the room, heading out into the hall. Paul, Brian, and Toshio are staring at me, and Toshio immediately gets up to give me a hug, holding me tight. I thought I was out of tears but being in his embrace is enough to bring more out of me.

"Your turn," I whisper to him. I look over at Paul, at his red eyes and nose. "And then we all say goodbye together. At the very end."

Paul nods and Toshio pulls away, head down, looking so lost.

"She's waiting to hear from you," I tell him, putting my hand on his shoulder. "Just try not to bitch about Sean too much, okay? She has a lot to process from five children already."

"She's used to it." He smiles sadly then walks off into the room.

I sit down beside Brian and Paul, and wait.

I sleep curled up in a chair.

Two p.m. rolls around, the twenty-four hour mark. Of course this is something that doesn't have to follow an exact schedule or timeline. If we tell the nurses we need more time, they will give us more time.

But we've all said our goodbyes now.

The time is up.

"Are you okay about this?" I ask Toshio gently as we head into the room with the doctor.

He nods. "She's not coming back. I know this now."

I put my arm around him, my head on his shoulder while we stand around the foot of the bed, staring down at her.

We each offer our little goodbyes.

I raise my hand, palm out, and tell her I'll miss her every day for the rest of my life.

I guess that's not a little goodbye at all. It's the biggest one you can ever say.

The nurses go about, gently removing whatever things were keeping her alive. I know that we were told it could take a few hours or even a few days for her to pass away. The doctor had said our mother would go when she's ready to go, and it's hard to know how long the body will cling to life for. But the heart monitor shows her blood pressure dropping rapidly. Her heart rate slows and slows and slows.

She's going.

She's been waiting.

And we're watching her leave before our eyes.

And just like that, she's gone.

She's really gone.

The stillness of death lingers in the room.

"I'm so sorry," the doctor says, and I know she means it.

I sob against Toshio. Paul and Brian come over, and we hold each other in a circle by the bed.

"I love you guys," I whimper, gutted. Absolutely gutted. Absolutely *ruined.* "You're my brothers. And you're my blood."

"We love you, too," Paul says softly. "It's just us from now on. I'll need you all more than I can tell you at times."

"Do you think she'll be proud of us?" Toshio asks, sniffing hard into his sleeve.

"Always," says Brian. "As long as we don't forget what we are to each other."

"Otherwise both her and Dad will deliver the smackdown from up above," I say, attempting a joke. We pull away from each other, and even though their smiles are sad, at least they are smiling.

I feel like I might not ever make a genuine smile again.

We leave the room, and I look over my shoulder at my mother one last time.

Gone from us forever.

But so, *so* loved.

I step out into the hallway.

And Lachlan is standing there.

I stop in my tracks, trying to see through the haze of my tears, to see if it's really him or some sort of apparition.

But my brothers all stop and regard him, wary, tired, and I know that he's actually here. How can you not see a tall, inked, beast of a man standing in the tiny waiting area?

"Lachlan," I say, my voice raw. I can't believe it. His beard has grown in more, and he looks as tired as I feel, but he's *here.* He's actually here. How is this even possible?

"I didn't want you to go through this alone," he says quietly. He opens his arms for me, and I immediately rush into them, collapsing against his chest, my feet giving way. He holds me with strength I desperately need, and I cry into his chest. So overwhelmed in so many, too many, ways.

"I'm here," he says softly, his voice gruff, sinking into my burdened soul. "I'm here." He breathes in deep, his chest rising against my face. "I'm so sorry for your loss, Kayla." He squeezes me tighter and I grip his back, my fingers twisting into his shirt.

"How did you get here so fast? What about your rugby?" I mumble into him, and then I can't believe I'm actually saying these words in his arms.

He's here.

God, I had no idea how much I needed him, needed this, until I got it.

"I took the first plane out in the morning. Came straight here," he says quietly. "We don't have a game for a few days. Alan said it was fine. But I would have come even if it wasn't. I don't ever want you to think that you have to handle everything on your own. I'm here for you, I always will be."

"Thank you," I say, feeling so much sorrow and so much gratitude just swirling around in my chest. My skin is burning beautifully under his touch. I've missed him so much. Slowly, I pull back and stare up at him. There he is.

I'm not sure if he's my Lachlan anymore.

But he's here.

So he's mine for now, for a brief time, once again.

Chapter Twenty-Nine

LACHLAN

I've wished a lot in my thirty-two years but I've never wanted anything more than to be the one who could take away her pain.

The moment she called me, I knew nothing would prevent me from reaching her. I got the first plane out in the morning, then I called Alan and told him I was missing a practice. He wasn't happy about it, but I told him I was doing it anyway.

I packed my bags, dropped the dogs off with Amara, and then got my arse over to San Francisco. I'd hoped to be there in time before Kayla had to say goodbye, but I got there just after.

Seeing her walk out of that room, a world of agony on her thin shoulders, heartbreak ravaging her face, undid me like a spool of thread. I could barely stand the sight of her in that much pain and sorrow, but I needed to be as strong as I could for her.

She collapsed into my arms. She collapsed into my heart.

I held on to her with both and told her I was there.

There was no protest, no anger. She accepted me, and just for one small flash of a second, I had her and everything was right in the world.

My beautiful world.

But of course, everything is still so very wrong.

I go back with Kayla that evening to her apartment. I told her I'd gladly stay in a hotel, that if she didn't need me around, I wouldn't be around. But she wouldn't hear any of that.

It's weird being back at her place. It feels like decades ago when I first came in here, blind with my lust for her, with no idea what could happen between us. I must have known, deep down, that she was going to be the love of my life. I just didn't know that our love would be fraught with so many challenges.

Or maybe I did know that. I still said "fuck it" and went for her anyway.

I can't say I would ever do it differently.

"I'm going to take a shower," she says, dropping her purse on the table. "I haven't been clean for a long time."

For a moment I think she might invite me, like she always did in the past. But she just gives me a tired smile and closes the door behind her.

I sit down on her couch and let it all sink in.

I wish I knew what we were to each other.

She said she loved me over the phone.

Could that matter right now, through all of this?

And if it could, what does that mean for us?

She's in the shower for a long time, and when she steps out, her hair wet around her shoulders, her towel wrapped around her, she takes my breath away. So beautiful that it feels like a knife.

"Will you come to bed with me?" she asks. Her voice is quiet and she looks at me shyly, like she's unsure if I'll say yes, unsure that she should even ask to begin with.

I nod, getting up. "Of course."

I follow her into her bedroom. Even in the dark it's a disaster zone, the product of someone who has been living through hell and can't be bothered with much. I can imagine her sleeping here at night, so alone and in so much pain.

She removes her towel and gets under the covers, and I stare blindly at her naked silhouette, both terribly turned on and hopelessly in love.

But I don't want to make any presumptions. I take off my boots, socks, and my pants, but keep my underwear and shirt on. I know there's the stirrings of an erection—it can't be helped when she's naked around me, especially when I haven't seen her for a month—but I ignore it. I don't want to be inappropriate with her, not now, when she's so close to breaking.

I get under the covers, staring at her warily, unsure how to act, how to be. She turns to me and settles into my arms, her face on my chest, her hand on my heart.

I want to live in this moment, the quiet comfort of her skin against mine.

"Thank you for coming," she says after a few beats.

I rub my hand down her back, wincing when I can feel her ribs. She's gotten so thin.

"Anytime," I tell her. "Thank you for telling me you love me."

She pauses, and I worry I've said the wrong thing. "On the phone," I add. "Whether it's true or not, thank you for that. You can't know what it meant to me."

A few heavy moments tick by, seeming so long in the darkness.

"I still love you," she says, pressing her hand on my chest. "Here. I love you here, your big, beautiful heart."

Those words, those words.

Hope flies within me.

"But it's not enough," she says, and as quickly as it had risen, the hope is dashed, fallen from the sky, wings cut to the bone.

"I understand," I tell her, voice ragged with pain, even though I don't understand. I can't. Because my love for her can conquer anything.

Then again, not many things can conquer death.

"It's just…it was so hard, you know? At times. And I know we could have worked through it, but you needed help that I couldn't give you."

"I know," I tell her. "But it's different now. I'm seeing a psychologist. I've been sober. I spent a few weekends at rehab. I'm making the changes, I really am. I want to be a better man, not just for you, but for my family, for myself. For life."

I can feel her smile against me. "Good. That…that brings me relief like you wouldn't know." She sighs heavily. "But it's done. You know? I don't think we can come back from it. Or, I can't come back from it. Not now. Not with my mom…it's too hard. I don't know how I'm going to get through tonight, let alone tomorrow. And the next day. And the next. How am I even going to put one foot in front of the other? I'll fall. And I'll stay down on the floor. I can't ever pick myself up from this."

"Kayla," I whisper to her. "Take your time. There's nothing to rush through. I'm always going to be here for you, always going to feel the same. I will wait."

"But I don't want you to wait for me," she says almost sharply.

I close my eyes, absorbing the pain.

She's breaking.

I'm breaking.

"Okay," I say hoarsely.

"It's not fair to you. I have my own shit to deal with here and I can't deal with any more guilt than I already have. I can't deal with knowing you're across an ocean, waiting for me, loving me, when I know I'll give you nothing. I can't give anything anymore. Don't you understand?"

I nod, knowing completely what she means and hating it. *Hating* it. "Aye. I understand. You know, there's something about me I never told you."

She stills against me, waiting for my confession. I bite the bullet. "When I decided to get clean, when I decided to come back to Jessica and Donald and beg for their mercy, to take me back in, it wasn't a gradual choice. It was an immediate one. I had a friend. Charlie. A junkie just like me. All his bad faults were due to the addiction. If you took that away, he was a kind, charming young man. Funny as fuck. And he was loyal, though his loyalty was always to the drugs, to that high, first." I lick my lips and realize that the story isn't ripping me apart like I thought it would. The pain and shame and guilt of what was done has been pushed aside. "Charlie really wanted to get into heroin. I never did it, though Brigs and a few other people think otherwise, but I never did. Not that that makes me anything special—meth is just as disgusting, maybe more so. But I didn't do it, and when Charlie wanted to get high that way, I refused to help him. I didn't want any part of it."

I pause and look down. She's listening, wide-eyed. I go on. "But then I saw him shoot it up and saw how happy he was. And when he came down, it didn't seem like meth. It seemed harmless. I told myself that. I told myself a lot of lies.

So when he wanted some more a few days later, I told him I'd get it for him. We helped each other like that, and now, well, now I believed I was really helping Charlie. So I went to some people I knew, the wrong people, but they had it and I got it for Charlie...used money I made begging on the street. It felt better than using it for food. We rarely fucking ate, you know. We could, but it just wasn't important. There was only one thing that was. The bloody high. So I went back to Charlie, gave him the smack. He shot it up in front of me. But...I don't know what went wrong. Maybe he used too much, maybe it was bad stuff, maybe his body couldn't take any more. The problem was, I was so fucking high on meth myself that I had no idea what was going on. He died in front of me."

"No," she whispers breathlessly. "Lachlan..."

"Aye," I tell her, reveling in how much stronger I feel for admitting it. "He died and I watched him die before my eyes. Me and my stray dog. We watched him die, and I couldn't do a single thing to help him. I couldn't even help myself. I just sat there beside him, rocking back and forth, until my high wore off. Then I got up and ran. I just ran away. I don't remember the next few days, though I'm working through them with my psychologist now, but I know I made the choice to save my own life. I remember knocking on Jessica and Donald's door and everything after that. It was the day I realized I only had one life, and that's when I was born all over again."

She breathes heavily against me and the darkness creeps closer. But I feel no fear over what I've told her. The truth has set me free.

"Why are you telling me this?" she finally says, her voice barely audible.

"Because I know what guilt is. And I know what death is. And I've finally learned that you should never attach one to the other. Or it will fucking destroy you." I kiss the top of her head. "I know you're going to hurt for a long time and you're going to hate yourself, but please. None of this was your fault. Don't let the guilt tell you otherwise. Grieve for your mother with all your heart, but never poison that very heart with shame. There's no room for it there. Let it go."

She trails her fingers down my chest but doesn't say anything.

There's nothing more for either of us to say.

We just breathe. Our hearts beat.

We cling to this sliver of time until she falls asleep against me.

I hold her in my arms, the truth setting me free.

I just hope that same truth can save her heart.

Just as her heart saved me.

...

I decide to stick around for the funeral.

Alan is not happy.

Thierry is not happy.

Edinburgh is not happy.

No one is happy with this decision. It means I'm missing a game. It means I'm in big fucking shit and that I've potentially screwed the team over, especially since we're up against Leeds.

But I'm not about to leave Kayla yet. Not when she still needs me. And she needs me more than anything. I'm there by her side as she navigates funeral arrangements and her brothers and lawyers and wills. I'm there to hold her when she breaks down, and she breaks down time and time again. The strain is sometimes too much for me to bear but I handle it all because she *can't.*

After my confession over Charlie's death, we don't discuss our relationship anymore. She's said what she needed to say. She doesn't think she can be with me, even though she loves me, and as much as I want to shake her, to explain that I'll be there waiting anyway, I know there is no getting through to her. Right now, there is no us. Right now she thinks there never will be. Right now I'm just the arm around her shoulder, holding her tight. She's walking through a sea of death and the current isn't letting go of her anytime soon.

I see Bram, Nicola, Linden, and Stephanie at the funeral. It's the only bright spot as of late, even though none of us quite feel like celebrating our reunion. I talk with Bram a bit about his development and how well it's doing, how Justine's father has brought in more investments from society folk. He's forever grateful to me, but I can only tell him to maybe shoot some of those investments over my way. I could sure use them for the dogs.

Saying goodbye to them is hard, especially to Bram. Saying goodbye to Kayla's mother, as the casket is lowered into the ground, is hard too.

Saying goodbye to Kayla, probably for the last time, is the hardest thing I'll ever have to do.

She takes me to the airport and I'm flooded with the memory of the last time we were here. I was just about to check in, nervous as hell that she wouldn't show up, that I'd have an empty seat beside me on the plane back home.

And then I felt her behind me, like the sun rising on your back, and I turned around to see her gorgeous face, full of hope and nerves and wonder, pulling a ridiculously bright suitcase.

I fell in love with her at that moment.

And every moment afterward.

Now everything has changed. Even my feelings for her.

Because that was just a taste of love. What I feel now is the whole spectrum.

"Lachlan," Kayla says to me while we stand by the security checkpoint. She reaches for my hand, grabbing it tight, her eyes on the floor. "I can't thank you enough, you know. For everything."

"No need to thank me," I tell her, squeezing her hand back. "I'll always be there for you. I hope you know that now."

She nods. Sniffs. "I know." When she looks up at me, her eyes are gleaming with tears. "I want to be ready. I want to be with you again. I just don't know how."

I give her a half-smile. "Oh, love. You know where I'll be. If you ever need me, want me, you know where I'll be."

"Would you even take me back then?"

I shake my head, fighting back tears. "How can you even ask that?"

I pull her into my arms, holding her with as much strength as I can. "How can you even question it?" I whisper harshly. "I love you. My heart is yours." I pull back, knowing the tears are running down my cheeks. I grab her face in my hands, rubbing my thumbs along her skin as she stares at me with the love I know is buried deep behind her grief.

I kiss her softly, yielding, never-ending, a kiss that says so much. More beautiful than any kiss before. I whisper against her lips, "Please come back to me. When you can, when you're ready, if you're ready. Please come back."

Then I step back, unable to stand there for one minute more. She's seen my ruin once. She doesn't have to see it again. I grab my carry-on, turn, and go.

I wonder if she'll stay until I'm gone.

Or if she's already left.

I'm too afraid to look, as if that will give me any indication of our future together.

I show my boarding pass to one of the guards, then quickly look over my shoulder before I disappear behind the wall.

She's still standing there.

Palm up.

I raise my palm in response.

And smile.

Chapter Thirty

LACHLAN

Three months later

My phone rings as I'm walking down Queen Street, barely audible over the barrage of Christmas carols that practically scream from the stores. I fumble for it out of my leather jacket, trying to juggle that, a bag of groceries, and Lionel, Emily, and Jo as they pull eagerly at their leashes. Even with their muzzles, Lionel and Jo seem to charm the pants off of everyone they pass. Emily is still a snarling little mess, but you win some, you lose some.

"Hello?" I answer, not really able to check who is calling. It's hopefully one of two things: one of Britain's biggest footy players wanting to donate to the organization, or it's Kayla.

"Hey," Kayla says, her voice sounding spring sweet over the air. "Catch you at a bad time?"

"Not at all. Just being a superhero, that's all," I tell her. "How are you doing? We haven't talked since...the dawn of man, I'm guessing."

"It was four days ago," she says dryly. "And you know on my salary I'm not exactly rolling in the long distance money."

"I can always call you back," I tell her as I've told her a million times. But she's stubborn. No surprise there.

"I know, but I like the air of spontaneity," she says. "So how are things?"

"Good," I tell her. Over the three months since I last saw Kayla, things have been a bit challenging, a tad tumultuous, but otherwise great. Good changes are happening anyway, and with change always comes an adjustment period.

I've been sober for nearly four months now. Four long, difficult, challenging months, but I'm fighting the good fight, day in and day out. The only thing I'm taking is a low-grade, non-addictive medication for my anxiety. I see my doctor once a week, and because of that I don't have to use any antidepressants. It's hard though, digging deep through my past and pulling up a million memories that I would have rather stayed buried. But at the same time, it's making me more self-aware. It's letting me accept the blame where it needs to be and to pass it off when it doesn't. It's helping me come to terms with the cards I've been dealt and why exactly I act the way I do. It's painful, but it's fascinating and it's worth it just to be able to manage my depression and anger without medication. Addiction starts from somewhere and you can't ever get better until you attack the cause.

I've also taken up boxing. I know it's not exactly something that flows well with rugby and I know my body doesn't want to be under any extra strain, but boxing is something I'm naturally good at and it's another way for me to get my aggression out. And, according to my physiotherapist, I'm still in excellent shape, maybe more so now than I was in my late twenties thanks to the absence of alcohol and the extra exercise. It might be more of a brain/body thing too, where your body responds better when your head and heart are happier, but I'm not too sure about that.

Because my heart...well, it's happy enough. It's beating. But it not operating at full capacity, to put it mildly. Kayla and I have been talking at least once a week, and texting, emailing, and messaging way more than that. But the space between us is always there. It's not that we even have a long distance relationship because we stopped referring to ourselves as *us* a long time ago. After everything that happened, her mother's death was too much for us to survive. The last time I told her I loved her was over a month ago, and I got no answer. A few weeks after that, she casually mentioned that she met a guy at a bar and was going on a date. I guess she was asking me permission or something.

Obviously I wanted to be sick at the thought. It took a long time before I had the courage to talk to her again. I'm guessing nothing ever happened with the guy because she never mentioned him again, and I've never seen anything on her social media either. I've even talked to Bram a few times and asked him. He said she's been single, just trying to move on. I don't know if that's moving on from her mother's death, from me, or both.

But my love for her has never wavered. Never ebbed. I might not say it anymore but only because I don't want to make her uncomfortable if she's clearly moved on. And the last thing I want is to rush her when she's been through so much.

So I keep it to myself. But I hope she knows. I hope she can hear it in my voice, the way I laugh at her silly jokes, because bloody hell, can she still make me laugh.

And I know it might be easier if I didn't talk to her at all, but that's not what I want. I would rather love her, unrequited, secretly from afar and still have her in my life, then never talk to her again. That's not life to me. Life is something that she's in, in any way, shape, or form.

Loving Kayla saved me in the end. I owe her everything.

"Just good?" Kayla asks, bringing the conversation around.

"Well, the dogs are good and boxing is going well," I add. "My old rugby mate Rennie is back volunteering, so that's fantastic. Other than that…nothing has really happened in four days."

"I quit my job," she says.

I'm stunned. "Really? I thought you loved it."

Kayla quit her last job, the one at Bay Area Weekly, a week after her mother died. They were going to fire her anyway, she thinks, and it was time. That much I could see. She then applied to be a staff writer for a local magazine. To her surprise, they took her in and have been teaching her the ropes. It's an online magazine about Northern California and I read every article she puts out. She really does have the talent, even though I know it will take time before it really pays off. The only downfall is that she had to take a massive pay cut, but Kayla rolled with the punches. She gave up her apartment and moved in with her brother Toshio.

"I did love it," she says. "But it was time to move on. I got the experience I needed. Now I want a different kind of experience. I've been applying to every publication for the last two days here."

"Any luck?"

"I have an interview tomorrow," she says.

"Where? What's it called? I'll spy on them."

"Twenty-Four Hours," she says. "It's like a daily free newspaper."

"Sounds familiar," I tell her.

"They're in every major city. They hand them out at the train stations."

I nod. "Ah yes, I've seen them. Good for you. Pay raise I hope?"

"We'll see. I'm hoping it will be enough to continue sharing an apartment. Otherwise sometimes it's about more than money." She pauses. "Where are you?"

"Eh, I just took the dogs out for a bit, picked up some groceries. Coming up Frederick Street now. It's bloody cold out."

"I know," she says, and I can almost hear her shivering. "Any plans for tonight?"

"Not really. Stay in, maybe watch a stupid Christmas movie since it's the damn season and all."

"You're positively Grinchy. Are you watching the movie alone?"

"Well, me and the pups, yeah."

"No woman to join you?"

I swallow. "No," I say softly.

"Are you sure?" she asks.

I frown. "I'm pretty sure I'd remember if I invited a woman over. You're still the last, uh, well anyway. My memory is sharp now. It's just me."

She seems to think that over and I swear I can hear a sigh of relief. "What are you wearing?" she asks.

"What am I wearing?" I can't help but smile at that. "Well that's a question I haven't heard in a bloody long time."

"Let me guess," she says. "Your old leather jacket. Dark grey jeans. Olive green sweater. Looks slightly Norwegian, like it would itch a lot. Camel Timberland boots. Oh, and fingerless black gloves."

I look down at myself, as if I'd forgotten I dressed myself. "That's exactly what I'm wearing," I tell her, confused. "How did you…"

Then I look up and see my flat across the road.

I see Kayla standing outside of it.

The bag of groceries drops from my hands.

Somehow I clutch the phone and the leashes.

It can't be her.

But Emily starts wagging her tail excitedly and Kayla raises her hand, giving me a small wave. She's dressed in a bright purple peacoat, jeans, boots, and a beanie pulled over head. She's smiling and pulls the phone away from her ear.

I walk toward her in a daze.

"Your groceries!" she yells at me happily.

As if on autopilot I quickly turn around and scoop them up, then march on over to her. She's not real until I can feel her. And the closer I get, the more real she becomes, until I'm standing on the curb, staring at her, utterly dumbfounded.

"What are you doing here?" I ask, my words floating away like in a dream.

"I was wondering if maybe you needed a roommate," she says, putting her hands in her pockets and looking away with a sly smile on her face.

"A roommate?" I frown.

"Yeah. My job interview. If I get it, well, I'll need a place to live."

I can only stare at her, blinking, thinking it's a prank of some sort.

She bites her lip, brow furrowed. "If you'll have me, of course. I don't blame you if I'm the last person you want to see."

"Kayla," I say softly, coming toward her. I stop a foot away, the dogs sniffing her legs. She smiles down at them, absently petting them while she looks back to me. "How are you here?" I ask her.

"I told you. I quit my job," she says, giving me a hopeful look. "I was ready to move on. Move on from the life I was living the last three months. That wasn't really a life at all. I just…I know I should have told you over the phone or something, but I was so afraid, you know. I was so afraid that you'd not believe me or you'd tell me not to come. I was so afraid that it wouldn't happen. So I quit my job and I bought a plane ticket, and I'm just…hoping for the best. Because really, I needed to tell you in person."

I can barely swallow, my mouth is so dry. "Tell me what?"

She stares at me with wide eyes, like I've somehow struck fear in her.

"Tell me what?" I repeat desperately.

She gives me a half-smile. "That I'm still in love with you."

I cock my head. I couldn't have heard her right.

She goes on, licking her lips. "And I know I might have waited too long, but…I couldn't ignore it. I tried, you know. I did. I even went on a date with someone else. I thought that maybe it would help. It lasted a minute, then I got up and left. I couldn't do it. I couldn't even *look* at him. Lachlan, you have literally ruined all other men for me. None of them compared to you before. None of them will compare to you after. There's just you and only you."

My heart is beating like a frightened bird, but I do what I can to keep as much control as possible. "I don't understand," I tell her. "You knew how I felt all this time. I kept telling you I loved you…until you stopped saying it back." I blink hard, remembering the burn. "Why? Don't you know how that felt, to not hear that from you?"

She looks away, nodding with a wounded expression. "I did. I don't know. I was so fucked up, Lachlan, and I still am. There isn't a day that goes by that I don't think about my mother and how much I miss her, how much I would give to have her back, even for one single second, just enough to smile at her." She stares up, her eyes watering. "I tried to move past the grief but I couldn't. But it didn't mean I stopped loving you. I just didn't *want* to love you anymore. I didn't want for you to have my heart, all the way over here. How would I ever get it back? It was already so fragile. It was easier to just…shut it all away. But I was wrong. Because it hurt me more to pretend that I didn't care. And in return, you did the same."

"But it was just pretending," I tell her, clearing my throat. "I never stopped loving you."

She stares at me, pained. "Then why are we standing here like this?"

"Because," I start to say.

But the words die on my lips. She's on me in a flash. She grabs my face in her hands and pulls my head down toward hers, until my mouth is pressed against her lips.

I drop the groceries again.

I drop the leashes.

I don't care. I'm sure the dogs' heads are in the bags, eating the food, and I don't care.

I give myself to her, to feeling the warmth and the ferocity of her kiss. It brings me back to a beautiful world, one I never thought I'd live in again. I bury my hands in her hair, holding her head, feeling her as our mouths move sweetly against each other in a slow, intoxicating hunger. I can't believe I'm kissing her again, touching her again, feeling her again.

I can't believe she still loves me.

I have to pause, have to breathe, have to know.

I pull back, staring deep into those soulful brown eyes of hers.

"You love me?" I whisper.

"I love you," she whispers back, running her hands down my arms. "My beautiful beast."

I grin so wide, I think my face might stay that way forever. "You love me."

She laughs, so happy. "Yes, yes, I love you. I don't want to be anywhere but right here. This is the only place I'm supposed to be."

I put my arms around her, holding her tight against me in a bear hug, her own arms slipping around my waist. I press my lips into the top of her head and pinch my eyes shut. I feel like a whole new dawn is rising in my chest.

Another new beginning.

Another road to go down.

"Let's go inside," I say to her after a moment, the December chill settling around us. "Get warm."

Her eyes twinkle deviously at that. It's been so long since I've seen that look. The reaction is pure chemistry in my blood. I grab her hand, unlock the door, and hustle her and the dogs inside.

I feel like there is no time left.

That all the time that has passed before has never happened.

The need to be inside her again, to be with her from the inside out, is so addicting, so intoxicatingly urgent, that the moment we're back in my flat—*our* flat—and the door is locked behind us, I'm hauling her to the bedroom.

I kick the door shut, throwing off my jacket, sweater, and pants, undressing as if my clothes are on fire, and I'm on her in seconds, my fingers fumbling along her every inch, frantically trying to get as close as possible. I want the heat of her hips pressed against mine, that silken feel of her skin, the way she perfectly holds me when I'm deep inside her, as if we were made purely to fuck each other, to love each other.

She's shucking off her clothes too and grabbing me with frenzied hands, our mouths meeting hot, wet, and so fucking desperate. I am wild to the touch and she is burning under my hands, and I'm lighting her fires like an arsonist.

"Kayla, Kayla, Kayla," I moan into her neck, tasting her. I sound so damn hungry for her that it both scares me and thrills me to the bone.

We fall onto the bed, and I'm climbing on top of her, pinning her between my thighs, wishing I could go slow and absorb every single carnal second, but there is no time. There will be—tomorrow. In a few hours from now, even. But right now, in this moment, where I have my love back, time is a precious thing, and if I can't have her now, I fear I never will.

She wraps her legs around me, one hand ghosting over my neck and into my hair, the other skimming down my back, and we kiss again, deep and savage, our tongues sliding over each other in a wild war.

"I can't wait," she whispers to me, and I pull back, lost in her eyes, knowing she feels just as delirious as I do. "Please, come inside me."

I close my eyes, resting my forehead against hers, and position myself between her legs, my cock thick and throbbing and hard as concrete. I push into her, slipping slick and rough until all the air leaves my lungs and it's almost too much.

I am purified, sanctified, inside her.

"Fuck," I growl, nipping at her neck now as I thrust in again. This time my arms are starting to shake, my body overloaded. I'm the greedy one, craving every part of her, and it's my soul that's just as hungry as the rest of me.

"Harder," she pleads, her nails digging into the back of my head as I'm biting along her breasts, flicking her nipple with a stiff and merciless tongue. I roughly grab her hips and shift her up, my cock sinking in hard and deep, and I'm grunting with exertion as I drive myself in again and again.

"Harder," she cries out again, meeting my eyes, telling me she needs to feel everything.

I give her all of me.

A savage growl rips from my throat and I'm fucking, fucking, fucking her like I might die if I don't. I'm a relentless machine, pounding her over and over and over again, then I'm leaning back down, my chest pressed against hers, slick with sweat, our hearts beating against each other in a rabid race, wanting so much I don't know what to do with myself.

I bite at her collarbone, her shoulders, her chest, her nipples, and she's crying out softly, wanting more, wanting all of me. My fingers are clamped onto her hips, a vise, and I fear I might just break her right in two.

Then it all starts to swirl together. I slip my hand along her clit, rubbing in frenzied circles that make her eyes roll back, and the sounds out of her delicate throat are among the most erotic, primal ones I have ever heard.

She undoes me.

She always will.

Bloody hell.

So I go and go until I can't, until my savagery snaps, and with one rough, final push I'm pouring into her, my hoarse shouts filling the room. We succumb to our pleasure at the same time, riding the current together, our bodies and hearts hopelessly intertwined. I empty into her and yet I've never felt so full.

I collapse onto her with nearly my full weight, breathing so hard that the bed is still shaking, and she's gripping my back with all her might, like I'm a raft and she'll drown if she lets go.

But I've got her. I do.

We hold on to each other like this for seconds, minutes. We hold on to each other because we didn't hold on to each other tight enough before. This time, this time, I know neither of us will let go.

"You know it hasn't been proven yet," I say, my voice thick and lazy as I brush her damp hair off her face. "But I believe I can exist on you alone. No food, no water. Just Kayla. Care to test this theory out over the next few days?"

She grins up at me and my heart beats something fierce for her. "I would love to help you with this experiment," she says, her eyes vivid, so beautifully full of life again. "Give me another few minutes and we can try again."

"I have a feeling this experiment might last a very long time," I warn, smiling.

"Good," she says, running her thumb over my lips. "Because I'm not going anywhere."

And this time I know it's true.

This time she's here to stay.

Epilogue

Nine Months Later

KAYLA

Lachlan is a sweating, grunting, tireless machine. The way his limbs move in all the right ways, his muscles tightening as he dips and lunges and plows his way through. He's a beautiful beast to watch, the kind of effortless skill that takes your breath away. And hell, does it ever turn me on.

I can't be the only one that thinks this. I look all around me, at the stadium of screaming spectators waving their red and black scarves, and I know that at least most of the women are thinking what I'm thinking, and maybe some of the men, too.

It goes without saying, Lachlan McGregor is a force to be reckoned with. And boy, do I ever know it. Now more than ever. And I mean that in the best possible way.

Moving to Scotland was the best decision I ever made. Nine months ago I had no idea what would happen with my life—all I knew was that there was a man I loved and a man who loved me, and I needed to be with him. It didn't matter that he was wrought with demons and I was stumbling in grief, and aimless except for him. I didn't care that I was risking it all for something that might not work out. I'd risked it all before and it worked out the only way it could.

My mom once told me that my life is on the track it's mean to be on. I think she's completely right. My old track led me to Edinburgh with Lachlan where I fell madly in love. But life has other plans, plans that we might never understand, and the track changed. It took me a moment to reroute it. It took some time to figure out what exactly I needed.

It was Lachlan all along.

A lot has changed in nine months. Lachlan has remained sober the whole time, though it's something neither of us take for granted. I know it's something that will never leave him completely. He has good days and bad days, and on the bad days we go for long walks and I make him talk to me until we can figure out a way through it. We're in this together now, and I make sure he knows that he doesn't have to face any of it alone.

His psychologist has helped a lot. So has his healthy lifestyle. He's doing extremely well in boxing, still just for fun, a form of exercise that has nothing to do with his career, and it's something to get his anger out better than any medication or booze.

I like to think that it's because of all this that he's gotten better at rugby. When I first met him, he was so worried about his career and age, thinking he couldn't possibly last much longer. That doesn't seem to be the case. Not only is he performing at his best, but he's the longest-standing member of the team and going into this new season, the team captain.

He handles his new responsibility beautifully.

As for me, we'll I'm still struggling, but it's a fun struggle.

I never did get the job at Twenty-Four Hours, but I did get a job writing for an online Scottish fashion and lifestyle magazine. I get paid per article, which supplements the income I get from working part-time with Amara at Ruff Love. The two of us are currently trying to put our heads together and come up with a PR position at the organization. Maybe she'll take it, maybe I will, but if it comes to light, it will really help Lachlan get all the love, funding, and attention he needs for the dogs.

Speaking of dogs, Lionel and Emily are still around, still licking us to death and sniffing everything in sight. Unfortunately, Jo died a few months ago. Cancer. There was nothing we could do, and once Lachlan saw she was suffering, he put her down. It hurt like hell, to be honest, to see that beautiful, sweet dog so fearful on that table at the vet's office. But at the last minute she looked up at Lachlan, and he smiled tearfully at her, and she seemed to smile at him. She calmed down. The vet gave her the shot and Jo died peacefully.

Naturally it brought up every fresh, painful memory of my mother's death. That's something that will never go away. Ever. I wish it could. I wish it would. But in some ways it feels wrong because someone like my mom should always be in the forefront of your thoughts. To feel that loss, that pain, is just a testament to the kind of person that she was.

Though sometimes it really is hard to just get out of bed. Sometimes you wake up with dreams of that person, and there's that blissful moment between sleep and reality where you think everything is as it always was. And then it sinks in how much everything has changed. I realize she's gone and my chest is filled with stones.

On those mornings I reach for Lachlan, and he's always there. Because he's my rock. He's my love and my everything. There's nothing I wouldn't do for him and nothing he wouldn't do for me, and god, it's scary to have that kind of love, it really is, but I would never trade it for anything.

I know I used to think that the kind of love that my mother had for my father was the kind that would ruin you. So big and bold and powerful that it would take over your life. And it's true. Because the love I have for Lachlan is like that. It's bigger than the both of us. It has the power to collapse us, like the darkest star imploding on itself, too great for its own good. But what a beautiful thing to have, a love so deep that it can bring people to their very knees. A love that can rise from the ashes, greater and stronger than ever before.

Amara elbows me in my side, bringing my focus back to the rugby game. I'm sitting with her in the lower stands, though I know that Jessica, Donald, and Brigs are up in the box seats.

"One more try and they have it," Amara squeals, clutching her beer even though there's nothing left since she's been chugging them down like a madwoman, along with the rest of the stadium.

I've pretty much stopped drinking in support of Lachlan. Maybe I'll have some wine when it's a girl's night with Amara at her place, but when I'm with Lachlan I'm as sober as a jaybird. It doesn't really have an effect on my life, it's just something I need to do for him, and I do it without him asking. Because I want to. Because he would do anything for me.

Amara has become a good friend though. She's actually a lot like me, totally opinionated and speaks her mind, even though her love life is a bit lackluster. Still, Lachlan and I are always trying to set her up with some rugby player of the moment, and I don't think she can complain too much about that. Naturally, she still does.

Of course I talk to Nicola and Steph all the time, so I don't feel like I've lost them at all. They both want to come out and visit with Linden and Bram, but…well, there's a complication now.

Stephanie is pregnant.

I know, I'm sad about it in a totally selfish way because it means that she's moving on to a part of her life that I can't relate to, and I'm afraid that our relationship will change. But at the same time, it's Steph. She's always going to have my back, no matter what, and I know I can always be real with her. And really, she's just so happy that she and Linden are going to be parents that her excitement is contagious. It's enough that I'm buying every Scottish baby item I can find, including the tiniest little kilt in the MacGregor tartan. I figure, girl or boy, it's wearable.

Either way, Stephanie is going to be an excellent mom, and I can't wait to see what kind of terribly attractive human being she's going to pop out. I think I'll have to fly back to San Francisco just for that.

I'm also in constant contact with all of my brothers. In fact, I'm far closer with them than I ever was before, and I think that wherever my mother is hanging out with my father, they're probably happy that we've all finally found each other.

The people beside us start chanting something in favor of Edinburgh as the teams come together on the field. We watch as the scrum takes place, Edinburgh pushing Munster back until Thierry gets the ball at the back of the players and quickly tosses it under to another guy who then tosses it to Lachlan who is waiting in the wings.

Lachlan makes a run for it, the ball under his arm, even though the other team has players going for him, watching his every move. They're always on him like a hawk.

But they never have his speed.

Watching him run is as impressive to me now as it was the first time I ever saw him on the field. He moves with such passion that you can't help but compare him to a wild stallion or a feral bull, galloping toward freedom, moving like he was born to move.

I hold my breath as he goes. So does everyone.

A player tries to tackle him, but Lachlan makes a move to sidestep before changing his mind and plowing through him. The guy goes down and Lachlan keeps running, legs and arms pumping, moving so fast I think he might break the sound barrier. He's a hot blur of ink and muscle.

Someone else moves in front, blocking him, but Lachlan only bounces off and keeps going. He punts the ball down the field, sidesteps someone else, then keeps running until he meets up with the ball again.

By now we're all screaming, on our feet, waving everything we can wave because he's feet from making a try and winning the game.

And Lachlan just picks up that ball like it was always there waiting for him and runs across the line, making a dramatic dive onto the grass and sliding on his stomach. I know that was just for show, but the crowd fucking loves it.

I fucking love it.

It's rare to see him showboat, so I know he's got to be feeling good right now.

So am I. I'm screaming my head off, jumping up and down with Amara.

Lachlan gets to his feet, tossing the ball on the ground, and I'm smiling so big that happy fucking tears are running down my face. The rest of his team jogs out to hug him, jumping around, celebrating their win during the first game of the season.

He's so getting laid tonight.

But then he does something funny. He runs away from his mates, away from the opposing team who is ready to shake hands, and heads toward the camera men on the sidelines. His coach Alan follows him, quickly passing something off into Lachlan's hands before he runs back to the team. Lachlan then talks to one of the camera men until a reporter comes over, seeing an opportunity for an interview.

Lachlan smiles at her, whispering something in her ear.

He takes the microphone.

Suddenly the giant screens in the stadium fill with the sight of Lachlan's handsome face. He smiles broadly at the screen, something that makes him look so much younger, softer, dare I say goofy. He brings the microphone to his lips and speaks into it but no sound comes out.

He tries again but nothing. His lips are moving, he's smiling, his eyes crinkling joyfully, but that's all we in the stands can know.

"What is he doing?" I ask Amara.

She shakes her head. "I haven't a bloody clue."

Finally he waves at someone, and they come out with a clipboard and a pen. He takes the pen, is about to write something down, and then he pauses and looks up at me. Right at me in the stands.

I can feel Amara's eyes on me too, as well as the people below us as they all crane their necks to look at what the hell Lachlan McGregor, savior of the game, is staring at.

It's me.

Always me for him.

Always him for me.

Our eyes are locked together.

Then he writes something down.

He looks back at me while he displays the paper and clipboard in front of the camera. I know that the screens are showing a message because people are gasping, but I can't take my eyes off of him. His gaze always holds me, as strong as his hands.

"Kayla," Amara whispers, grabbing my arm. "Oh my god."

I finally look at the screens. At the paper Lachlan is holding, still smiling, albeit a bit more nervous now. The paper is shaking.

It reads: *Kayla Moore, will you do me the honor of becoming my wife?*

Signed: *Lachlan McGregor.*

Then the clipboard drops away, and the camera focuses on the grass.

My head swivels back to him but he's gone, running forward, across the field.

Up the stairs.

Down the row.

Stopping right in front of me.

I'm still sitting down. I haven't moved. I haven't really formed one coherent thought.

I honestly can't figure out what's going on. Is this really my Lachlan, my reserved, subdued Lachlan? Am I caught in the middle of a play or something?

He gets down on one knee so he's at my level. His damp hair clings to his sweaty brow, his eyes clear green, piercing through me.

"What are you doing?' I ask him, so stunned.

He holds out one of his hands, and held between his fingers is a ring. A gorgeous, beautiful emerald and silver ring.

"Oh my god," I think I say, maybe I just breathe it.

"I thought it would be some grand romantic gesture," he says. "But it didn't really work out that way. Technical difficulties." He has a way of staring at me that makes the rest of the world disappear, like I have blinders on. I'm hanging on to his every word, tunnel vision of his face. "They say you should always do something that scares you, pushes you out of your comfort zone. You did that a lot with me. Every time you came here to Scotland, you left behind the life you knew. You were brave. You took a risk. Many risks. Now, I know the surest thing I could ever do is ask you to marry me. Because I know I'm supposed to be with you, and you know you're supposed to be with me. I knew it from the moment I asked you to come here, I just didn't know how to deal with it. But now I do. Now I know. So I'm doing it like this, because it's bloody frightening."

His eyes dart from side to the side, at all the people, all *his* fans that are listening to his every word and watching us like a television program. "I mean, I don't know any of these people. But I do know that I want them all to know just how much I love you. That if it wasn't for you, if it wasn't for Kayla Moore, I wouldn't be here today. I wouldn't be the man I am today. A better man. And yes, a man that's terrified you might just say no in front of the entire world. But that's the risk I'm willing to take for the chance that you might say yes." He swallows hard, his eyes measuring me. "Will you marry me?"

"Are you serious?" I whisper, still feeling like this is some kind of dream, like someone is going to pull the rug out from under me and I'll fall flat on my face, humiliated. But I guess he has to be feeling the same way too. Every moment that the ring, shining beautifully, is held out there in his hand, waiting for my finger, is a moment that he dies a little inside.

What the fuck am I even waiting for?

As if there was ever anything to think about.

"Yes," I tell him gleefully.

It hits me once, twice.

Oh my god, he's asked me to marry him.

Oh my god, I'm going to marry my lover, my best friend, the man of my dreams.

"Yes!" I say louder now, smiling so wide it hurts. "Yes, I will marry you, Lachlan. I love you. I love you."

He grins at me with so much joy that it takes my breath away. "You're sure?"

"Yes, yes, yes," I tell him, shoving my ring finger toward him. "Put the damn ring on it already."

He laughs, his eyes watering, and slips the gorgeous ring on my finger. His hands are shaking. It might just be the most adorable, most vulnerable moment, and we're sharing it among so many people.

But it doesn't matter. Because it's our moment.

I stare down at it on my hand. It's so beautiful. Not because of how it looks, because it really is gorgeous, but because it came from him. Because he chose it for me when he knew he wanted me to be his wife.

I look up at my future husband and I can't even believe it.

"I'm so lucky," I say, beaming at him, my cheeks hot and stretched from smiling so hard.

"Aye," he says with a sly smile. "But then again, so am I."

The next few hours pass by in a blur. I can't really believe what happened. Pictures are taken because obviously the local paparazzi is going to go a little bit nuts, and Lachlan's family comes by to congratulate us, and I can tell they knew he was going to do it. I was the only one caught unaware, and boy was I caught.

Finally we manage to break free of all the hoopla, and we're on our own and heading back to the flat in a cab. We don't speak much in the back. I just stare at my ring while he holds my hand and stares out the window. I'm still coming to terms with how surreal the day has been. First he wins an epic game for the team, then he proposes to me in front of thousands. He fucking proposed! On one knee and everything.

I'm getting fucking married!

It hits me even harder once we get into the flat and I realize that this is really, truly my home now. All of the beautiful cornices and designs, everything will be my home.

More than that, he's my home.

Always will be, wherever we are.

Emily and Lionel greet us at the door as usual, wanting attention, perhaps feeding off our happiness, but Lachlan quickly whisks me away into the bedroom. He closes the doors behind him and peels his shirt off, displaying tattoos and abs for days. One of his latest tattoos is the word "love" across his chest.

The *love* is for me.

He strides across the room, grabbing me and pulling me toward him, and gazes at me so intensely that I fear I may spontaneously combust. "I love you," he says to me, his burning eyes roaming over my skin. "And this us, this will be forever."

"You promise?" I whisper.

"Always," he says.

He kisses me long and deep. Beautiful. Our lips are sweet with love.

We fall back into bed.

And find each other again and again.

The End

Acknowledgments

It's no secret that my muse for the character of Lachlan is none other than the magnificent actor, Tom Hardy. But it's also Mr. Hardy himself that inspired me to do more than just write a book. An advocate for adopting shelter dogs and a warrior against the unfair stigma and treatment of pit bulls, Hardy uses his fame and stature to try and help educate people on the matter. And while my own fame and stature is absolutely miniscule, especially compared to a mad genius like him, it did inspire me to speak out and do more for a cause I deeply believe in.

I rescued a pit bull mix from a high-kill shelter in San Bernardino, California. Or, I should say, the lovely ladies at the non-profit Vancouver Island Flirting with Fido organized a rescue run, trucking up dogs from various shelters and bringing them up to Canada to find a fit for them with various loving families. Most of the dogs are pit bulls or mixes, bully breeds that are misunderstood and usually cast aside, the first ones to be put down in a shelter alongside the sick and the old. Because these dogs do have a terrible reputation, the organization takes special care to let people foster the animals first so they can find out if the dog is meant for them. Not every dog is for everybody—especially rescue dogs who may or may not have been abused and have behavioral issues—and dog ownership is a lifetime commitment. It's not just until you have a baby and then you decide you don't want your dog anymore. It's not just until you have to move and you don't want to bother finding an apartment that takes dogs. It's not just until the dog is old and can't play anymore and just isn't as cute. A forever home is a forever home.

So my husband and I took this scared little pit bull mix, Bruce, into our home. And it wasn't easy. There were times at the beginning where I thought I couldn't handle it. Bruce wasn't like the dogs I grew up with. He was terrified of everyone and everything. Tail always between his legs, shaking like a leaf. He didn't bark, he didn't make any sounds. He just wanted to run away and be on his own, away from human hands that he thought would only hurt him.

But we persevered. I wanted to be that forever home for Bruce. I was afraid that in any other hands, he would never be happy, never trust, never come out of his shell.

Slowly but surely though, he did come out of his shell. With lots of patience, lots of love, and, yes, lots of frustration, Bruce learned to trust us. He learned his commands. He learned to be a big puppy in such a way that makes me think when he was living on the streets as a young dog, he never got a chance to even be one.

Now Bruce is a completely different dog. He barks at strangers who come to the house, which is both bad because it's annoying and good because it means he finally has confidence. He's protective of us and we're protective of him. He's better with people in general too, once he figures out they aren't to be feared. And of course he adores being around other dogs. One day soon we'll be rescuing another dog in need so he can have a little buddy to love on and play with.

But, of course, I feel that it's not enough. That's why I decided to donate $1 from every pre-order of The Play to animal charities who need the funding. From major ones like Best Friends Animal Society, Battersea Dogs & Cats, SPCA and others, to smaller ones like the aforementioned Flirting with Fido, Villalobos, and more. So if you're reading this book because you pre-ordered, THANK YOU. Your money is going to help dogs, cats, and other animals get the loving homes they need. You've helped save a life.

And if you didn't pre-order, there is still time to make a difference. My check from this book will come at the end of January, and it's then that I'll be making the donations to the various charities. You'll be able to follow along with this on my website: www.authorkarinahalle.com under "News." If you want to give, you can always donate to the charities I'll have listed. If you don't see a charity listed that you think is worthy, please email me at authorkarinahalle@gmail.com with the subject line "Save the Puppies" and I'll see what I can do. My goal is to donate to as many deserving organizations as possible. Depending on how fundraising goes, I may even donate all of my release day sales to the charities as well, so if you also bought this on release day, THANK YOU FOR BEING AWESOME. Also, buying a book on release day is super special to authors like myself, so thank you again.

Of course, I can't just thank generous readers, Bruce, and Tom Hardy for this book, so without further ado: Scott Mackenzie, I'm sorry I spent all of our Hong Kong, Australia, and New Zealand trip writing. Who knew this book would be this big? Who knew I could actually write a 150,000 word book while freaking CAMPING? Yeah, I'm not sure if this is a good or bad thing. Are no vacations safe anymore? First, I write The Pact while in Hawaii, now I finish half of The Play while gallivanting around New Zealand in a camper-van. What's next? You know what…don't answer that. But I promise to make it up to you. *wink*

Many thanks to my parents, Kara Malinczak, Laura Helseth, Stephanie Sandra Brown, Sandra Cortez, Kelly St-Laurent, Dani Sanchez, Taylor Haggerty, K.A. Tucker (this table of contents is all her, she can write AND format, who thunk it), Mark Coker, everyone in Hallewood for their enthusiasm, feedback and talent, Instagram (it's where it's at), and of course my loyal crew of Anti-Heroes. You're the best bunch of readers an author could ever have. I am truly, truly lucky and extremely grateful to have you. Let's have Tom Hardy Parties for the rest of time!

CPSIA information can be obtained at www.ICGtesting.com
Printed in the USA
BVOW05s0527260216

438160BV00012B/33/P